He had to have her, and he had to have her *now*.

He got to the front door and knocked hard.

Once, twice, three times.

Grace opened the door and frowned at him from the other side. "Jax?" she said confused.

"I'm your person, Grace. Me, not anyone else," he said stepping into her apartment.

She looked up at him startled as he closed the door behind him and locked it. And then he grabbed her and pushed her up against the wall. She gasped before his mouth landed hard on hers, his hands grabbing onto the fabric of her jeans. Her arms wrapped around his neck, her fingers digging into his hair and holding him in place as she opened her mouth to his.

Acclaim for
Shannon Richard's Country Roads Series

UNDENIABLE

"Shannon Richard's Mirabelle, with its quaint Southern charm, sweet, sassy heroines, and sexy country boys, is quickly climbing my list of places I want to be."
—ScandaliciousBookReviews.com

"A great read...a sweet love story, with some steamy moments and lots of drama...Once I picked it up, I couldn't put it down."
—DarkFaerieTales.com

"HOT! Richard's tempting second addition to her Country Roads series puts a clever spin on the small-town romance trope with great effect. The chemistry between her main characters is indisputable...a heartwarming story with clever twists that will please Richard's fans and win her new devotees."
—*RT Book Reviews*

UNSTOPPABLE

"*Unstoppable* is a great romance story filled with inspiring characters, sexual tension, and heartfelt moments...a fun and steamy series."
—DarkFaerieTales.com

"Shannon Richard is a rising star...and I cannot wait to read more by her."
—TheBookCellarx.com

"A charming read that warms the heart on a chilly afternoon."
—KTBookReviews.blogspot.com

UNDONE

"Richard's page-turner marks her as a contemporary romance author to watch." —*Publishers Weekly*

"A fun, feel-good story and perfect for a quick, entertaining escape!" —ABookishEscape.com

"4½ stars! These characters are rich and deep, so expertly written that they feel like friends, and the best news of all is that this small-town series is set to continue!"
—*RT Book Reviews*

Also by Shannon Richard

Undone
Unstoppable

Undeniable

SHANNON RICHARD

A Country Roads Novel

FOREVER

NEW YORK   BOSTON

Copyright © 2013 by Shannon Richard
Excerpt from *Unstoppable* copyright © 2013 by Shannon Richard
All rights reserved. In accordance with the U.S. Copyright Act of 1976, the scanning, uploading, and electronic sharing of any part of this book without the permission of the publisher is unlawful piracy and theft of the author's intellectual property. If you would like to use material from the book (other than for review purposes), prior written permission must be obtained by contacting the publisher at permissions@hbgusa.com. Thank you for your support of the author's rights.

Forever
Hachette Book Group
237 Park Avenue, New York, NY 10017

www.hachettebookgroup.com
www.twitter.com/foreverromance

Printed in the United States of America

OPM

Originally published as an ebook
First mass market edition: June 2014

10 9 8 7 6 5 4 3 2 1

Forever is an imprint of Grand Central Publishing.
The Forever name and logo are trademarks of Hachette Book Group, Inc.

The publisher is not responsible for websites (or their content) that are not owned by the publisher.

The Hachette Speakers Bureau provides a wide range of authors for speaking events. To find out more, go to www.hachettespeakersbureau.com or call (866) 376-6591.

To Gloria Berry,
who inspired a lot of Grace.
You have more strength and
courage than you know.
You're one of the greatest friends
I could ever ask for.

Acknowledgments

To my parents, I'll never be able to thank either of you enough. You've helped me so much through the years and I wouldn't be doing this without the two of you.

To Kaitie Hotard, I can't tell you how much you mean to me. You've been on this writing journey with me from the start. You're an amazing friend and I love you so, so, so much.

To Katie Crandall, for being the best distraction in my times of need. No one makes Mario Kart quite as entertaining as you do, and you play a mean Princess Peach if I do say so myself. I appreciate you in more ways that you can imagine.

To Gloria Berry, thank you for pushing me further and helping me get past a lot of the brick walls. I wish I could say that the deadlines are what have made me crazier than usual, but let's face it, I was crazy long before any of those and you've had to deal with it for years. You've been there from the very beginning of my writing, and I hope that you'll be there until the end. I'm blessed to count you as one of my friends.

I also want to say how much I appreciate all of you going to New York this past October. It meant the world to me that you took the time to celebrate this accomplishment with me. I love you all beyond words.

To Selina McLemore and Megha Parekh, I enjoy working with both of you and I'm glad that you've been a part of the creation of my stories. I am so thankful for your continued efforts to make my writing better.

To Lieutenant James McQuaig of the Leon County Sheriff's Office, who had the patience to sit down with me and answer all of my questions, and oh, there were a lot of them. Thank you for listening to me go through all of the law enforcement scenarios that Jax had to deal with. Any mistakes in *Undeniable* are my own.

To my lovely Beta readers, especially Catie Humphreys, Jenna Robinson, and Ronald Richard. It means a lot to me that all of you took the time to read.

To Kip Moore and Dan Couch for writing "Hey Pretty Girl." Your words inspired so many of mine and this song was instrumental in the writing of *Undeniable*.

And last but certainly not least, I have to thank my agent but more importantly my friend, Sarah E. Younger. You continue to go past above and beyond. You were there all through the writing of *Undeniable* and this book wouldn't have been the same without you and your incredible feedback and advice. I always look forward to our chats and talking about *Game of Thrones* and the wonder that is Khal Drogo.

Undeniable

Prologue

The Princess

At six years old there were certain things Grace King didn't understand. She didn't understand where babies came from, how birds flew way up high in the sky, or where her father was. Grace had never met her dad; she didn't know what he looked like, she didn't even know his name, and for some reason this fact fascinated many people in Mirabelle.

"What's a girl bastard?"

Grace looked up from the picture she was coloring to see Hoyt Reynolds and Judson Coker looming over the other side of the picnic table where she was sitting.

Every day after the bell rang, Grace would wait outside on the playground for her brother Brendan to come and get her, and they'd walk home together. Today, Brendan was running a little late.

"I don't know." Judson smirked. "I think bastard works for boys and girls."

"Yeah." Hoyt shrugged. "Trash is trash."

Brendan was always telling Grace to ignore bullies, advice he had a problem following himself. Half the time she didn't even know what they were saying. Today was no different. She had no idea what a bastard was, but she was pretty sure it wasn't anything nice.

Grace looked back down to her picture and started coloring the crown of the princess. She grabbed her pink crayon from the pile she'd dumped out on the table, and just before she started coloring the dress the picture disappeared out from under her hands.

"Hey," she protested, looking back up at the boys, "give that back."

"No, I don't think I will." Judson slowly started to rip the picture.

"Stop it," Grace said, swinging her legs over the bench and getting quickly to her feet. She ran to the other side of the table and stood in front of Judson. "Give it back to me."

"Make me," he said, holding the picture up high over her head as he ripped it cleanly in half.

Grace took a step forward and stomped down hard on his foot.

"You little bitch!" Judson screamed, hopping up and down on his uninjured foot.

Grace had one second of satisfaction before she found herself sprawled out on her back, the wind knocked out of her.

"Don't ever touch her again!"

Grace looked up just in time to see a tall, freckled, red-haired boy punch Hoyt in the face. It was Jax, one of Brendan's best friends, who had come to her rescue. And boy did Jax know what he was doing, because Hoyt fell back onto his butt hard.

"And if you ever call her that word again, you'll get a lot more than a punch in the face, you stupid little scum bag," Jax said as he put himself in between Grace and Judson. "Now get out of here."

"I'm going to tell my father about this," Hoyt said. This was a legitimate threat as Hoyt's father was the principal.

"You do that." Jax shrugged.

Apparently the two eight-year-olds didn't have anything else to say and they didn't want to take their chances against a big bad eleven-year-old, because they scrambled away and ran around the side of the building and out of sight.

"You okay?" Jax asked, turning around to Grace.

It was then that Grace realized the back of her dress was covered in mud and her palms were scraped and bleeding.

"No," she sniffed before she started to bawl.

"Oh, Grace," Jax said, grabbing her under her arms and pulling her to her feet. "Come here." He pulled her into his chest and rubbed her back. "It's okay, Gracie."

She looked up at him and bit her trembling lip. "They called me names." She hiccupped.

"They weren't true," he said, looking down at her.

"What's a bastard, Jax?"

Jax's hand stilled and his nose flared. "Nothing you need to worry about. Grace, sometimes dads aren't all they're cracked up to be."

She nodded once before she buried her head back in his chest. By the time she'd cried herself out, Jax's shirt was covered in her tears. She took a step back from him and wiped her fingers underneath her eyes. Jax reached down and grabbed the two halves of her picture from the ground.

"We can tape this back together," he said, looking down at the paper. He studied it for a second before he looked back to her. "This is what you are, Grace. A princess. Don't let anyone tell you different. You understand?" he asked, lightly tugging on her blond ponytail.

"Yes." She nodded.

"All right," he said, handing the papers back to her. "Get your stuff together and we'll go wait for Brendan."

"Where is he?" Grace asked as she gathered her crayons and put them back into the box.

"He got into trouble with Principal Reynolds again."

Grace looked up at Jax and frowned. She really didn't like the Reynolds family. Principal Reynolds wasn't any better than his son.

"No frowning, Princess. Let's go," Jax said, holding out his hand for her.

Grace shoved her crayons and drawing into her bag. She grabbed Jax's outstretched hand and let him lead her away.

Chapter One

The Protector

The nightmares felt so real. They always started off the exact same way as the accident had, but then they morphed into something so much worse, something that haunted Jax even when he was awake.

As a deputy sheriff for Atticus County, Jaxson Anderson was no stranger to being the first person to arrive at the scene of an accident. What he wasn't used to was being the first to an accident that involved two people he cared about. That day it had been Grace and Paige King. Grace was the little sister of Brendan King, one of Jax's best friends. Paige was Brendan's wife.

It had happened over six months ago. Violent storms had raged across Mirabelle for days, and the rains had flooded the river that ran through the town, making the current swift and deadly. By some miracle Jax and been driving right behind Paige and Grace. Jax and his friend Bennett Hart had watched as the SUV the girls were in swerved off the road, crashed through a barrier, and disappeared down to Whiskey River. The only thing that had stopped the car from being swept under the water was a tree growing out of the bank. The tree was barely strong enough to hold the car back.

That day Jax had experienced a panic like no other. He'd gone into the river desperate to pull them out. And that was when the second miracle of the day happened. Brendan, along with Nathanial Shepherd and Baxter McCoy had shown up. It took the efforts of all five men to pull the girls out of the car before it was swept under the water. It had been just a matter of seconds of getting them out before the tree gave way.

Jax went over those moments, over and over again, replaying everything from what he'd said to what he'd done. The one thing he was absolutely sure about was that getting those girls out of that river alive was miracle number three.

But Jax's nightmares didn't play out like the miracle. No, in his nightmares he watched as Grace died.

When the accident happened, they had to pull Grace out from the car before Paige. In the nightmare, it was Grace who was pulled out second. Paige was safe in Brendan's arms, and Jax would go to get Grace, but the tree would snap right before his hands touched hers. Jax would scream her name as the river dragged her away and she disappeared under the surface of the water.

Jax woke up, Grace's name still on his lips. He was breathing hard and drenched in sweat, the sheets sticking to his skin. He blinked, his eyes adjusting to the darkness as he slowly began to realize that what he'd seen wasn't real. That it was just another nightmare. That Grace wasn't lost. She'd walked away from the accident with a dislocated shoulder and minor scrapes and bruises.

Jax lay there and when he got his breathing under control and his heart stopped pounding out of his chest, he turned to look at the alarm clock. It was ten to five in the morning. He didn't need to be up for another hour, but it was pointless for him to even attempt to go back to sleep. Whenever he had a nightmare about Grace, he was on edge until he saw her and knew she was okay.

So instead, Jax threw back the sheets that were tangled around his legs and sat on the edge of the bed. He rubbed his face with his hands before he got up and padded into the bathroom. He brushed his teeth and splashed his face with cold water. He looked into the mirror as water dripped off the end of his long, freckled nose. The hollows under his eyes were tinged a light purple.

Mirabelle had a whopping five thousand people in its six hundred square miles, half of which was water. The little beach town made up sixty percent of Atticus County's population, and boy did those five thousand sure know how to keep the sheriff's office busy. Deputies worked twelve-hour shifts. Two days on, then two days off; three days on, then two days off.

Jax had worked only the first day of his three-day shift, and he'd had to deal with plenty already: a kid who'd stolen his mom's car to go joy riding with his girlfriend, more drunken college kids on spring break than he could count, and three house calls for domestic disturbances, two of which had ended in arrests. He was also investigating a string of burglaries that had been going on in Mirabelle. Five alone in the last two months, and they all looked to be connected.

The day before had been a long one and he left work exhausted. For normal people that would mean sleep would come easier, but that wasn't the case for Jax. For him, deep sleep brought on his nightmares. He'd been having nightmares for as far back as he could remember, and at twenty-nine years old, that was a long time. It was hard not to have nightmares when you grew up in an environment that was less than friendly.

Haldon Anderson was one mean son-of-a-bitch, and he took great pleasure in making his son feel like shit as often as possible. When Haldon wasn't in jail, he was out on a fishing boat making money to drown himself in a bottle of liquor and whatever pills he could get his hands on. And when Haldon got on one of his benders, there was absolutely nothing that was going to stop him. Whether Haldon used his fists or his words, he knew how to make a person bleed.

Haldon had laughed when Jax became a deputy seven years ago. He'd thought it was one of the greatest jokes of his life.

"This is perfect," he'd said, wiping his fingers underneath his eyes. "A worthless boy doing a thankless job. Working for justice my ass, you're not going to do anything to make this world a better place. The only thing you could've possibly done to achieve that was to have never been born."

Yup, Haldon Anderson, father of the *fucking* year.

As a child, Jax couldn't understand why his mother let his father get away with all the abuse. But Patricia Anderson wasn't a strong woman and her greatest weakness was Haldon. She hadn't protected her child like a mother should. Actually, she hadn't done anything that a mother should do.

Jax shook his head and pulled himself out of the past. That was the last thing he wanted to think about.

He put on a sweatshirt, a pair of gym shorts, and his sneakers before he headed out into the chilly April morning. He stretched for a minute before he hit the pavement and attempted to run from his demons.

* * *

Grace King inhaled deeply as she pulled out a fresh batch of Bananas Foster muffins. The rich smell filled her nose before it expanded her lungs. She smiled as she set them on the counter to cool. These muffins were going to sell out with the morning breakfast rush.

Grace didn't care if she was making cookies, pies, or

cupcakes; she never got tired of it. One of her first memories was sitting in the kitchen at her grandparents' house while she watched her mother stir chocolate cake batter. Grace's fondest memories of her mother were the two of them baking together. Claire King had lost her battle to breast cancer almost fourteen years ago. But before she died, she'd passed on her love for baking to her daughter.

Grace had been working in her grandmother's café since she was eight years old. Now, at twenty-four, she helped her grandmother run Café Lula. The café was a small, brightly painted cottage out on Mirabelle Beach. The promise of freshly baked food kept customers from all over town and the county pouring in no matter the time of day or the season.

The day promised to be a busy one, as Grace had to fill up the dessert case with fresh goodies. She'd been experimenting with cupcake recipes the past couple of weeks. She'd wanted to make something amazing for her sister-in-law's baby shower. Grace had eaten dinner at Brendan and Paige's the night before, and she'd been the one in charge of dessert. For fear of disappointing a sassy pregnant woman, she'd brought her A-game and made two different types of cupcakes.

"I think my favorite is the Blueberry Lemonade," Paige had said as she'd rubbed her ever-growing belly. "But Trevor seems to like this Red Velvet Cheesecake one. I think he's dancing in there."

Trevor Oliver King was supposed to be gracing the world with his presence around the middle of May. Grace couldn't wait to meet her nephew. Paige was over seven months pregnant, and she was one of those women who still looked beautiful even though she was growing another human being inside of her. If Grace didn't love her sister-in-law dearly, she would've been fifty shades of jealous. As it was, she was only about twenty shades.

But really, Grace couldn't be happier for her brother and

sister-in-law. Brendan was going to be an amazing father. Much better than his or Grace's had been.

Neither Brendan nor Grace had ever had their fathers in their lives. Brendan's dad had gotten their mother pregnant when she was seventeen. When he'd found out, he promptly split town and never looked back. But while Brendan at least knew who his father was, Grace had no idea about hers. It was one of the great mysteries, and a constant source of gossip in Mirabelle.

There were many things in life that Grace was grateful for, her brother and Paige topping the list. They were a team and they worked together. They loved each other deeply. And Grace envied that stupid dopey look they always got on their faces. She wanted that. And she knew exactly who she wanted it with. It was just too bad for her that the man in question was stubborn and refused to see her as anything besides his best friend's little sister.

Grace took a deep breath and shook her head, bringing herself back to the muffins that she had to take to the front of the café. There was no need to concern herself with frustrating men at the moment. So she loaded up a tray with an already cooled batch of muffins and went to load the display case before the eight o'clock rush of customers filled the café. But when she pushed her way through the door she found the frustrating man in question on the other side, staring at her with her favorite pair of deep green eyes.

* * *

Jax's whole body relaxed when he saw Grace push through the door from the kitchen. The moment she saw him her blue eyes lit up and her cupid's bow mouth split into a giant grin. She'd always looked at him that way. Like he was her favorite person in the whole world. God knew she was his.

"Heya, Deputy. Let me guess," she said as she put the tray down on the counter, "you came here for coffee?"

No. He'd come here to see her. He always came here to see her. But coffee was a legitimate enough excuse, especially since he hadn't gotten that much sleep and was at the beginning of another twelve-hour shift.

"Please," he said, drumming his long, freckled fingers on the counter.

"Did you eat breakfast?" she asked as she pulled a to-go cup off the stack and started pumping coffee into it.

"I'm fine."

"Hmm." She looked over her shoulder at him and pursed her lips. "You know that isn't going to fly for a second. I got just the thing to go with this." She put the steaming cup and a lid down on the counter. "Go fix your coffee while I bag up your breakfast."

Grace turned around and pushed through the door to the kitchen as Jax grabbed his cup and went over to the end of the counter where the sugar and milk was.

Since Jax was four years old, the King women had been feeding him. Between them and Shep's mom, theirs were the only home-cooked meals he'd gotten after his grandmother died. If it hadn't been for them, he would've gone to bed with an empty stomach more nights than most.

Patricia Anderson wasn't much of a Susie Homemaker. Between her long hours working at the Piggly Wiggly, and drinking herself into a stupor and getting high when Haldon was on parole, she sometimes forgot to stock the freezer with corndogs and mini pizzas for her son.

"Here you go."

Jax turned to find Grace by his side. She hadn't gotten the height gene like Brendan. She was about five-feet-four and came in just under Jax's chin. Her petite stature and soft heart-shaped face inspired an overwhelming urge in him to protect her. She'd always inspired that feeling in him, ever since her mother brought her home from the hospital all those years ago.

"They're Bananas Foster muffins and they're fresh out of the oven," she said, holding out a bag.

"Thanks, Princess," he said, grabbing the bag and letting his fingers brush the back of her hand.

God, he loved the way her skin felt against his.

"Anytime, Jax." She smiled widely at him. A second later she stepped into him and grabbed his forearms for balance as she stretched up on her toes and kissed his jaw.

It was something Grace had done a thousand and one times before. She had no concept of personal boundaries with him, and she was wide open with her affection. And just like always, when her lips brushed his skin he had the overwhelming desire to turn into her. To feel her lips against his. To grab her and hold her against him while he explored her mouth with his.

But instead of following that impulse, he let her pull back from him.

"Eat those while they're hot," she said, pointing to the bag.

"I will," he promised.

"Do you need something for lunch? I can get you a sandwich."

"I'm good."

"Really?" she asked putting her hands on her hips and narrowing her eyes at him.

He couldn't help but grin at her attempt to intimidate him.

There was no doubt about the fact that Grace King was tough. She'd had to grow a thick skin over the years. Even though Jax, along with Brendan and Shep, had done everything in their power to try to protect her, they couldn't be there to shield her from everything. So Grace had done everything to even up the score with whoever tried to put her down. She wasn't a shy little thing by any means, and she'd tell anybody what was up without a moment's hesitation.

"I'll stop somewhere and get something," he said.

"Or I can give you something now," she said, exasperated. "I'm getting you a sandwich." She turned on her heal and walked back into the kitchen.

"Grace, you don't have to do this," Jax said, following her.

"I know." She looked over her shoulder as she opened the refrigerator. "But I'm going to anyway."

Jax watched as Grace filled a bag with two sandwiches, a bag of chips, a cup of fruit salad, and his favorite, a butterscotch cookie.

"This should last you till dinner."

Jax didn't say anything as he pulled his wallet out to pay for everything.

"Oh, I don't think so," Grace said, shaking her head. "You are *not* paying."

Before Jax could respond the side door in the kitchen opened and Lula Mae walked in.

To the casual observer, Grace and Brendan's grandmother wouldn't strike a person as someone to be feared. She had a kind face and bright blue eyes that, when paired with her ample stature and friendly disposition, inspired a feeling of warmth and openness. But Lula Mae was fiercely loyal, and those blue eyes could go as cold as ice when someone hurt anyone she loved. Lula Mae had declared Jax as one of hers over twenty-five years ago, and she'd marched down to his parents' house more than once to give them a piece of her mind.

Jax had spent more nights sleeping at the Kings' house than he could count. It was one of the few places he'd actually felt safe growing up. And even now whenever he saw her or her husband, Oliver, he had that overwhelming feeling of being protected.

"Jaxson Lance Anderson," Lula Mae said, walking up to him, "what in the world is your wallet doing out? Your money is no good here."

"That's what I just told him."

Jax turned back to Grace, who was wearing a self-satisfied smile.

"Your granddaughter just gave me over thirty dollars' worth of food." He indicated the stuffed bag on the counter before he turned back to Lula Mae.

"I don't care," she said, shaking her head. "Now give me some sugar before you go and keep the people of Mirabelle safe."

"Yes, ma'am." Jax leaned down and gave Lula Mae a peck on the check.

"And next time I see that wallet of yours make an appearance in this establishment, you are going to get a smack upside that handsome head of yours. You understand me?"

"Yes, ma'am," Jax repeated.

"Good boy." She nodded, patting his cheek.

"Thanks again," he said, reaching for the bag of food and his coffee. "I'll see you two later."

"Bye, sugar," Lula Mae said as she rounded the counter.

"See you later." Grace gave him another of her face-splitting grins.

Jax headed for the door, unable to stop his own smile from spreading across his face.

* * *

Grace stared at Jax's retreating form as he walked out of the kitchen, and she appreciated every inch of it. He had a lean muscular body. His shoulders filled out the top of his forest green deputy's shirt, and his strong back tapered down to his waist. His shirt was tucked into his green pants that hung low from his narrow hips and covered his long, toned legs.

And oh, dear God, did Jaxson Anderson have a nice ass.

Though her appreciation of said ass had only been going on for about ten years, the appreciation of Jaxson Anderson had been discovered a long time ago. He was the boy who saved her from bullies on the playground. The boy who gave her his ice cream cone when hers fell in the dirt. The boy who picked her up off the ground when she Rollerbladed into a tree. The boy who let her cry on his shoulder after her mom died.

Yes, Brendan and Shep had done all those things as well, but Jax was different. Jax was hers. She'd decided that eighteen years ago. She'd just been waiting for him to figure it out.

But the man was ridiculously slow on the uptake.

Grace had been in love with him since she was six years old. She loved his freckles and his reddish brown hair. His hair that was always long enough to where someone could run their fingers through it and rumple it just a little. Not that she'd ever rumpled Jax's hair, but a girl always had her fantasies, and getting Jax all tousled was most definitely one of Grace's.

Jax was always so in control and self-contained, and so damn serious. More often than not, that boy had a frown on his face, which was probably why every time Grace saw his dimpled smile it made her go all warm and giddy.

God she loved his smile. She just wanted to kiss it, to run her lips down from his mouth to his smooth, triangular jaw.

Grace sighed wistfully as the door shut behind him and turned to her grandmother.

"You get your young man all fed and caffeinated?" Lula Mae asked as she pulled containers out of the refrigerator.

"I don't know about 'my young man,' but I did get Jax something to soak up that coffee he came in for."

"Oh, sweetie," Lula Mae said, looking at Grace and shaking her head pityingly, "that boy did not come in here for coffee."

"Hmmm, well he sure didn't ask for anything else," Grace said as she walked over to the stove and started plating the rest of her muffins.

"Just give it time."

"Time?" Grace spun around to look at her grandmother. "How much *time* does the man need? He's had years."

"Yes, well, he'll figure things out. Sooner than later I think."

"I don't think so. To him, I'm just Brendan's little sister."

"There's no *just* about it," Lula Mae said, grabbing one last container before she closed the fridge and walked back to the counter where she'd piled everything else. "He doesn't have brotherly feelings for you, Gracie. I've never seen anyone fluster that boy the way you do."

"Oh, come on, Jaxson Anderson doesn't get flustered," Grace said, shaking her head.

"If you think that, then he isn't the only one who's blind."

"What's that supposed to mean?"

"You see, Gracie, you've never had the chance to observe him when you aren't around."

"And?" she prompted, gesturing with her hand for her grandmother to carry on.

"He changes when you're around. Smiles more."

"Really? Because he still frowns a whole lot around me."

"Well, that's usually when some other boy is trying to get your attention, and he's jealous."

"Jealous." Grace scoffed. "Jax doesn't get jealous."

"Oh, yes, he does. Grace, you need to open your eyes; that boy has been fighting his feelings for you for years."

And with that, Lula Mae went about fixing her menu for the day, leaving Grace even more frustrated than she had been the minute before.

* * *

"Holy hell, that girl can bake."

Jax bit into his second muffin and chewed slowly. He hadn't realized how hungry he'd been until he'd taken that first bite, and then he'd promptly inhaled the first muffin. This one he intended to savor. He let the warm richness of the bread rest on his tongue for a moment before he swallowed and took a swig of his steaming coffee.

It was amazing how much better he felt with food in his stomach, or maybe he just felt better because he'd seen Grace. He *always* felt better when he saw Grace. She made everything so much brighter, so much *more*. Like swallowing a warm liquid that settled in his stomach before it shot out to his fingers and toes and made him feel like he could take on anything.

The power of caffeine had nothing on Grace King.

She was loud and vibrant, and it was almost impossible to escape her enthusiasm. She'd always had the ability to draw whoever was around into her atmosphere and keep them there. She'd drawn Jax in when she was a baby, and he'd been hooked ever since.

Though how he was hooked had changed in recent years. It hadn't been a slow gradual change, either. It had been about as subtle as Grace. Jax remembered the day vividly. She'd been eighteen years old; he'd been twenty-three.

He'd stopped by the Kings' house for dinner one night and Grace was out in the yard, washing her vintage yellow Bug. She had the radio blasting music so she hadn't heard him pull up on the street. She was wearing short cutoff blue jeans and a bright blue bikini top, the strings tied around the middle of her back and around her neck. Her light blond hair had been up in a ponytail, but a few strands had escaped and were sticking to the side of her neck. It was then, as Jax studied the slope of her neck, that he felt it. He'd wanted to come up behind her and put his mouth to that neck, taste her warm skin against his tongue.

He remembered stopping so suddenly at the thought that he'd almost tripped and landed on his face.

Grace was Brendan's little sister. Jax had watched her grow up, been there when they'd brought her home from the hospital, heard her first laugh as a baby, watched as she'd taken her first steps, sang happy birthday to her as she blew out candles on every single birthday. This was Grace, the girl he'd always thought of as his little sister. But damn if every single one of those brotherly feelings was gone.

Every. Last. One. Of. Them.

And then he'd watched, paralyzed from the revelation, as she turned to dunk the sponge in her hand in a bucket of soapy water, and he got a glimpse of her side.

"What the hell is that?"

Somehow he'd found his tongue and his voice had carried over the beat of the music.

Grace looked up and turned to him, her usual grin spreading across her face. But he'd only had a moment to register her smile because his eyes darted back down to her side where a blue swallow about the size of his hand was tattooed on her upper ribs. It was diving down; one of its wings spanned her side, the other wrapped around to cup under her right breast.

Jax had never thought much of Grace's breasts. They were small, not even a handful. But now? Now he wanted to know what those felt like, too. His fingers were itching to untie those straps.

What the hell was wrong with him?

"Why, Jaxson Anderson," Grace drawled, "are you star-ing at my chest?"

Jax looked up, and he could feel the flush coming to his cheeks. But he was determined to play this off, because he would go to the grave before he admitted to wanting one of his best friends' baby sister.

"No, I'm looking at that tattoo on your side," he said, let-ting his anger boil over into his voice. "What the hell did you do? Does Brendan know about this?" he almost screamed at her.

Why the hell was he so pissed off?

Because that tattoo was sexy as hell and he didn't want anyone looking at it. Or God, touching it. Touching her.

Her smile disappeared in an instant and her blue eyes turned icy. "He was there when I got it a month ago," she said, narrowing her eyes at him.

"He let you?" Jax asked, incredulous.

"Brendan doesn't *let me* do anything," Grace said, cross-ing her arms under her chest. It made her small breasts more prominent.

How had he not noticed how amazing they were before that moment?

"In case you hadn't noticed, I'm not a child anymore, Jax."

And that had been precisely the problem, because he *had* finally noticed. And it had tortured him every single day for the last six years.

Jax sighed before he took another bite of his muffin, because boy did Grace ever like to torture him.

Grace's friendliness tended to come off as flirting, and nothing got under Jax's skin more than when he saw Grace flirting with some little schmuck. He'd had to watch as guy after guy paraded through her life. Okay, so there hadn't been that many guys who'd gotten past the flirting stage. But none of them had been good enough for her, not a single one.

Jax wasn't good enough, either, so he'd resigned himself to doing what he *was* good enough for, watching out for her. And man was watching hard.

Chapter Two

Mr. Monosyllabic vs. the
Red High Heels

Jax, Brendan, and Shep had all met on their first day of preschool almost twenty-five years ago. They'd been best friends ever since. Brendan was a mechanic and helped his grandfather run King's Auto. Shep's family owned a bar called the Sleepy Sheep out on the beach.

The Sleepy Sheep had been a landmark in Mirabelle for the last sixty-five years. The bar had a Scottish pub feel to it, and the locals and tourists loved it. Shep's grandparents moved to the area after his grandfather had gotten out of the air force following WWII. Owen Shepherd bought the land and built the bar with his own two hands. It had survived a number of hurricanes and more bar fights than anyone could count. Not that it was a rowdy place or anything. As it went with most establishments that served alcohol, some people just couldn't handle their liquor, and Jax had been called down a number of times to deal with the drunks.

But tonight Jax wasn't on duty. Tonight he was going to drink a beer and watch the Yankees demolish the Red Sox. When he was in the second grade, he'd had to do a report on a famous person. He'd stumbled across a biography on

Mickey Mantle and he'd been a Yankee fan ever since. This had also inspired Jax to start playing the game.

Baseball was good for Jax. He'd channeled his anger into his pitching and when that wasn't enough, he used it for batting practice. Jax, Brendan, and Shep had all joined the county baseball league as children. Jax was always a pitcher, Brendan a catcher, and Shep played shortstop. The Kings and Shepherds had split all of the fees so Jax could play, and they drove him to all of the practices and games.

In high school, the three boys had been pretty unstoppable. All of them had made varsity their sophomore year. They'd gone to the playoffs all three years, and had even won state their senior year. They all continued to play on the adult league for the county, but that wouldn't start up until July.

Jax parked his truck in the lot and walked up to the front of the building. On either side of the front door were two large paned windows that gave a clear view into the crowded bar. The sign above the door creaked in the cool April breeze that blew in off the Gulf. The sign read THE SLEEPY SHEEP in big green letters. Two sheep slept in the corner, Z's trailing above their heads. Jax pushed open the door to the comforting sounds and smells of one of his favorite places.

While they were growing up, Jax, Brendan, and Shep weren't allowed in the bar when alcohol was being served. But in those few hours before it opened, Shep's parents gave them root beer in chilled mugs and let them play pool and darts to their hearts' content.

The walls, floors, and ceilings of the inside of the bar had been built with the same dark wood as the outside. Over the years the walls had been covered with signed dollar bills and framed cartoon pictures of drunken sheep. The bar was located at the back of the room, running along the wall.

Booths lined the walls to the left, and tables surrounded by chairs were scattered across the floor. The right side of the room housed two pool tables and a dartboard. There was a stage in the far corner where a live band sometimes played. The rest of the time music would blare from the jukebox. Tonight there was the added noise from the TVs hanging from the walls.

Jax made his way to the back of the bar and slid into an empty stool next to Bennett Hart. Bennett had been a year younger in high school and he played third baseman Jax's junior and senior year. Bennett had joined the air force right out of high school. He still sported his short hair that eight years in the service had ingrained in him. During his last tour, he was on a mission when the helicopter he was in was shot down. Only one other man had survived.

Bennett had been back for almost two years now. He was doing better than he had been, but Jax recognized the signs of a man trying to battle his demons. Now, Bennett did construction work to make a living, not to mention a few side jobs restoring antique furniture and building some of his own creations. He'd also come out for the county league last year and now played for the Stingrays, along with Jax, Brendan, and Shep.

"Really?" Jax said, looking over at Bennett and shaking his head at Bennett's bright red Boston Red Sox shirt.

"What?" Bennett took a sip of his beer as he turned his head to the side to look at Jax.

"You a Red Sox fan now?"

"Nah." Bennett grinned. "But I'm not a Yankee, either. I'm Braves through and through. I figured I'd root for the Sox tonight so Grace wasn't all alone."

When Grace was six years old she decided she was going to be a Red Sox fan just to spite Jax, Brendan, and Shep. The only person that it continued to bother was Jax.

"Grace is here?" Jax asked, looking around.

"Not yet, Romeo."

Jax turned back to the bar to see Shep grinning at him. At least Shep hadn't fallen back on his loyalties. He was wearing a navy blue Yankee T-shirt.

"When are you going to get over yourself and just ask her out already?" Shep asked.

Jax frowned. He'd been dealing with these comments from Shep for the past couple of years. Brendan tended to join in, too, but he wasn't nearly as bad as Shep.

"Mind your own damn business." Jax drummed his fingers on the bar.

"Which means," Bennett said, rubbing the condensation from his own mug, "shut up and get him a beer."

"You're hopeless," Shep said, shaking his head at Jax before he turned. He grabbed a frosted mug and went to the tap, filling the mug with a rich amber liquid. "You know," Shep said as he set the mug down in front of Jax, "if you don't do something, and soon, you're going to miss your opportunity."

"Are you speaking as a wise bartender who knows all?" Jax asked, not hiding his sarcasm.

"No," Shep said seriously. "I'm speaking as a man. I'm not blind to Grace. And neither are most of the men in this town, or this bar for that matter." He indicated a spot behind him with his chin.

Jax turned, and as always, the instant his eyes landed on Grace, he felt the intensity of it everywhere, and did he mean *everywhere*. She was wearing a white T-shirt with a big red "B" on the front, skintight jeans, and red high-heeled shoes that made her at least four inches taller. She was pretty much completely covered, but every single article of clothing hugged her small curves in amazing ways. And her face and hair completed the entire picture. Her eyes were smoky;

the black and gray stuff she'd used around her bright blue eyes made them look impossibly brighter. Grace's hair fell just past her shoulder blades, but tonight she'd curled it. Thick, soft strands swirled around her face and the top of her shoulders.

He wanted to plunge his fingers through it.

Instead he tried not to swallow his tongue.

* * *

Grace walked into the Sleepy Sheep, and as always, her eyes zeroed in on the one man she always wanted to see. She'd known he was here. She'd seen his red truck in the parking lot. But something had to be said for the fact that she'd known exactly where he was when she'd walked into the bar. He turned around and his eyes met hers for a moment before they traveled the length of her body. She felt that slow, lingering gaze *everywhere*.

He swallowed hard and took a deep breath as his eyes settled on hers again, and the frown on his face deepened.

Interesting.

Grace had decided she was through playing fair. She had long ago figured out how to play to her strengths, so tonight she'd pulled out all of the big guns. She had a small chest, something she hadn't inherited from her mother or her grandmother. But an ingenious push-up bra gave her A-cup breasts a little boost. Grace had a tiny waist, but below that, her hips flared out into a rather round butt that didn't look half bad in a good pair of jeans. She was short; something she knew could only be fixed with heels. And the power of red high heels was not to be trifled with.

As she made her way toward the bar, she was aware of a surprising number of eyes that were on her. But she could care less about any of them except for one deep green pair, the same green pair that appeared to get more agitated the closer she got.

"You okay?" she asked, stopping in front of Jax. "You look tense."

"And that's different how?"

Grace looked behind the bar to find Nathanial Shepherd grinning at her. But no one called him Nathanial. Well, besides his mother, grandmother, and Lula Mae. Everyone called him Shep. Jax and Shep were on opposite sides of the spectrum in many ways; Brendan fell somewhere in the middle.

Out of the three of them, Shep was most definitely the bad boy of the group. Tattoos were scattered across both of his arms and forearms. He had perpetual scruff on his wide, chiseled jaw and above his lips, which were usually quirked up in a smile. He had the darkest blue eyes that Grace had ever seen on a man and thick wavy black hair that was always shaggy and rumpled.

There was no doubt about it, Shep was hot. But Grace had never had any romantic feelings for him. No, those were reserved for the scowling redhead in front of her.

Grace tilted her head to the side and studied Jax's scowl, which reached all the way up to the corners of his eyes and wrinkled his forehead.

"More tense than usual," Grace amended.

"Something that could be so easily remedied," Shep said.

"Shep's remedies for life," someone said, sliding an arm around Grace, "most likely include sex."

Grace looked up into the smiling face of Brendan. Claire King had passed on her light blue eyes to both of her children, but Brendan had inherited Claire's wide smile. Whenever Grace saw it, she was intensely grateful she could still see small pieces of her mother were still alive.

"Hey, Gracie." He kissed her temple.

"You would know all about my remedies for life." Shep smirked. "Speaking of which, I wasn't expecting you tonight. Where is your *very* pregnant wife?"

"Paige is spending some quality time with her mother."

"How's Denise doing?" Bennett asked.

"It's still hard for her without Trevor. But working part-time at the health clinic is keeping her a little busy. I think the baby will be good for her. When Paige is done with her maternity leave, Denise is going to watch him a couple of days a week," Brendan said, letting go of Grace and sliding onto the stool on the other side of Bennett.

Last September, Paige's father had lost his battle with pancreatic cancer. Grace could relate to Paige's loss; she knew what it was like to have a parent die. But she couldn't relate to what Denise was going through. She couldn't imagine losing the love of her life. And with that thought, Grace's gaze flickered back to Jax, who was still frowning at her.

"Seriously, what's up with you?" Grace whispered to Jax as she sat down on the stool next to him.

"Nothing." He took a drink of his beer.

"Long day?" she asked.

"Yeah."

"Busy?"

"Yup." He nodded.

"You working tomorrow?"

"Uh-huh."

So he was in monosyllabic form tonight. Not that Jaxson Anderson could ever be considered talkative. But still, he really was the most frustrating human being. Ever.

"I need a tall drink, or a tall man."

Grace turned to find Harper Laurence sliding onto the seat next to her.

Grace had been friends with Harper for twelve years. The Laurences had moved down to Mirabelle when Harper's dad had inherited his uncle's veterinary practice. Harper had been one of those girls who had taken a little time to grow into her body. She'd been slightly overweight when she'd started the sixth grade. Grace had known exactly what it was like to be bullied, and she, along with Melanie O'Bryan, had brought Harper into their circle.

Harper had grown into her body in high school. Her curves had come into full bloom, and those same guys who had bullied her started drooling over her. Along with those curves, she had thick black hair that flowed down to the middle of her back, and violet eyes. Add to that the fact that she was a massage therapist with magic hands, and any man was a goner.

"Oh, jeez, not another one."

Grace turned back to Jax who was shaking his head at Harper's bright red Boston Red Sox T-shirt.

"The numbers are even now. Three to three. Drink your beer and shut up," Grace said before she turned back to Harper. "What's wrong?"

"Guess who came in today," Harper said, raising one of her perfectly plucked black eyebrows.

"Who?"

"Bethelda Grimshaw."

"We're going to need something stronger than a beer down here," Grace called down to Shep, who was filling a mug up for Brendan. "Harper had to deal with the dragon today."

Bethelda Grimshaw was Mirabelle's resident bitch. She'd worked for the town newspaper fifteen years ago. Back then she had a tendency to report on things that were less than savory, her stories focusing on the people of Mirabelle. When her articles turned downright nasty people demanded that Bethelda be fired; Oliver King, Brendan and Grace's grandfather, had been the loudest. Grace and Brendan's parentage had been the subject of many articles.

Now Bethelda used her online blog to spread her trash. Her blog was one of those things that no one in Mirabelle would admit to reading, yet everyone knew what she wrote about.

Brendan leaned back in his chair to look at Harper. Grace recognized the look on his face. It was the one that meant he was barely holding in his anger. Brendan had a bit of a temper, and a surefire way to light it up was to mention Bethelda Grimshaw. Brendan and Paige had been the focus of quite a few of Bethelda's articles over the last year and a half.

"She write an article about you?" he asked.

"Oh, I'm sure it's just a matter of time, but no, not today. She's one of my new clients, though. Do you think 'horrible hag' is contagious?" she asked, looking at Grace a bit pathetically. "I don't want to grow scales on my hands."

"I know just the cure for that," Shep said, putting down two glasses filled with ice. "Tequila." He poured a generous amount of the golden liquid into a metal container that he pulled out from under the bar. He added many other brightly colored liquids from bottles behind the counter before he put a metal top on the container and shook it. He poured his concoction into the glasses; it was an orangish red that reminded Grace of a sunset. "Drink up," he said, putting a straw in each glass and pushing them across the bar to Harper and Grace.

Grace grabbed her drink and took a long sip. It tasted like citrus, strawberries, something else that she couldn't quite put her finger on, and a healthy dose of tequila.

"Mmm, what is this called?" Harper asked, sounding like she was in heaven.

"The Dragon Killer."

"This is amazing," Grace said, closing her eyes and taking a long pull.

When she opened her eyes again, she saw Jax staring at her out of the corner of her eye.

"What?" she asked, turning to him.

"Nothing," he said, shaking his head and turning his focus to the TV that was mounted on the wall behind the bar.

"He seems moodier than usual," Grace whispered out of the side of her mouth at Harper.

"That's probably because of what you're wearing, darling. He can actually see the outline of your boobs and he doesn't know what to do with himself." Harper talked around the straw that was still in her mouth.

"I have a few ideas," Grace whispered back.

"Oh, I'm sure you do."

"What are you two conspiring about?" Shep asked, moving in front of them again.

"How the Red Sox are going to kick your beloved Yankees in the ass," Grace said, pasting on her customary smart-ass grin.

"You want to bet, Princess?" Jax asked.

Grace looked at Jax over her shoulder and batted her eyes at him. "Absolutely, big boy. How much?"

"We get to make the terms," Harper burst out before Jax could say anything.

"What?" Grace asked, turning to look at her.

"We get to make the terms, me, Shep, Brendan, and Bennett. And you two don't get to see what the wager is until the game is done."

"I don't know about that," Jax said.

Grace turned to look at him and grinned wickedly. "Scared?" she taunted.

"Not on your life. Fine, you guys make the terms." He leaned back and took another sip of his beer.

"Give me a napkin," Harper said as she dug a pen out of her purse.

She scribbled something down, her hand covering what she wrote from everyone's view. She folded the napkin in half and passed it to Shep. Shep unfolded the napkin, and his mouth split into a grin before he passed it to Bennett, who laughed before he handed it to Brendan.

"Boy am I ever so glad I came out tonight," Brendan said, passing the napkin back to Shep, who shoved it in his back pocket.

"Shake on it," Harper demanded.

"Prepare to be walloped," Grace said as she stuck out her hand.

"Princess, you're the one who's in for a world of pain," he said as his long, strong fingers wrapped around the back of her hand. Their hands pumped once, before they let go.

Jax's words affected Grace because she knew that far beyond this bet he had the power to hurt her more than anyone else.

* * *

It was the bottom of the ninth, and the score was 7–5, the Yankees leading. The Yankees had been pitching a fairly good game, but with only one out and a Red Sox player on both first and second, it wasn't over.

Jax was on edge, but it had less to do with the game and more to do with the woman next to him.

What the hell was wrong with him?

From the moment she'd walked into the bar he'd been a freaking mess. It was taking everything in him to focus on the game, and not the constant feel of her leg brushing up against his, or the ever-present smell of her soft perfume. He just wanted to push his nose into the hollow of her throat and inhale.

And what the hell were the terms of the bet? What the hell had he agreed to? He'd lost his damn mind.

It was all Grace's fault. Her too tight T-shirt was

distracting him. But it wasn't like she could take it off or anything.

And then he had an image of her taking off her too tight T-shirt.

"Shit," he mumbled, rubbing his eyes with his palms. But that image wasn't going anywhere.

Grace turned to look at him, her knee brushing his thigh for the hundredth time that night.

"What?" he asked, looking at her.

"Nothing," she said, shaking her head, looking more than slightly amused. "You just keep mumbling to yourself over there. It must be a fascinating conversation."

"Grace, pay attention," Harper said, leaning over the bar to get a better view of the TV.

Jax turned just as the batter for the Red Sox took a swing and the ball sailed past the outfield and into the stands.

"Shit," Jax repeated, but Grace's and Harper's loud cheers drowned it out.

"Okay, what do I win?" Grace asked, sticking her hand out toward Shep.

The grin that spread across Shep's face made Jax more than a little nervous. Shep pulled the napkin out of his pocket and placed it in Grace's hand. She opened the napkin, her eyes gleaming.

"Perfect," she said, slapping the napkin down in front of Jax so he could read it.

The loser has to ask the winner to dance to a song of the winner's choosing.

"I don't dance." Jax looked up at all the eyes now focused on him.

"You shook on it," Bennett said. "That's a verbal contract. As a man of the law you can't back out."

God, how the hell was he going to last three minutes with Grace pushed up against him?

"Don't worry, Jax," Grace whispered in his ear, "it'll be painless."

Nope, that wasn't true. He'd been in quite a bit of pain for the last three hours. Dancing with Grace was going to be excruciating.

"Go pick your song, Princess." He turned to her, his face just inches away. He was so close to her that he had an up-close and personal view of her blue eyes.

Grace slid off her seat and Harper followed her to the corner.

"You guys suck." Jax finished his beer. What he really needed was a shot of whiskey, but that wasn't in his best interest since he would be driving soon.

"Yeah," Shep said, shaking his head. "You have to dance with a beautiful girl. Your life is so hard."

"I don't know how you do it," Brendan said.

A soft slow song picked up over the speakers and Jax stood up as Grace made her way across the bar. She stopped in front of him, her smile suddenly shy. It made his chest tighten.

"Can I have this dance, Princess?" he asked, holding out his hand for her.

"Absolutely," she said, putting her hand in his.

He led her away from the four pairs of prying eyes onto the nearly empty dance floor. He slowly spun her around and pulled her to him, her body right up against his. He placed his free hand at the small of her back, and she rested hers on his shoulder.

Jax had danced with Grace before, but he could never fully prepare himself for the feeling of having her so near. How her hand felt in his, or what it did to him when she rested her head on his chest, or how every time he breathed he inhaled her. He could dance with her every day for the rest of his life, and it would still feel like this. Like his world was here in front of him, like the most important thing in his life was in his hands. And then the music would end, she'd walk away, and he'd be surprised he was still standing.

Jax moved his head, and his nose skimmed the top of her hair. He closed his eyes and inhaled deeply as he continued to move them slowly across the dance floor.

"Jax," Grace whispered as she pulled back from his chest and looked up at him, "are you going to tell me why you're in such a mood?"

"Your clothes are too tight."

"What?" she asked, confusion wrinkling her forehead. "You don't like what I'm wearing?"

"No," he lied. Problem was he liked it *way* too much. "Every guy in this place is looking at you," he said, looking down at her.

"Why do you care?"

"Because I don't like the way they're looking at you."

"Is this you doing your big brother thing and trying to protect me?"

"Yes," he lied again. This had nothing to do with any *big brother thing*. He was pretty sure that if Brendan ever got an idea of all of the non–big brother things he wanted to do to her, Brendan would punch him in the face. "None of them are good enough for you. They only want to get in your pants."

Hurt flashed through her eyes before they hardened and turned icy. "So what you're saying is, I dress like a slut?"

"I didn't say that," Jax said.

"I can take care of myself, you know."

"I'm sure you can," he said, maybe a little bit too patronizingly. But what did she expect? He would go to the grave trying to protect her. Especially from all the assholes eyeing her like she was dessert.

"You don't believe me?" she asked.

"I do believe you. But old habits die hard."

"You can say that again," she said, clearly beyond pissed off.

"Grace?"

"You know, I could care less about getting anyone's attention, except for one person who is clearly an idiot. Or maybe I'm the idiot. You tell me no one is good enough for me?" she asked, raising her eyebrows. "Well, why don't you do something about it?" She pushed away from him, leaving him standing in the middle of the dance floor.

"Grace," he called after her.

"I'm out of here." She grabbed her purse from the bar and turned around.

"What's wrong," he said, blocking her path to the door.

"Don't, Jax." She refused to meet his gaze.

"Grace." He said her name again, needing to see her eyes.

When she looked up at him, the wetness that he found in her eyes brought him up short.

"Just let me go, Jax," she whispered desperately.

He nodded, stepping out of her way. He turned and watched her walk away, completely baffled as to what had just happened.

Chapter Three

The Dangers of Flour

Grace pounded her fists into the dough in front of her. But it wasn't helping. The harder she pounded, the angrier she got.

Yes, she was pissed at Jax, but she was more pissed at herself.

Stupid, stupid, stupid.

How many times had she told herself that Jax didn't look at her that way? And yet she'd pushed it and made an idiot of herself. Oh, she'd gotten him to notice her, but only because he thought she dressed like a slut. And to top it off he'd pulled out his go-to brotherly advice and made her feel like a child. Like his best friend's baby sister.

Perfect, just perfect.

Every time her fist hit the dough, a canister of metal utensils jumped and clanged together.

He doesn't want you. Not in the way you want him. Let it go. Let him go.

Grace stopped and closed her eyes. She dropped her head between her shoulders and leaned forward. She gripped the counter with both hands and took a deep breath, trying to find an ounce of composure.

The very idea of letting go of Jax was impossible, and she was lying to herself if she thought it was possible.

But she was so good at lying to herself. The few relationships she'd been in had been a lie. How could a person give themselves to someone truly and completely when they were in love with someone else? Grace had never been able to do it, which had ultimately led to the end of those relationships. But she kept trying to find that *someone* who would make her get over Jax.

That *someone* didn't exist. He was a mythological creature, because for Grace, there only was Jax.

Suddenly, Grace wanted her mother so desperately she couldn't breathe. She swiped uselessly at the tears streaming down her face.

Yes, Grace could always go to Lula Mae, and her grandmother would give her a wealth of advice. But Lula Mae had never dealt with anything like this before, having your heart broken by a man.

Grace's grandparents had been married for fifty-two years, and they'd been in love long before that. Grace knew it hadn't always been easy; they had to bury their only child, and that sadness plagued them every day. They knew heartache of an entirely different kind.

But Claire had dealt with the heartache of loving someone who hadn't loved her back. Claire had loved Brendan's father, but Crayton Dallas had never returned that love. He'd abandoned Claire, left her without a second thought. He'd never been capable of love. At least that's what Grace believed, because what other explanation could there be for a man who could walk out on the mother of his unborn child.

And as for Grace's father? Well, that was a whole other topic of conversation.

Claire died when Grace was ten years old. Grace had

been too young to demand to know who her father was then. And now the only person who could tell Grace was gone. But whoever he was, he'd either not known, or not cared. Grace didn't know for sure, but she had a hard time imagining her mother not telling Grace's father. So she went with the notion that he just hadn't cared.

Had this man broken Claire's heart, too? Had she loved him? How had she dealt with it? How had she moved on? All of this would be helpful information to know so that Grace could figure out how to move on from Jax, because she had no freaking clue how to do it.

Grace took another deep calming breath before she opened her eyes and straightened. She wiped away the remaining tears from her cheeks and dried her hands on her apron.

She was tired; that's why she was being so emotional. She hadn't slept very well after she left the bar. Her mind had been full of useless thoughts that hadn't gotten her anywhere, and had kept her from sleep until well after one in the morning. She'd woken up at five, and instead of lying in bed for an hour and a half, she'd decided to go to the café and cook.

Pies were on the agenda for the day, thus her dough pounding. At least the café wasn't going to open for another thirty minutes. She had a little bit of time to collect herself and down another cup of coffee.

Yes, coffee would help her nerves.

As she reached for her empty mug, a knock from the side door in the kitchen had her spinning around. Through the light blue sheers covering the windows, she could just make out the dark green uniform of an Atticus county deputy.

"Oh, awesome. Just what my morning needs, more humiliation," she whispered as she walked across the kitchen and unlocked the door.

* * *

Grace had been crying.

If there was anything that brought Jax to his knees, it was Grace crying. She had flour on her face, and he could see the path the tears had taken down her cheeks.

"Grace, what's wrong?" Jax asked, stepping into the kitchen, not waiting for her to invite him in.

"Nothing," she said, turning around and walking away from him. "Did you come for coffee?" She grabbed her mug from the counter before she walked through the swinging door and out to the café.

God, he hated it when she walked away from him. That's all he'd been able to think about last night. Well, that and all of the disappointment from his friends. Harper had declared him an idiot before she'd followed Grace out of the bar. Shep had asked him what his problem was, Brendan had told him he better fix it, and Bennett had just frowned and shaken his head.

"No," he said, pushing through the door behind her, "I came to talk to you about last night."

"There's nothing to talk about," she said as she pumped coffee into her cup. "I got upset, now I'm over it. Case closed."

"If you were over it, why are you still upset? You've been crying, don't try and hide it. I know that I—"

"Contrary to popular belief, *Jaxson,*" she interrupted as she grabbed a to-go cup from the stack and started to pump it full of coffee, "not everything is about you."

Jax crossed the space between them and came up behind her. He put his hand over hers and stopped her vicious pumping. "Grace," he said in a low voice, "I've never once believed everything was about me. And you damn well know it."

Grace took a deep breath, her shoulders rising and falling.

"I'm sorry, Jax. I was thinking about my mom," she

whispered before she pulled her hand out from underneath his. She grabbed her mug from the counter and carried both steaming cups of coffee over to where they kept the cream and sugar.

Well, damn. Claire was a tough subject for Jax to dwell on. She'd always treated him and Shep like her sons, too. And for Jax, Claire had been the mother he'd never had.

"I'm sorry, Grace," he said softly.

She was silent as she fixed both cups of coffee. But after a moment, the stubborn set of her shoulders fell and she sighed. "I just miss her," she said barely above a whisper.

"Grace." He reached for her, but she turned quickly and pushed him away before he could touch her.

"I'll be okay. Talking about her is only going to make me more upset right now." She grabbed a cap on the stand and snapped it down on the to-go cup. "Here you go," she said, holding it out for him.

"You know this isn't why I came?" he asked, taking the cup from her. "I want to know why you got upset last night."

"It isn't important." She grabbed the handle of her mug and walked around him. She pushed through the door to the kitchen and disappeared again.

She was infuriating. Not one to give up, Jax followed her. He was *going* to get an answer from her before he left.

"Is this your new tactic?" Jax asked, setting his cup down on the counter and folding his arms across his chest. "Avoidance?"

"It's worked out just great for you," she mumbled as she tossed some scones in a bag. No doubt for him to take when he left.

"What the hell is that supposed to mean?"

Grace threw the bag down onto the counter and looked up at him. "Are you honestly going to stand there and tell me that this clueless persona you have going on is the real deal? Are you honestly going to tell me that you have *no* idea?"

"No idea about what?"

"You want to know why I got upset last night?" Grace asked, marching over to him. "Why it infuriates me that you treat me like a little sister?" she shouted, shoving his chest hard. He was surprised by it and he fell a step backward. "I *don't* have sisterly feelings for you, Jaxson; I don't and I never will. But you're too blind and stubborn to see what's standing right in front of you!"

It was then Jax did the most impulsive thing he'd ever done in his life. He knew exactly where the impulse came from; he'd had the desire for years. He just wasn't sure how the overwhelming need overran all of his sense. He grabbed Grace before he even realized what he was doing. He gripped her elbows and brought her body flush up against his. His mouth came down hard on hers. She inhaled, startled, and Jax took full advantage of the tiny opening of her mouth, dipping his tongue in and finding hers.

Holy shit.

Never in his life had Jax kissed a girl and felt like his whole body was on fire, burning from the inside out. This was incredible, like nothing he'd ever known. She was warm, and sweet, and soft. How could the inside of someone's mouth feel this way? Taste this good?

Grace sighed in pleasure as her body relaxed against his. Her arms wound around his neck. He wrapped his hands around her waist as he walked her backward. When her back hit the counter he put his hands on her bottom and pulled her up to sit on top of it, their mouths never breaking.

Holy shit, his hands were on Grace's ass. Her perfect, incredible ass.

Her shoes hit the floor a second before she pulled her legs around him, her bare feet running up the back of his thighs. Her hands were on his chest, as one of his pulled out the tie in her hair so that he could run his fingers through it. She grabbed on to his side, and her hands slid around and lowered until they were on his butt. She squeezed and he thought he was going to go off, right then and there.

He pulled away from her mouth, letting his lips travel down the slope of her neck. How many times had he fantasized about this? About feeling her skin underneath his lips? God he loved her neck, the soft delicate space at the hollow of her throat.

"Jax." She said his name with so much need that he abandoned his exploration of her neck.

He palmed the back of her head in one of his hands as he slanted his mouth over hers. Grace moaned when their tongues found each other again. The sound of it rumbled in Jax's chest and settled low in his abdomen.

Jax wasn't sure how long they stayed like that, wrapped around each other in more ways than one, before a crackling noise filled the kitchen. Mary Landers's voice squawked through the speaker attached to Jax's shirt.

"Seventeen, what's your location?"

Jax pulled back from Grace, both of them breathing hard. Grace's hair was everywhere, courtesy of his hands. She opened her eyes slowly, as if she was delaying coming back to reality, but Jax slammed into it hard.

What the hell had he just done?

* * *

Grace was having an out of body experience. Or at least that was what it felt like.

Jax had kissed her.

God, his mouth had been on hers, his hands every-where, *her* hands everywhere. Grace's hands had been on

Jaxson Anderson's ass. And it was just as spectacular as she'd imagined.

But as Grace brought herself back down to earth, she registered the look on Jax's face and her eyes snapped open as everything inside of her crashed.

He did not look happy.

"Jax?" Grace asked, searching his face for something, anything besides the regret that shone plain as day in his eyes.

He didn't answer, just disentangled himself from her as he took a step back. There was no warmth in his eyes as he pushed the button on the microphone on his shoulder. "Seventeen, on Sandy Beach Drive."

"Seventeen, shoplifter at Forty-Nine Brooks Avenue. Deputy needed on location."

"Ten-four."

"Jax," Grace said, sliding off the counter and taking a step toward him.

"I have to go." He took another step back from her.

"You're not even going to say anything about what just happened?" she asked, trying to keep calm.

His mouth tightened before he shook his head. "It was a mistake. It shouldn't have happened."

Grace inhaled sharply, pulling back from him like he'd just hit her. And really he had, because those words were a slap in the face.

I'm not going to cry. Not in front of him.

So Grace did the only thing she could do, she walked away from him.

She stepped around him and pushed through the door out into the café. She closed her eyes as she leaned against the wall and tried to breathe past the tightness in her chest.

It was a mistake.

She reached up and grabbed her throat. The wall behind Grace shuddered slightly as the side door in the kitchen closed. He was gone and he didn't want her. She slid down the wall and pressed her face into her bent knees.

It shouldn't have happened.

God it hurt. It hurt so damn much.

Grace gave up trying to fight it and let the pain wash through her. She wasn't sure how long she sat on the floor hugging her bent knees. She kept reliving what had happened in the kitchen.

He'd grabbed her. *He'd* kissed her. Not the other way around. But he'd also decided that it had been a mistake.

Grace was done. She was done waiting for a man who didn't want her. She was done living with this constant ache. She refused to let him break her. She wasn't going to let that man affect her anymore.

Grace wiped the remaining tears from under her eyes and pulled herself up onto her feet. She took a deep breath before she pushed through the door and walked back into the kitchen. Jax's cup of coffee was still sitting on the counter, so was his bag of scones. Grace stared at them for a second before she grabbed both of them. She threw them into the trash can with so much force that the coffee exploded up and around the sides.

Okay, starting *now* she wasn't going to let him affect her anymore.

* * *

Haldon Anderson had never been a model citizen. He'd never been a model *anything*. He dropped out of school when he was sixteen and started working off of various fishing boats that came in and out of Mirabelle. He also started drinking, heavily. Haldon had a short fuse, and it was even shorter when it was soaked in liquor. He spent eight years doing whatever the hell he wanted, not caring about the consequences. And then when he was twenty-four, his actions caught up with him.

Patricia Stanton was seventeen when she'd gotten pregnant. She lived with her God-fearing grandmother, who gave Haldon an ultimatum. He could either marry Patricia or go to jail for statutory rape. He chose marriage. Haldon moved into Grandma Stanton's house after the marriage. The only reason being he no longer had to pay rent and had more money to spend on alcohol.

The first five years of Jax's life, Grandma Stanton raised him. If it hadn't been for her, he probably wouldn't have survived. She might have despised Haldon with every fiber of her being, but she'd loved Jax. She'd been the person who named him, the person who tucked him in at night, the person whose lap he crawled into when he wanted a hug.

Getting attention from Patricia was hit or miss; sometimes she'd want to be in her son's life, other times she'd just ignore him. For the most part Haldon ignored Jax, too, which had been just fine with Jax. Whenever Haldon did acknowledge his son, there was a sneer on his face. Never one to take responsibility for his own actions, Haldon blamed Jax for being forced into a marriage he never wanted. He blamed Jax for ruining his life and he had absolutely no problem telling Jax that at every opportunity he got. But Haldon knew better than to mess with Jax when Grandma Stanton was in the room. He'd always wait until he could corner Jax.

Jax remembered one time when he'd been playing with his toy cars under the dining room table. Grandma Stanton had gone outside to pick some herbs from her garden to add to the chicken she was baking for dinner, leaving Jax alone for only a few minutes. Haldon had walked into the kitchen and made a beeline for the fridge, just like he did every night. Jax had stopped playing, trying to be as quiet as possible, not wanting his father to know that he was in the room. But Haldon had noticed him.

"I hope you know just how worthless you are," Haldon said, leaning back against the counter.

His cold eyes didn't leave Jax as he tipped his head back and took a long pull on his beer. He stared at Jax for a few more moments before he pushed off the counter and walked over, crouching down so that he was on eye level with Jax. Jax remembered being too terrified to move or speak.

"Did you hear me, boy?" Haldon asked.

"Y-yes."

"You ruin everything you touch," Haldon said as he reached down and grabbed one of the cars. He turned it in his long fingers before he stood up, dropped it onto the ground, and crushed it under his boot.

Jax knew now that he didn't ruin everything he touched. No, it was Haldon who did. Problem was Jax was included in that category of messed up and broken things. Which meant he wasn't good enough for Grace, no matter how much he wanted her.

Jax closed his eyes and leaned his head against the headrest. He let his thoughts wander to a little kitchen that he wished he'd never left.

Kissing Grace? There were no words for it. It'd been better than he'd ever imagined it could be, and he'd imagined it for what felt like forever. He wasn't sure what had pushed him over the edge to finally grab what he wanted, grab Grace and kiss her like his life depended on it. It didn't matter, though, because if one thing hadn't changed, it was the resounding fact that Jax couldn't have her.

So instead of focusing on all of the kissing that had blown his mind, he focused on the image of Grace, staring at him with wide, wounded eyes. That was the reality, Jax hurting Grace. The only way he could protect her from himself was to not be with her. Because if there was one thing Jax refused to ruin, it was Grace.

Jax opened his eyes and shook his head. No use dwelling on this now. He put his truck in reverse and pulled onto the road.

The shoplifter had been at a gas station. Fourteen-year-old Dale Rigels had purposefully spilled a soda in the back of the store so that when the attendant went to clean it up, the boy could steal a *Playboy* that was kept behind the counter. He'd been unsuccessful in his endeavors.

Jax waited until Mrs. Rigels and Clark Trellis, the owner of the store, had gotten there. Mrs. Rigels had been mortified and furious with her son, but she'd worked it all out with Clark. He wasn't going to press charges and Dale was going to paint the entire outside of the store in retribution.

Jax headed downtown. He needed to stop by Farmers Drugs and talk to the Harolds.

Hugh Farmer had opened the little store almost sixty years ago and worked there until the day he died. The Farmers had sold it to Lewis and Veronica Harold seven years ago. Lewis ran the pharmacy and Veronica ran the front of the shop.

Two days ago, the Harolds had left the pharmacy at six o'clock, the time they left every day. They'd set the alarm and locked the doors. At around two that night, someone broke in.

The alarm system had a sixty-second delay. Once it was triggered, a remote company in Tallahassee received the alert. By the time they contacted the Atticus County sheriff's office and a deputy responded, the thieves had already been and gone. They'd stolen morphine, OxyContin, Ritalin, and all the other class two drugs they could get their hands on. They were going to make a lot of money selling what they'd taken.

This incident held similarities to the other breaking and entering cases Jax had been investigating. The people involved were getting more confident, and if Jax knew anything it was that confidence led to stupidity when it came to criminals. And stupidity was always dangerous.

Jax pulled into a spot across the street from the store. He walked in and nodded to Mrs. Harold who was in the middle of helping a customer. Loud bangs echoed from the back, so Jax made his way through the store, following the sounds.

The only signs of forced entry to the pharmacy were the scratch marks on the dead bolts to the back door. The inside was a whole different matter.

Bennett worked for Marlin Yance Construction and he was working on the repairs. The thieves hadn't been minimal in their destruction. They'd knocked down the door that led into the pharmacy, completely ruining the door frame, and ripped a metal cabinet off the back wall, destroying a pretty good section of the drywall.

Bennett had already removed the damaged portion, leaving the structure and insulation of the back wall exposed. Bennett was building a sturdier frame that would make the new reinforced cabinets harder to break into. The Harolds were also having him install a reinforced steel door.

"Hey," Bennett said, spotting Jax in the doorway as he turned to the worktable.

"Hey. You find anything?" Jax asked, indicating the mess on the floor with his chin.

"Nothing you guys didn't." Bennett shook his head.

"How long do you think it took them?"

"From the time they got in the front door? Five minutes."

"Yeah." Jax nodded. "That's what I figured."

"They knew exactly how much time they had, which means they knew what to expect with that alarm system."

"I was thinking the same thing."

"Can you grab another box of nails for me?" Bennett said, indicating with his chin a spot somewhere behind Jax. "They're in my toolbox on the counter."

Jax turned and walked the few steps. He grabbed a box from a stack inside of Bennett's black toolbox. When he turned around, Bennett was grinning.

"You stop by Café Lula this morning?" Bennett asked. There was nothing nonchalant about Bennett's question. Somehow he knew something.

"Yes. Why?" Jax narrowed his eyes as he handed Bennett the box.

"You and Grace talk?"

Among other things. God, that kiss would forever be ingrained in his brain.

"Yes. Why?" Jax repeated, not liking where this was going.

"So it was a good talk then?"

No, the talking hadn't been good. Every time Jax had opened his mouth he'd said something stupid. Who was he kidding? Everything he'd done with his mouth had been stupid.

Incredible? Yes. But also incredibly stupid.

"Is there a point to this?" Jax asked.

"Yeah. Two as a matter of fact, and they're on your ass."

"What?"

"You've got some nice Grace-size handprints."

"Shit," Jax said, wiping his hands vigorously on the back of his pants.

"It's on the back of your shirt, too, and on your collar. You two roll around in flour or something?"

Jax looked up and glared at him. "You finished yet?"

"Sure." He shrugged, still grinning.

"Good, 'cause I don't want to talk about it."

"Well, that just sucks for you, doesn't it? I'm pretty sure this is going to be talked about for a while."

"You planning on informing everyone about it?"

"No, you took care of that all on your own. Where did you go after you left the café?"

"The Gas-N-Go. Then here. Maybe no one saw," Jax said hopefully.

"Not likely."

"Shit," Jax repeated.

This was all he needed, for everyone in Mirabelle to know that Grace had grabbed his ass. It was perfect, just perfect.

* * *

Grace tried to eat her salad, but all she was doing was pushing it around her plate. She'd failed spectacularly in her mission to not let Jax affect her. She'd been affected all freaking day, burning two batches of cupcakes, spilling a five-pound bag of sugar all over the kitchen floor, and making butter instead of whipped cream when she blended the cream too long.

But how the hell was she supposed to concentrate on anything when all she could think about was Jax? How he'd grabbed her. How he'd kissed her. How he'd explored her mouth with his. How his hands had traveled all over her body. How her hands had been all over his body.

But those thoughts were also accompanied with the burning reality that he'd proclaimed it all to be a mistake. That *none* of it should've happened.

Her stomach churned again and she shoved her salad away. She looked up at the table of women who surrounded her, trying to focus on the conversation she'd hardly contributed to.

Every Thursday, for as long as Grace could remember, a group of women got together to eat lunch at Café Lula. Originally, it had been Lula Mae, Claire, and Lula Mae's cousins, Pinky and Panky Player. Grace had been able to come during the summers, but she hadn't officially joined the ranks until she graduated from high school, but by then, Claire had passed away.

Pinky owned a hair salon, but she also styled the hair and did the makeup for the deceased at Adams and Family Funeral Home. She had short strawberry blond hair that she gelled so it stuck up all around her head. She had a tendency to wear bright eye shadow under her overly plucked eyebrows. Her propensity for biker clothes was pretty appropriate since she drove her Harley Davidson whenever weather permitted, which was most of the time.

Pinky and her boyfriend, Reginald, or Reggie, had been together for thirty-four years and refused to get married. They'd had two kids together, always had a barrage of fluffy mutts running around their house, and traded in their Harley's every five years for a newer model. And they were more than happy.

Panky shared her twin's strawberry blond hair, big green eyes, and overly ample chest. But that was pretty much where the resemblance ended. Panky was way more conservative. Her hair flowed down to her shoulders in big, thick curls. She always wore bright red lipstick and 1950's housewife dresses that made her look like Lucille Ball. Panky was a florist, and while she owned her own shop, she also arranged the flowers for the Adams and Family Funeral Home.

Panky was currently enjoying her new status as the owner of the funeral home's new wife. Burley Adams was a huge man, bald and beefy with a thick neck and wide shoulders. Panky had been in love with him since grade school, but they'd never gotten together. He'd married Jan Clemont, and Jan had died five years later giving birth to their son. Burley had been devastated by the loss and refused to date or get involved with any woman. He'd devoted himself to his son and the family business.

Panky had gotten married, too. And after thirty years

of marriage and three sons, Sydell Dryer had decided he was done with Panky. She'd been on the market for four years before Burley had opened his eyes to the fact that she still wanted to be with him. They'd gotten married four months ago.

Tara Montgomery had been invited to join the luncheons five years ago when she was hired as a receptionist at the funeral home. She'd moved down to Mirabelle from South Carolina when she'd met her husband, Juris, on a dating Web site. Tara was a Southern belle through and through. But, boy, did she have a smart mouth on her, so she fit right in with the rest of them.

Tara had short reddish brown hair that was cut at a slanted angle, framing her face. The cut of her hair made all the sharp angles of her nose, cheeks, and chin stand out even more. She was tall and had a tendency to wear heels, making her well over six feet. Which was a good thing since Juris was a mountain man, or a mountain of a man.

Juris was a taxidermist, which skeeved Grace out. He also did the embalming and cremation at the funeral home, which *really* skeeved her out. But plain and simple, the man was a strange bird. He reminded her of Sasquatch with his long scraggly hair and just as scraggly beard. He and Tara were such an odd pairing.

Tara was very well groomed, with her makeup always in a state of perfection, while Juris's idea of sprucing up was to put his brown hair into a braid that stretched down his broad back. Juris was also a man of very few words, while Tara could probably have struck up a conversation with one of the deceased at the funeral home.

But, hey, who was Grace to judge? People couldn't help who they fell in love with. She knew that firsthand.

Paige had started coming to the lunches about a year and a half ago about the time she began working at the funeral home. That was also when things started between her and Brendan. Denise, Paige's mom, began coming to the lunches last October.

It had been almost seven months since Denise's husband, Trevor, passed away. She was doing better, but she couldn't hide her sadness all the time. Sometimes it made an appearance in her eyes or the set of her mouth. But today, she was laughing and talking with the rest of the women. Her dark brown bob bounced around her shoulders as she talked animatedly with her hands.

"And then would you believe it, but he pulled his pants down in the middle of the store, in front of God and everybody, to show me this spider bite that was on his rear end. He said he couldn't be bothered to go down to the doctor and would I just tell him what he needed to get to treat it."

"Tell me you're joking," Lula Mae said as everyone laughed.

Paige reached for her glass of lemonade, her eyes dancing with laughter. But as she pulled back she looked up and made eye contact with Grace. Paige's smile faltered as her eyes narrowed on Grace and then fell to the barely eaten salad.

"Who wants dessert?" Grace asked, throwing her napkin on the plate to hide the evidence of her lack of appetite.

"What did you make?" Tara asked.

"Blueberry pie." Grace pushed her chair back from the table. It was one of the few things she hadn't ruined.

"Absolutely," Tara said.

Grace looked around to see everyone else's nod of assent, but she avoided looking at Paige.

"Coming up," Grace said, grabbing her plate and heading for the kitchen.

She pushed through the door and dumped the food from her plate into the trash before she put it with the stack by

the sink. She washed her hands and grabbed a pie cutter
from a drawer. As she made her way to the counter where
the pie was cooling, she heard someone pushing through the
kitchen door.

"So, are you going to tell me what's going on?"

Grace turned to find Paige leaning against the counter.
She stretched to the side, the green material of her dress
pulling over her belly as she rubbed at her ribs.

"Trevor kicking?" Grace asked as she reached above her
for a stack of plates.

"He's just making camp in my ribs. What's going on,
Grace?" Paige repeated.

"Nothing."

"I didn't know you were lying to me these days."

"I don't want to talk about it."

"Does this have to do with what happened at the bar last
night with Jax?"

"I swear Brendan gossips like an old married woman,"
Grace said, turning to frown at Paige.

"He's worried about you."

"About what?" Grace asked, focusing on the pie and slicing it. "There's nothing to worry about."

"Bullshit."

Grace's hand stilled and she looked over to Paige again.
Brendan's hadn't been the only heart Paige had made her
way into. Paige had quickly become one of Grace's best
friends, and she truly did think of her as a sister. She trusted
Paige in every sense of the word.

"Jax came over here this morning to apologize about last
night. Except he didn't really know what he'd done to upset
me. And then I started yelling at him about not seeing what
was right in front of his face. And then he kissed me."

"He *what*?" Paige asked, her mouth falling open.

"God, Paige, he kissed me," Grace said, dropping the

cutter in the pie and turning to her. "And it wasn't just a simple little peck on the lips. It was a full body attack. He pushed me back against the counter, picked me up, and sat me down on top of it. His hands were everywhere, and so were mine. It was so much more than I'd ever imagined. It was...it was *everything*. Up until the part where he told me it shouldn't have happened. That it had been a mistake."

"He said *what*?" Paige asked as the softness on her face disappeared. Her eyebrows came together in an angry line and her lips bunched up. "If that man were standing in front of me right now I'd slap him in the face."

"Right, you'd hit Jax," Grace said skeptically.

"Fine, I wouldn't. But I would throw a drink in his face and I'd blame it on my pregnancy hormones."

"Now I'd pay to see that."

"Well, you just wait. Jaxson Anderson will have a cold drink in his face very soon."

"Oh, I'm sure," Grace said, returning to her pie slicing. She started dishing it out, placing the plates on the counter. "Promise me you won't tell Brendan. All I need is for him to find out and give Jax a lecture or something."

"I don't tell Brendan everything," Paige said, feigning offense.

"Really. Tell me something you've never told him."

Paige's mouth bunched to the side and her brow furrowed. "I've got nothing," she said, shaking her head.

"That's what I thought."

"I'm sure there's something; I just can't think of it. I'm going to blame it on pregnancy brain. But, don't worry. I won't say anything to Brendan, even though I think Jax needs a good smack upside the head. I don't think I've ever met a man more clueless in my life. I'm glad your brother isn't."

"Oh, Brendan has had his fair share of clueless moments.

He just didn't have any when it came to wanting you," Grace said as she handed Paige two plates of pie.

"Yeah, I was the clueless one for a while. I snapped out of it though. Maybe there's still hope for Jax."

"I seriously hope so," Grace said. But she seriously doubted it.

Chapter Four

The Power of Jack Daniel's

Grace pulled into the parking lot of Adams and Family Funeral Home just before five o'clock that evening. Café Lula did the catering for the funeral home, and Aberdeen Butelle's wake was that night. Grace had made three batches of cookies while Lula Mae put together a platter of sandwiches, and a cheese and fruit tray.

Grace got out of her car and walked around to the passenger side to grab the trays from the front seat. As she opened the door her brother's big black pickup truck pulled into the spot next to hers.

"Hey," he said, hopping down from his truck and slamming the door behind him. He was in his customary King's Auto navy blue short-sleeved button-up shirt, which hung loose over his navy blue pants. His baseball cap was firmly in place on his head, and his sunglasses were perched on his nose.

"Hey, what are you doing here?"

"I'm doing some work on Paige's Jeep and I had to order a part. So I'm driving her while it's in the shop. You need help?"

"Absolutely," Grace said, pulling out the tray and balancing it on the roof. She pushed the passenger seat back and leaned in to the backseat to grab the other trays. She handed them to Brendan before she straightened.

Brendan grabbed them. He opened his mouth to say something else and hesitated for just a second too long.

"What?" Grace asked.

"What happened with you and Jax this morning?"

Grace closed her eyes and let out a long breath before she opened them again. "How did you find out?"

"Delta Forns came in this afternoon to get her oil changed."

Oh, great, this was only going to get worse. Delta Forns was Denise Morrison's nosey old neighbor. She was also a bitter old shrew. When Brendan and Paige had started seeing each other, Delta had given Bethelda Grimshaw plenty of commentary for her blog.

"How did *she* find out?" Grace asked as her stomach dropped down somewhere to the region of her knees.

Brendan frowned. "There was a blog post today."

"Oh, God," Grace said miserably. It really couldn't get any worse. "What did it say?"

"I don't know exactly as I didn't read it. But apparently Jax was walking around for a good part of the morning with flour handprints on his ass."

She was wrong, so *totally* wrong. It could get a whole lot worse. Grace's stomach fell the remaining distance to her feet. She felt sick.

"What happened with him?" Brendan asked.

"Nothing important," she said, turning again to the backseat and grabbing the last tray. She shut the door before she grabbed the other tray from the roof of her car and made her way up to the porch.

"If you don't tell me I'll just ask him," Brendan said, coming up next to her.

"Like he'll tell you anything." Grace scoffed. Jax was the most tight-lipped man she'd ever met. Well, except when he was kissing. When he was kissing his lips were wide open and wonderful. Oh, God, just *so* wonderful.

Grace slid the tray back on her arm so she could open the front door. They walked in and Tara looked up at them and smiled, giving them a friendly wave as she continued to talk to someone on the phone.

"No, I understand Mr. Molten, we just don't do that," she said, turning back to her computer.

Grace made her way into the kitchen, Brendan hot on her heels.

"If you think this conversation is over, you're sorely mistaken," he said, putting the trays down on the table as she did the same thing.

"You know, you're the pushiest person I've ever met." She took the tray of cheese and fruit to the refrigerator.

"I think you two tie for that."

Grace spun around as she shut the refrigerator door, the cool air blowing around her in a gust, to find Paige standing in the kitchen doorway. Her arms were folded on top of her belly and she was looking straight at Grace.

"No, I'm not," Grace said, her voice going up an octave.

"If I remember correctly you did a couple of things to push Paige and me together." Brendan leaned back against the wall. He pulled his sunglasses off and hooked one of the stems in the front of his shirt.

"I was just trying to help out."

"Mmm hmm," Paige hummed, raising her eyebrows.

"Well, that's what your caring, loving brother is trying to do. Tell me what happened, Grace," Brendan said seriously.

"Jax came over to the café this morning to talk and we might've kissed."

"Might've?" Brendan asked.

"We kissed. And then he said it was a mistake."

"He said *what*?"

"I know, unbelievable, isn't it?" Paige shook her head. "You should go set him straight."

"Oh, by the time I'm done with Jax, he's going to be a little bent up," he said, making his way to the door.

"Stop it, Brendan." Grace stepped in front of him and pushed his shoulders back.

Grace was much smaller than her brother. Brendan wasn't a full foot taller than her like Jax was, but he made up for those inches Jax had on him with about thirty extra pounds of muscle.

"All I'm going to do is tell him to stop wearing his ass as a hat."

"Actually you're not, because this doesn't concern you."

"*Everything* about you concerns me, Grace," he said as his eyebrows bunched together. He looked at her with so much concern it made her heart squeeze painfully.

"Not this," she said, shaking her head. "I don't need you to get involved with this."

"Grace—"

"No." She cut him off firmly. "It's done. Over. We're not talking about it anymore."

"Sweetie," Paige said, shaking her head, "you know that isn't true. Everyone knows about this because of Bethelda."

"No, they just think they know about it. I'm sure Jax has kept quiet. So as far as you two are concerned," Grace said, looking between her brother and Paige, "you know nothing. Got it?"

"Grace—"

"Got it, Brendan? Nothing."

"He's an idiot," Brendan said, grabbing Grace and pulling her into his arms. Grace pressed her face into her brother's chest as he wrapped his arms around her. He leaned down and kissed the top of her head. "The word mistake should never be said in reference to anything that involves you," he said softly. "Do *you* understand that?"

Grace closed her eyes and nodded. She didn't want to say anything for fear of losing the last bit of composure she had. Brendan's arms loosened from around her and he looked down at her as he took a step back. He held on to her arms and studied her face for a second before he nodded. It was a small gesture, but just enough for Grace to know that he was going to do what she asked.

* * *

Jax was starving. His stomach had been rumbling for most of the day. Apparently the two protein bars and cup of coffee he bought at the Gas-N-Go that morning weren't enough to hold him over. Nor was the wilted and slightly soggy tuna salad sandwich he'd eaten for lunch. His stomach had been pretty annoyed with what he'd tried to give it, having had the best food the day before. But he wasn't going to be having any food from Café Lula or any King women for a little while. And with that thought his stomach started to roar, both in hunger and anger.

Jax was a moron all right, and for so many reasons. But that wasn't going to get fixed anytime soon, so he decided to deal with the problem at hand, or at stomach. The prospect of going back to his house with its pathetic food supplies was not a happy one, so instead he pulled into the Floppy Flounder parking lot. The smell of fried fish and hush puppies hit his nose as he opened the door to the truck. Jax made his way up the cracked and creaking floorboards and pushed the bright blue front door open. The delicious fried food smells got stronger and the roaring in Jax's stomach cranked up a notch. He walked to the bar in the back and slid onto one of the stools.

"Deputy Anderson." Stacey Frampton smiled, coming up to him on the other side of the bar.

"Hey, Stacey," Jax said, giving her a polite nod.

"What can I get you?" She pulled out a pad of paper from the front of her apron.

"Fried grouper with fries, hush puppies, and double the coleslaw. To go please."

"Coming right up," she said, writing it all down before she slipped out of the bar and walked to the kitchen.

Jax sat there for a couple of minutes, staring at the TV above the bar but not really watching.

"Why, if it isn't the big, bad deputy."

Jax turned to the side to see a man with shaggy, beach-blond hair slide onto the barstool next to him.

Fantastic. Chad Sharp was a royal asshole. The guy had dated Grace for about a second when they were in high school, but as far as Jax knew it hadn't gone further than a couple of dates. Jax had never liked anyone that Grace dated, and Chad had been at the top of that list.

Last year, Chad had done his best to mess with Brendan and Paige's relationship. Brendan had even gotten into a fight with Chad, one that landed them in jail, along with Shep and two of Chad's friends, Hoyt Reynolds and Judson Coker. Somehow they'd all gotten out with little more than a warning.

Jax had no doubt that this little visit was going to be the icing on top of his shitastic day.

"What do you want, Chad?" Jax asked, looking away.

"Just a little chat."

"I really have no desire to talk to you."

"Well, apparently you do have a desire for something. I hear you scored with Grace."

"What are you talking about?" Jax asked, unable to stop himself from looking back at Chad.

"Everyone knows," he said, raising his eyebrows and smirking. "What was my favorite line from Bethelda's article?" He put his finger to the corner of his mouth like he was pondering. "Oh, yeah, it was that Grace tried to get your attention *'with her hooker shoes and her negligible breasts on display.'* I'm going to have to tell you, man, I've seen what Grace has to offer up close and personal, and it isn't that impressive."

"Chad, I don't care what your opinion is. Never have. Never will. So how about you just go away," Jax said calmly. But really it was taking everything in him not to sock the guy in the face.

Chad had talked about Grace, and that was a surefire way to set Jax off. But Jax knew how Chad worked, and Jax wasn't going to fall for it. Not today at least.

"Here you go, Jax," Stacey said as she put a plastic bag on the counter.

"Keep the change." He handed her some cash before he slid off the stool and got the hell out of the restaurant and away from Chad.

* * *

Ten minutes later, Jax pulled up in front of the tiny two-bedroom/one-bath house he'd been renting for the past two years. The house was a good reflection of him because it was also pretty pathetic.

There were no curtains on any of the windows, just yellowing cracked blinds that were probably older than he was. The carpet was a matted dingy brown but at least it didn't clash with the white walls. The kitchen housed a set of six mismatched plates and bowls, a set of silverware that was missing half its counterparts, one pot that cooked up a decent batch of spaghetti, and a frying pan that worked just fine for scrambling eggs. He had a pretty nice coffeepot that he rarely used because he'd rather just go to the café, a stove that had all four burners working, and a nearly empty refrigerator with an automatic ice dispenser.

It wasn't home. Jax had never really known what a real home was. Well, that wasn't exactly true; the King's house had been a home to him. But the tiny house he currently resided in was just a place to lie low every night before he started the next day. But hopefully all of that would be changing very soon.

A house just west of Mirabelle had gone into foreclosure, and Jax bought it the year before. The people who'd lived there for years hadn't taken care of it, and it showed. The roof had massive leaks, the walls and carpet had acted as filters for the constant stream of cigarette smoke, and the yard was overrun with weeds and overgrown trees. He'd gotten it for a steal.

The house was over two thousand square feet and it sat on two acres of land. It was surrounded by massive oak trees, which gave the whole property the kind of privacy that fences could never achieve. The view from the back of the house was of Whiskey River. Like many houses on the water in Mirabelle, it was built on ten-foot pylons. Before Jax had signed the paperwork, Bennett had gone over to check it out, reporting back that the foundation and overall structure of the house were solid and the plumbing in top condition. When you added in free labor, it just couldn't be beat.

Jax, along with Brendan, Shep, and Bennett, had been working on rebuilding the house for the last five months. Even Oliver and Shep's dad, Nathanial Senior, had come down a couple of times to help wherever they could. The inside of the house had been gutted, the roof and deck had been rebuilt, and the outside had been refurbished but not repainted yet. It was really coming along. All of Jax's free time was spent there, and when it was finished, the plan was he'd continue to want to spend time there.

Jax grabbed his dinner before he got out of his truck and made his way into the lonely, little house. He flipped the hall light on and locked the door behind him before he went into the kitchen, dropped his dinner on the counter, and grabbed a beer from the fridge. He twisted the cap off and threw it in the trash can as he walked to the back of the house. He turned the light on in the spare bedroom, which consisted of a desk for his computer and a weight-lifting bench.

Talk about pitiful offerings.

Jax sat down and hit the mouse a couple of times until the screen came to life. He pulled up the Internet and typed in the address for Bethelda's blog. He knew that he shouldn't bother with it. Knew that what he read was only going to piss him off more. But for some reason he just needed to know what Bethelda had said about him and Grace. It didn't take long for him to get the urge to throw the computer across the room.

THE GRIM TRUTH

NO ONE'S GOING TO BUY THE COW...

Little CoQuette has been a topic of conversation for years around Mirabelle. The mystery of who exactly her father is has been discussed in a wide variety of circles, but that secret has yet to be revealed. Her mother, Jeze Belle, took that to her grave. Probably for the best, if as it's suspected, said father is a married man that the late home wrecker had set her sights on. But with two children from different daddies, what else could be expected?

If CoQuette learned one thing from her mother, it was how to entice men. Just last night she made an attempt to get in good with the law, or the law's pants. CoQuette showed up at our local watering hole, the Den of Iniquity, with her hooker shoes and her negligible breasts on display. Apparently, Deputy Ginger took notice though, because the two were seen out on the dance floor right before CoQuette stormed off in a fit of passion. Lovers' quarrel? Maybe.

Deputy Ginger has never been one to stand out in a crowd. Growing up in a family of meager means and affections he's been more of a standing in the shadows kind of guy. Probably, because if you can't be found then your drunken father can't beat you. But those shadows haven't hid him from the likes of Little CoQuette. Oh no, she's noticed him just fine. And thanks to her, so have a number of our other towns-people.

Deputy Ginger was seen running around downtown this morning with handprints on his derrière. And what might you ask were those handprints made by? Well, according to our more than delighted eyewitnesses, because let's face it Deputy Ginger has a mighty fine caboose, those handprints were slapped on with flour. And where else could those flour handprints have originated but the Illegitimate Buns where CoQuette whips up her sinful concoctions. I just wonder if Deputy Ginger got a free glass of milk with his slice of cherry pie this morning.

Jax stared at the screen, trying to blink back the red rage that clouded his eyes. His first instinct was to drive over to Grace's, to talk to her, to comfort her, to throw back a couple of beers, and rip into Bethelda. Stuff that they'd always done. But that wasn't an option anymore, not after the stunt he'd pulled that morning.

Yup, his day had been freaking-phenomenal.

* * *

Grace was going on a week of not seeing Jax. She hadn't gone that long without seeing him in years. He came in regularly to get a cup of coffee from Café Lula, either at the beginning of his shift or just after it ended. Grace and Lula Mae would always load him up with food before he left. But for the past week there'd been none of that. What there had been was this massive void in Grace's heart, a massive void that was the absence of Jax.

At first she'd been sad about it, moping around the kitchen every day because she missed him. Now she was just pissed.

"We're going out on Saturday," Mel declared one night when they were holed up in Grace's apartment. For Grace it had been the seventh night running. She'd had absolutely no desire to go out since the whole disastrous episode with Jax, or that awful post from Bethelda.

But the truth was, she was getting tired of seeing the walls of her tiny apartment. Granted they were pretty walls, Grace had painted them the instant she'd moved in. Light blues and citrus greens in the kitchen and living room, periwinkle in the bathroom, and a bright sunshine yellow in her bedroom. She had woven rugs on the hardwood floors, jeweled green drapes hanging in the living room, and a wooden rack that Brendan had attached to the minuscule ceiling space in her kitchen where pots and pans hung. It wasn't her dream kitchen by any stretch, but she'd made do with what she had.

"I'm fine, Mel," Grace said, shaking her head. She might

be sick of hibernating in her apartment, but she was not going to have her friends throw her a pity party.

"This isn't about Harper and me feeling sorry for you," Mel said, reading Grace's mind like she always did.

Grace and Mel had been together since they were infants. Mel's mother Corinne had been Claire's best friend, so by turn, Mel was Grace's best friend. Mel was older, having come into the world exactly two months before Grace. Maybe it was because they'd shared everything growing up that they were able to share brain waves. They'd never been able to hide anything from each other. Ever.

"*I* want to go out," Mel said, winding one of her corkscrew blond curls around her finger. "I don't know if you remember this, but I deal with teenagers on a daily basis, and I need to unwind." She let the curl loose and it bounced up around her face. "Not everything is about you," she said as she raised her eyebrows.

Grace had a flashback to when she'd said those exact same words to Jax a week ago. Mel had said it playfully, but it still made Grace wince.

"What?" Mel asked, her mouth falling into a frown.

"Nothing," Grace said, shaking her head.

"I don't believe you," Mel said as her eyebrows bunched together. "Look, Grace, I'm not stupid, so don't try to play off your avoidance of the world as something besides Jax."

"It isn't about Jax," Grace lied.

"Oh, really?"

"Yes, really. Let's go out Saturday. What's the plan?"

"Dinner and then drinks at Shep's," Mel said.

Grace knew that Mel was waiting for her to back out. Odds were fairly good that Jax would be there.

"Fine," Grace said, not caving.

So on Saturday night, Grace stood in her bathroom, leaning over the sink as she applied her mascara. She wasn't nervous or upset. No, she was in full hell on heels mode, and if Jax was there, she was going to show him exactly what he was missing.

* * *

Jax walked into the Sleepy Sheep just after nine. He'd had a day that felt like it just wasn't going to end. There'd been another burglary the night before. Since Jax was the lead on the investigation, he'd been called in at four that morning to go down to a specialty shop on the beach where over five thousand dollars' worth of merchandise had been stolen. After that he was called down to the high school because a kid had been caught smoking a joint behind the gym, and then he was needed for backup to a traffic accident.

The accident was on the main road in Mirabelle, blocking both lanes. A truck had plowed into a little two-door Honda. The truck hit the empty passenger side, and the driver of the car suffered a broken arm. Which was pretty lucky considering the fact that when the vehicles crashed the Honda caught fire. The passengers got out before both car and truck went up in flames. But for two hours traffic stood still until the charred remains could be towed off the road.

But ever since Jax had seen that accident, he'd been anxious. It brought him back to last September, to seeing Lula Mae's SUV in the river, to pulling Grace and Paige out just in time. Jax hadn't seen Grace in over a week, and he felt like he was drowning. Without Grace in his life Jax couldn't breathe.

The Sleepy Sheep was packed, as per usual on a Saturday night. Jax pushed through the people and made his way to the bar. There was an empty seat next to Tripp Black and Baxter McCoy. Tripp was Mirabelle's new fire chief. He moved over from Panama City a couple of months ago to take the job. Jax had seen Tripp earlier that day when he'd been called down to the accident. Baxter was a deputy for the county, too. He and Jax had joined the force in the same class. Baxter also played baseball on the county team with Jax, Shep, and Brendan.

"Hey." Tripp nodded as Jax slid into the seat next to him.

"You look like you need a drink," Baxter said, leaning forward so he could see Jax. "Tripp just told me all about the accident."

"It was a freaking disaster," Jax said, shaking his head.

"Sounds like it." Baxter nodded before he took a sip of his beer.

"Here you go." Jax looked forward as Shep set down a frosted mug of beer. "You're going to need this. Drink up."

"You heard about the accident?"

"Yeah, but that's not why you're going to need that," Shep said, pointing to the drink.

"Then what is?"

"That." Shep pointed to other side of the room where the pool tables were.

Jax turned in the direction Shep was pointing and had the weirdest feeling as two opposing emotions ran through his body.

The first was relief at seeing Grace. Her head was thrown back and she was laughing loudly, the smile on her face making him feel warm. The constricted feeling around his lungs loosened and he was able to breathe for about a second. Then the rest of the scene registered and he felt like he'd been punched in the stomach. All that warmth turned into a boiling anger.

Grace was standing next to a pool table, pool cue in one hand, while her other hand rested on the arm of Preston Matthews. There was a crowd of people around them, and someone bumped into Grace, pushing her into Preston. His arm shot up to her waist to steady her. His palm pushed up the side of her shirt and his fingers traced her bare skin.

The top of Jax's head was going to blow off.

To make matters worse, she was surrounded by a group of Preston's friends. They were probably from law school because Jax didn't recognize any of them. To be fair, it wasn't just Grace they surrounded. Harper and Mel were with her, too, and all three had pulled out all the stops tonight.

They stood in towering high heels, which put Grace on more of an eye level with the guys. Harper and Mel weren't as short as Grace, but their heels sure did add to both of their figures. Mel and Harper were both in tight jeans and tank tops. Grace had gone for a miniskirt and some kind of flowy shirt that exposed her shoulders and showed just a hint of her stomach and back when she moved.

Damn she was hot.

"I'm going to need a shot," Jax said, spinning back around to the bar.

Preston *freaking* Matthews, stupid little prick that he was, was genuinely a good guy. A genuinely good guy who currently had his hands all over Grace. So naturally Jax hated him.

With his sandy blond hair and bright blue eyes, Preston was the golden boy in every sense. He'd been a star basketball player his last three years of high school and he'd gotten a full ride scholarship to Florida State University. He'd then gone on to FSU law, where he graduated with honors. He'd moved back to town three months ago and was now practicing at his father's law firm in Mirabelle.

Preston and Grace had never dated, much to Jax's relief, not that she hadn't dated other guys Jax had never liked. But those other guys didn't matter at the moment, because none of them had their grubby *golden* hands on Grace.

Shep put down a shot glass and flipped a bottle of Jack

Daniel's over it. When it was full Jax reached across the counter and poured it down his throat.

He was a moron. He wanted Grace more than his next breath, but he refused to go and get her. Refused to get off his barstool, march across the bar, grab her, and make her his. She couldn't be his. Why? Because, well, it just wasn't in the cards.

"Again," he said, slamming the glass down.

Yup, a freaking idiot. But he was going to have to just get over it, wasn't he? It wasn't like she was over there pining away for him. No, she had her hand on another guy. She was laughing with another guy. She was flirting it up with another guy with absolutely no second thought about Jax.

"You sure?" Shep asked, raising an eyebrow.

"Yes," Jax said as he nudged the glass a couple of inches forward.

"Well, this is going to be an interesting night." Shep flipped the bottle of whiskey over the glass again.

* * *

Grace had known the second Jax walked in. She'd seen his red head moving through the crowd before he sat down at the bar. Her stomach had done a little flip, and the fist that had been squeezing her heart since the last time she'd seen him eased up. But her concentration was shot for shit.

She'd been playing a pretty good game of pool up until about an hour ago when her eyes had landed on a stupid freckled face. Yeah, now she was shooting crap.

"You okay?" Preston asked, coming up next to her.

"I'm fine," Grace said as she grabbed her beer off the table.

"She's a liar, is what she is," Harper whispered to Preston.

"What's going on?" Preston asked, turning to Harper.

Preston had been out of town for the last two weeks. He'd had to go up to Montgomery to deal with his late great-uncle's estate, and it was a *massive* estate, so he'd missed all of the tantalizing gossip.

Grace downed the rest of her beer as Harper filled Preston in on all of the gory details. Grace didn't care if Preston knew what had happened. She would've told him anyway, he was one of her best friends, had been ever since he'd sat down next to her freshman year of Spanish. Well, her freshman year, Preston's sophomore year.

And after that first year, they'd made sure they stayed together for the following two years. They'd had to have a companion to battle the bat-shit-crazy that was Señora Darwimple. The woman had dyed purplish red hair, smelled of patchouli, and spoke Spanish like she had a British accent. Yeah, Grace and Preston were bonded for life.

"Seriously?" Preston asked, looking up and over Harper's head to the bar. He turned around to Grace with a frown on his face. "No wonder you're all uptight tonight."

"I am not uptight!"

"You keep telling yourself that," Preston said, grabbing his own beer. "I thought something was up. Why didn't you call me when I was gone? Tell me what was going on?"

"I didn't want to bother you, and it's *nothing*."

"How's the water in the Nile this time of year?" Preston asked. "Warm?"

"Shut up," Grace said, punching his shoulder.

"Ow." He rubbed the spot with his hand.

"That didn't hurt you big baby."

"I know." He grinned his megawatt smile. "But seriously, you should've called me."

"She's not talking about it," Mel piped in. "Not to anyone."

"Can we not have this conversation here?" Grace whispered.

"Not likely," Harper said. "Because you will not talk

about it here, or there. You will not talk about it anywhere. You will not talk about it in a house. You will not talk about it with a mouse. Or in a boat, or with a goat."

"Cute, you're *real* cute," Grace said, snatching the pool cue from where she'd leaned it against the wall and went to the table to take her shot.

* * *

Grace and Preston headed up to the bar to get more drinks. They stood in the empty spot next to Baxter McCoy. Grace could feel Jax's eyes on her from two seats down, but she didn't look at him. He could be quiet and surly to his heart's content, she didn't care.

"What can I get you?" Shep asked.

"Two more pitchers," Preston said.

"Coming right up," Shep said as he grabbed two pitchers to fill.

"Hey, Baxter, Tripp," Grace said.

She saw the corner of Shep's mouth twitch at her obvious attempt at ignoring Jax.

"Hey, Grace," Baxter said while Tripp merely nodded.

Tripp was a big man, with big muscles. He had warm chocolate-brown eyes, thick brown hair, and a decent amount of dark scruff across his jaw. He was all man and flat out hot. Grace might be in love with the moronic redhead seated next to Tripp at the bar, but she wasn't blind. Baxter wasn't lacking in the looks department, either. He had sandy blond hair, hazel eyes, and a killer grin.

"You guys know Preston, right?" she asked the two men.

"I remember Preston," Baxter said. "Mirabelle's basketball star." He held out his hand toward Preston.

"Yeah, not so much these days," Preston said, shaking Baxter's hand.

"This is Tripp Black," Baxter said. "He's our new fire chief."

"Nice to meet you," Tripp said as they shook hands.

"Likewise." Preston nodded.

"You done with law school?" Baxter asked.

"Yeah, graduated in December. So I'm back here now."

Jax mumbled something from his seat.

"What was that?" Grace asked, unable to stop herself. She wasn't sure what had gotten into her, but she apparently really wanted to play with fire tonight.

"I said, *fantastic*," Jax repeated clearly.

"What's your problem?" she asked.

"I don't have a problem," he said, shaking his head.

Grace pushed away from her spot at the bar and went to stand next to Jax, getting right up in his face.

"Yeah, you do. So why don't you tell me what it is?"

"Why would you care what I think? You've never consulted me about the guys you've slept with before. And you've got golden boy over there to keep your bed warm tonight, so what I think about you shouldn't really matter."

Everything in Grace went cold, like she'd been plunged into a tub full of ice water. A shock to her system, and the sudden coldness made her inhale sharply. Jax had pretty much just called her a whore. Grace didn't even realize what she was doing, but a second later she reached over and grabbed Jax's full beer from the bar, throwing the amber liquid in his face before she slapped him soundly across the jaw.

He stared at her in shock, his green eyes going clear and wide as they focused on her.

"Fuck you, Jax," Grace said, slamming the glass down on the bar. She turned around and went to grab her things. She had to get out of there and as far away from Jaxson Anderson as possible. She needed to be alone when she lost it, which was inevitable, because she apparently didn't know the man she loved at all.

Chapter Five

No Going Back

Wake up jack-ass."

There was a pounding in Jax's head, a deep throbbing hammer working in tandem with the churning in his stomach. Jax cracked an eye to a sea of navy blue. He was face first in a pillow, but it wasn't his pillow. He rolled to the side, slowly, and looked up at Shep, who was frowning down at him.

"What time is it?" he croaked. His mouth was like sandpaper.

"Eight."

"Why am I here?"

"'Cause your sorry ass couldn't drive home. I wasn't going to drive you home just to have to pick you up in the morning so that we could go get your truck at the bar."

"What the hell happened last night?"

"You honestly don't remember?" Shep asked, raising an eyebrow.

"I remember Grace and..." Jax trailed off trying to picture the night before. It made his head hurt. An image of Grace laughing with a guy came to him vividly. "Preston

Matthews," Jax mumbled, bringing his hand up to rub at his eyes. It was like his arm was attached to a marionette string as it flopped down onto his face.

"Yup, that was when you started to shoot doubles."

"And you didn't stop me?"

"Nah, I figured it was about time you got knocked on your ass."

"How nice of you. What happened after the shots?" Jax asked, bringing his hand down.

"You got slapped."

And then with picture-perfect clarity Jax remembered everything from the beer thrown in his face all the way to the look of pure loathing on Grace's face before she told him to fuck off.

"Shit," Jax said as he slowly tried to sit up.

"Yup. Now drink up." Shep handed Jax a cup of coffee when he became vertical. "You need to take a shower and change, 'cause you smell like a brewery. Then we're going to pick up your truck at the bar before we go up to your new house where Bennett and Brendan are meeting us."

Oh, great, he had to do construction with a hangover. It was going to be a *long* day.

"Clothes?" Jax asked.

"I put some in the bathroom," Shep said, pointing to a door off the guest bedroom.

Jax stood up on wobbly legs and made his way into the bathroom, desperate to wash away the night before. What the hell had gotten into him?

Such an easy answer.

Grace had gotten into him. She made his life so freaking complicated. He'd seen her with another guy and something in him had just snapped. It was becoming clearer to him that his relationship with Grace was changing, and he most definitely wasn't ready for it.

* * *

Twenty minutes later, Jax felt relatively human again. He'd never been one to underestimate the power of a shower and a strong cup of coffee. Shep was only an inch shorter than Jax, so the pants were long enough, if not a size too big, but Jax's belt took care of that problem.

When Jax walked into the kitchen, Shep was at the stove frying something up.

"Smells good," Jax said, easing himself down into a seat at the kitchen table.

"You're lucky we've been friends for so long, otherwise I wouldn't give you anything," Shep said as he spooned some fried potatoes onto a plate and forked on a few pieces of bacon. He loaded up another plate and made his way to the table.

"I was that bad?" Jax asked, grabbing the plate Shep handed him.

"Do you not remember anything after we left the bar?"

Jax tried to think, but after Grace slapped him everything was a blur. But he had a brief image of Shep helping him up the stairs.

"Not really," Jax said as he forked up a mouthful of potatoes. The salty, crispy pieces were just what he needed.

"You get pretty chatty when you're trashed."

Jax's fork froze on its return journey to his mouth. He looked up at Shep, who was smirking at him.

"What did I say?" Jax asked as the fork resumed its course.

"Oh, you know, just that you're a moron. You said that multiple times. And you mentioned something about Grace and the taste of her tongue."

Jax swallowed his mouth full of potatoes, not really chewing them. The sharp edges and heat made his eyes water. He put his fist to his mouth and coughed as he reached for his cup of coffee.

Jax wished he could say Shep was lying, but the taste of Grace's tongue had been a constant thought of his since he'd kissed her. He wouldn't be surprised if he'd finally voiced it.

"Not denying it?" Shep asked.

"Did I say anything else?" Jax asked, ignoring Shep's question.

"A couple random mumblings," Shep said, waving his hand in the air. "Nothing memorable."

Shep was full of it, and Jax had a feeling that those *random mumblings* were going to be revealed slowly, and most likely at the worst possible times for Jax.

"Also, I had no idea how ticklish your feet were. When I was taking your boots off you kept flailing your legs around like I was going to pin you town and take a feather to you."

"Now you're just making shit up," Jax said as he resumed eating.

"You'd like to think that, wouldn't you, but I'm not."

"You're going to keep all of this information to yourself, right?"

"Not a chance." Shep grinned.

* * *

When Jax had decided to buy and remodel the house on the river, he had the brilliant idea that he'd just do it himself. Brendan and Shep had put the kibosh on that little plan pretty quick.

"This isn't some small favor, like helping you move or watching your dog. This is rebuilding an entire house. Something that will take months to do and will be extensive and exhausting," Jax had said.

"I'm glad you clarified. I thought this was going to be a

piece of cake," Shep said. "If you only were like a brother to us or something, then maybe this wouldn't be such a *massive* inconvenience."

"Yeah, it isn't like you've done *anything* for us over the years," Brendan added. "Like rebuilding Shep's mustang, or helping me build an art studio for Paige. Or hey," Brendan said, snapped his fingers in the air, "remember that time you went into a river and saved my wife and little sister's life? That wasn't a big deal at all, either."

"Stop being an idiot. We're going to help you build your house, because if anyone deserves a place to call home, it's you," Shep had said seriously.

Even Bennett had offered his services, which was a godsend really because Bennett worked in construction so he knew exactly what he was doing when it came to just about everything.

Sometimes blood wasn't the strongest bond. Sometimes your friends were your real family.

But despite that fact, Jax was a little unsure of how Brendan was going to react to the events of the night before. Jax had seen Brendan since the flourgate episode. He knew that Brendan had gotten that full story. It wasn't that he thought Grace was incapable of keeping a secret; it was more along the lines of Brendan forcing the truth out of her.

That first couple of days after the incident had consisted of Brendan's jaw bunching up every time he saw or spoke to Jax. But he hadn't said a word to Jax on the subject of Grace. Jax had the feeling that this wasn't going to be the case for much longer. He and Grace were having too many collisions of late, and if there was one thing that nobody messed with, it was the women in Brendan's life. Jax might've been one of Brendan's best friends, but there was no doubt in Jax's mind that the man would grind his ass into the pavement.

After Shep had taken Jax to go pick up his truck, Jax

stopped to get ice and drinks to fill up the cooler. When he pulled into the driveway, Shep, Brendan, and Bennett were standing around the tools that they'd already pulled out for the day.

They got to work right away, and Brendan didn't say a word about anything to do with Grace. Apparently the events of the night before were being kept from the big bad brother.

Jax's hangover eased up and he was able to get some work done on the house. By the time everyone parted ways at five that afternoon, the windows and doors were replaced and the new insulation installed. The next thing on the agenda was putting up the walls.

Jax stopped for a pizza on the way home. He threw it in the oven before he got in the shower and washed off the sweat and dirt from the day. After changing into a fresh pair of jeans and T-shirt, Jax grabbed the box of pizza and plopped down on his couch.

The labor of the day had kept his mind occupied, and off Grace. Well, for the most part. She'd managed to slip in a couple of times, as was the norm. But now, sitting in front of the TV and watching an action movie that he'd seen twenty times, he couldn't think of anything besides her.

He needed to talk to her. Even if they couldn't be together romantically, they could still be friends. He had to fix it. Had to have her back in his life. He missed her too damn much.

* * *

Grace slept in until after ten that morning. The café was closed on Sundays, and she really didn't want to leave her apartment. She didn't want to be around anyone. So she'd spent the day doing a little spring cleaning. And by a little, she'd cleaned every inch of her apartment from top to bottom, blasting music and singing at the top of her lungs.

Now she was curled up on the couch, a glass of white wine in one hand and a Kit Kat in the other. Yup, Grace knew exactly what delicacies to pair up with her liquor. She'd put on an action movie that wasn't centered on a love story and felt a deep satisfaction every time something blew up.

"And that's what you get," she said to the TV as the hero punched the villain in the face.

Just as another building blew up, Grace's doorbell rang. She muted the movie and put her half-empty glass of wine and candy wrapper on the table. She padded over to the front door and stretched up on her tiptoes to peek out of the peephole.

Of course it's him.

"Can I help you?" Grace asked, opening the door.

"I was hoping we could talk," he said, shifting on his feet.

"Well, that's entirely up to you since you're the one who avoids conversations."

"Grace, please."

"Come in," she said, moving to the side and opening the door wider so he could squeeze in past her.

The fresh scent of him, and whatever soap he used, wrapped around her as he walked by. She closed her eyes and inhaled deeply, but not audibly. She closed the door behind him and when she turned to face the room, he was standing there just looking at her.

"So talk," she said, waving her hand in his direction.

He studied her for another moment before he said, "I'm sorry."

"For what?"

"For the kiss at the café and for last night."

"You're going to have to be a little more specific in both of those instances."

"What do you mean?" he asked as his eyebrows bunched together.

"What about the kiss are you sorry about? That it happened or what happened afterward?" she asked as she folded her arms across her chest.

"Both."

Grace flinched. That sucked. She had a desperate need to cross the room and throw back the last of her wine. That was the only way she was going to get through this conversation.

"Grace—"

"And what about last night?" she asked, cutting him off.

"For what I said to you. It's none of my business what's going on between you and Preston. I shouldn't have said anything."

"No," Grace said, shaking her head, "you shouldn't have."

"Well, I'm sorry for that." He shoved his hands in his pockets.

"Nothing is going on."

"What?"

"Nothing is going on with Preston and me. Not that it even matters," she said, shaking her head. "It's not going to change anything. And neither is this conversation."

"What do you mean?" Jax took a step forward.

"What did you think tonight was going to accomplish? That you'd just come down here and apologize and we'd go back to the way things were before?"

"I was hoping that would be the case."

"Then you're delusional, Jax. I don't want to go back. I *can't* go back. Can you honestly tell me you don't know how I feel about you?"

"Grace," he said, closing his eyes and shaking his head.

"Can you?"

He opened his eyes slowly and just looked at her for a second before he shook his head again. "We can't."

"Why?"

"Because we just can't."

"That's not good enough," she shouted at him.

"You're right and neither am I," he yelled back.

Grace's legs were moving across the room of their own accord. She plowed into Jax, and he stumbled backward. They would have been on the ground if the sofa hadn't broken their fall. Grace scrambled onto Jax's lap, straddling him. She grabbed his face in her hands and kissed him hard. He didn't resist for even a second. His mouth opened to hers instantly. His arms wrapped around her back, his hands sliding up and down her spine.

This was right. So. Damn. Right.

Grace's hands traveled up to his hair, her fingers sliding through the soft strands. She started to move her hips against him, her body grinding down on a spot that made both of them groan. And within an instant she found herself flat on her back, Jax now completely in control as he moved between her thighs. Their mouths hadn't separated once. Their tongues moved together in a rhythm that mimicked their bodies.

Wow. Just. Wow.

Jaxson Anderson was on top of her. He was touching her, kissing her, surrounding her. She never *ever* wanted it to end.

His hands traveled down to the hem of her sweatshirt and he worked it up her sides, pushing it up past her breasts, leaving them covered by only the thin material of her tank top. She let go of his hair and stretched her arms above her head. She was all for less barriers being between them. As far as she was concerned the clothes needed to start flying, like *now*.

Their mouths broke apart as Jax pulled the sweatshirt up and over her head. He threw it to the floor, and the second his hands were free he cupped her jaw with one palm, while the other brushed her now errant hair out of her face. He stared down at her for just a second, the look of desire in his eyes so intense Grace thought she was going to explode.

Jax didn't say anything as his mouth went down to hers again. Grace pulled her knees up so her legs cradled his moving hips. His hands went to the back of her thighs, his fingers sliding under the thin material of her pajama shorts. She grabbed his shoulder blades, her fingers pushing hard into his muscles.

Jax's mouth left hers and started a journey down her neck, making a path across her skin. He traced her collarbone with his tongue and descended lower to the top of her tank top. His teeth raked the material, tugging at the edge. He didn't pull it down though. Instead his lips traveled to Grace's chest, where his mouth opened wide on one of her breasts.

Holycowholycowholycow.

She arched up into him, her hands going back to his hair.

Cold air hit the wet material as Jax switched sides, his mouth showing equal admiration to both breasts. He kept at it for a couple of minutes, switching back and forth, before he moved back up her body. His lips were on hers again, his tongue diving into her mouth.

Grace moved her hands down Jax's chest. She slipped them underneath his shirt, touching his skin. He groaned deep in his throat, the vibrations of it rumbling through her body. She traced his abs with her fingertips before she followed the trail down his jeans. She pulled on the top button and then worked down his zipper. She slipped her hand into the opening and stroked him through the soft cotton of his boxer briefs.

And then everything stopped. Jax was off her in a second. He was standing on the other side of the room panting. His chest rising and falling like he'd just sprinted a couple of miles. The look on his face had the sexual heat that had been running through Grace the moment before turning ice cold.

He was doing it again. The stupid jerk was doing it *again.* He was chickening out, pulling away from her, *leaving* her.

"Grace I—" he said, shaking his head, still trying to catch his breath.

Grace scrambled up and grabbed the blanket off the back of the couch. She wrapped it around her shoulders as she stood up. She really didn't want to have whatever conversation they were about to have with her nipples popping through the front of her now very wet tank top.

"Grace—" Jax said, trying to talk again, but he just swallowed hard as he ran his hands through his hair, his T-shirt straining at the top of his shoulders.

"Just spit it out, Jax."

"We can't do this," he said, making a motion between their bodies.

"This?" she asked, trying to hide her shaking hands in the fabric of the blanket.

"We can't be together this way. It isn't an option."

"Because you think you're not good enough for me? Is that why?"

"I don't think it, Grace, I know it."

"Oh, you *know* it. The all powerful and enlightened Jaxson Anderson. You just know all, don't you?" Her voice cracked under the strain of not losing it.

"Grace," Jax said, taking a step toward her.

"No." She cut him off, her hand slicing through the air to stop him. "You want to know what your problem is? You've convinced yourself that all of the garbage your father drilled into your brain is the truth. You've turned them into facts, into reality. *You've* decided that you're not worth it, and I'm done trying to prove to you otherwise. I can't do the friend thing with you anymore. It's not an *option* for me."

"Grace—"

"Get out, Jax," she said with so much finality that it even shocked her.

Jax inhaled sharply before he nodded and walked to

the door. He didn't say anything, didn't even hesitate as he opened it and walked outside.

The moment the door closed all the air left Grace's lungs. She staggered to the door and flipped the dead bolt before she fell onto the couch. The blanket that was still wrapped around her shoulders did absolutely nothing for the cold that was raking her body. She pulled her knees up to her chest and buried her face in a pillow, trying to muffle the sobs that just wouldn't stop.

Chapter Six

Haunted

On Monday morning, Grace was in the kitchen of the funeral home setting up for the Guerdon wake. The food was already made, so it was just a matter of putting it out. She was in the kitchen with Panky, who was making fresh flower arrangements.

Normally the two of them would be talking, but not today. Grace was in a mood because of Jax, and Panky was in a mood because of the assistant funeral director, Missy Lee. Missy was in micromanage mode, and every two minutes she would stick her head in the kitchen and say something to Panky.

"I just think you're overstuffing the arrangements," Missy said. "You could use cheaper flowers. We don't need so many roses and lilies. How about more carnations and daisies? And baby's breath?"

"I'll take it into consideration," Panky said, not even looking up from her arrangement.

"That's all I ask." Missy turned and left the room.

Missy Lee might be the assistant funeral director at Adams and Family Funeral Home, but that was just her day job. Her real profession was gold digger. At the age of forty-eight, the woman had been married five times and engaged seven. For a while Missy had found her conquests around town, but with the Internet now at her fingertips, she'd turned to the world wide web to find her new victims.

Three months ago Missy had married Clive Burdgen. He was a furniture salesman in Montgomery, Alabama, with a beamer and a full head of hair. Missy and Clive had known each other for all of about five minutes before they'd gotten hitched. But a month into their marriage, Missy discovered that Clive Burdgen was really Gill Seamore. Gill Seamore had a wife and kids in Atlanta and had fled with the beamer when his Laundromat had gone belly-up. Oh, and also, that head of hair was all hair plugs.

So the conner became the conned, and Missy hadn't taken it very well at all. As the great, great, great niece of Robert E. Lee, she didn't deal very well with defeat. After Missy's *heartbreak* she'd gone on a full-out rampage. The woman had always been crazy, but now she was crazy with a vendetta, and it wasn't just against her most recent ex-husband, or whatever he was, as technically they'd never really been married.

For a while Missy had targeted Mr. Adams for a merger, so that she could liquidate his assets. Burley Adams wasn't hurting for money. As the owner of the only funeral home in Atticus County, he was making a pretty penny. Missy had known it, and she'd wanted all of that money for herself. Interestingly enough, Missy had married Clive/Gill exactly a month after Burley and Panky had tied the knot. Coincidence? Most likely not.

"What if we start using silks?" Missy asked, coming back into the kitchen. "Then we could reuse the flowers. No one ever pays enough attention to know the difference anyway."

"Excuse me?" Panky asked, looking up. Her eyes narrowed on Missy and her cheeks started to turn red.

"I'm just saying, they aren't that important."

"Excuse me?" Panky repeated.

"We can charge the families the same price for less flowers."

"That's it," Panky said, slamming her scissors down on the counter. "I'm going to talk to my husband." With that she stormed out of the kitchen. Missy followed, the two of them arguing as they went down the hallway.

"What was that all about?"

Grace looked up to find Paige waddling into the kitchen.

"Missy is being a pain in Panky's ass."

"Well, that's new and different." Paige grinned.

Grace didn't return the smile.

"What's going on?" Paige asked, a frown now pulling down her lips.

"I'm fine," Grace said.

"Grace, fess up. You look worse than you did after Jax kissed you."

Grace's face fell more. She wasn't even sure how that was possible at this point.

"Come on," Paige said, grabbing Grace's hand. She led her out the back door of the kitchen and onto the porch.

"All right," Paige said, letting go of Grace's hand and rounding on her. "Did the two of you..." Paige trailed off, not finishing the question.

"No, we didn't have sex," Grace whispered.

But oh, they'd been so freaking close.

"Almost though," Paige said, giving a small nod of her head.

"What are you? A mind reader these days?"

"No, you just look really upset. What happened?" Paige reached out, running her hand up Grace's arm.

"You *can't* tell Brendan. Promise?" Grace asked.

"I won't tell him," Paige said seriously.

"Last night, Jax came over to my apartment to apologize about the kiss at the café and the incident at the bar on Saturday."

"What incident at the bar?"

"We got into an argument," Grace said.

"Why am I not surprised?"

"He said some stuff. I threw a beer in his face and slapped him."

"I told you he was going to get a cold drink thrown in his face. But what did he do?"

Grace told Paige all about what had happened at the Sleepy Sheep. Paige's mouth fell open in shock.

"You should've slapped him twice," Paige said angrily.

"He was so mean. He's never talked to me that way before. I just don't get it, he doesn't want me, but he doesn't want anybody else to have me, either. How does that make sense?"

"When it comes to you, I think all of Jax's sense goes out the window."

"I don't think I can do it anymore," Grace said sadly as she reached up and rubbed a spot over her heart.

"Grace?" Paige said her name with so much concern that Grace had to close her eyes for a moment. She only opened them again after she regained some semblance of her composure.

"I can't wait around for him to figure it out anymore, because I don't think he ever will figure it out. He doesn't think he's good enough. That's what he said yesterday. He came over and we started kissing and...God, Paige, it felt so right. Him and me, it felt *so* right, *so* real. But *too* real for him, because he stopped and left. I've wanted that man for so long, but I think I'm done waiting."

"Oh, sweetie," Paige said sadly.

"It's fine. I'll be fine," Grace said, but she knew she was just lying to herself.

"Grace, can I ask you one thing?"

"Yes." She nodded slowly.

"Do you think you can get over him?" Paige asked seriously, doubt written all over her face.

Grace laughed, except there was absolutely no humor in it. "Ohhh, if it were only that easy. No, I'll never get over him. Jaxson Anderson will haunt me for the rest of my life."

* * *

The day proved to be a long one. All of the days felt long when Jax wasn't in them. After Grace left the funeral home, she went back to the café and kept up her routine of secluding herself in the kitchen. She finished her last batch of cookies, cleaned the kitchen, and left before Lula Mae closed up. She pulled into the parking lot of her apartment just after five.

"Oh, fantastic," she mumbled to herself as she spotted the man leaning against his black BMW. He really was a sight, with his thick, windswept blond hair and his long tanned legs that shot out of his khakis and ended in his worn-out dock shoes. Wouldn't her life be so much easier if she could just be in love with him?

"What do you want?" she asked as she got out of her Bug and closed the door.

"You and I are going to dinner," Preston said, pushing himself off the door of his car.

"Oh, are we?" Grace raised her eyebrows.

"Yup, you're not sulking by yourself for the rest of the night."

"I'm not sulking," she said, folding her arms across her chest.

"Riiight, and I'm your fairy godmother."

"Well—"

"Shut up, and get in my car."

"You're such a pain in the ass. Remind me why we're friends again?" she asked as she made her way around to the passenger side.

"It's my charm and magnetism. You can't resist me." He grinned.

"Now who's delusional?" Grace slid into the tan leather seats and buckled herself in.

Preston turned the car on and pulled out of the parking lot. "You ready for this?" he asked as he rolled down the windows.

"Always," she said, leaning back in her seat.

Preston leaned forward and turned the stereo on. A deep, rich voice, that knew the meaning of a broken heart, filled the car and blasted out the windows. Grace's blond hair whipped around as she opened her mouth and sang as loud as she could.

* * *

Never in Jax's life had he done anything more difficult than walk away from Grace. For so long it had been her walking away from him, giving him that empty feeling that settled in his chest and made him ache.

He'd gone over to her apartment to fix things. Instead, he ruined everything. She'd said there was no going back to the way things had been before. She told him there was only one direction their relationship could go. But he just couldn't let it go there.

Truth be told, there was no going back for Jax, either. Not after he'd kissed her that first time in the café, and definitely not after that episode on her couch. They'd been so close to having sex, so freaking close.

He'd been too shocked to do anything when Grace tackled him to the couch. The second she straddled him, all his inhibitions had gone out the window. And now he knew. He knew what it was like to be on top of her, knew the sounds she made when he sucked on her breasts, knew what it felt like to have her stroke him. Yeah, there was absolutely no going back for him. *Ever.*

But he wasn't wrong. Grace deserved someone better than him.

She'd already had a difficult enough life. She had no father and then she lost her mother to breast cancer when she was only ten years old. She deserved her happy ending. No, she deserved the whole package. She deserved a guy who wasn't damaged, a guy who wasn't screwed up beyond repair, someone who could give her a house and a family, someone who would always keep her safe. She deserved a life with someone who could give her every single one of her dreams.

That someone *wasn't* Jax. He could never be that guy. He would never be able to give her *happily ever after.*

But letting go was going to be a bitch. Every time Jax thought about Grace being with some other guy he wanted to hurt someone, punch his fist through a wall. It was a shame that the demolition portion of the house was finished, because he would have loved to pound a sledgehammer through a wall. Instead he'd spent the day channeling his aggression with a nail gun.

He'd met Shep at the house under construction early on Monday morning. As they worked that day, Shep was unusually quiet. Jax knew it was just a matter of time before the questions came. And they came at the end of the day.

"You talk to Grace?" Shep asked as they started to put the tools away.

"Yeah." Jax would've laughed, but nothing about life was funny at the moment.

"You made it worse, didn't you?"

"Why do you say that?"

"Because you're about as cheerful as a sleeping bear that just got poked in the eye," Shep said as he closed the toolbox.

"You have such a way with words."

"You're worse today than you were last week, so I'm guessing you fixed nothing with Grace. The two of you still aren't talking, are you?"

"There's nothing going on. So how about you not worry about that?" Jax asked as he put the last of the tools in the garage closet. He locked the door and turned around to find Shep looking at him. Shep's arms were folded across his chest and he was shaking his head, his face filled with pity.

"What?" Jax asked before he could stop himself.

"When are you going to figure it out?"

"Figure what out?"

"Nothing," Shep said, shaking his head again. "You ready? I'm starving."

They pulled into the parking lot of Potbellied Portman's Barbeque fives minute later. Jax hopped out of his truck and walked around to where Shep had parked. Brendan and Jax had helped Shep restore his '67 Mustang, and it still looked like it did ten years ago. That car was Shep's baby and he treated it as such.

As they made their way up to the front door, it opened and two people stumbled out laughing.

"Oh, shit," Shep said coming to a halt.

Oh, shit didn't even begin to cover it. It was Grace and Preston. He had his arm around her shoulders and was grinning down at her while she beamed right back up at him.

Jax's blood began to pound in his veins, and he wouldn't have been surprised if steam was coming out of his ears. That smarmy prick was all over her, and she was all over him. Jax wanted to break something, and Preston's face was at the top of the list.

Grace looked up and came up short when she saw Jax and Shep, the grin disappearing from her face like she'd been slapped. He knew the feeling; he felt like he'd just been slugged in the face, too.

They all stood there for a second before Preston cleared his throat. "How you doing, Shep?" he asked as he stuck his hand out to Shep, while the other stayed firmly in place around Grace's shoulders.

"Doing good," Shep said, taking the outstretched hand and shaking it. "You?"

"Same old, same old," he said as they let go. "Jax, how have you been?" He stuck his hand out for Jax.

Jax's hesitation before he grabbed Preston's hand was obvious. He didn't want to be friendly to the jackass. He also had the urge to squeeze the shit out of Preston's hand, 'cause if it was broken, he couldn't have it on Grace.

"Staying busy," Jax said before he let go.

"Yeah, I heard about the house remodel. I'd like to see it when it's all done."

Preston would come into Jax's house over his dead body. But Jax only nodded because he couldn't unhinge his jaw to say anything else.

"All right, well," Shep said, slapping his hands together. "Good seeing you, Gracie." He swept in and kissed her on the cheek. "We're off to eat dinner. You two have a good night."

Preston led Grace away, and it took everything in Jax not to follow. Not to pull her out of Preston's arms. Were they going back to his place? Or hers? Were they going to sleep together?

Oh, God.

Jax looked back, he couldn't stop himself, and he saw

Grace looking over her shoulder at him. She closed her eyes and turned away, and Jax felt a punch right in his stomach.

"Yeah, nothing going on my ass."

Jax turned around and didn't even look at Shep as he walked into the restaurant. It wasn't crowded so the hostess showed them to a table immediately. Shep waited until after they ordered before he started the third degree.

"What the hell happened? And don't say nothing. Something is going on between you and Grace. Between that incident at the bar and what just happened out there, you can't honestly think I'm going to believe you when you say nothing. You two could barely look at each other, and I thought you were going to crack a molar you were grinding your teeth so hard."

Jax leaned back in his chair and drummed his fingers on the table.

"Grace and I kissed."

"At the café? I figured as much. But that was over a week ago."

Jax checked to make sure no one was in hearing distance before he continued.

"No. Well, yes, we did kiss at the café, but that's not what I'm talking about. Last night I went over to her house to talk to her, and we did a little bit more than talking."

Shep raised his eyebrows.

"It didn't go that far," Jax said, shaking his head. "I stopped it before it did. Told her we can't be together."

"Why the hell not?" Shep said loudly. The couple a few tables over looked up at them for a moment before they went back to their ribs.

"Can you not be so loud?" Jax asked as the waitress came over and gave them their beers.

"Fine, why the hell not?" Shep whispered as she walked away.

"She can do better than what I can offer her."

"You're serious? With who? Preston? He's a good guy, but he isn't for Grace."

"No, not Preston," Jax said, grabbing his beer and taking a long pull.

"Then who? Because as far as I can remember you've never approved of any guy Grace has brought home. And that's saying something considering the fact that Brendan hasn't shown as much dislike to the guys as you have. So tell me, who's she supposed to be with?"

"I don't know, all right, but it isn't me."

"Look, I'm not going to bust your ass about this the rest of the night, because I'm sure we'll both get tired of it. But I hope for your sake that you figure things out before it's too late. If you lose that girl you're never going to forgive yourself. And you want to know how I know this, Jax? Because I did. I lost the girl I was supposed to be with."

"Hannah," Jax said knowingly.

"Hannah." Shep nodded. "You never forget," he said, grabbing his beer and downing half of it.

Hannah Sterling had come to Mirabelle the summer after Jax, Shep, and Brendan graduated from high school. She was a year younger than them, with strawberry blond hair and eyes the color of green sea glass. Shep had fallen for her the moment he'd seen her.

But Hannah's dreams had extended much further than a boy in a small Southern town. She'd left at the end of those three months, and Shep had let her.

"Would you change it? If you could go back, would you do things differently?"

"No," Shep said, shaking his head. "I had to let her go. If I hadn't she would've never followed her dreams. I couldn't hold her back."

"How is that any different from this?"

"Because you think you're not good enough for Grace. But the thing is, you're the only one who *is* good enough for her. Her life is here and she wants to spend it with you. You're holding her back from her dreams by doing what you're doing."

Jax didn't say anything. He just sat there and drank his beer in silence. Shep was quiet, too, now in his own head, haunted by his own memories of the girl he couldn't have.

Chapter Seven

Desperately

When Jax walked into the Sleepy Sheep on Wednesday night it was pouring. Sheets of rain fell from the sky. Lightning danced in the background, and thunder boomed overhead. Jax had had another long day, but it wasn't because he'd been busy with work. He'd woken up at four that morning, another nightmare about Grace making him feel like he was dying.

In this one, she'd been trapped in the funeral home. The entire downstairs was in flames and she was in a room on the second floor, banging on a window and screaming, as the smoke got thicker around her. He woke up choking on air that felt like fire.

He needed to see Grace, *had* to see her. But he couldn't. It wasn't an option. Nope, the only thing he could do was try to stay busy. Too bad work had moved at a sloth's pace. All he'd been able to do was think of Grace, and he was so damn twitchy he thought he was going to go crazy. He was now running on three hours of sleep and more cups of coffee than he could count.

He really wasn't in a socializing mood, but the idea of

going back to his house and sitting alone with his thoughts sounded like torture. Besides, he needed to go over the new plans for the kitchen with Bennett and Shep, so they'd decided to meet at the Sheep for a drink.

Bennett wasn't there when Jax walked in, but Shep was working behind the counter.

"Hey, what do you want? More Jack?" He grinned.

"No, just a beer. And only the one," Jax said, taking an empty seat.

"No more late-night benders for you?" Shep asked as he grabbed a frosted mug.

"Nope."

"Yeah, we'll see about that."

"What?"

"Your friend's here," Shep said, looking past Jax as he placed the full mug of beer down on the counter.

Jax turned to see Preston walking up to the bar, and he took the empty seat right next to Jax.

The guy was wearing pressed black slacks, probably some designer brand that cost more than Jax's rent, and a blue button-down, still wrinkle-free from the day's work. But he had rolled up the sleeves to the elbows and taken off his tie. Somehow he'd managed to stay completely dry. How the hell was that even possible with the lakes that had formed in the parking lot?

"Can I get one of those?" Preston asked, pointing to the beer in front of Jax.

"Coming right up," Shep said. He put a beer down in front of Preston a minute later and went down to the other end of the bar to get some drinks for a group of guys.

"Those the plans for the house?" Preston asked.

"Yup," Jax said looking straight ahead. Maybe if he didn't have to see the prick he would be okay.

"You decide on the plan yourself?"

Yeah, that wasn't going to be the case. The guy's smooth, *I'm too cool* voice grated on Jax's nerves.

"Yup." Jax took a drink from his beer.

"Can I take a look at them?"

"Nope," Jax said, putting his mug down with a little bit too much force. The beer frothed and spilled over the side.

"You don't like me very much, do you?"

"Nope."

"That's rich," Preston said.

"And why's that?" Jax asked, unable to stop himself from looking at the guy.

"You have absolutely no reason to dislike me, whereas I have every reason in the world to despise you."

"Really, what did I ever do to you?"

"It's not what you did to me, it's what you've done to Grace. What you're continuing to do to her," Preston said.

"I don't think that's any of your business."

"Actually, asshole, it is."

"Excuse me?" Jax turned in the stool so that his whole body faced Preston.

"You heard me," Preston said, looking a tad-bit aggressive himself. His ability to stand his ground, and not look the least bit intimidated, made Jax respect him just a little. "I've watched Grace cry over you since she was fourteen years old. Now, that's not really an accurate span of time as to how long you've messed with her mind and her emotions; I didn't witness it from the beginning. But I've been around for ten years of it, and nothing has been as bad as the last couple of weeks. So, since you're too chicken-shit to do anything about it, why don't you just do her a favor and leave her the hell alone. Did you hear that? Was I clear enough?"

"You going to make your own move on Grace now? Is that what this is about? I've seen you. Hanging all over her, laughing, and carrying on. So how about this you self-righteous prick, you hurt her and you'll get a lot more than a threat from me."

Preston laughed and grabbed his beer. "God, if you weren't so stupid, we could be friends."

"Yeah, I don't know about that."

"And why's that?" Preston asked.

"I could never be friends with someone Grace was with."

"Then there might be hope for us yet."

"How's that?" Jax asked skeptically.

"Because Jax, I've never had feelings for Grace. Well, romantic ones that is. I've never had romantic feelings for *any* woman actually."

"You mean..." Jax trailed off, looking at Preston.

"Yeah." He nodded. "And Grace knows. I came out to her in high school."

"Oh," Jax said, still trying to process that little piece of information. "I, uh, I had no idea."

"Really, is that why you thought I was trying to make a move on her? Look, Jax, she's one of my best friends, and I'll always try to protect her."

"You don't think I'm trying to do that?"

"No, I think you're trying to protect yourself," Preston said, shaking his head. "I know what that's like, the whole self-preservation thing. Denying yourself what you want because you're too scared of what might happen. But all you do is lose out and it's such a waste of time. You want to be with her, she wants to be with you."

"It's not that easy."

"Yeah, it is. You're the one making it so complicated."

Jax and Preston sat for a minute in silence, drinking their beers.

Jax was still reeling from the information he'd just gotten. Preston was gay? Yeah, Jax hadn't seen that one coming. Not from a mile away. And Preston wasn't interested in Grace romantically. Relief had washed through Jax at the news, and he felt oddly buoyant.

"You take any of your own advice into action?" Jax asked, looking over at him.

"I'm working on it." Preston nodded. "I'm actually meeting someone tonight. I just thought I'd set you straight first."

Jax choked on his beer. "You know," he said when he could breathe again, "you aren't half-bad after all."

"You're just saying that because now you know I'm not trying to mack on your girl."

"True." Jax nodded.

"So, you going to let me see those plans?" Preston asked, pointing to the blueprints again.

"Sure." Jax handed them over.

Preston grabbed some napkins from the corner of the bar and wiped the bar down. He put the plans down on the now dry counter and unrolled them.

"So you completely gutted it, right?"

"Yeah." Jax nodded.

"How many rooms was it originally?"

"Four, but I knocked down a wall that was here." He reached over, tracing a spot. "I'm only going to rebuild three rooms, because this is going to be used for the kitchen."

"What's the kitchen going to look like?"

"This," Jax said, pulling out another plan from the stack.

The room was going to be massive, with granite counters, hardwood floors, glass cabinets, new appliances, and two islands—one in the center, the other at the edge of the kitchen where bar stools would make it a good breakfast table.

"Huh," Preston said, looking at the plan. "It's a pretty elaborate kitchen."

"Yeah, kind of more than a guy who has zero culinary

skills needs," Shep said, coming up to them and taking a look at the plans himself. "It kind of looks like something that a chef or baker would dream of, doesn't it?"

"Sure does," Preston said, looking back up at Jax. "Plenty of counter space for cooling pies and cookies."

"It's just a kitchen." Jax turned from the men and took a long pull from his beer.

"Riiight," Preston said, leaning to the side and pulling out his ringing phone. He looked at the display and his mouth split into a grin. "And if it isn't someone who could put that counter space to use." He pressed a button and put the phone to his ear. "Hey, Grace, what's up?"

A moment of silence as she said something.

"Where are you?" The concern in Preston's voice brought Jax to the edge of his seat. "All right, I'm at the Sleepy Sheep. I'm leaving right now." His eyebrows lowered and pulled together as he listened to something Grace said. "Are you crazy? You're not walking in this storm. I'm coming to pick you up. Just wait for me."

Jax was on his feet before Preston hung up the phone.

"Where are you going?" Preston asked, getting to his own feet.

"To go get her. What happened? Where is she?"

"Her car wouldn't start. And she didn't call you, Jax. She called me."

"Well, she should've called me. Tell me where she is so I can go get her."

"You might as well tell him," Shep said. "Otherwise he's just going to follow you there."

"Yeah, and you have plans, remember?" Jax said.

"Oh, I didn't forget," Preston said, studying Jax. "Fine." He sat down at his stool again. "She's at the café. But if she gets mad I'm telling her it was all your doing."

"Can you give those to Bennett?" Jax asked Shep,

pointing to the blueprints. He didn't even wait for an answer before he turned around and made his way to the door.

* * *

Grace was cold, wet, and miserable. She'd stayed late at the café, experimenting with a new cookie recipe, and by the time she'd finished it had been almost nine. It had been a good use of her time, because staying busy was the only way to keep her mind off her hurting heart.

She'd forgotten to bring her umbrella from her apartment, so there was no hope in staying dry. The second she'd stepped out from under the overhang she was soaked. And then, to top it all off, her car wouldn't start. The engine didn't do anything besides make a clicking noise.

Dead battery most likely.

Her first instinct was to call Jax. He'd always been the first person she'd called. But she shoved that stupid impulse into a corner. Jax wasn't her rescuer. She would've called Brendan, not that he could've done anything to fix her car in the storm, but he and Paige were currently on their way back from Tallahassee. Paige's best friend Abby was flying in from Washington, D.C., for the baby shower.

Shep was working, so he was a no-go. Mel was in Tampa for a math tournament with her students, and Harper was in Georgia visiting family. Grace would've called her grandparents but neither of them drove really well at night anymore and the storm would make it ten times worse.

Her only option was Preston. She felt genuinely awful about it, too, because he had a date. Well, not a date so much as a "let's get a drink" with Baxter McCoy. Apparently after the whole bar incident with Jax on Saturday night, the two had struck up a conversation, and Preston had picked up a vibe from Baxter.

She would've smiled at the thought of Preston finally meeting a guy, but at the moment her lips were numb and her teeth were chattering. It might be April, but she was soaked and freezing. She just wanted to go home and take a hot shower.

Yeah, she was going to owe Preston big time.

But a moment later, every warm feeling Grace had ever had for Preston went out the window as Jax's big red pickup pulled in next to her dead car.

"You've got to be kidding me," she said, staring at it for a second. "Oh, whatever." She shook her head as she got out of her car and bolted for the passenger door.

She was literally in the rain for less than ten seconds, but it was like she'd just stepped out of a pool. Jax's truck was blessedly warm as she slammed the door behind her.

"What are you doing here?" she asked, shivering inside of her freshly soaked clothes. "I called Preston."

"I know," Jax said, turning the heat up. "I was sitting right next to him when you did."

"What?" Grace asked, rubbing her hands up and down her arms.

"We were having a friendly chat." Jax put his truck in gear and backed out of the spot.

"You? Friendly? Right."

"I'd give you something to dry off with but I don't have anything."

"I'm fine," she said, waving off his words.

They sat in silence for a couple of minutes, her body temperature slowly going up. Her mind and heart were playing tug-of-war with her emotions. Her mind was pissed. She was mad that she was in the same car as Jax. Furious that he was sitting next to her and acting like everything was just fine, like nothing had happened.

But her heart? Her heart was rejoicing that he was so

close to her. Just goes to show how stupid a person's heart could be. Because the second he left her, it was going to feel like he'd ripped said heart out of her chest again.

"Why did you come?" she asked.

"Why didn't you call me?" he countered.

She turned and looked out the window into the darkness.

She closed her eyes and took a deep breath. "You can't be the person I call, not anymore," she said quietly, but her words echoed in the cab of the truck.

"Grace..."

"Just take me home, Jax," she said, keeping her back turned to him.

* * *

Jax pulled into the parking lot of Grace's apartment and put his truck in park. They sat there for a second, the rain pounding against every inch of his truck, the pings echoing in the silence.

He wanted to reach across the distance and touch her, to gather her up in his arms and kiss her, but his hands stayed firmly on the steering wheel.

"Thanks, Jax," she said before she opened the door and went out into the rain.

He watched her sprint away from him, up the stairs and to the second floor. She fumbled with her keys before she got them in the lock of her door and then she disappeared from his view.

Jax stared at that empty landing for about ten seconds before he let go of the wheel and opened the door. He stepped outside and was soaked instantly. But he didn't care; he had other way more important things on his mind.

He wanted Grace, plain and simple. Preston was right. It was just that easy.

Jax was so tired of watching her walk away from him. So tired of not having what he wanted. So tired of not being with her. He was done letting his life pass him by without Grace in it. He had to have her, and he had to have her *now*.

He got to the front door and knocked hard.

Once, twice, three times.

Grace opened the door and frowned at him from the other side. "Jax?" she said, confused.

"I'm your person, Grace. Me, not anyone else," he said, stepping into her apartment.

She looked up at him startled as he closed the door behind him and locked it. And then he grabbed her and pushed her up against the wall. She gasped before his mouth landed hard on hers, his hands grabbing onto the wet fabric of her jeans. Her arms wrapped around his neck, her fingers digging into his wet hair and holding him in place as she opened her mouth to his. His hands traveled up under her shirt, his fingers wrapping around her bare sides.

He was eating at her mouth, and she seemed to be on the exact same page as he was, because she was trying to consume him as well.

He moved his hands to the hem of her shirt and slowly started to peel the wet fabric from her skin as he moved it up, up, up. His mouth broke from hers as he pulled the material over her head and threw it to the floor.

"Jax," Grace said, grabbing his face before his mouth could land on hers again. "I swear, if you have any thoughts in your head about walking out that door tonight after spouting some stupid theory that you aren't good enough—"

He shut her up by sealing his mouth over hers. He brought his hands up to her breasts and squeezed gently. She moaned deep in her throat and grabbed his shoulders, her fingernails digging into his skin.

He moved his mouth to her ear, grazing her earlobe with

his teeth. "I'm not going anywhere, Grace," he whispered. "Well, at least not anywhere farther than your bed."

"Let's go," she said, making a move to go down the hall to her bedroom.

"Wait a second." He held her in place.

"Why?"

"Because, we're both in wet clothes. Let's get rid of those first," he said, moving his mouth down her neck to her collarbone.

He needed to pace himself so that he could remember this moment for the rest of his life. To enjoy it. Savor it. Savor *her*.

He moved down the center of her breasts with his tongue, going lower until he was kneeling in front of her. He ran his hands up her sides, needing to just look at her for a second, to take her in. It was then that he noticed her new tattoo. *Still Breathing* was inked in inch-high script writing. It started just under her left breast and ran horizontally out across her ribs.

"When did you get this," he asked, tracing the words with his fingertips.

"Last September after the car accident," she said, playing with his hair.

"I like it," he said right before he kissed the words.

"Really? I thought you'd hate it after your reaction to my other one."

"Hmm. I never hated this tattoo," he said, switching sides and kissing the outstretched wings of the swallow. "The problem was I liked it just a little bit too much." He looked up at her as his thumb moved gently over the spot.

Grace was staring down at him. Her cheeks were flushed. Her breasts were rising and falling rapidly, and her nipples were poking out of the wet fabric of her bra.

To hell with pacing himself. He needed her to be under him. *Now.*

He reached up and unbuttoned the front of her jeans. He pulled them down, peeling the wet fabric from her legs. He lifted her feet up, first one, then the other, and freed her completely. Then he was on his feet again in front of her. She fisted her hands in his dripping T-shirt and pulled it over his head, the fabric making a squelching noise as it hit the wood floor.

Grace pulled Jax back to her. She slipped her tongue into his mouth and found his. Her hands were all over his chest, her fingertips tracing his pecks and his abs, around to his side and up his back.

Jax reached down and grabbed Grace's thighs, pulling her up as she wrapped her legs around his body. He moved his hands to her perfect ass as he pulled away from the wall and made his way down the hallway and into her bedroom. When his legs hit the bed he laid her down slowly. He unhooked the back of her bra and pulled it off. He groaned and his mouth was on her bare breasts in about a nanosecond. He stayed at if for who knew how long.

"Jax."

He looked up to see Grace arching her back, her head pressing into the pillows as she writhed underneath him. He made his way back up her body. He needed his lips on hers. He kissed her hard and started moving his hips in rhythm to hers.

All the while, her hands were traveling down to the fly of his jeans, working the button and the zipper, and moving under the elastic of his boxer briefs. And then those magic hands of hers were on him, stroking him, and he thought he was going to lose his damn mind.

He pulled back and stood up. The sudden move brought a look of doubt to Grace's face, but it disappeared when he kicked off his boots. He unstrapped his ankle holster and put his gun on her nightstand before he shoved his jeans, boxers, and socks to the floor.

* * *

"Please tell me you have a condom," Grace said, staring at Jax in all of his naked glory. She most definitely liked what she saw, and she couldn't stop herself from licking her bottom lip as she looked at Jax's very prominent, and very glorious, erection.

"Grace," he said, sounding pained. "If you keep looking at me like that, I don't think I'll last long enough to get inside of you."

"How am I looking at you?" she asked, letting her gaze travel all the way up his hard, muscled body to his eyes.

"All hot and hungry."

"I can't help it."

Jax grabbed his jeans from the floor and dug out his wallet. He pulled out a small package before he threw his wallet down on top of his jeans. He opened the package and rolled the condom on before he kneeled on the bed. He reached for the thin straps at her hips and pulled her panties down her legs.

"Good God, Grace, you're perfect," he said, looking down at her.

"Come here." She held out her hand. He grabbed it and let her pull him down to the cradle of her body.

Jax found her mouth again, his tongue sliding past her lips, searching for her tongue. He moved against her, and she loved the way her bare skin felt rubbing against his, her breasts against his chest. She was pretty sure nothing had ever felt this good before, and he hadn't even gotten inside of her yet.

He reached between their bodies, his fingers gently pushing her apart. "You're so ready," he groaned against her mouth as he slid two fingers inside of her. "So wet," he said as his thumb pressed against that little knot that had her writhing.

"Jax, please," she begged as her body arched up off the bed.

He covered her mouth with his as he stroked his fingers inside of her. Her hips pumped up against his hand wildly. Though Grace was a very big fan of Jax's fingers, that wasn't what she wanted inside of her. So she reached down and grabbed him. The second her hand closed around him, he pulled his hand out from between their bodies and Grace guided him to her. Jax pushed inside of her slowly, not taking his eyes off hers as their bodies joined. He stilled when he was all the way inside of her, letting her body adjust around his.

Grace had been imagining this moment for years. Dreaming of what it would feel like to finally have Jax this way. The reality blew her dreams right out of the water. Being with Jax was like coming home.

"You're so damn beautiful," he said, looking down at her. "You knock me off my feet, Grace. You always have." He lowered his mouth to hers and kissed her gently, slowly.

Grace's hands came up to the back of his head, her fingers sliding into his hair.

"Make love to me, Jax," she whispered against his mouth.

"You feel so good," he said as he began to pump his hips.

She pulled her legs up and wrapped them around his waist.

"And it just keeps getting better," he groaned as he slid even deeper inside of her.

He captured her mouth again, his tongue thrusting in. She wanted to stay there forever, wrapped around him in every way while he was buried deep inside of her. It was amazing. *He* was amazing. She knew without a doubt that she'd never in her life get enough of this man.

As Jax continued to move inside of her, he brought one of his hands back down between their bodies, searching for that sweet spot again.

"Oh, Jax," she said when he found it.

And it didn't take her long to go over the edge. She cried out as she pulsed around him. He continued to pump into her through the aftershocks, and when she finished she looked up at him, more than a little bit out of breath.

"You didn't..." she trailed off, feeling that he was definitely still hard inside of her.

"Not yet." He smiled down at her. "I'm not quite ready for this to be over," he said as he moved his hand from between their bodies and slid it underneath her bottom. He pulled her more firmly to him and started to swivel his hips, grinding into her. "We've only got one condom and I need to feel you do that again...and again...and again." He punctuated his words with kisses to her mouth.

"Oh, oh," she gasped as her head fell back into the pillow.

Jax was exactly a foot taller than she was, but their bodies fit together perfectly. He also had about eighty pounds on her, but she loved how his long, lean body felt pressing hers into the mattress.

"More, Jax. Harder," she begged. She knew she was getting close, knew she was on the verge of shattering.

"Grace, look at me," he said above her mouth.

Her eyes opened and focused on his as he picked up the pace, giving her what she wanted. And that was it. They were both swept under in a wave of pleasure. Grace screamed his name over and over again, and Jax groaned her name through his own release. He buried his face in her neck, kissing her skin as he caught his breath. Grace still had her arms and legs wrapped around him in a vice, keeping him from pulling out of her body.

"Gracie, I'm going to crush you," he whispered.

"I just want to feel you inside of me for a little bit longer," she said sleepily. She'd waited so long to be with him, so she hadn't been ready in any capacity to let him go.

"Drop this leg," he said, running his hand up her left thigh.

She did and he rolled them to their sides. His mouth was on hers again and he kissed her slowly. He brought one of his hands to her breast, cupping it and sliding his thumb over her nipple.

"Mmm," she hummed into his mouth.

"You're incredible, Grace," he said above her mouth.

"You're pretty freaking fantastic yourself." She pressed her lips to his before she buried her face in his chest. They stayed that way for a while, wrapped around each other, kissing and touching. She wasn't sure how long it was before she dozed off, but she awoke when he pulled from her body.

"No, don't leave," she said, reaching for him.

"I'll be right back." He kissed her mouth.

He padded lightly to the bathroom, and a minute later he was back, pulling her into his arms. She snuggled into him, and the last thing she remembered was kissing his chest before she fell asleep.

Chapter Eight

Something's Up with the Deputy

Grace came to slowly, her face pressed into a pillow while her arm was wrapped around another. She pushed up the pillow she was wrapped around and stretched her arm to the other side of the bed, searching for Jax. The soreness in her muscles made her mouth split into a grin. But that grin quickly disappeared as her hand came up with only cold sheets.

She sat up and stared at the empty side of the bed, her heart in her throat. She scrambled to the edge and looked over the side; Jax's clothes and boots were gone.

Grace sat down and pulled her knees up to her chest. She wrapped her arms around her legs and closed her eyes as she took a steadying breath. Maybe it wasn't what she thought it was. Maybe Jax hadn't woken up in the middle of the night and freaked out about what they'd done. Maybe there was a logical explanation.

Or maybe there wasn't.

God, she was such an idiot. She was a freaking moron. Of course he'd freaked out. This was Jax she was talking about, the boy who refused to accept that anything good could happen to him. And, oh, how good it had been last night.

Indescribable, it had been *indescribable*. No man was ever going to compare to Jaxson Anderson. Ever.

He'd taken his time, and thank God, because they'd only had the one condom. If it had been a quick push to the finish line, she might've cried. And he'd taken her to that finish line twice. And boy had it been spectacular, complete with banners and confetti and a screaming crowd. Well, maybe she'd just sounded like a screaming crowd. Yeah, she hadn't been quiet, and shockingly enough, neither had he. He'd said her name as he came inside her, said it with so much passion. And now he was gone.

She hadn't thought she'd needed to convince him that they worked together, that they were supposed to *be* together.

Grace pressed her face into her knees.

She couldn't do it. If this was what it was always going to be like, him always freaking out and leaving her, she just couldn't do it. She couldn't handle the constant disappointment, the hollow feeling in her heart when she looked at the empty space next to her.

She pulled back and wiped at her eyes. She didn't even realize she'd started crying.

Grace took another deep breath and shook her head. She was done with this. If this was how Jax was going to do things, she was just done.

Yeah right. All he was going to have to do was look at her and her resolve would disappear quickly, followed by her panties.

She looked at the nightstand. Seven o'clock. She needed to call her grandmother to get a ride to the café. She got out of bed and went into the living room. Jax had picked her clothes off the floor and laid them on the back of the couch. She walked over and ran her fingers over the shirt that he'd peeled her out of hours before.

She pulled her hand back, already frustrated with herself.

It didn't mean anything. It was just a meaningless gesture on his part.

She grabbed her purse from where she'd dropped it on the couch last night and dug into it, searching for her phone. She had a moment, between closing her hand around it and pressing the button to light up the display, where she thought that maybe, just maybe, Jax would've called or sent her a text.

No such luck.

"Hey sweetie," Lula Mae answered after a couple of rings.

"Can you pick me up?" Grace asked as she made her way into the bathroom. "My car didn't start last night."

"I'm leaving in about twenty minutes."

"I'll be ready," Grace said, turning on the shower.

When she got out ten minutes later, she stood in the doorway, wrapped in a towel, and stared at her rumpled bed. She and Jax had managed to pull the top sheet out from the end. It was in a pile on the floor, along with two toss pillows and the throw that she kept at the foot of her bed. Her quilt was upside down, the white and yellow stripes showing instead of the blue, green, and yellow floral print.

She'd have to wash everything when she got home. The thought of sleeping in a bed that still smelled like Jax was impossible.

She went to her closet and pulled out a navy blue cotton dress and a pair of canvas slip-on shoes. She was dressed and ready to go by the time her grandmother pulled into the parking lot.

"How'd you get home last night?" Lula Mae asked as she turned onto the main road.

"Jax."

"You two talking again?"

No, apparently they were having out-of-this-world sex

and then *not* talking about it because he'd pulled a disappearing act.

"I have no idea what we are," Grace said.

"I don't like the sound of that."

"Join the club," Grace said miserably.

* * *

Jax mounted the steps to Café Lula just before ten. He was still wearing his clothes from the day before, and they were more than slightly rumpled, but he hadn't had time to change. He'd been itching to see Grace, and the longer he waited the crazier he was feeling.

He'd gotten a call at four that morning to go in to work. Of all the days, it just had to be the one where he left a gloriously naked Grace in bed. As he'd fallen asleep with her in his arms the night before, he'd planned on convincing her to play hooky from the café, if not the whole day, then at least just the morning. He was supposed to have the day off and he'd known just how he wanted to spend it, and it involved her underneath him for the majority of it.

But that wasn't how things had worked out. Jax had woken up to a low, steady ring coming from his pile of clothes on the floor. Grace was sprawled across his chest, one of her hands resting dangerously low on his abdomen. It had been pure torture leaving her.

She only stirred a little when he'd pulled away from her, tucking a pillow into her arms to hold and kissing her on the forehead. But there was nothing he could do; he had to go. Three houses had been broken into.

Most of the houses on Mirabelle Beach were million-dollar properties, and a lot of them were empty because their owners only occupied them during the summer. The alarms had been triggered within seconds of one another.

The first house was about four miles away from the second and third. There hadn't been enough deputies on patrol to get to all three houses at once. Neal Sanders had gone to the first house and everything was still locked up tight. But the first house had just been a distraction. By the time he got to the second and third house, he was too late. The thieves had already been in and out and made off with thousands of dollars' worth of valuables.

Jax was pretty sure it was the same guys who had burglarized places all over the county. The locks were picked with the same quick efficiency, and again, they'd known exactly where everything was.

Sheriff Dawson assigned Neal Sanders and Baxter McCoy to start working on the case with Jax. By the time they'd finished going through all three houses, and Jax had gone over everything he knew about the case with Baxter and Neal, it was past nine.

Jax hadn't had time to call Grace, and really talking to her over the phone wasn't good enough. He had to see her. Had to bury his face in her neck and kiss that soft spot that made her sigh.

The café was busy when Jax walked in. Almost all of the tables were full and there was a line five people deep at the counter. Callie Armstrong was manning the register while Lula Mae filled the orders.

"Long time no see, Jaxson Anderson." Lula Mae narrowed her eyes at him.

"I know," he said, coming around the counter and giving her a kiss on the cheek.

"I'm not a fan of this disappearing act you've got going on. You done with the whole avoiding Grace thing?" she asked under her breath so the customers couldn't hear her.

Oh, was he ever done with that.

"Yes, ma'am."

"Good, now you get in there and fix it," she said, shooing him in the direction of the kitchen.

"Fix what?" he asked, confused as he glanced over at the kitchen.

"Whatever it is that you did. She's been in a mood."

"That doesn't sound promising."

"It sure doesn't. Now get in there." She pushed him toward the door.

Jax walked into the kitchen just as Grace was bending over to pull something that smelled like heaven out of the oven. Her dress was riding up high on the back of her thighs, and his mind immediately flashed to last night when he'd been between said thighs.

Grace put two chocolate cakes on the counter before she pulled the oven mitts off her hands and turned around. She froze when she saw Jax, a look of uncertainty in her eyes that Jax wasn't a fan of at all. Her whole body was tense and her guard was up.

"If you've come here to tell me last night was a mistake, save it. I don't want to hear it."

"Okay," he said slowly, "not why I'm here."

"It isn't?" she asked as her shoulders slumped in relief.

"No." He smiled, crossing the distance to her.

"So, you're not having doubts?" she asked as he stepped into her.

"No," he said, reaching out and tracing her jaw with his fingers. He pushed a stray piece of her blond hair behind her ear.

"Then why did you leave?" She studied his face.

"I got a call at four this morning. Three houses were broken into just up the street from here. I wrote it all in the note."

"You left a note?"

"Yeah, right by your head."

"I didn't see it," she said, leaning into him.

"I figured." He ran his fingers to the tip on her chin and pushed up. He was in desperate need of feeling her lips against his. He covered her mouth with his, his tongue sliding in between her lips. Her arms wrapped around his shoulders as he worked her mouth with his.

"Come here," she said, stepping back and grabbing his hand. She pulled him into the pantry where he promptly pushed her up against the wall. "No regrets?" she asked, looking up at him.

"My only regret is I only got to have you once last night."

"Hmm, I think we can rectify that," she said, grabbing the collar of his shirt and bringing his face to hers.

"Tonight?" he asked against her mouth.

"Yes, please."

"I'll pick you up at five," he said, letting his hands travel down to her hips. He grabbed her thighs and pulled her up, her legs wrapping around his waist. His hands skimmed up under her dress and he kept going until he got to the good stuff. "You don't play fair," he said when he found her thong.

"Never said that I did," she said, nibbling on his bottom lip. "You don't, either." She stroked his cheeks. He hadn't shaved and had a day's worth of growth on his face. "I like this. I like this a lot."

"Do you now?" he asked, his mouth quirking to the side.

"Oh, yeah."

"I'll have to keep that in mind."

"So, what did your note say?"

"Dear Princess," he said as his lips moved down to her neck. *"Last night was perfect."* His mouth went lower. *"There is nowhere I'd rather be than waking up next to you."* His tongue was tracing her collarbone. *"Well, maybe waking up in you,"* he said as his fingers explored the area

not covered by her panties, which was pretty much everything. *I got a call, break-ins on the beach. I'll stop by the café when I can. Jax. P.S. You have no idea how incredibly sexy you are, even when you're asleep.*

"That's a good note," she said as his mouth returned to her neck. Her head fell back against the wall and she arched her body into him.

"You're killing me," he said, making his way back up to her mouth.

"I try," she said right before her tongue found its way into his mouth.

"I have to go." He pulled his mouth from hers a minute later.

"Why?"

"Because if we don't stop, I'm going to have sex with you right here. Up against this wall. With your grandmother and a room full of customers in the next room."

"Yeah, maybe that isn't the best idea," she said, biting her lip.

"You think?"

"You going to work today?"

"Yeah just for a couple of hours. I had to see you before I went home to shower and change. Then I'm going in to the office for a little to try and make some sense of this case. If I have time I'm going to go work on the house."

"What are you doing tomorrow?"

"Waking up next to you. What are the chances you can come in here a little late and spend the morning with me?"

"I'd say they're pretty good. Grams and I need to start working on the food for Paige's baby shower, so I have to work a little late tomorrow anyway. You want to eat some breakfast before you leave?"

"I'd like to eat something else, but breakfast will do."

"Why Jaxson Anderson." She grinned, unwinding her

legs from around his hips. "You are a dirty, dirty boy. I had absolutely no idea."

"Grace King," he said, leaning into her mouth, "it's all you. You bring out the bad in me."

* * *

Jax was back at the café just before closing wearing jeans and a short-sleeved button-up flannel. He still hadn't shaved and it took everything in Grace not to crawl all over him. By the time they got back to her apartment she was in pounce mode. The second the door was locked behind them, they were stumbling to her bedroom, clothes flying everywhere.

When they resurfaced an hour later, Grace pulled on Jax's shirt and made her way into the kitchen to whip up something for them to eat.

"What are you going to make?" Jax asked, coming up behind her as she stared into the refrigerator. He kissed the side of her neck as he ran his hands under the shirt, up her bare thighs, and to her hips.

"What do you feel like?" she asked, leaning back into him.

"Anything, I'm starving." His arms wound around her waist.

Grace had to pause for a second to appreciate the magnitude of the moment. It might have been something small and insignificant to anyone else, standing in the kitchen wrapped up in this man, but to her it was huge. She finally had him. She finally had Jax in her life in the way she'd been dreaming about for what felt like forever.

She wrapped her arms around his and turned her face to look up at him. He leaned down and kissed her, and the only reason they broke apart a minute later was because his stomach growled.

"All right, let's get you fed."

She wound up making tomato, mozzarella, and basil sandwiches. Jax stood behind her the whole time she grilled them on the stove, nibbling on her neck.

"You are *very* distracting," Grace said as she flipped a sandwich, the cheese oozing out the side.

"Can't help it, I'm starving."

"Well, I'm almost done. Then you can eat."

"Food isn't the only thing I'm starving for," he said, switching to the other side of her neck.

"We can take care of that craving, too."

"Can't wait." He smiled into her shoulder.

After dinner, they returned to Grace's bed, where they stayed busy well into the middle of the night.

* * *

"Shit!"

Jax shot up in bed just in time to see Brendan banging off the door frame of Grace's room.

Shit was right.

There was no way Brendan was oblivious to what had been going on between Jax and Grace for the last couple of years, but there was no telling how he was going to react to the fact that his friend had just had sex with his little sister.

"What the hell are you doing here?" Grace asked, pulling the sheet up to cover her naked chest.

"I told you," Brendan said, shielding his eyes with one hand while he rubbed his knee with the other, "I was stopping by to get the keys to your car. Holy hell, there are so many things I've never wanted to witness and you in bed with Jax is pretty close to the top of the list."

"Did you ever think of knocking?"

"I did! You didn't answer. Nor did you answer your phone when I called you. I figured you weren't home."

"Crap, I forgot to charge my phone last night. It's probably dead."

"Kind of like my eyesight. Where are your spare keys so I can get the hell out of here?" Brendan asked.

"I have to find them. Go out into the living room so we can put some clothes on and I'll get them for you."

"Fine," Brendan said, closing the door behind him.

"So, Brendan knows about us." Jax turned to Grace. "I think he took it pretty well."

"Oh. My. Gosh," she said, turning to him, her cheeks on fire. "There couldn't have been a worse way for him to find out."

"That isn't true," Jax said, unable to stop himself from grinning. "He could've walked in while you were screaming my name."

Grace grabbed a pillow and hit him in the face with it. "Put on some pants, Smiley-McGee. You're going to need to have some coverage when you go out there." She got out of bed and walked to the bathroom.

"Smiley-McGee?" Jax asked as he got out of bed and started searching for his boxers among the clothes that cluttered the floor.

"I don't know if you've looked in a mirror lately," she called out to him, "but your characteristic scowl has been absent. I've never seen your dimples make this long of an appearance before."

"Actually, I haven't had a lot of free time to stand in front of a mirror. I've been kept *very* busy," he said, bending down to grab his boxers by Grace's dresser.

"Mmm," Grace hummed behind him.

He turned to find her in a bright blue robe. She was leaning against the doorway to the bathroom, staring at him with a very appreciative gleam in her eyes.

"How about you not look at me that way right before I go

out there and talk to your brother," he said, stepping into his boxers.

"Why?" She grinned. "Am I making things *hard* for you?"

"Oh, Princess, you just wait." He grabbed his jeans and pulled them on.

"For what?" she asked, waggling her eyebrows.

"Oh, you'll find out," he said, walking to the door and going out into the hallway.

Jax stepped around the corner and found Brendan leaning against the counter, his arms folded across his chest and a severe frown in place.

Huh, normally Brendan was Mr. Happy-Go-Lucky. Apparently that outlook in life had a tendency to disappear when you found your best friend in bed with your baby sister.

"I'm just going to tell you this once," Brendan said, narrowing his eyes. "It should go without saying, but I'm going to tell you anyway just so we are perfectly clear. If you hurt her, I will hurt you."

"I would expect nothing less."

"Good." Brendan nodded. "That was not what I expected to find when I walked in here."

"I'm sure it wasn't," Jax said, unable to keep his lips from quirking up.

"What the hell is that on your face? Is that an actual smile?" Brendan asked.

"Shut up, I smile."

"Not like that you don't," Brendan said, shaking his head. "I'm serious, Jax, don't screw this up. You deserve to be happy, too."

Jax didn't have a chance to respond to that before Grace came into the kitchen.

"Here you go," she said, holding her hand out to Brendan. He stuck his open palm out and she dropped a set of keys in it.

"I'll take a look at your car today," Brendan said, pushing off of the counter. "I'll give you a call when I figure out what's going on, but it's probably just a dead battery." He leaned down and planted a kiss on the side of Grace's head. "You should bring your new boyfriend around sometime," he said as he walked toward the door.

"Bye, Brendan." Grace shooed him with her hand.

"No, I'm serious. I'm sure the family would *love* to meet him." He opened the front door and turned around to look at them.

"Get out, Brendan."

"All right, all right, I'm going. See you two love birds later." He grinned as he shut the door behind him.

"So," Grace said, turning to the counter and grabbing a stack of mail. "What are your plans for the rest of the day?" She started to sort the mail without any real organization. Her shoulders were rigid and her voice was off, too high and unnatural.

"Grace?" Jax asked, coming up behind her and pulling the remaining mail out of her hands. He set the mail on the counter and turned her around. "You okay?"

"Yeah, I'm fine," she said. Except her voice went up just a little bit more and she was looking over his shoulder, refusing to look him in the eye.

"Look at me," he said, touching her chin and moving her head so she had to look at him. "What's going on?"

"Are you going to freak out?" she asked, looking terrified.

"What?"

"Brendan called you my boyfriend; he caught you in bed with me. There's no going back from here."

"Grace, there was no going back a long time ago. It started before that session on your couch, and way before that kiss in the café," he said, rubbing her jaw with his thumb. "I'm not going to freak out."

"You promise?" She looked up at him with wide imploring eyes.

"I promise."

"How are you so mellow and reserved about this? You? The guy who's been determined to keep me at arm's length, since forever."

"You've never been at arm's length," he said, shaking his head. "That was always the problem. Grace, I've wanted you for a long time now. Since you were eighteen. Well, that's when I figured it out. It probably started well before then. So, I'm not scared of the *boyfriend/girlfriend* label. It's about damn time actually."

"Who are you?" she asked, searching his face for an answer.

"A man who's finally taking what he wants."

"And what do you want?" she asked, a smile finally turning up her lips.

"You. Right now preferably," he said, bending down and throwing her over his shoulder. And then he proceeded to take her back to her bedroom in full caveman style, Grace laughing the whole way.

* * *

When Jax dropped Grace off at the café just before eleven, they sat in his truck making out for a good five minutes.

"Do you have to work today?" he asked, running his thumb across her bottom lip.

"I so wish I didn't," she said, pushing back from him and trying to catch her breath. "But just keep in mind while you slave away today, that you'll get me all to yourself tonight. We'll have dinner, then move on to dessert."

"Mmm dessert," he said, coming in for another kiss that turned into a couple more minutes of heavy tonguing and touching.

"Okay, now I really have to go. I have too much stuff to do," she said, pulling away from him.

"Call me when you're done tonight. I'm going to stop by the Sleepy Sheep and get a beer with the guys after I finish up at the house."

"Sounds good," she said, giving him one last kiss before she turned and scrambled out of his truck. If she didn't put some massive distance between them with a quickness, she wasn't going to be doing anything besides Jax. Before she closed the door she caught his grin and it spread to her mouth.

"Wow," Lula Mae said when Grace walked in. "That's a smile if I've ever seen one."

"I have no idea what you're talking about." Grace made her way behind the counter and into the kitchen.

"So you're not talking?" Lula Mae asked, following her through the door.

"Nope."

"Why? Mouth tired from the workout you just gave it in Jax's truck?"

"Grams!" Grace said, spinning around.

"What? Was it supposed to be a secret? Because if it was you should have chosen a different spot to suck the boy's face off. Also, I can't believe he didn't come in here and say hello."

"He was running late meeting Bennett up at the new house." Grace grabbed her apron.

"Doesn't matter, still going to give that boy a piece of my mind," Lula Mae said, stern look firmly in place.

"Oh, don't even act like you're not going to forgive him," Grace said, tying her apron.

"Well, that depends entirely on one thing." Lula Mae studied Grace for a second.

"What?"

"If he keeps that smile on your face. I like seeing it there," she said as her own mouth was overtaken by a grin. "I told you that boy was hopeless when it came to you."

"Yeah, it goes both ways, though." Grace opened the fridge and pulled out what she needed to make strawberry champagne cupcakes. "That boy makes all rational thought vacate my brain."

"Gracie," Lula Mae said, shaking her head. "There's absolutely nothing *rational* about love."

Oh, the L-word. Grace wasn't going to touch that one for a little while. Did she love Jax? Without a doubt. But she was going to keep that fact to herself. He might not have freaked out about being categorized as her boyfriend, but bringing love into the mix would be a whole different story.

"Why don't we keep that word to ourselves?" Grace asked, pulling out the mixer.

"Don't tell me you're in denial."

"I'm not. I'm in love with Jax. But I don't think he's there at the moment."

"Sweetie, he ran past that line a long time ago. He just hasn't realized it yet."

Yeah, and Grace was scared that when he did, he was going to start running in the opposite direction.

"Grams," Grace pleaded.

"All right, all right. I wouldn't say anything to him anyway. I'm not completely clueless."

"You're not clueless at all. It's just I've wanted this for so long, wanted *him* for so long, I don't want to do anything to tip the apple cart. You know?"

"I know." Lula Mae nodded.

"I'm still waiting to wake up. It all feels too much like a dream."

"Well, in that case," Lula Mae said, reaching over and pinching Grace's arm.

"Ow," she said, flinching away. "What was that for?"

"Just letting you know that you're wide awake. Now get cracking on those cupcakes. We have a café to run and people to feed."

"I know, I know."

"But I'm happy for you, Gracie," Lula Mae said as she swooped in and gave Grace a kiss on the cheek. "It's going to work out for the two of you."

Dear God, Grace hoped so.

* * *

"What?" Jax asked looking over at Shep. Shep had been staring at Jax since he'd walked in the door a half hour ago.

"Something's up with you," Shep said, narrowing his eyes.

"Nothing's up," Jax said. But that was a lie. Certain things had been up for days. He wanted Grace so bad it was insane, and he was counting down to when he got to see her.

Said countdown was currently at twenty-three minutes, forty-nine seconds.

Forty-eight seconds.

Forty-seven seconds.

"Hmm," Shep said, still studying him. "Yeah, I don't believe that. I'm going to figure it out, though."

"With your super detective skills?" Jax asked, raising his eyebrows.

"You spent the day with him," Shep said, turning to Bennett. "He's acting strange, right?"

"Yeah, it's almost like he's content with life, happy even," Bennett said.

"Now, why would that be?" Brendan grinned as he took a pull of his beer.

"I don't know, but I have a feeling it's about to disappear," Shep said as he wiped out a glass.

"Why's that?" Jax asked.

"Because Grace is here, and you two have been at each other's throats the last couple of weeks."

Jax turned around and saw Grace making her way up to the bar.

Jax turned back to Shep as he slid off his stool. "Yeah, that isn't a problem anymore," he said before he turned around and walked toward Grace, meeting her in the middle.

"Hey." She smiled up at him. But she didn't say anything else as Jax wrapped his arms around her and covered her mouth with his.

"You were supposed to call me so I could pick you up," he said, pulling back from her mouth.

"Don't get all upset. We finished a little early so Grams dropped me off." She ran her hands up his chest. "I wanted a drink, too."

"Let's go back to my place and I'll give you as many drinks as you want. *And* you can be naked while you drink them."

Grace laughed, shaking her head.

Jax frowned. "You think I'm joking but I'm not."

"Actually, I know you're dead serious. We won't stay long," she said, and grabbed his hand. His fingers automatically twined with hers and she turned, pulling him toward the bar.

Jax was more than a little disappointed that he was going to have to share Grace for a little while; he wanted her all to himself. But Jax couldn't stop himself from laughing as he took in Shep's shocked expression.

Shep's jaw was dropped open and he stared at them unblinking. His hands had stilled from drying the beer mug and he looked like a statue he was so still. It took him a second to find his voice. "All right, who are you and what have you done with Jaxson Anderson?"

"Shocking, isn't it?" Brendan asked.

"You knew about this?" Shep asked, rounding on Brendan.

"Believe me, the way I found out will forever scar me," Brendan said. "I walked in on them in bed this morning."

"We were sleeping," Grace explained, looking at Shep, then Bennett. Then she reached over and hit her brother upside the head.

"Ow." Brendan flinched.

"You have a big mouth, you know that?"

"When the hell did this happen?" Shep asked.

"When my car didn't start the other night."

"I think that Jax finally pulling his head out of his ass is a definite cause for celebration." Shep grinned.

"And let's just hope he doesn't have a relapse," Bennett said.

Yeah, let's just hope so, Jax thought.

Chapter Nine

Promises, Threats, Secrets, and Lies

Grace slept until nine on Sunday. She vaguely remembered Jax pulling away from her and kissing her temple before he left bed early that morning. He had to work and promised that he'd meet her at her apartment when he got off at seven.

All of the food for Paige's shower was already at Lula Mae's. Grace just needed to be there by eleven to help set up and decorate. Brendan had fixed her Bug on Friday and she'd picked it up on Saturday. It was good to have her car back, but she sure did love Jax playing her chauffeur.

It didn't take long for Lula Mae's house to fill up with people. Paige had made quite a few friends in the almost two years she'd lived in Mirabelle, and they filled the living room and kitchen laughing, eating, and having a good time.

They played many shower games. Guessing what kind of baby food was in diapers, stealing clothespins when the words *baby, Trevor, due date, daddy,* or *mommy* were said, guessing how many safety pins were in a mason jar, and they'd finished it all off with baby bingo. They ate an assortment of goodies: bacon and gouda quiches, spinach and artichoke puffs, and pesto chicken sandwiches. For dessert, Grace had made red velvet cupcakes. She'd added her own little twist to them, putting a cheesecake ball in the center.

"Grace, these are heaven," Paige all but moaned as she took another bite of the cupcake. "You're a genius, you know that? An absolute genius in the kitchen."

"Aw, Paige, you say the nicest things to me."

"Between you and Lula Mae," Abby said, grabbing a second cupcake, "I'm going to go back to D.C. twenty pounds heavier."

"Good," Denise said, giving an approving nod. "You are far too skinny, sweetie. That company is working you to the bone."

Abby was short, coming in at five-feet-two, and she'd had some decent curves on that frame of hers. But said curves had diminished slightly since the last time Grace had seen her over the Christmas holidays.

"I'm fine," she said, sweeping back a piece of auburn hair that had fallen from her elegant twist. "Don't worry about me."

"That's not going to happen." Paige shook her head. "I wish you were closer. This whole being thousands of miles apart thing isn't working for me."

"Yeah, well, I don't see that many PR crises happening here in Mirabelle."

"With the way this town likes to gossip you never know," Grace said.

"As long as Bethelda is writing her trash, there will be Public Relation crises," Mel said.

"Oh, that could be your job," Harper said. "You just deal with the messes that Bethelda makes. Should keep you plenty busy."

"Without a doubt," Tara added, taking a seat next to Grace.

"Horrible, gossiping hag." Pinky leaned forward and tossed her cupcake wrapper onto an empty plate.

"Truer words could not be spoken," Paige said, rubbing her belly.

"Have any of you been in the limelight lately?" Abby asked.

"A couple of weeks ago she targeted Grace," Lula Mae answered.

"Not that my name hasn't been in her blog over the last couple of years," Grace said.

"She writes about you a lot?"

"Oh, that's an understatement."

"Is it just the same stuff over and over again? Wouldn't that get boring?" Abby asked, looking around at the women.

"You'd like to think so, but her last article had new material in it," Grace told her.

"And what was that?" Abby asked.

There'd been about thirty women at the shower, but the remaining stragglers circled around the room were all in on the soap opera that was Jax and Grace. Though, they hadn't been informed of recent developments. Lula Mae knew what was going on, not that Grace had flat out said that she'd slept with Jax, but because Lula Mae had witnessed the two of them together and had seen a good portion of the kissing. Grace had no doubt that Paige knew, too. There was no way Brendan hadn't told her. Nor had Grace been oblivious to the looks that Harper and Mel kept shooting her. Both of them had gotten back into town late last night, and Grace hadn't had an opportunity to tell them yet. But Grace was pretty sure they knew something was up.

"Something happened between Jax and me...well, I guess it would be better to say something *is* happening between Jax and me," Grace said, unable to hide her smile.

"I knew it!" Mel said, shooting forward in her seat.

"So Jax finally got a clue?" Panky asked.

"About. Damn. Time," Harper said.

"Wait," Abby said, and held up her hand. "I've kind of picked up on something going on, but I want to hear this from the beginning."

And with that, all of the women were off telling the story. But Grace just sat back and ate another cupcake, so content with life it was ridiculous.

* * *

Mel and Harper had to run to the Piggly Wiggly to get groceries, and since Grace needed some as well, they all piled into Mel's car and went together. Mel would just swing by and drop Grace and Harper off at their cars afterward.

"So," Mel said as soon as she shut her car door, "you better spill."

"And like now," Harper added, sticking her head in between the front seats.

"When did it happen?" Mel asked.

"Wednesday night."

"And you didn't call us?" Harper asked, feigning outrage.

"I've been busy." Grace smiled.

"I'll bet you have," Harper said.

"Get on with the story," Mel demanded.

"Well, it was pouring down rain and my car wouldn't start."

"Thank God for dead batteries," Harper said.

"Wait, isn't that the opposite of your motto?" Mel smirked as she glanced over her shoulder.

"Oh, you're hilarious," Harper said before she focused on Grace again. "So how was it?"

"Meh," Grace said, shrugging her shoulders.

"Liar," Mel said. "You haven't stopped grinning all day. There is no way he is merely *meh* in bed."

"Okay, fine. He's incredible. He knows exactly what he's doing, and he knows exactly how long to do it for."

"That's what I'm talking about," Harper said, hitting her hand on the back of Grace's seat. "But I want to hear all of it. So start from the beginning, and spare no details."

Grace went into the story, starting with Jax pulling up in the café parking lot and going all the way to this morning. They'd both been the perfect audience, oohing and awing at all the right parts.

"He seems to like pushing you up against walls," Mel said.

"Yeah, well, I like it, too."

"I'm sure you do," Harper said.

"So, he's your boyfriend now? Like officially?" Mel asked.

"Yeah," Grace said, still feeling slightly stunned by her new reality.

"You must be on cloud nine," Harper said.

"Well, I'm happy for you." Mel reached across the center console. She grabbed Grace's hand and squeezed it.

"Me, too," Harper said, leaning over and smacking a kiss on Grace's cheek.

Mel pulled into the parking lot of the grocery store a minute later. The three girls made their way into the store, giggling like they were in seventh grade again as they walked down the aisles.

"You should get this." Harper threw a can of whipped cream into the cart.

"Really, Harper?" Grace said, shaking her head but laughing while she did it.

"What?" she asked innocently. "It goes really good with your *pound* cake."

"You are so much dirtier when you aren't getting any," Mel said.

"First of all," Harper said, holding up a finger, "I am always dirty. Second of all"—she flipped up a second digit—"I'm never getting any."

Grace laughed as they rounded the aisle and came up short when she saw two men in front of her. Hoyt Reynolds and Judson Coker were on the other side of the aisle putting a case of beer and some ice in their cart. Harper hadn't been talking that loudly, but judging by the identical smirks on Hoyt's and Judson's faces, they'd heard everything.

Grace couldn't help but cringe. She despised Hoyt and Judson. The two guys might've been considered attractive, but only until they opened their mouths.

"We could fix that dry spell for you." Hoyt smirked at Harper.

"Not only no, but *hell* no," Harper said, glaring at the pair.

"Oh, come on," Judson said. "It'll be fun. We could show you exactly what you're missing out on."

"Yeah, but just the two of you," Hoyt said, pointing to Mel and Harper. "We don't mess with dirty bastards." He indicated Grace with his chin.

Yeah, the sting of that slap wasn't made any less severe by the fact that she'd been called that name more times than she could count. But she absolutely refused to show weakness.

"That must make using your right hand pretty difficult then," Grace said.

"Oh, aren't you clever." Hoyt sneered.

"She likes to think so," someone said as he wrapped an arm around her waist. She was pulled back into a large, hard body. Grace's skin immediately started to crawl. She knew exactly who had his arms around her.

Chad Sharp.

Chad, Judson, and Hoyt had all been on the varsity football team their junior and senior years. They were popular and attractive, so it wasn't all that shocking that they dated their way through a good number of the girls at the school. What had been shocking was when Chad had started talking to Grace.

Grace had mixed emotions about Chad because of all the rumors she'd heard, but he was nice to her. Hoyt and Judson had always made fun of Grace, but when Chad came along he put a stop to it. He defended her, stood up for her, and won her over in the end with all his charm. They'd been dating for a couple of weeks before every single ounce of that charm disappeared. She still cringed when she thought about that last night with him. It could've ended way worse than it had.

After that, the shit had hit the fan, and the two ringleaders behind it all had been Hoyt and Judson. They told everyone that Grace was just as much of a whore as her mother, and that if she kept up at the pace she was going, she'd be popping out a bastard of her own one day. Grace was beyond grateful that Brendan had graduated from school, because by some miracle he'd never found out about it.

"Let go of me," Grace said, pulling at Chad's arms, but his embrace only tightened and he put his mouth to her ear.

"I hear you're screwing the deputy these days," he whispered, his hot breath in her ear making her want to gag.

"Get off her," Harper said.

"I bet your new fuck buddy doesn't know how to make you scream when you come. I can show you exactly what you're missing out on," Chad said, still talking low enough for only Grace to hear. "He's going to get tired of you, Grace. He's going to get tired of you and move on."

Grace jabbed her elbow back hard, but somehow Chad dodged it, laughing as his arms loosened and he let her go.

"I'll see you around, Grace." He smiled, looking her up and down with a lascivious gleam in his eyes. "Have a good evening, ladies," he said to Mel and Harper before he turned around and walked away, Judson and Hoyt following behind him with the cart.

"I hate those assholes," Harper said, glaring at their retreating backs. "There isn't anything even remotely redeeming about any of them."

"Grace?" Mel said softly. "Are you okay?"

Was she okay? She was millions of miles away from okay. If okay was the sun, Grace was somewhere around Jupiter. She could still feel Chad's hot breath on her ear, could smell his nauseating cologne on her clothes. She wanted to go home and shower. She wanted to find Jax and wrap herself in his arms.

"Not exactly," she said, shaking her head. "But I'll be fine. I just need to get out of here." She grabbed the cart and headed in the opposite direction from where the assholes had disappeared.

"Grace, what did he say to you?" Harper asked.

"Disgusting perverted Chad-like things. It's fine. I'll be fine," Grace repeated.

Maybe if she said it enough times it would be true. She was going to get over this, just like she'd gotten over everything before.

* * *

Jax was at Grace's apartment a little after seven on Sunday night. She made the most mouth-watering stuffed tilapia he'd ever eaten. She was quieter than usual, though. When he asked her about it, she said she was tired. It wasn't all that surprising, as he'd kept her pretty busy, but he just couldn't get enough of her.

After dinner, they sat down on the couch together. Jax had spent many a night watching something or other with

Grace, but he'd never spent it with her curled up into his side, her head resting on his chest and her hand on his knee. He tried to be good. Tried to keep himself from laying her out on the couch and covering her body with his. So she had only herself to blame when halfway through the movie her hand slid up the inside of his thigh.

"I thought you said you were tired?" he asked, looking down at her.

"I think I've rested long enough."

And that was all the invitation he needed to pull her off the couch and to the bedroom, where he kept her thoroughly occupied.

On Monday morning Jax woke up before the alarm, and he had absolutely no complaints about it. Grace was pressing open mouth kisses down his abdomen. It was the best damn wakeup call he'd ever gotten.

They spent a good half hour rolling around in bed before they were ready to face the day. Jax had brought his uniform over so that he could get ready at her place and go directly to work from there. They took separate showers, which was a necessity; otherwise they would've been late. Jax tended to get distracted when Grace was naked, wet, and soapy. Really he just got distracted when she was around him, period, but the naked part was his real weakness, the wet and soapy just added fuel to the inferno.

"I'm going to be late tonight," Grace said as they sipped coffee in the kitchen. "I have a bunch of orders that I have to fill for tomorrow."

"All right, I was actually thinking we could go over to my place tonight."

"Yeah?" she asked, raising her eyebrows as she lowered her cup.

"Yeah," he said. "And I'll take care of dinner. Give you a night off."

"Hmm," she hummed, running her hand up the front of his forest-green shirt. "Just a night off in the kitchen, right?"

"Only in the kitchen," he agreed.

They were heading out the door ten minutes to seven and Grace locked up before they went downstairs. Jax was paying attention to the way that Grace's shorts molded to her butt that he loved oh-so-very much, so when she stopped suddenly he almost ran into her.

"What the hell," she whispered.

Jax looked up and over her shoulder in the direction she was looking. Her little yellow Bug was covered in red flyers. Every single inch of it.

Jax stepped around Grace and went to the car. He pulled off one of the flyers and read.

THE GRIM TRUTH

SOILED DOVE DIRTIES OTHERS

Little CoQuette hasn't had the best examples in life. Her parents seriously lacked on the role model front. Before her tragic demise, CoQuette's mother Jeze Belle was known to get around town. Like her mother, CoQuette is spreading much more than her dirty wings. And now she's corrupting a man of the law with her scandalous tricks.

For the past few nights, Deputy Ginger's pickup truck has been parked outside of CoQuette's apartment. When it comes to sex men are weak by nature. They can't really help it as they're controlled by the head between their legs and not by the one on top of their shoulders. But Deputy Ginger has always seemed to be so levelheaded and mild mannered. I suspect this will not be the case for much longer as he's been lured into the bed of one of our town's most promiscuous residents.

Deputy Ginger was "raised" by a drunken father who spent more time behind bars than at the dinner table. His mother is a piece of work too, still living in the same bottle as her husband and thriving on being his punching bag. Deputy Ginger has worked so hard to change the circumstances that he was born into. He's an inspiration really, and it's a shame that CoQuette has contaminated such an upstanding man. Not that illegitimacy is contagious and there is a vaccine for it, but CoQuette very well could bastardize Deputy Ginger, bringing him down lower than he ever was before.

Jax couldn't believe it. Couldn't believe that not only would someone write this crap but would cover Grace's car with this shit. He looked over at Grace who was standing right next to him. She reached forward and started ripping off the flyers, filling her arms with the red pieces of paper. Jax started to grab pieces of paper, too. They'd been taped on with masking tape and made a very audible ripping noise as they were being removed.

Grace gasped and Jax looked over. *Bastard* was written in big black letters across the front windshield. The papers dropped from her hands.

"Shit," Jax said as the papers were picked up with the breeze and scattered out across the parking lot. "Go get something to clean the glass. I'll take care of this."

She just stood there and stared at that word.

"Grace," Jax said softly.

But she didn't move. Jax walked over to the Dumpster and emptied his arms of the flyers before he walked back to her.

"Grace," he said again, reaching out to her.

She shook her head, like she was trying to shake it all off. "I'm okay," she said. "I'll be okay." She bent down and started picking up the scattered flyers.

Jax bent down, too, and stilled her hands. She looked at him and it almost knocked the wind out of him. There was so much pain and hurt in her eyes.

"I'm so sorry, Grace," he said, leaning in and kissing her temple. "I'm going to find out who did this," he promised.

And he was going to beat the shit out of the asshole when he did.

* * *

It took them a good thirty minutes to get the flyers in the trash, and the car chalk off the windshield. The black letters smeared, leaving thick streaks across the glass, and it took a good deal of Windex and scrubbing to get it all off.

Jax was fuming. If there was anything to send him into a barely controlled rage, it was Grace being upset. She'd looked so damn lost, so damn lonely. It tore Jax up, made his chest hurt painfully, and he wanted to take that hurt out on somebody. He would've done just about anything to prevent her from experiencing that whole episode.

Jax wanted nothing more than to go down to the Mirabelle Information Center and rip into that horrible hag. But Jax didn't think this was Bethelda's handiwork. Bethelda targeted a wide variety of people, but she only did it from the safety of her blog. Whoever did this to Grace's car specifically didn't like Grace.

So instead Jax headed to work. He went down to the

station to file a report on Grace's car. After that, Jax headed to Lock and Load Security.

Six of the places that had been broken into had an alarm system from the same company, which wasn't saying much considering the fact that there was only one place in Mirabelle that provided the service. Lock and Load Security had been around for twenty years, and not only did they install security systems and locks, but they sold plenty of guns and ammunition for those who wanted to have that extra sense of security.

Jax had talked to the owner Ray Pittman last week, and he hadn't found anything suspicious. Ray had been incredibly helpful and had given the sheriff's office all the information they'd asked for. But something wasn't sitting right, especially with the three houses that had been broken into on the beach. Ray was a good guy, and Jax didn't suspect that he was behind anything. But whoever had done this was familiar with the system, and Ray had employees.

When Jax walked into the small shop his uneasy feeling intensified. Judson Coker was standing behind the counter. Jax had never liked the asshole. Judson and his pal Hoyt Reynolds had always picked on Grace, and they would forever be on Jax's shit list.

"Can I help you?" Judson asked, giving Jax a disdainful look.

"I'm here to see your boss," Jax said.

"Ray is in his office." Judson indicated a hallway to the left.

"Thanks." Jax walked down the hall.

"Deputy Anderson," Ray said when Jax walked into the office. Ray was in his late forties with bushy gray hair on his head and his face. He'd inherited the store ten years ago from his father-in-law. "How's it going?" he asked as he stood from behind his desk and held out his hand.

"Good." Jax shook the man's hand.

"Have a seat," Ray said, letting go and motioning to one of the chairs in front of his desk. "What can I help you with today?"

"I need a list of all your employees. Everyone who has access to the system."

Ray's eyes widened. "You think someone here is involved?"

"At this point I have no idea. Your alarm system hasn't been in all the places that have been broken into. But it's been in the majority of them. I'm just trying to cover all my bases."

"Understood. Let me get you that list." Ray tapped a few keys on his computer. He hit another couple of buttons before he stood up. "The printer's out there," he said, indicating the front of the shop.

Jax stood up and followed Ray down the hallway. Ray went behind the counter to a giant printer that started making a humming noise. Judson was still behind the counter, talking on the phone as he typed something into the computer.

"Huh," Ray said, turning around. "I can't say that we normally use this type of paper, but here you go." He handed Jax the list, which was printed on a bright red piece of paper.

Jax's hand shook as he held it. It was the exact same paper that all those damn flyers had been printed on.

"Son-of-a-bitch," Jax said, looking up at Judson who was now off the phone. Judson just stared back, no visible reaction.

Ray looked back and forth between the two men.

"It was you," Jax said, barely keeping his anger in check. It was taking everything in him not to leap across the counter and pummel the asshole.

"I have no idea what you're talking about, *deputy*," Judson said with no small amount of contempt in his words or his gaze.

"What's going on?" Ray asked.

Jax looked over at Ray, needing to take his eyes off Judson. "This morning, someone printed out an article of Bethelda's about Grace and me. They made multiple copies on red pieces of paper just like this and covered her car in them. Is there a way to check the printing history?" Jax asked, looking at the computer.

"Yes," Ray said. He looked at Judson who moved out of the way, an expression on his face that said *you aren't going to find shit*.

Ray clicked a few buttons and shook his head. "The printing history has been cleared."

"What a coincidence," Jax said.

"Hold on, let me try something else."

When Ray turned around something flickered across Judson's face, but it was gone almost as soon as it had appeared.

Ray hit a few buttons on the printer and it kicked to life again. Some more red pieces of paper shot out. He grabbed them and sorted through them. His jaw bunched together when he got to the second page. He looked up at Judson and held up the piece of paper. It was the article all right.

"You still want to deny it?" Jax asked.

"It wasn't me," Judson said, shrugging his shoulders. "I'm not the only one who has access to this printer. There are a number of people that work here. It could've been any of those guys. And considering the way that Grace got around in high school, I'm sure that they would want to *spread* that message."

Must. Remember. To. Breathe.

Must. Not. Go. Crazy.

Must. Stay. Calm.

Breathe.

Brrreeeeaaaathe.

"Or maybe you should go straight to the source and get

Bethelda to stop. It sounds like that's where your real problem lies," Judson said.

"Oh, I'd say that someone using company resources, my
resources as it is, is most definitely part of a problem," Ray
said, taking a step forward and frowning at Judson. "Deputy
Anderson, I promise you that I'm going to look into this situation thoroughly."

"Thank you," Jax said.

"You're going to have to do a lot of looking. I think you'd
be surprised about what the King women have done, or more
specifically *who* they've done."

"That's enough of that," Ray said, looking at Judson, his
face flushing red.

"Do you enjoy pushing your luck?" Jax asked. "Because
sooner or later it's going to catch up to you." And Jax hoped
he was there when it did.

"Is that a threat?"

"No," Jax said, shaking his head, "it's a promise."

And with that, he turned around and walked out the door.

* * *

The whole article and car situation put Grace into a deep
funk. She tried to distract herself with baking and was somewhat successful with it, but more often than not it would all
come rushing back to her, like a slap in the face. Her eyes
would start to sting and she'd have to pull herself back from
the verge of tears.

Grace needed a bigger distraction than baking. She
needed Jax. He'd worked wonders last night. He had a way
of making her forget everything when his hands were on her.
Of making all of her troubles disappear when he was just in
the same room. She hadn't told him about what happened at
the grocery store, and there were several reasons why.

One, she hadn't run to him for every single problem before they started sleeping together, and she wasn't going to start now. Two, he would overreact. Three, he would tell Brendan and Shep and they would all overreact together. Jax might be capable of not doing stupid things, but Brendan didn't share that quality.

So Grace had sucked it up and gotten over it. Sort of.

Okay, really she hadn't gotten over the whole thing with Chad, Judson, and Hoyt at all. It was just that it had been pushed to the back of her mind while she dwelled on other things.

Grace really wished she could just not care about what other people thought about her. She'd been dealing with crap like that article her entire life. And it was more than just Bethelda behind it. Growing up, there'd been a couple of mothers who refused to let their daughters be friends with Grace. They didn't like Claire. They thought all the stories were true, that Claire was a home wrecker that would try to steal their husbands. But that wasn't, and had never been, Claire's MO. Grace had never seen her mother date anyone, and Brendan said he hadn't, either.

Both Grace and her mother were painted in these horrible, scandalous images that weren't even true. That was probably one of the most frustrating things for Grace. Certain people continued on with this idea that she was a whore. They said she was jumping in and out of all these guys' beds, but she wasn't. Grace had been with exactly two guys before Jax.

After everything with Chad, good guys had been few and far between. All the guys at Mirabelle High School had believed the rumors that Grace was easy, and they only asked her out because they thought she would put out. After a couple of dates, Grace had given up on guys from school.

The first serious boyfriend Grace had was when she was

seventeen. Eric Tanner was a student at Florida State University and they'd met at the beach. They'd been together for about a year when she gave him her virginity, and they stayed together for a year after that before she ended things.

When she was twenty-one, she dated Mark Abernathy. He was another good guy who worked for his father's fishing company in Mirabelle. He was five years older than Grace, so he'd missed out on all the high school rumors. They were together for about eight months when she again ended the relationship.

What it all came down to was that Grace had been in love with Jax. She'd known it hadn't been fair to continue dating either Eric or Mark when her heart belonged to someone else.

It hurt more than anything that within less than a week of Grace's *finally* being with Jax, more than one person was out to try to ruin things. Was out there trying to take away from her something she'd been dreaming of for years. It infuriated her.

And she wasn't the only one it pissed off. Brendan had come by the café that morning, his temper barely in check. It had taken the combined efforts of both Lula Mae and Grace to calm him down and get him to go to work. Oliver stopped by for a late breakfast claiming that he wanted to see Lula Mae, though he spent a good twenty minutes in the kitchen with Grace and only five with his wife.

It wasn't long before Shep was in the kitchen, drinking a cup of coffee and eating a muffin. Shep had claimed he'd only come for the food, but when he'd said good-bye, he hugged Grace hard and told her not to listen to worthless opinions from worthless people.

Grace was making bread when Harper came into the kitchen around two.

"So you saw the article?" Harper asked.

"It goes way beyond the article," Grace said.

"Oh, dear, what happened?"

Grace told Harper about what she and Jax had discovered that morning. When Grace finished, Harper's mouth was hanging open.

"You've got to be kidding me?" Harper asked, horrified.

"Nope."

"I hate that stupid cow," Harper said.

"Me, too," a deep voice said from the door that led to the front of the café.

Grace looked up to find Jax.

"Hey, Princess," he said as he rounded the island in the center of the kitchen and came up behind her. He put his hands on her hips as he leaned down and pressed his lips to hers in a quick open-mouthed kiss before he pulled back. "Hey, Harper."

"Hey, Jax. You here to check up on your girl?" She gave him a smile.

"That and tell Grace something I found out."

"What?" she asked, going over to the sink to wash the flour from her hands.

"I went over to Lock and Load first thing this morning. Ray Pittman had to print something off for me, and it printed on the same red paper as the flyers. Whoever did it works there and they'd cleared off the printing history on the computer. But Ray hit some button on the printer and it reprinted the article."

"Are you serious?" Grace asked as she grabbed a towel to dry her hands.

"Yup. And you know who works there, and who just happened to be behind the counter when I went in?"

"Who?" Grace and Harper asked at the exact same time.

"Judson Coker."

Grace's hands froze and before she could say anything, Harper was talking.

"Oh, my gosh, I bet this has to do with them harassing us at the Piggly Wiggly on Sunday."

"What?" Jax asked.

"It wasn't anything." Grace looked at him.

"Harper just said someone harassed you?" Jax asked, his mouth going thin and firm.

The kitchen was deafeningly silent for a moment.

"Is that Lula Mae calling my name?" Harper said, taking a step back before she turned and quickly retreated out of the kitchen.

"Care to explain?" Jax asked.

"Jax, really it wasn't that big of a deal."

"Apparently it was, Grace. I'm pretty sure Judson is connected to all of this, and what did Harper mean by *them*?"

Grace sighed heavily before she relented to his hard stare. "Hoyt and Chad were there."

"Why didn't you tell me?"

"Because I didn't want you to get upset. I knew if I told you, you were going to tell Brendan and Shep and—"

"What happened?" Jax asked, interrupting her. He was clearly furious, talking through clenched teeth.

Grace told him what had happened, his eyebrows drawing closer and closer together the further she got into the story. When she got to the part where Chad touched her, Jax looked like he was going to explode. When she told him what Chad had said to her, Jax had to close his eyes and take a deep breath.

"I'm going to kill him," Jax said. When he opened his eyes he focused on her, and Grace saw something beyond anger. Jax was hurt. "You lied to me."

"No, I didn't. I just didn't tell you," she said.

"No." He shook his head. "I knew something was going on last night, and I asked you if you were okay. You told me you were tired. You were upset. You were upset about this and you didn't tell me. You *lied* to me."

"Jax," Grace said, reaching out for him as she took a step closer.

But it was then that Alice Myers's voice came through the speaker on Jax's uniform and echoed through the kitchen.

"Seventeen, what's your location?"

Jax pressed the button as he took a step toward the door and turned his mouth into the speaker. "Seventeen, on Sandy Beach Drive."

"Accident on Pine and Ninth. Possible injury. Ambulance on the way."

"Ten-four. On the way," he said as he let go of the button. "I have to go," he said as he turned around and walked out of the kitchen.

Chapter Ten

Making Up: Apparently It Isn't So Hard to Do

Grace pulled into Jax's driveway just after seven thirty. She hadn't talked to him since he'd left her in the kitchen of the café, and she had no idea what to expect. He was angry and hurt. He'd been angry with her in the past, which was nothing new or different, but never hurt. She'd had her reasons for not telling him the truth, but she really needed to explain it to him. All of it. She just wasn't sure how receptive he was going to be.

She was more that slightly nervous as she walked up to his house. She hesitated before she knocked, her stomach flipping uncontrollably. Jax opened the door a minute later wearing a pair of jeans, a white T-shirt, and a scowl.

"Hey," Grace said cautiously.

He didn't say anything, just stepped to the side to give her enough room to walk in. He closed the door behind her, and as she turned to face him she found herself pushed up against the wall and Jax's mouth came down hard on hers.

She dropped her purse to the floor and her arms came up and around his neck as he kissed her aggressively. Apparently it didn't matter how mad he was at her, he still wanted to kiss her, and damn could he kiss. After a minute, he pulled back and looked at her, running his thumb across her jaw.

"Why did you lie to me?" he asked.

"I'm sorry, Jax," she said, looking up at him. "I should've told you what happened, it was just that..." She trailed off. She'd been thinking about how to explain things since he'd walked away from her hours ago, and she still wasn't sure how to word it without making him even angrier.

"It was just that what?"

She took a deep breath and just plunged in with both feet. "I've wanted you for as long as I can remember. Waited to be with you. And now we're finally together and it hasn't even been a week and there's already all of these strikes against us. I know it isn't supposed to be easy, relationships aren't easy, but yesterday those jerks were saying things. Saying that you were going to get tired of me and I just—"

She was cut off by Jax's mouth pressing against hers slowly, tenderly. She moaned deep in her chest and let his tongue work its magic against hers. When he pulled back again, she was surprised to find that he had a slight twinkle in his eye and his mouth was quirked to the side.

"First of all, I'm not going to get tired of you. And second, I don't think I've ever heard anyone talk so fast in my life. Calm down for a second, Gracie," he said, kissing her again.

"That's not going to help me catch my breath," she said when he pulled back a minute later.

"I didn't think so. Talk to me." He looked deep into her eyes.

"Jax, when I was growing up you and Brendan and Shep always tried to be my defenders. Always tried to keep me from getting hurt. But I knew that you couldn't protect me from everything, so I tried like hell to grow a tough skin, tried to learn to deal with the small things, and later with the bigger things."

"Why?"

"Why?" she repeated, laughing incredulously. "Because every time something happened to me, Brendan wound up in detention or suspended, and you and Shep often weren't that far behind him. So if I just learned to deal with things maybe all of you wouldn't be getting into trouble all the time. *And* I didn't want to be this helpless girl who couldn't take care of herself, because one day you guys wouldn't be around and it was only going to be me."

"I don't think you're helpless, Grace," he said shaking his head. "And that day isn't going to happen, the day that none of us are going to be around. I'm always going to try to protect you. And so are Brendan and Shep; it's just how it is."

He covered her mouth with his again and reached down to pick her up. Her legs wrapped around his waist, and he carried her into the kitchen where he sat her down on the counter.

"What were the bigger things you had to learn to deal with?" he asked.

She looked at him for a second, her heart picking up speed and pounding in her chest. If he was upset about the Piggly Wiggly incident, she wasn't sure how he was going to react to what had happened eight years ago.

"Grace?" he pressed.

"Some of this stuff with Chad, Judson, and Hoyt has been going on for a while."

"How long?"

"If I tell you, you can't tell Brendan or Shep."

"I already don't like where this is going, but I won't tell Brendan or Shep." He promised.

"And you can't freak out and do something stupid," she added.

"I'm not Brendan; I think before I act."

"Promise me," she said.

"I promise. Geez, Grace, you're making me really nervous."

"So Chad and I dated in high school."

"Yeah, I know." He frowned.

"He was this big senior and I was this little sophomore, and for some reason he wanted to date me. I didn't get it. And he was just so damn charming. A couple of weeks in we'd been on a few dates, where we did nothing more than kissing."

Jax's frown deepened.

"Well, one night he drove his mother's Cadillac out to Alligator Lane to park. He brought beer. I'd never had alcohol before and the beer hit me pretty fast, and we moved to the backseat. He…" Grace hesitated when she saw the fire in Jax's eyes. "He stuck his hand under my shirt and it was all moving too fast for me, so I asked him to stop, but he just grabbed me harder. I started to struggle, and I kneed him in the crotch."

Jax was frozen as he listened to her, his eyes wide and blazing.

"I got out of the car and he left me there," Grace continued. "I called Preston to come pick me up. And it took a lot of begging to get Preston to promise not to do anything to Chad. Because I knew that if you, Brendan, or Shep found out, chances were that one of you would've done something incredibly stupid."

Jax just stared at her stunned, not saying anything.

"Please don't be upset," she said, feeling desperate.

"Upset?" he asked, finally finding his tongue. "I'm not upset. I'm *way* beyond upset. I now know what the drive for *murder* feels like."

"Jax, you can't do anything. It was eight years ago."

"I don't care when it happened. He could've raped you," he snapped out harshly.

She closed her eyes and flinched back.

"Grace," he said, his voice calmer.

She opened her eyes and he reached up to cradle her face.

"I'm sorry," he said, shaking his head. "I...I'm not taking this information very well at all."

"No kidding."

"How do Judson and Hoyt factor into this?" he asked.

"They spread some pretty vicious rumors about me in high school. That was really it."

"What rumors?"

"Jax, it was a long time ago. It doesn't matter anymore," she said.

"Can you please stop acting like something that hurt you doesn't matter and tell me what happened?" he asked, more than a little exasperated.

"It was the same stuff that was in that article today," she said, maybe a bit too loudly, but Jax was frustrating the hell out of her. "That I'm a whore just like my mother. That I'll crawl into bed with any guy at any time. That I'm not good enough." Her voice broke. "That I wasn't good enough from the beginning, because otherwise my father would've wanted me."

She couldn't stop the tears that sprung to her eyes or the tightness in her throat. She didn't want to cry about this. Didn't want to show Jax just how much this stuff affected her. But it was no use because once that first tear fell more followed.

"Grace," Jax said, sounding pained.

"It's okay," she said barely above a whisper.

"No, it isn't." He shook his head as he reached up and cupped her face. He swiped his thumbs underneath her eyes to wipe away the tears, but as soon as they were gone more followed. "It isn't okay, Gracie. You are good enough, and it has absolutely nothing to do with your father, and everything to do with you." He pulled her into his arms and she rested her face in the crook of his neck. "Why didn't you ever say anything? Why didn't you tell us? Why didn't you tell *me*?" he asked as he held her, running his hands up and down her back trying to soothe her.

"What were you going to do?" Her lips brushed across his skin as she talked. "What was anyone going to do? They were seventeen. If any of you had laid a hand on any of them, it would've been bad. I didn't want you guys to get in trouble."

Jax just sighed. "They aren't seventeen now."

A huff of laughter escaped Grace as she pulled back to look at him. "What are you going to do to them?" she asked, raising her eyebrows.

"I don't know." He frowned. "But I can follow you around to make sure they don't do anything to you."

"My personal bodyguard?"

"Yup," he said, bringing his mouth to hers. He kissed her for a minute before he pulled back and rested his forehead against hers. "Will you just promise me that you won't keep anything like this from me again? And no more lies."

"No more lies," she said softly. "I'm sorry, Jax."

"I am, too." He kissed her forehead before he disentangled himself from her arms and legs. "Want a drink?"

"Please," she said desperately.

Jax went over to the fridge and opened the door. He turned a second later holding up a bottle of Pinot Grigio.

"Wine?"

"Don't sound so shocked," he said. "I like things other than beer."

"And Jack Daniel's?"

"Yes." He pulled out a corkscrew.

"Really? How long has that bottle of wine been sitting in your fridge?" She suspected it had been in there for months. Probably a Christmas gift from someone he worked with.

"Since I went to the store on my day off," he said, holding the bottle to the side as he started to twist the corkscrew. "I got this fancy cheese, too, and that ice cream you always get. I figured I should have some stuff here that you like."

"You bought me double fudge mint ice cream?"

"And I also got a jar of maraschino cherries and a big bag of M&M's," he said as he poured a generous amount of wine into a glass.

Grace just stared at him. She couldn't really make her throat move at the moment, because it was so tight.

Jax looked up as he reached for the other glass and froze when he saw what she was sure was a stunned expression. "What?" he asked as he grabbed the glass and started filling it.

"I'm just . . . I'm a little surprised."

"That I know what kind of ice cream you like?"

"No," she said, shaking her head. "That you know me. I didn't know you paid that much attention to me."

"Really?" Jax said, shaking his head as he walked over to her, "because when you're around you're all I can pay attention to. God, Grace, you're on my mind even when you aren't around."

He held out one of the glasses and she grabbed it, downing half of it in one fell swoop.

"You aren't getting a refill until you eat," he said, eyeing her half-empty glass.

"I'm not that hungry."

"Tough, you're eating."

"When did we switch roles? I thought I was the one always trying to feed you."

"You are. And it works in my favor as you are a fantastic cook and my skills are very limited," he said, turning and opening a cabinet.

"Your skills in the kitchen might be limited," Grace said, admiring his ass as he bent over and pulled out a skillet. "But your skills in the bedroom are above and beyond."

Jax turned and grinned at her. "You're pretty talented, too."

"So what are you making me?"

"Scrambled eggs," he said, holding up the skillet.

"All that you know how to make?"

"All that I have the supplies to make. It's either that or pasta, but I'm all out of mac and cheese," he said, putting the skillet on the stove before he went to the refrigerator and started pulling things out.

"So it's slim pickings here at casa Anderson?"

"I have what I need," he said as he laid out the ingredients.

"Yes, but do you have anything that you want?"

"I do now," he said, looking up at her and staring at her with so much intensity that her head suddenly felt light. It probably had a little to do with the wine, but it was mostly Jaxson Anderson.

"I'm going to need more of this wine if you keep saying things like that." She took another healthy sip.

"Food first," he said, cracking open a carton of eggs.

"Well, then hurry it up."

Twenty minutes later they sat down at his table with two plates that were loaded with buttered toast and scrambled eggs, smothered in cheese, ham, salsa, and sour cream. Grace took one bite and as the warm, melty goodness hit her tongue she realized just how hungry she was.

"Okay," she said around a mouthful of toast, "you know your way around a scrambled egg."

"When's it's one of four dishes that you know how to make, you learn to perfect it."

"Well it's delicious. What are the other three dishes you can make?"

"All in good time, Princess, all in good time," he said as he took a bite of eggs.

When they finished dinner, they cleared the dishes and cleaned the kitchen. Jax brought the bottle of wine out to the living room and they snuggled up on the couch. Grace threw her legs across his lap and he wrapped his arm around her shoulders. She rested her head against his chest as he flipped through the channels on the TV.

"Oh, can we watch this?" she said as he landed on a marathon of her favorite TV show.

"Anything you want." He kissed her head.

For the next thirty minutes they watched as two of the characters stole a cheesecake from a neighbor and proceeded to eat it all. When the next episode started, Jax poured a little bit more wine into each of their glasses. Grace was feeling a whole lot better about life than she had earlier, and it had everything to do with the man whose arms she was in.

* * *

Something was biting into Grace's ribs, not hard or anything. Just incredibly annoying.

She opened her eyes to darkness. She was lying in bed. In Jax's bed. She must've fallen asleep on the couch. Or more like passed out because she didn't remember being carried to Jax's bedroom, or being put into his bed. Apparently this was the effect three glasses of wine had on her.

The man might have skimped on kitchen utensils, but he'd splurged on his bed. It was way more comfortable than hers, some sort of foam material that molded to her body. And the pillows were heaven. But the best part of the whole bed was the man pressed up against her. He had one arm draped over her hip, his hand palming her thigh. A thigh that was now bare.

Damn, she'd missed the part where he'd taken off her shorts, too.

Every time he exhaled, his breath washed over her bare shoulder. He hadn't taken off her tank top, or her bra. And the under wire was the annoying poke that was digging into her ribs.

The bra in question was strapless and normally it was

comfortable enough, but not after sixteen hours. She needed to get it off, like now. The problem was, Jax was wrapped around her and she just couldn't bend that way.

She shifted forward a little bit, and bent her arm awkwardly to try to unhook the back. She fumbled with it for a minute before she gave up.

On to plan B.

She grabbed the side of her bra and slowly started to spin it.

"What are you doing?"

Dear God, that man's gravelly, half-asleep voice was not to be messed with.

"My bra is digging into my skin. I was trying to take it off and not wake you up in the process."

"Now where's the fun in that?" he asked as he moved his hand from her hip and slipped it under her shirt. "I'd be more than happy to help with such endeavors."

His hard body shifted down hers as he worked her tank top up and over her head. He kissed her shoulder while his fingers traced up her spine. He kept moving down until his mouth was in line with the back of her bra. He used his teeth to hold the material in place while he slowly unhooked the clasps with his fingers. When her bra was undone, he moved his hand to the front of her chest to pull it free. His fingers glided over her breasts and she couldn't help it when she arched into him. He groaned deep in his throat as his mouth moved from the center of her back.

"Where was it digging into you," he asked as he planted kisses across her skin.

"Up and to the right."

"Here?" he asked before he opened his mouth on the side of her breast.

"Yes," she moaned as he flicked his tongue across her skin.

"I think it might have dug into your skin here, too." His mouth started moving under her breasts.

A second later, Grace found herself on her back, Jax between her thighs.

"So just for future reference," he said as he soothed her skin with his tongue, "I'm allowed to take your bra off when you pass out drunk on my couch?"

"I wasn't drunk," she said as her hands found their way into his hair.

"Well, you were most definitely asleep, which was highly disappointing because I was so looking forward to make-up sex. We really do need to celebrate surviving our first fight."

"Our first fight?" she asked, tugging on his hair so that he would have to look up at her.

"Our first fight as a couple," he amended as his mouth moved across the space to her other breast.

"I was going to say, that was probably our four hundred and fifty ninth fight."

"Hmm," he hummed into her chest as his hands found their way to her hips and he started to pull down her panties. "Probably," he agreed, sitting up on his knees.

"And Jax, you have permission to take my bra off whenever you want," she said as he pulled her legs together and skimmed her red lace panties the rest of the way down her legs.

"Really? Whenever I want?" He came back down between her thighs again.

"Well, I mean not in public. Or around people."

"I knew it was too good to be true. You put all of these stipulations on it. It's a shame."

"No," Grace said as she reached around and palmed his butt. "What's a shame is that you still have these on. Do you normally sleep in clothes?" she asked as she started to pull his boxer briefs down.

"No." He shifted to the side so that he could kick the boxers down his legs. "I normally sleep naked."

"You? Sleep naked?" Grace asked, trying to sound shocked as he resettled in between her thighs. "Who would have thought reserved Deputy Anderson would sleep in the buff? What were you trying to do? Shield me from your scandalous ways?"

"No." He smiled down at her. "You see I've had this problem the last few days of being constantly turned on. It's what happens when you have the best sex of your life. So you can imagine my predicament when said woman, who has provided said sex, is passed out in my bed and I can't do anything to take care of the constant need I have for her. I had to provide myself with some sort of barrier, or I'd lose my damn mind."

"Best sex of your life, huh?" she asked, raising her eyebrows.

"Absolutely. Also, I thought I was going to short-circuit when I pulled your shorts off to find red lace whatever those were."

"Boy shorts?"

"Yes, boy shorts. I'm a *huge* fan of those," he said, kissing her neck.

"I think I have an idea of just how *huge* a fan you are." She bumped her hips up. "And for your sanity's sake, maybe you should stop talking and take care of this need of yours."

His grin widened as his mouth descended on hers, and he proceeded to take care of said need with gusto.

Chapter Eleven

A Changed Man

On Saturday morning Jax met up with all the guys at his house that was under construction. Tripp, Preston, and Baxter joined Brendan, Shep, Bennett, and Jax for a day of hard labor. The goal for the day was going to be finishing up the walls. The plan for the following week was working on the bathrooms. He'd ordered the tile and fixtures months ago, and it was scheduled for delivery on Thursday.

When he pulled up in front of the house, Tripp, Shep, and Brendan were already there. Jax got out and grabbed the bag of goodies Grace had baked the night before and made his way over to the guys, who were all nursing cups of coffee.

"Breakfast," Jax said, holding up the bag.

"You stop by the café this morning?" Brendan asked as he helped himself to a cranberry-orange scone.

"No, Grace made them last night."

"How does it feel to eat like a King?" Brendan asked.

"Probably not as good as it feels to be sleeping with one." Shep smirked.

"Hey, that's my sister," Brendan said. "I might've accepted the fact that she's with Jax, but I have absolutely no desire to hear about it. I've already seen it, and my eyes still haven't recovered."

"Oh, give me a break. You caught Grace and me in her apartment. Behind closed doors," Jax said.

"And you can't really talk," Shep said. "Remember that time Jax caught Paige dry-humping you in your truck?"

"Vividly." Brendan grinned.

"Wow, I've missed so much," Tripp said with raised eyebrows.

"It's a harrowing life we live here in Mirabelle," Shep said. "Glad you've joined us though." He clapped Tripp on the back before he grabbed the bag of scones and helped himself to two.

When the rest of the guys showed up, they all got to work. As the hours passed, Jax was amazed, and incredibly grateful, at the amount of work they were getting done. He'd been a little concerned about finishing everything that he needed to before the delivery, but not anymore at the rate they were going.

Just after one, Grace's Bug came rumbling up the packed dirt driveway. Jax had asked her to bring them lunch, and since she had this thing about feeding him, she'd jumped at the chance. Plus she said she wanted to see the work that he'd done on the house. She hadn't seen it since they'd gutted it out. Yeah, they'd made more than a couple of changes since then.

"Hey," he said, abandoning Tripp and Baxter at the saw and walking up to her.

"You got a whole crew here today." She put her hands on his hips and stretched up to kiss him.

"Yeah, we're getting a lot done. Want to see it before we eat?"

"Yes, please," she said eagerly.

"Well, then come on." He held his hand out for hers. She

grabbed it and they twined their fingers together as they walked up the driveway.

The house was on ten-foot pylons, so there was a wooden staircase that led up to the porch, which wrapped around the right side of the house and to the back. One of the first things Jax replaced had been the rotting steps and porch.

"This looks good and safe," Grace said as they made their way up to the house.

"What? You don't have that overwhelming feeling that you're going to fall to your death anymore?"

"Nope. What color are you going to paint the house?" she asked as they walked through the open front door.

"I haven't decided yet. I was actually going to ask for your help on that. Well, help on all of the paint actually."

"Really?" she asked, her eyebrows stretching up to her hairline.

"Don't look so shocked. I'd like a second opinion, and I value yours more than anybody else's."

"Yeah?" She beamed.

"Yeah," he said, leading her down the hallway.

The kitchen was directly to the left where the hallway ended. At the moment it was just an empty space with pipes sticking out of the walls where the sink and dishwasher were going to go. It opened up to the living room at the back of the house. Two bay windows framed the French glass doors that opened to the back deck. Whiskey River was a good fifty yards away, and the land that led up to it was scattered with mossy oak trees.

Their shoes shuffled across the dusty unfinished floor as they walked across the room.

"Wow," Grace said as she looked out the windows. "The view is amazing."

"I thought I heard your voice," Brendan said, coming out of the master bedroom that was to the right of the living room. It too was on the back of the house, so it had the same incredible view.

"I brought lunch," she said as Brendan went over to the toolbox and grabbed some more nails.

"Awesome," Bennett said, coming out of the room, too. "I'm starving."

"Help yourselves. It's all in the front seat of my car."

"We will. We're just going to finish up this room really quick. We only have a couple more panels to put up," Bennett said, grabbing a sweating bottle of water off the ground and downing half of it.

Jax continued his tour, showing Grace the two spare bedrooms and bathroom that made up the left side of the house. Shep and Preston were in one of the bedrooms, the nail gun firing as they put up a piece of the wall.

"Hey," Preston said when he saw her.

"Getting a good look at your man's new place?" Shep asked.

"Yeah, it's really coming along. What are you going to work on next?" she asked, looking at Jax.

"The bathrooms."

"Do they work at all?"

"No," Jax said, shaking his head.

"What do you do when you have to go to the bathroom? You guys don't hold it all day."

"Guys don't have the same plumbing issues as you do." Preston grinned.

"What, you guys just pick a spot and whip it out to pee?" Grace asked, wrinkling her nose.

"I really don't understand why this shocks and disgusts you. You grew up with us, Gracie, not a lot has changed," Shep said.

"I never saw you guys peeing in the bushes."

"Really?" Shep asked, surprised. "'Cause we did it all the time."

"Well, you must have waited until I wasn't around. Ugh, you boys are so gross." She shuddered.

"Come on," Preston said, putting down the nail gun. "Let's go eat. We can scratch our chests and belch while we do it."

"You're annoying." Grace rolled her eyes.

"But that's not a man trait," Shep said. "That's just Preston."

"Really?" Preston asked as they left the room. "I'm the annoying one?"

Jax picked back up on his tour, showing Grace where the dining room and den were going, and then he pulled her into the master bedroom. It had a walk-in closet, and when the bathroom was finished it would have a stand-up shower and a Jacuzzi tub.

"Jax, it all looks amazing," she said, beaming at him. "You've done a lot with this place."

"Yeah?" he said, feeling more than a little bit proud.

"Yeah." She stepped into him.

"I'm all hot and sweaty."

"I don't care." She pushed her body against his as she stretched up and wrapped her arms around his shoulders. "Besides I'm used to you being hot and sweaty, otherwise the sex would be very boring."

As her mouth closed in on his there was a loud thump from the closet, and a second later a very agitated Brendan emerged. "Bennett and I are still in here. How hard is it to check a room?"

Grace bit her lip, most likely holding back a laugh.

"Oh, geez. I'm never going to get used to this," Brendan said as he stormed out of the room.

"Sorry 'bout that." Bennett smiled over at them as he followed Brendan out.

Grace laughed and turned back to Jax. "Now, where were we?"

"Right about here," he said as he leaned down and kissed her.

Her hands started to roam all over his chest and he couldn't stop himself from groaning into her mouth.

"Do you enjoy torturing me?" he asked.

"You're really sexy when you're hot and sweaty. You think we could go have a quickie in the closet?" she said, motioning her head in the direction of the closet that Brendan and Bennett had been working on.

"As much fun as that would be, if Brendan happened upon us he'd really lose his mind. And there are too many other men wandering around. I don't really want any of them to see you naked."

"You wouldn't have to worry about Preston."

"I'm beginning to think I wouldn't have to worry about Baxter, either."

"So you picked up on that?" Grace asked.

"Yeah. Preston had mentioned something to me that night I talked to him at the bar, the night your car wouldn't start."

"Aw," she said, getting a dreamy look in her eyes. "That was a good night."

"It sure was. But he said that he'd had a date. And I've seen him and Baxter out a couple of times."

"You think the other guys know?"

"I don't know," he said, shaking his head. "We haven't talked about it."

"You think they'd care?" she asked, worrying her bottom lip.

"Not even a little," Jax said, reaching up and pulling her lip out of her teeth with his thumb. "I've worked with Baxter for years. He's a really great guy, and though my feelings toward Preston have only recently changed—"

"Recently because you found out that he has no desire of getting into my pants," Grace clarified.

"Yes." Jax nodded. "But he was a good guy before that. I just have this jealous streak when it comes to you."

"No kidding?" Grace asked with mock exaggeration. "Well, if I'm not going to get sex in the closet, I'm going to have to ask for a couple more kisses before we go down and eat."

"I think I can handle that," he said, bringing his mouth back to hers.

When they emerged a couple of minutes later, all the guys were crowded around the back of Jax's truck. They were chowing down on sandwiches and potato chips, laughing loudly about something.

"I know I said it before, but you guys have done an amazing job with this place."

"She's right." Preston nodded. "I saw this place when it got condemned. It was trashed; it's going to be incredible when it's finished."

"It's mostly been Jax and Bennett," Brendan said, popping a chip in his mouth.

"With the planning, yeah," Jax said. "The labor has been a significant portion of you and Shep, too."

"When do you think it will be finished?" Grace asked.

"I'd say June, July at the latest," Bennett told her.

"Here's hoping," Jax said, taking a step back toward the cooler. "I'm going to get a drink. What do you want, baby?" he asked as he turned around.

All of a sudden everyone went silent. Jax halted and turned back. Brendan, Shep, and Preston were staring at him open-mouthed, Bennett looked just slightly surprised with his eyebrows raised, and Baxter and Tripp had grins on their mouths.

"What?" Jax asked.

"Really? You just called Grace *baby* and you need to ask us *what*?" Shep asked.

"She's my girlfriend."

"Yes, Jax, but the reason we're confused is because it's a term of endearment," Brendan said. "From *you*."

"Grace, I don't know what you've done to that man over there," Shep said pointing to Jax. "But keep it up."

"Oh, I plan on it." Grace gave Jax a look that left him in no doubts as to what exactly she wanted to keep up.

* * *

Sunday was the first day that Jax and Grace had off together, and he was going to spend every single minute with her. He woke up with her sprawled across his chest. The ends of her hair tickled his jaw as he looked down at her. Her face was turned up to him, her cupid's bow mouth slightly opened. A piece of her hair fluttered in front of her mouth as she breathed steadily.

He watched her sleep and marveled at how beautiful she was. How had he gone this long before making her his?

He'd made love to her twice the night before, but it did nothing to lessen his need for her. If anything the need was just intensifying.

He reached up and pushed the strand of hair away from her mouth. The light touch made her burrow farther into him. Her leg rode up between his, the bottom of her foot running up his calf, her knee rubbing up against the inside of his leg.

Yeah, he was going to wake her up in *five*...

Four...

Three...

"Morning," she said, running her hand across his chest as she slowly opened her eyes and smiled up at him sleepily.

Thank God.

He rolled her beneath him and she inhaled sharply as his mouth latched on to one of her nipples.

"What is it with my breasts that fascinates you so much?" she asked as she made room for him between her thighs.

"You just answered your own question," he said, looking up at her. "One, they're breasts. Two, and more importantly, they're *your* breasts."

"Yes, but mine are so small and insignificant."

"Nothing about you is insignificant. You're beautiful."

"Right." She rolled her eyes.

"Is that sarcasm I detect?"

"Um, yes."

Jax moved before she even had a chance to react. He had her hands pinned above her head, and his legs were now on the outside of hers, locking her legs down. She gasped, startled, and her eyes opened wide as he looked down at her.

"So here's the thing." He adjusted his hands so only one held hers down. "You, Grace King, are beautiful. From here," he said, reaching up and tracing her hairline, "to the tips of your toes, and everything in between. Now your breasts are in the between. So they are therefore part of the beautiful." He ran his fingers across one of her nipples and she took another unsteady breath. Her legs squirmed between his, aligning things *perfectly*. "Are you trying to torture me?" he asked, resting his forehead against hers.

"You're the one making me do it," she said, moving her hips some more as he continued to touch her breasts.

"Then let's see you really move," he whispered in her ear before he moved his hand to her side and started tickling her.

"Oh, my God, Jax, nooooooo," she cried out, laughing.

She was helpless beneath him, her hands and arms still pinned down but her body writhing against his.

"I give up. You win. You win," she panted.

"I like the sound of that." He let go of her hands.

But the second her hands were free they were on his sides and she was tickling him.

So apparently Jax *was* insanely ticklish and not just on the bottom of his feet. Grace might be a whole lot smaller than him, but she had quick hands and nimble fingers that found every single spot that drove him crazy. He could have stopped her if he'd really tried but the sound of her laughing did funny things to him, and he wanted to hear her make that sound for as long as possible. For the rest of his life.

He wasn't sure how long they wrestled around the bed, or when Grace managed to get on higher ground straddling him, or at what moment everything changed from playful to passionate.

She reached down and stroked him.

"Ahh, Grace," Jax groaned as his head fell back into the pillow. Her grip around him tightened and he couldn't stop himself from pumping his hips up. He knew he wasn't going to last long, so he reached down and stilled her hand. "I really don't want to come that way."

"No?" she asked.

"No," he said, shaking his head.

She let go of him and lifted slightly as she reached over to the nightstand and pulled out a condom. She opened the little package and he groaned when her hands were on him again, rolling the latex down.

A second later she was lowering herself down onto him, and Jax was thrusting up inside of her. He grabbed her hips to help steady her, and she proceeded to ride him. Hard.

It still amazed Jax that Grace's small body could take him, could take all of him. He'd never gotten this much pleasure out of sex. It had never been like this before. So out-of-his-mind indescribable. And it appeared that Grace got a good amount of satisfaction out of their joining as well.

It was a couple of minutes of pure joy before Grace's head fell back between her shoulders and her hips picked up their pace. She cried out as her body throbbed around him, and Jax just let himself go.

Grace collapsed onto him, their sweaty skin sticking together. Jax wrapped his arms around Grace, holding her to him and never wanting to let her go.

* * *

Grace watched as Jax looped his jeans with a belt. He looked good in jeans and an emerald-green T-shirt. No, that was an understatement. He looked incredible. Edible. The top of his shirt was tight across his shoulders and chest, a chest that she happily had her mouth all over that morning.

After their wrestling match in bed, they'd taken a shower together. There hadn't been any wrestling in the steady stream of hot water, though Grace might have gotten pinned up against the wall at one point. When they surfaced sometime later, Grace stole one of Jax's T-shirts and pulled on her shorts from the day before.

"Are you going commando?" he asked, sounding pained.

"Just until we go to my apartment so I can change," she said as she buttoned the top button. When she looked up, Jax was staring at her hands as she pulled up the zipper.

"Oh." He nodded, not taking his eyes off her zipper, or more accurately her crotch.

"You sound disappointed by that fact."

"Well," he said, looking up at her and grinning. "I mean, it's kind of hot, the idea of you not wearing anything all day."

"Really?" she asked, laughing. "Well, I'm not going to spend the day out and about sans panties. Besides, I thought you really liked taking them off me."

"I do." He grabbed her and pulled her into him.

"You know you can't have it both ways."

"Yes, I know. But both options are pretty fantastic," he

said as he ran his hands up her thighs to her waist. "So either way I'm happy."

"You're ridiculous."

"Mmm hmm," he hummed into the soft spot under her ear.

"You know what else could be pretty hot?" she asked, placing her palms on his hard chest.

"What's that?" He continued to slowly run his hands up and down her waist.

"You could pick out the panties I'll wear all day."

Jax's hands stilled and he looked like he might've just swallowed his tongue.

"Oh, Princess," he said, smiling wide, "you have no idea what you do to me. Let's go before I tackle you again." He spun her around and ushered her out of the bedroom.

When they got to her apartment, Jax searched her underwear drawer while she changed into a yellow cotton dress. When she came out of the bathroom, he was grinning as he stretched out his arm, a peach cotton thong with white lace around the top dangling from his index finger.

Grace smiled back as she lifted up the skirt of her dress. "Would you like to put it on for me?"

Jax's smile transformed into something hot and hungry and he looked like he was going to combust. He dropped to his knees in front of her and ran his tongue around her navel as he pulled the thong up her legs. When it was in place, he kissed the tiny little bow that was sewn onto the front of the lace. Then he reached up and pulled the skirt of the dress from her hands, straightening it around her thighs.

He stood up and kissed her, his tongue sweeping the inside of her mouth. "You sure do keep things interesting," he said above her lips before he pulled back. "I'm now going to have the image of you in that thong all day long."

"You're welcome."

He laughed, shaking his head. "Come on. Let's go." He grabbed her hand, their fingers lacing together.

She was never going to get over how it felt when her hand was in his.

* * *

They headed up to Tallahassee to look at new furniture for when Jax's house was finished. He told Grace that most of the stuff he had wouldn't be making the move with him. Bennett was building a couple things that Jax wasn't going to need to buy, like the coffee table and side tables for the living room, the dining room table, and a new headboard for Jax's bed.

So Grace walked around the store with Jax helping pick out a sectional, bar stools, bedroom furniture, and a recliner for the den. The significance of it all wasn't lost on Grace. She just wasn't sure whether it was lost on Jax.

When they finished there, they went to a couple of stores Grace wanted to go to. At one of them Jax headed toward electronics and Grace made her way to the women's section. She picked out some new panties whose only possible function was Jax taking them off her. She was sure both of them were going to enjoy said panties thoroughly.

And then it was time for the best part of the day. Jax was taking Grace on their first official date. It might've only been dinner and a movie, but she was beyond excited.

There wasn't a theater in Mirabelle, and Grace loved movies. So it was a treat for her to see one on the big screen, especially a movie that was relatively new. They agreed on a recent Oscar winner, and bought a small popcorn and Coke that they shared. Jax pulled up the armrest between them and put his arm around her shoulder while she snuggled into him.

Every time their hands brushed against each other in the popcorn tub, a ridiculous giddy feeling flared up in Grace's stomach. This moment was every high school fantasy she had come to life. She was on a date with Jaxson Anderson.

The movie was amazing, and they talked about it for a good part of dinner. He took her to a small restaurant that was known for its steaks. They both ordered filet mignon, which was so tender it melted in their mouths. The garlic mashed potatoes were amazing, and the tiramisu had Grace moaning around her fork.

And then Jax took her back to his house, where he made love to her. He was so sweet to her, so tender, so *perfect*. He blew every one of her fantasies out of the water.

Chapter Twelve

Little Surprises

Grace woke up on Monday alone. She was flat on her stomach, her head on Jax's pillow and her arm draped across his side of the bed. It was dark in the room as it was just after six and the sun hadn't risen. She pushed up from the mattress and looked over her shoulder to the bathroom across the hall. The door was open and it was unoccupied. But there was a light shining from down the hallway, the floorboards and wall reflecting just a little bit of the soft yellow glow. The refrigerator closed quietly and a drawer was opened and then closed.

Grace sat up, pulling the sheet with her to cover her bare chest. She drew her knees up and rubbed the sleep out of her eyes.

It was still a little disorienting waking up in Jax's bed. She hadn't gotten over the feeling that being with him was all still a dream. She kept thinking that any moment she was going to wake up. Either that or Jax was going to freak out again. She couldn't get over the fear that he was going to come to her and tell her they couldn't be together.

She was just about to get out of bed when footsteps echoed

down the hallway and then Jax was standing in the doorway, wearing his uniform and holding two cups of coffee.

"Morning," he said, coming into the room.

She stared at the incredibly yummy man in front of her and pushed her fears to the back of her mind.

"Morning," she smiled as he sat down on the bed facing her, his hip pressed against hers.

She reached for a cup, but he shook his head.

"You have to pay the toll first."

She leaned forward and kissed his cheek.

"That's not going to cut it."

"You're so demanding in the mornings," she said, shaking her head as she came in for another kiss. This time she pressed her lips against his.

"That's more like it." He handed her a cup.

"I was just trying to spare you from my dragon morning breath," she said before she took a sip of coffee. "Mmm," she hummed as the warm, rich, hazel-nutty goodness hit her tongue.

"You don't have dragon morning breath," he said, shaking his head before he took a long drink.

"Oh, you're just being nice, and in more ways than one. Thanks for the coffee. You make a pretty good cup. I didn't think you could, based on the fact that you come to the café almost every day to get your fix."

"I have ulterior motives." He leaned forward and kissed her neck. "You're better than coffee," he said, moving to her ear and nibbling on her earlobe.

"Why didn't you wake me up before you got dressed?"

Jax laughed as he kissed her throat. "You were sound asleep. I thought you needed some rest after last night."

"Mmm, last night was nice." Grace turned her head and his mouth opened over hers. "We're going to spill coffee everywhere," she said against his lips.

"Probably," he said, pulling back.

"You getting off at seven?"

"Yup."

"I'll make you dinner."

"What is it with you and this need to feed me?" he asked.

"What is it with you and your need to protect me all the time?"

"I'm a deputy sheriff; it's my job to protect people."

"Do you get all moody and overbearing with them, too?" she asked.

"No, but I'm not sleeping with any of them."

She froze, the mug halfway to her mouth. "Right," she said softly before she brought the mug up and took a drink.

"Grace? What's wrong?"

"Nothing."

"Yeah, I don't think so. What's wrong?" he repeated, looking down into her face.

"I'm just being stupid, don't worry about it." She took another sip of coffee.

"Like that's going to happen. Talk to me," he said seriously.

She chewed on her bottom lip for a moment before she sighed and let it fall from her teeth. "I just...it's more than that, more than us sleeping together. At least it is for me. So when you simplify it, I...I don't know."

"Grace, it's more than that. It's a hell of a lot more than that," he said as he grabbed her coffee and put both his and her cup down on the nightstand. He grabbed her face in both of his hands, and his fingers wound into her hair. "That's just the newest facet of our relationship, so it was what came to mind first. But if you'll remember correctly, I've always been moody and overbearing when it comes to you. It didn't take us sleeping together for me to start acting that way around you. Baby, I know this just started, but I've known you for most of my life, *all* of your life, and when it comes right down to it, there is no way to simplify it. Not with words."

She just looked at him, unable to stop her mouth from turning up at the sides.

"What?" he asked, and the corner of his mouth quirked up.

"I love it when you call me *baby*."

"That's the *one* thing you got out of what I just said to you? That was a really good speech. I was all eloquent and stuff, and you know I don't do eloquent."

"That wasn't the only thing I got from your speech." She smiled, running her hands up his chest. "This is about more than just sex for you, too," she said seriously.

"I mean, don't get me wrong, some of it's about the sex." He grinned, something he was doing a lot more of these days. "I have to get going." He leaned in and kissed her sweetly on the mouth.

Too bad she didn't want sweetly. She wanted to push him down on the bed and get him out of that uniform.

"You should've woken me up," she said just a little bit pathetically.

Jax laughed as he pulled back. "I should go before you make me late. There's more coffee in the pot. Lock up before you leave," he said as he stood up.

"With what?" she asked, reaching for her cup.

"With the key I put on your keychain."

For the second time that morning, Grace's mug stopped halfway to her mouth. Had she heard him correctly? He'd given her a key to his house?

"When you go to your place, you should grab a few things to leave over here," he said.

"What? You're serious?"

"I'm serious." He laughed again as he planted his hands on either side of Grace and leaned in close to her face. "I'll see you tonight," he said before he pressed his lips to hers. "Have a good day at work, *baby*." He smiled as he straightened.

"You, too," she said still just a little bit stunned.

Jax grinned at her one more time before he turned and walked out of the room. The second the front door closed Grace bolted out of bed and ran down the hall completely naked. Her purse was on the counter, and next to it were her keys. She grabbed them and immediately noticed the new key on the ring. How could she not? It was bright blue, her favorite color.

* * *

Grace's mind was still spinning seven hours later as she drove to the Adams and Family Funeral Home. She needed to talk to somebody, and who better than Paige? It might've been a year and a half ago, but Paige had gone through the whole key thing more recently than anybody else. It might've been with Grace's brother, but Paige was pretty good about keeping certain details to herself...sometimes.

Grace pulled into the parking lot, right next to a Pepto-Bismol-pink Mercedes convertible. It read *Missy* on the license plate. Well, that was new. And it made sense, an obnoxious car for an obnoxious person.

Grace grabbed the tray of cookies for that night's funeral from the back of her Bug and made her way up the porch and in the door. Tara was behind her desk while Pinky leaned her hip against it, the two of them whispering conspiratorially.

"Oh, let me get that," Pinky said, pushing off the desk and closing the door behind Grace.

"What are you two gossiping about? And what's up with Missy's new ride?"

"Go put those cookies down and we'll fill you in," Tara said.

Grace put the cookies in the kitchen and when she got back Pinky and Tara were standing at the base of the stairs.

"Come on, let's go visit the lonely pregnant woman. She's to the point where she only attempts these steps once a day," Tara said as she started her way up the stairs.

When they walked into Paige's office she was sitting at her desk, her eyes closed as her head rested on the back of her chair.

"You better not let Missy catch you sleeping on the job."

"What is she going to do? I'm done for the day. I have a doctor's appointment and I'm just waiting for Brendan to come and get me," Paige said slowly opening her eyes. "Please tell me you brought something chocolaty and covered in frosting."

"What kind of sister-in-law would I be if I didn't?" Grace reached into the canvas bag that hung from her shoulder. She pulled a Tupperware container of birthday cake brownies covered in butter cream frosting out and set it on the desk.

Paige eyed the container for a second before she looked back up to Grace. "Milk?"

"Puh-lease, I know who I'm dealing with," Grace said, reaching back into the bag and pulling out a thermos of milk and some plastic cups.

"You not getting enough sleep?" Pinky asked, sitting down in one of the chairs in front of Paige.

"I don't remember what sleep is anymore. This child keeps me up half the night," Paige said as she reached for the Tupperware.

"You make me sick," Tara said, shaking her head. "If I ate like you do I'd be a whale."

"I am a whale." Paige pulled out a brownie and bit into it. "Oh, my God," she moaned around the brownie as she closed her eyes again and leaned back in the chair. "This is incredible."

"Thank you, and you're not a whale," Grace said, unscrewing the top off the thermos and pouring four glasses of milk. "All of your weight is where the baby is at, and your boobs. Your butt and thighs have barely changed. It's disgusting how good you look." She handed a glass to Paige.

"Really it is," Pinky said, shaking her head as she helped herself to a brownie. "I was a house for mine. What do you do? Surely sex with Brendan doesn't burn that many calories."

Paige inhaled her milk and started coughing.

"Oh, God," Grace said, grabbing a tissue and handing it to Paige. "Can we *not* talk about that?"

"What?" Pinky said unabashedly. "Pregnant sex is pretty amazing."

Paige coughed harder and Grace turned and looked at Pinky. "You're going to make her go into premature labor."

"I'm fine, I'm fine," Paige said, wiping at her eyes. Her cheeks were flaming and Grace had a pretty good idea that it wasn't from lack of oxygen.

If the sex hadn't been with Grace's brother, she would've asked Paige just how good pregnant sex was. But really, after Brendan had walked in on Grace in bed with Jax, both of them completely naked, what boundaries were left?

"Can we talk about something else?" Paige wheezed out.

"Yeah, didn't we come up here to talk about that pink Mercedes that's outside?"

"What pink Mercedes?" Paige asked.

"Hold on," Tara said, walking over to the door. She peeked out into the hallway before she came back inside and shut the door.

"Is the gossip really that good?" Grace asked, perching on the side of Paige's desk as Tara sat in the other seat next to Pinky.

"Yes," Tara said in a hushed voice, grabbing a small piece of brownie.

She handed the Tupperware to Grace, who took a fairly substantial brownie out. She knew that she was burning a ton of calories between the sheets with Jax, so that bad boy would be gone by the morning.

"Missy has a brand-new ride," Tara said.

"That car has to be over fifty thousand dollars," Grace said.

"Where the hell did she get that kind of money?" Paige asked.

"That is the question, isn't it?" Pinky said.

"Have you noticed that her wardrobe has gotten a little fancy, too?" Tara asked. "She's been wearing Prada shoes, Dior purses, and fancy suits that she isn't buying from anywhere around here."

"I think that those conferences she goes to are just excuses to go on shopping sprees. She probably just buys a book on tape and listens to it when she drives to Atlanta or Tampa or wherever the hell it is that she goes," Pinky said.

"So where do you think the car came from?" Grace asked. "You think it's from a guy?"

"Is she dating someone again? I thought she'd *sworn off men*." Paige made air quotes over the last part.

"Riiight," Grace said. "The day that Missy Lee swears off men is the day that Bethelda grows a conscience."

"But where is the money coming from? There's no way that she makes that kind of money," Paige said.

"You think she's doing something illegal?" Tara asked.

"Please tell me you are going to start playing detective," Pinky said, grinning at Tara.

"Don't you dare doubt my sleuthing skills." Tara raised her eyebrows and pursed her lips.

"Oh, I don't doubt them, Sherlock," Pinky, said shaking her head and still grinning. "I just think that this is going to be *very* entertaining."

"You just wait, Paige is going to be my Watson."

"I am?" Paige asked, looking alarmed. "I'm a horrible sleuth."

"Oh, you'll be fine. No one will assume that you're up to anything 'cause you're pregnant," Tara said.

"Yeah, I highly doubt that. I think I'll just attract more attention to the scene."

"Or," Pinky said, "you can just stand in doorways and block anyone from seeing Tara snoop. By the time you waddle out of the way no one will know what she was doing."

"All I wanted was chocolate. That was all I wanted. How in the world did I get roped into playing backup for Inspector Clouseau over here?"

"It's because you're here all the time," Pinky said.

"Between you, Grace, and Panky, you guys can play backup, too," Paige said.

"Oh, all right," Pinky agreed.

"Hey, I didn't agree to this," Grace said.

"Too bad, you're involved. Now let me have another brownie." Paige held her hand out for the Tupperware.

"So, how are things going with you and Jax?" Pinky asked, changing the subject.

"We're doing good." Grace grinned.

"Well, I'd hope it's still good. It's only been a couple of weeks," Tara said.

"No," Pinky said, shaking her head. "It's been twenty-four years."

"That it has. He took me on a date yesterday."

"And?" Paige asked.

"It was perfect," Grace said, and then told them all about it.

"Well, it sounds like he's doing pretty good so far." Pinky smiled and stood up. "I've delayed long enough. I need to be getting back to the shop. I'll see you guys on Thursday at the latest," Pinky said, heading out the door.

"I'll walk you out," Tara said and followed.

Paige leaned back in her chair with a blissed out expression on her face. Her eyes were half closed. She was probably coming down from the sugar high.

"Have I told you you're my favorite sister-in-law?" Paige asked.

"I'm your only sister-in-law."

"That's true. But you're still my favorite."

"Because of the brownies?" Grace asked.

"No, but those don't hurt your cause. So how *are* things going with Jax?" Paige asked.

Grace didn't say anything. She just reached for her keys and placed them on the desk in front of Paige.

"What am I looking at?" Paige asked, leaning forward.

"You see that bright blue one?"

"Yes."

"It's to Jax's house. *He* had it made and *he* put it on my key ring."

Paige's eyes were wide open as she looked up at Grace. "Seriously?"

"Yup. He also told me he wanted me to bring some of my stuff over to his place."

"Wow," Paige said, picking up the set of keys and looking at the blue one closer. "How do you feel about all that?" she asked, reaching across the desk and handing them back to Grace.

"I can't believe it," Grace said, shaking her head, still shocked. "The man has jumped in with both feet. I didn't expect this. I wanted it, believe me, but I didn't expect it. It's *Jax* for crying out loud."

Paige laughed. "I get it, sweetie. Brendan shocked the hell out of me when he gave me a key to his place." She smiled as her face warmed.

"What?"

"I'm just remembering what happened after he gave me the key."

"Spare me the details."

"I've never given you the details."

"The details are evident," Grace said, eyeing Paige's stomach.

"That they are." Paige winced and closed her eyes as her hand came to rest on her belly.

"You okay?"

"Yeah," Paige said, opening her eyes and rubbing a spot on her side. "I swear this child has some sort of fascination with my ribs. But anyway, the key is exciting. He obviously wants you around."

"He wants me in his bed."

"And there isn't anything wrong with that." Paige grinned. "But he wants you in his house, Grace."

"But for how long?" Grace asked, finally voicing her fear.

"Oh, sweetie, you can't look at it that way. I was so scared that your brother was going to realize he didn't want me in his house, in his life. It's one of those things, though, if Jax is the guy you're supposed to be with, he isn't going to get tired of you, he isn't going to want you to leave."

"I know, but it's Jax," Grace said softly. "It's stupid, it hasn't even been two weeks, and I'm already being ridiculous."

"Grace, it's been much longer," Paige said seriously. "Pinky was right, Jax has always been in your life."

"Is it too much to ask for him to always be in it?" Grace asked.

"No," Paige said, shaking her head. "It isn't too much to ask for. I pray that boy knows how worth it you are, Grace."

"Thanks, Paige." The thing was, Grace had been praying that she was worth Jax for years.

"Excuse me."

Grace and Paige looked to the door where a glowering Missy Lee stood.

Missy had overly teased blond hair and a pointy nose. She wasn't a tall woman. She was about Grace's height but always wore heels to make up for the lost inches; it helped her out when she needed to look down at people.

"Can I help you, Missy?" Paige asked sweetly.

"Is this how you spend your time on the clock? Eating and talking? Don't you have things you need to do? Like actual work?"

"Have they ever taught you how ineffectual micro-managing is at any of these seminars that you go to?" Grace asked.

"Making sure someone does their job isn't micromanaging. Don't think I'm not going to report this to Mr. Adams," Missy said, coming into the room, her hands on her hips.

"Report away. And I'm actually done for the day."

"So you're just wasting time here and getting paid for it?"

"I clocked out."

"So you're leaving early? Under whose authority?"

"Her doctor's," an agitated male voice said from behind Missy. Brendan came into the room and walked over to stand next to Paige. "In case you haven't noticed, my wife is pregnant."

"It's kind of hard not to notice," Missy said rudely as she looked over at Paige.

"What's that supposed to mean?" Brendan asked, narrowing his eyes.

"It's okay, sweetie," Paige said, reaching up and putting her hand on Brendan's arm. "Missy was just calling me fat. But that's fine. In a couple of months I'll have Trevor and lose the weight. Whereas for Missy, in a couple of months she'll still be the same bitter shrew she is today. Feel free to report *that* to Mr. Adams, Missy." Paige smiled sweetly.

Grace had to cover her mouth with her hand to keep from bursting out laughing.

Missy inhaled sharply, her face turning red. "Oh, believe me I will," she said before she vacated the room.

Brendan turned to Paige and held his hands out for her. She grabbed them and he helped her stand.

"Do you have any idea how beautiful you are?" he asked her, pulling her into his body. "Every single part of you." He placed his hands lovingly on her belly as he pressed his mouth to hers in a sweet kiss.

"I love you," she smiled as she reached up and touched his face.

"I love you, too." He kissed her again.

"You know," Grace said, "sometimes you two are nauseating."

"Oh, really?" Brendan asked, rounding on her. "You're a fine one to talk. You and Jax are pretty awful yourselves."

"I have no idea what you're talking about."

"You two spent a night apart yet?" Brendan asked.

"Are you asking me about my sex life?" Grace grinned and raised her eyebrows.

"God no. I was just making a point. It's just a matter of time before he gives you a key to his place."

Grace froze, her mouth dropping open. This time it was Paige who had to cover her mouth to keep from laughing.

"He already did, didn't he?" Brendan asked.

"This morning," Grace said.

"Good for him and you for that matter. I'm happy for you, Gracie."

"Thanks, Brendan." Grace smiled at him, so freaking happy it was ridiculous.

* * *

Over the next couple of weeks, Jax and Grace settled into a routine. Jax marveled at the fact that it happened so fast, they fit into each other's lives so easily, so perfectly. They were up in the mornings together, and after a quick, or sometimes not so quick, round in bed or the shower, they had a cup of coffee and were out the door. They alternated between his house and her apartment, both of them accumulating a pile of things at each other's place. Jax actually cleared out an entire drawer for her in his dresser, and he'd felt much more than a small amount of satisfaction when Grace had done the exact same thing for him. The icing on the cake was her giving him a key to her apartment.

Grace's stuff accumulated in more than just Jax's bedroom. She'd actually brought over more pots and pans than clothes. She cleared out space in one of the cabinets and now had all her spices lined up and alphabetized.

They went grocery shopping one day to stock up Jax's rather pathetic food rations. He followed behind her, pushing the cart and watching in fascination as she quickly and efficiently shopped. And it was more than a little surprising at how fast the cart filled up.

"Do we really need all this stuff?" He frowned as he helped her stack everything onto the conveyor belt at check-out.

"This isn't even a dent of what you need in that kitchen."

"I don't use this stuff to cook."

"Yes, but I do. So why don't you worry about the things that you know, and I'll worry about the things I know," she said, raising her eyebrows and giving him just enough sass for him to keep his mouth shut.

So Jax did just that. Good thing, too, because he'd never eaten so well in his life. He was surprised that he hadn't gained any weight over the last month. Maybe it had to do with the fact that he wasn't eating takeout that consisted mainly of meat and fried potatoes. Or it could have had something to do with the sex marathon he and Grace were currently partaking in. They were seriously burning up the sheets multiple times a day. It was awesome.

Another big change was that his kitchen was finally being put to use. The first time he'd opened the refrigerator door after their shopping trip, all he'd been able to do was stare.

He'd never seen it so filled with food.

A gallon of milk, coffee creamer, butter, cheese, orange juice, a package of hamburger, fresh strawberries, lemons, and so much more. He watched Grace put it all into the cart. He helped her load it into his truck and bring it into the house, but for some reason it just looked different all laid out in his normally barren fridge.

And it was more than just a filled fridge. With Grace, his *life* was full. He didn't come home to an empty house anymore. He came home to her.

On days that Jax was working, Grace was always home before him. Whether it was her kitchen or his, when he walked in the door she was cooking dinner ninety percent of the time. Music would be playing and she'd be dancing around the kitchen as she threw stuff into a skillet or stirred something in a bowl. The way Grace moved around *any* kitchen was an art form. The way she handled the food, cutting it with fast precise motions, the knife acting like an extension of her arm. She was amazing. He could watch her cook for hours and still find it fascinating.

One Sunday night Jax came home to find Grace in his kitchen making fajitas. He changed out of his uniform, and when he came into the kitchen he leaned against the door-jamb and watched as Grace dumped a plate full of tomatoes into a bowl. She ripped off a few sprigs of something green and leafy from a bushel on the counter and began dicing.

She dropped that into the bowl, too, and then squeezed in half a lemon before she stirred. She grabbed a chip from an open bag on the counter and dipped it in before she brought it to her mouth.

She'd made guacamole, and a small green dab of it was at the corner of her mouth. She absentmindedly wiped it with her finger before she put said finger into her mouth and licked it.

Jax pushed off the wall, needing a little taste himself.

"Looks good," he said, coming up behind her, resting his chin on her shoulder and his hands on her waist.

"Tastes good, too," she said, grabbing another chip from the bag and dipping it into the bowl. She turned in his arms and leaned back against the counter as she popped the chip into his mouth.

Holy guacamole. It was rich and tangy and just *incredible*. It burst on his tongue and made him want more, except he had a better idea of how to eat it than on a chip.

"Sure does." He reached around her to grab another chip and scooped a generous amount of dip up. He brought the chip to her mouth and purposely bumped it against her lips, leaving a green smudge.

"You going to clean up your mess?" she asked after she swallowed.

"Absolutely." He brought his mouth down to hers and sucked her top lip into his mouth.

Her arms wrapped around his neck as she stretched up. He pressed his body into hers, pushing her up against the counter.

"The meat's going to burn," she said against his mouth.

"Is that a euphemism for something? Because I've never heard it."

"You're ridiculous." She pushed on his chest. "Stop trying to distract me."

"I have no idea what you're talking about," he said as he stepped back from her and let her pass by him.

"How was work today?" she asked, and went to the stove to stir the steak that was sizzling in the pan.

"Mind numbing. I was going over files for the burglary cases." He leaned against the counter and helped himself to another chip.

"Anything new?"

"Not at the moment. I'm trying to find some link, but I just don't see one."

"You'll figure it out."

"Here's hoping." He dipped his finger into the bowl of guacamole. He came up behind Grace and ran his finger along her neck.

"What are you—"

But she stopped talking when he bent his head and ate the dip off her neck. She tilted her head to the side, giving him greater access.

"Mmm," he hummed into her throat. "Tastes perfect."

"Don't get any ideas," she said, turning to look at him.

"Too late."

"Dinner will be ready in about five minutes. And I made tortillas from scratch. So no funny business."

"Come on, we could have a lot of fun with that guacamole." He grinned.

"I made dark chocolate custard for dessert; I think we could have more fun with that."

"I like the way your mind works. All right, I'll try to control myself."

"Well, while you control yourself why don't you fix the margaritas? They're ready, you just need to salt the glasses and pour."

"That I can do." He went to the refrigerator and pulled everything out that he needed.

"Done," he said, sidling up to her a couple of minutes later as she pulled a skillet to the side of the stove and turned off the burner.

"Thanks." She turned to him as he handed her a glass. They both sipped at their drinks. Grace knew how to make a mean margarita; it was loaded with tequila.

They ate dinner and as they were clearing the dishes, Jax's cell phone rang. It was another deputy.

"Give me a second," Jax said to Grace before he stepped out of the kitchen to answer the phone.

Roy Hough's mother-in-law had passed away and he and his wife had to go up to Memphis. He needed Jax to cover the evening shift for him the following week.

"That won't be a problem, Roy," Jax said.

"Thanks, man. I owe you one."

When he walked back into the kitchen, Grace had finished cleaning and was wrapping something up in aluminum foil. There was an identical package sitting on the counter.

"What's that?" he asked, coming up behind her and wrapping his arms around her waist as he looked over her shoulder.

"Your lunch for tomorrow."

"Why do you always worry about me eating?"

"Because a protein bar and a banana is not a lunch. And you're going to be working on your house all day. You need sustenance."

"Hmm," he hummed into her throat. "I might just have to keep you around."

"For food purposes? I provided that before."

"That's true." He kissed the spot just under her ear.

Grace pulled out of his arms and went to put the last of the food and his lunch in the fridge. He leaned back against the counter and watched her.

"You know you've never answered my question," he said.

"Which question?" she asked, turning around. Her hair was up and in a ponytail, but a couple stragglers had fallen out and framed her face.

"Why you feed me all the time," he said, crossing to her.

Something flickered in Grace's eyes. "I'm a cook, Jax. I like to feed people."

"I believe that." He took a step forward and caged her in against the counter. He reached up and pushed a strand of hair behind her ear. "But you have this *need* to feed me."

She hesitated for a second before she cleared her throat. She reached up and put her palms down on his chest. "Growing up, I saw you hungry a lot. My mom and Grams started this mission to feed you whenever you were in their sight. You were always so much smaller than Brendan and Shep. I thought that the bigger you were, the *stronger* you would be, and the less likely it was that your dad could hurt you. You've always been so hell-bent on protecting me, it was the only way I knew I could protect you. The only way I still know how to protect you."

There were no words that were good enough at that moment. There was nothing Jax could say to express just how much Grace meant to him. This beautiful, caring, compassionate woman standing in front of him knocked him on his ass.

He looked at her, stunned, for a moment, before he leaned down and pressed his mouth to hers. He was desperate to show her just how much she meant to him. The problem was he had no idea how to do that. He didn't deserve her, didn't deserve anything like her in his life. But he kept that thought to himself and just kissed her.

* * *

Since Jax had switched shifts for the week, he was working from seven at night until seven in the morning. Which meant that out of the last six nights, Grace had not slept by her man for four of them. She was not a fan of it. Not. At. All.

To make matters worse, Grace's period had fallen on Jax's days off, so they were now going on day six of no sex. She was about to climb the damn walls.

But Grace's need for Jax went *way* beyond sex. They'd been together for almost a month and a half, and her need for him had grown leaps and bounds in that time. She'd grown *very* accustomed to going to bed and waking up in his arms, and not having him next to her at night left her aching throughout the day.

Grace would've taken some days off to spend with Jax, but it was the end of May and the summer season had started. This meant that the café's business had almost doubled and Grace was pulling longer shifts herself. The café would stay that busy until the middle of September before it died down to a normal pace again.

Grace finished up at seven on Tuesday, the last night of Jax's late shifts, and went over to Brendan and Paige's house to have dinner.

"What's wrong with you?" Brendan asked when he opened the door.

"Got to love *that* greeting." Grace frowned and walked into the house.

Brendan and Paige's dog came skidding into the hallway and stopped right before she plowed into Grace. Sydney was half husky, half something else, and she was gorgeous with bright blue eyes, and black and gray hair.

"Hey, pretty girl," Grace said, dropping her purse on the floor and getting down on her knees to give the dog a proper chest scratching.

Sydney's eyes dropped shut and her back leg started to thump on the wood floor. Grace looked up at her brother, who was currently standing in front of her, a towel draped over his shoulder and a frown on his face.

"Did you and Jax have a fight or something? You have an agitated look on your face."

The look she had on her face was an *unsatisfied* one.

"No. We didn't have a fight. We're doing well, thank you very much for asking."

"Then what the hell is wrong with you?"

"You really don't want me to answer that question."

"Why not?" he asked, folding his arms across his chest in his customary *I'm scary as hell* big-brother way.

"Probably because it has to do with sex," Paige called out from the living room.

"Oh, God," Brendan said as his arms dropped to his sides and he looked horrified. "You're right, I don't want to know. Go talk to Paige." He turned around and headed toward the kitchen.

Grace continued to show Sydney some loving for a moment. Grace had wanted to get a dog over the last couple of years. The problem was she had no yard, and she really wanted a dog like Sydney. A lab, or a retriever, or something that was bigger than a cat. Jax could get a dog. Well, when his new place was finished he could. A dog would have a field day in that yard of his. So would kids.

Grace froze. She had the image of Jax chasing a giggling little girl with strawberry blond hair around the yard.

She was brought back to reality with a furry swat to the face. She looked at the dog in front of her, who looked very put out that she wasn't being scratched anymore.

Grace gave her one more good rub before she got up off the floor, grabbed her purse, and headed into the living room, still a little dazed from her recent vision.

"Do you enjoy getting him all flustered?" Grace asked as she walked into the room.

Paige was sitting on the couch, her back leaning against the armrest and her legs stretched out across the cushions. "Immensely." She grinned.

"I'm glad it entertains you so much," Grace said, taking a seat at the opposite end of the couch. She, too, leaned back against the armrest, but she curled her legs up underneath her.

"Me, too." Paige adjusted herself on the couch. She inhaled sharply and closed her eyes in pain.

"Are you okay?" Grace leaned forward.

"Yeah." Paige nodded. "It's nothing. So, what's going on?" Paige asked, fidgeting with her T-shirt and stretching it over her belly.

"I think the correct question would be what's not going on?"

"Don't tell me you've already hit a slump."

"I can still *hear* you," Brendan called out from the kitchen.

"Then put some music on or something," Paige called back.

"No slump," Grace said, shaking her head as country music began to play in the kitchen. "It's just this week and these stupid late hours he's been working."

"But tonight's his last night. And it's only been a couple of nights, right?"

"Six nights. I was on my period during his days off," Grace explained.

"Isn't Mother Nature a bitch sometimes?" Paige asked.

"Not always," Grace said, nodding to Paige's big belly.

"Oh, this isn't always a picnic."

"Yeah, but you get a pretty big prize at the end."

"That's true," Paige said, putting both hands on her belly. She glanced down and gave her belly a warm smile. "I just can't wait until he's here."

"Me, either."

"So," Paige said, looking up again, "you're going crazy I take it?"

"Paige, I've had more sex since we've been together than ever before in my life."

"Okay," Brendan said from the doorway, "I'm just going

to start announcing myself before I walk into rooms. This is getting absolutely ridiculous."

"What's up, sugar?" Paige said sweetly.

"Dinner's ready." He turned back around and disappeared into the kitchen.

"So as it turns out, I like messing with him, too. I saw him in the doorway." Grace grinned, getting up from the sofa and holding her hand out for Paige to grab.

"It's fun, isn't it?" Paige asked as she grabbed Grace's hand and leveraged herself up with the other hand on the armrest. But as soon as she stood all the way up she stilled.

"Are you sure you're okay?" Grace asked.

"Yeah, I'm fine." Paige took a deep breath and waddled into the kitchen. She went to the dining room table and Brendan was beside her in a second, pulling out her chair and helping her sit. He leaned down and whispered something in her ear and she turned to him. He kissed her softly on the mouth before he pulled back. It still marveled Grace how much her brother had changed since Paige. It was crazy what love did to a person.

They all sat down at the table and had Chicken Marsala for dinner.

"You know, Brendan, you can give me and Grams a run for our money sometimes," Grace said before she savored her last bite.

"Yeah, he's pretty good around the kitchen." Paige leaned back in her chair. "That was delicious. Now, Grace, would you mind cleaning up for us?"

"What?" Brendan asked, looking at Paige confused.

"You need to drive me to the hospital," Paige said calmly. "I'm in labor."

Chapter Thirteen

Something 'Bout a Truck

W hat?" Brendan repeated, his confusion quickly turning to panic.

"I'm in labor," Paige said as if they were talking about the weather. "I have been all day, but the contractions are finally getting close enough that we can go."

"All day?" Grace asked.

"And you didn't tell me?" Brendan asked, standing up so suddenly that his chair fell back onto the floor.

"They weren't close enough to cause concern until about thirty minutes ago."

"And why didn't you tell me then?" he asked, his voice getting louder.

"Because I was hungry and I wanted to eat dinner," Paige answered, still sounding perfectly calm. "Now would you like to continue to discuss this? Or take me to the hospital?"

Brendan just looked at Paige like she was the craziest person he'd ever met.

"We need the bags," Paige said, turning to Grace. "They're in the bedroom. Could you grab them since your brother seems to be having a stroke?"

Grace got up from the table and walked into the bedroom,

both amused and in shock. Paige never failed to surprise her. By the time Grace was walking out of the bedroom, Brendan was leading Paige down the hall. He had a look of sheer frustration on his face, but he'd apparently decided to keep his opinions to himself. Sydney was walking next to them, whining softly as she looked up at Paige.

As Paige was slipping her shoes on, she inhaled sharply and bent over, obviously in pain. Brendan's look of frustration disappeared and was replaced with concern.

"Paige?" he said, placing one hand on her back.

She took a moment to breathe past the contraction and then straightened. "It's okay," she said, looking at Brendan. "Everything is okay." She reassured him as she reached up and touched his face. "Our son is coming."

"Our son is coming," he repeated, his mouth turning up into a smile. "Grace, you got everything here?" he asked, opening the front door and leading Paige out.

"Yes."

"Can you and Jax watch Sydney?" he asked as they descended the stairs.

"Yeah, I'll drop her off at his house before I head over to the hospital, and I'll call everyone to tell them that Paige is in labor."

Grace helped Brendan get Paige loaded in his truck.

"Thank you. You're amazing." He gave Grace a peck on the cheek before he hopped up into the driver's seat of his truck.

"Love you both," Grace said before he shut the door and started backing up. Grace and Sydney watched until the truck disappeared from the driveway. "All right, girl, it's just you and me." Grace looked down at the dog sitting by her feet.

Sydney whined and looked back and forth at Grace and the empty drive.

"She's going to be fine," Grace said, reaching down and

patting the dog's head. "And in a couple of days you're going to have a new human to protect. Come on." Grace turned around to head up the stairs. Sydney followed and when Grace shut the door, Sydney sat down and stared at it.

Oh great, so now she was going to have to deal with a heartsick dog.

Grace left Sydney at the door and went to grab her purse. She called Denise, Oliver, and Lula Mae before she called Jax. He answered on the second ring.

"Hey, everything okay?" he asked, sounding concerned.

"How do you always know when something's up?"

"I'm just that good. What's going on?"

"Paige went into labor."

A beat of silence. "Is she okay?"

"Yeah," Grace said. "She's apparently been in labor all day and she decided to tell Brendan after dinner. You should have seen his face."

"Oh, I'm sure it was something to behold," he said, clearly amused. "So what's the plan?"

"Well, once I get off the phone with you I still have to call Shep, Bennett, and Abby. Then I'm going to drop Sydney off at your place, because we're playing babysitter, and then I'm off to the hospital. You still getting off at seven?"

"Yeah, unless I can get off earlier. Keep me posted. If she still hasn't had the baby by the time I get off, I'll stop by and let Sydney out before I go to the hospital."

"Sounds good. Be safe."

"*Always,*" he said before he hung up.

* * *

Grace showed up at the hospital just after ten. Lula Mae was walking around the small waiting area, while Oliver sat in a chair sipping a cup of coffee.

"What's going on?" Grace asked as she sat down next to her grandfather and gave him a kiss on the cheek.

"They're getting settled in their room." Oliver pointed to a closed door within view of the waiting room.

"How's she doing?"

"Denise was walking her around while Brendan checked them in," Lula Mae said, continuing her rounds.

"Grams, if you do that until the baby's born you're going to wear a path in the floor."

"I'm just so excited I can't sit still."

"Was she this bad when Brendan and I were born?" Grace whispered to her grandfather.

"No," Oliver said, giving his wife a loving smile. "She stayed very calm with your mother. Well, on the surface at least."

"So now she can let out all her crazy?"

"Yup." He grinned.

"What are you two whispering about?" Lula Mae asked, narrowing her eyes at the pair of them as she made another lap.

They were spared having to answer by Shep coming into the room.

"Paige have the baby yet?" he asked, catching Lula Mae before she started around again and giving her a big hug and a kiss on the check.

"Not yet." Grace shook her head. "I have a feeling we're in for a long night."

"I figured," he said, walking over to where Grace and Oliver were sitting. He shook Oliver's hand before he sat down next to Grace and stretched out his long, jean-clad legs. "When's your boy toy getting here?"

"Really?" Grace asked, looking at him. *"Boy toy?"*

"Yup," he said, and waggled his eyebrows. "I feel like that's a pretty good description of Jax."

Oliver snorted. "That sounds like more of a good description for *you*," he said, looking over at Shep.

"Hey, I've calmed down in my old age," Shep said.

The old age was debatable, but the calming down was definitely true. Grace hadn't seen Shep with his normal plethora of women for a while now. It had been over two years since he'd dated anyone, longer than that since he'd had a girlfriend of any kind.

"What *is* going on with you?" Grace asked, studying him. "You've been flying solo lately. What happened? All your charm dried up?"

"My charm is part of my DNA, Gracie."

"So it's not going anywhere?"

"And don't you forget it." He grinned.

"When *is* Jax getting here?" Lula Mae asked, finally giving up on her pacing and sitting down.

"His shift ends at seven. He's going to try to get here earlier if he can. Did you talk to Bennett?" Grace asked Shep.

"Yeah, he should be here soon."

"Who's working the bar tonight?" Oliver asked.

"My dad. But Austin Gammons is working there now, so he's going to close up."

"When did he start working there?" Oliver asked.

"About a month ago. He's working out well. It's also giving my dad a little bit of a break. He and my mom don't like to leave Grandma El alone a lot. She gets really lonely."

"How is Ella doing?" Lula Mae asked.

"She's okay," Shep said, rubbing a spot on his jeans. "Last month was really hard on her."

"I'm sure." Oliver nodded his head sadly.

Last month marked two years since Shep's grandfather died. Owen and Ella Shepherd had been married for almost sixty-five years. They'd built a life together, literally. Owen built the Sleepy Sheep and the house Shep currently lived in with his own two hands. Everyone in Atticus County knew who Owen and Ella were. They were institutions, and beloved ones at that. They were part of the legacy of the Sleepy Sheep.

Shep and his grandfather had been incredibly close. Shep pretty much worshiped the man. Owen's death had been really hard on Shep. The only person it hit harder was his grandmother. In fact, it was just after Owen passed when Shep eased up with the ladies.

Grace looked up at Shep, studying the side of his face like she was going to figure the man out by some insight hidden under the scruff on his jaw. Grace loved Shep like a brother. Always had. But he'd been a little too carefree. Grace had asked Brendan about it. He said it all stemmed back to Hannah Sterling, the one and only girl who had gotten in Shep's heart, and ultimately broke it.

Grace knew what it was like to only want one person. To have her heart belong to someone so completely that there was no chance it could ever be anyone else's. Grace knew that she would never be able to move on from Jax, never look at another man the way she looked at him, never love someone more than him. If that was how Shep felt about Hannah, Grace's heart hurt for him. Not that she'd ever tell him. He was too badass, alpha man for any of that nonsense.

Deep blue eyes were suddenly focused on her. "What?" he asked.

"Nothing." She put her arm through his and rested her head on his shoulder. "I'm glad you're here."

"I wouldn't miss this for the world," he said, kissing her head. "No matter how long it takes."

"We taking bets on time?" Bennett asked coming into the room and sitting directly across from Grace.

"Hour increments?" Shep asked.

"That works." Bennett nodded. "Ten dollars each?"

"I can't believe you're betting on my great-grandbaby like he's a horse at the race." Lula Mae frowned.

"I'm calling the six o'clock hour," Oliver said.

"Oliver!" Lula Mae slapped his arm.

"What." He shrugged. "We're going to be here for a while. Might as well make it interesting."

"Three o'clock," Shep said.

"I've got seven," Grace said, picking it because it was Jax's favorite number.

"Grace Elizabeth!" Lula Mae glared at Grace and shook her head.

"I'm taking eight," Bennett said.

"Then I've got four."

Everyone looked at Brendan who was standing in the entryway of Paige's room.

"And I've got two," Paige called out from their room. "And I swear, Bennett, if I'm in labor until eight in the morning, I'm blaming *you*."

"Well, in that case I'll say that Trevor is going to be born by one," Denise said, coming out into the hallway.

"Really?" Brendan asked. "You think it will be that quick?"

"No," she whispered, shaking her head. "Put me down for nine." She mouthed the words, holding up nine fingers.

Grace looked at Lula Mae. Her grandmother's eyes were narrowed like she was having an intense internal battle.

"Fine." She stood up and smoothed out the front of her pants. "I'm calling the five o'clock hour," she said not meeting anyone's eye.

"What happens if it goes past the last hour?" Shep asked.

"You hush your mouth, Nathanial Shepherd. Do not even put those thoughts out there into the universe," Paige said, appearing on the other side of Brendan wearing a bathrobe over a hospital gown. Her hair was thrown up in her customary Paige-crazy-up-do-bun-thing that only she could pull off and not look like a bag woman.

"Wow, Paige." Grace grinned. "That was some Southern sass coming out of your mouth."

"She's always had the sass, but the Southern sure is a development," Denise said.

"Why aren't you in bed?" Brendan asked, concern evident in every feature of his face.

"Because I don't want to be. They said I could walk around for a little bit longer, so calm yourself," she said, patting his arm.

"Brendan? Calm? Oh, Paige, that's never going to happen." Grace shook her head.

"I know. My dear hot-headed man." She sighed and looked up at her husband. "How about we go on a walk around the hospital so we can calm your nerves. You're going to have a very hard night watching me push a tiny human out of my body." She smiled sweetly.

Brendan's lips quirked up and he shook his head. "Come on, woman. Let's go." He looped his arm around her back and led her down the hall.

They made a couple of rounds before Paige's contractions got to be too much for her to stay upright and then they were back in the room. Over the next couple of hours Brendan and Denise were in and out getting Paige ice chips and keeping everyone updated. By two in the morning, Paige had a couple more centimeters to go before she was dilated enough to even start pushing.

Grace didn't even remember closing her eyes, but when she woke up she was using Jax's shoulder as a pillow.

"Hey," she mumbled, grabbing his hand as she pressed her face into his arm and inhaled.

"Hey." He kissed her head.

"What time is it?" she asked, tilting her head back to look up at him.

"Almost four. I got someone to cover for me." He leaned down, kissing her mouth. He hadn't shaved and his scruff brushed her face.

"I'm guessing there's still no baby?" she asked, reaching up and running her thumb across his jaw.

"Still no baby," he said, shaking his head.

"So no more late nights?" she asked hopefully.

"No more late nights." He grinned.

"You're all mine again?"

"I'm always all yours." He leaned down and pressed his mouth to hers.

* * *

Brendan won the bet. Trevor Oliver King was born at four fifty-eight in the morning. He weighed eight pounds two ounces, had a full head of dark brown hair the exact color as Paige's, and Brendan's nose. He was currently bundled in a light green blanket that was covered with monkeys, his teeny tiny little body cradled in Brendan's massive arms.

Everyone who had been in the waiting room was now standing in a circle, staring at the father and son duo.

"He's *perfect*," Brendan whispered in an awed voice as he looked down at his son. "He's *absolutely* perfect." He reached up and wiped at his eyes.

As Grace watched her big brother hold his son, she was completely baffled that any man, or woman for that matter, could walk out on their child. Could leave behind something that was so tiny, so defenseless, so in need to be *loved*.

Grace hadn't known her father, neither had Brendan, but maybe that was for the best. Jax knew his father, and Haldon Anderson wasn't a good man by any standards. Jax would've been better off never knowing him. Really, unless a father looked at his child the way Brendan was looking at Trevor, he didn't deserve to be in his child's life.

"You want to hold him?" Brendan asked, looking up at Grace. He had to be exhausted, there was no doubt about that, but the sheer joy in his eyes completely overpowered everything. Grace had never seen him look so happy.

"Yes," she said, taking a step forward.

Brendan gently put the little bundle in her arms. His delicate little eyelids fluttered as he slept.

"Wow," Grace whispered, looking up at Brendan. "He's you in miniature."

"I hope he has Paige's gray eyes," Brendan said.

"Well, he has her hair." Lula Mae sniffled.

Grace looked back down and put her finger in Trevor's little hand.

"Hey, Munchkin, this is your Aunt Grace," she whispered. "Now don't let this go to your cute little head, but you're pretty much the most adorable thing I've ever seen in my life. You're going to get spoiled by everyone in this room, but just remember that I'm your favorite."

Brendan laughed as he pressed a kiss to Grace's temple.

"How's Paige doing?" Jax asked as he came up behind Grace and looked over her shoulder at Trevor.

"Good. Exhausted, but good."

"Is she still awake?" Grace asked as she passed Trevor to a clearly anxious Lula Mae, who promptly started sniffling in full force the moment Trevor was snuggled in her arms.

"Yeah," Brendan nodded.

"You think it'd be okay if I went and saw her?"

"Absolutely."

Grace took a step back from the circle and ducked into the door that was behind them. The blinds were still drawn, so the only light in the room was coming from a lamp in the corner.

"Hey." Paige smiled sleepily from the bed.

Denise was settled in the chair next to her, her head resting on the back, her eyes closed.

"Hey, yourself," Grace said, coming over and kissing Paige's forehead. "He's beautiful, Paige." She brushed a stray hair from Paige's cheek.

"Isn't he?" she said, closing her eyes as Grace continued to stroke her hair back. "That feels good." She sighed.

"You guys are going to be great parents."

"You think so?"

"I know so."

"Brendan's been worried," Paige said, opening her eyes. "He said something a couple of months ago. Something along the lines of he doesn't want to be anything like his father."

"Have you seen the way he looks at that little boy? There's no way," Grace said, shaking her head.

"I told him before that he's nothing like his father. But yeah, I saw the way he looks at Trevor." Paige smiled. "Like he's never seen anything more perfect."

"You both mean the world to him. You've given him so much."

"He's given me a lot, too," Paige said sleepily.

"Like that little angel out there?"

"Yeah, and you. I always wanted a sister."

"Me, too." Grace smiled.

"Love you, Grace."

"Love you, too."

"You can keep rubbing my head like that for as long as you want." Paige closed her eyes again.

"Will do," Grace said, and she kept at it until Paige was soundly asleep.

* * *

Jax and Grace left the hospital just before seven. They went back to his house, where Grace had just enough time to take a shower and head out the door to work. She was going to be surviving off caffeine all day. But so was he. He'd scheduled a delivery for nine o'clock that morning weeks ago. Installing the wooden boards for the ceilings and floors was the next step. If he rescheduled the delivery it would get pushed back another two weeks.

Jax had gone with amber wooden planks for the ceiling in the living room, kitchen, den, and master bedroom. They were just a little bit darker than the hardwood floors that would be in all the rooms of the house, except for the tile in the bathrooms and the carpet in the spare bedrooms. But the floors would be installed after the painting was finished.

At least Jax had picked out the colors. He and Grace had done that the week before. They'd decided on dove gray for the kitchen, living room, and hallway, butter cream yellow for his bedroom, lime sorbet for his bathroom, ocean water blue for the second bathroom, and so on, and so on. He couldn't wait to see everything painted.

"What time will you be done tonight?" Jax asked as he snatched Grace up before she walked out the door. He pulled her into his body and kissed her before she had time to answer and she melted into him. Her tongue was in his mouth and her hands were traveling to the back of his head, her fingers playing with the hair at the base of his neck.

"Around six," she said, pulling back a minute later. She was breathless and her cheeks were flushed. He could tell by the look in her eyes that she was as desperate for him as he was for her.

"So I'll see you here?"

"Yes, and I'll take care of dinner. Something we can just

throw in the oven, because as soon as I walk in that door I'm going to tackle you to the floor."

"Sounds promising." He grinned and kissed her one more time before she left.

* * *

By five o'clock, Jax was in countdown mode. He wanted Grace underneath him, now. Ten minutes ago. This morning. Yesterday. He just wanted her.

He'd had Grace on the brain all damn day. Who was he kidding? She was always on his mind because he always wanted her. Bennett and Tripp came by to help out at around twelve, and they had to ask Jax questions three or four times before he answered. They'd been working on the ceiling and Jax was lucky he hadn't been hit in the head with a piece of wood at this point.

"So I think we should call it a day," Tripp said as he nailed the last board in the ceiling of the den.

"Scared for your life?" Bennett grinned.

"Well, yes. But Grace just pulled up," he said, nodding to the window in the kitchen that looked out into the front yard.

Jax's head whipped around, and sure enough there was Grace, getting out of her little Bug wearing a red sundress. She'd gone home and changed.

Jax was out the front door in five seconds flat, grinning like an idiot as he made his way down the steps.

"Hey, stranger," she waved as she walked up the drive.

He didn't even respond, just grabbed her and pulled her into him as he laid a big old kiss on her mouth. Grace's arms wound around his neck.

Jax would've loved nothing more than to bend down and grab Grace's thighs so that she could wrap her legs around his waist. But there was some sense of sanity still buzzing around in his brain, because he really had no desire to give Bennett and Tripp a show.

"I thought you weren't going to be done until six." He pulled back and placed his hands on her hips, thinking about what color underwear she was wearing under her dress.

"I was, but apparently patiently waiting for you for eighteen years has led to all of my patience drying up."

"Oh, really?" He grinned.

"Yes." She smiled, leaning into him and stretching up onto her toes so she could put her mouth by his ear. "But I can assure that's the only thing that's dry," she whispered.

Jax inhaled sharply just as a hand came down hard on his back.

"We're out of here," Tripp said, walking by them. "Good seeing you, Grace."

"Yeah, you two have a good night," Bennett said, putting his hand in the air and waving as he headed for his truck.

"Bye, boys," Grace called out after them. "They scattered pretty quickly," she said as her hands journeyed up under the hem of Jax's shirt to his abdomen.

"Yeah." He nodded. "I think they caught the vibe."

"What vibe is that?"

"The *I'm about to jump you* vibe."

"Oh, that one." Grace looked over her shoulder as both men backed out of the driveway and disappeared through the trees. "Coast is clear," she said, turning back to Jax. "Let's go." She grabbed his hand.

"What? Here?" he said, looking around like someone was watching from the trees.

"Absolutely."

"You can't be serious," he said as she dragged him toward the house. "There is *nothing* for us to do anything on up there. At least not comfortably."

"We aren't going up to the house," she said, bypassing

the stairs and heading around the back to the river. "I think we should take a dip. You seem a little hot."

"I don't think a swim is going to cool me off."

"Good," she said, looking over her shoulder and grinning at him.

"We can't go skinny-dipping. The sun's still out; some-one will see us."

"I never said anything about skinny-dipping."

"You going to go in that dress?"

"No," she said, shaking her head. "My black lace panties and bra."

Jax about tripped over his feet. He could just imagine what Grace was going to look like in all that wet lace.

And all his objections went out the window.

When they got to the water's edge Grace turned to him and her hands immediately found the hem of his T-shirt. She began working it up his sides. He lifted his arms, and she pulled the clothing up over his head. He pulled off his boots as quickly as possible before he reached for her again.

His mouth found hers as his hands traveled behind her back. As soon as he found her zipper it was down and so were the straps at her shoulders. She dropped her arms, and the dress pooled at her feet.

Oh, jeez, she was wearing those black lace boy short things that made him forget his name.

"Your tongue is hanging out of your mouth." Grace smiled as she reached for the front of his pants and undid his belt. His zipper was down a second later, and she was pushing his jeans down his legs. He pulled his socks off as he freed his legs from his jeans so that he was only wearing his navy blue boxer briefs.

Grace eyed him appreciatively for a moment before she turned and ran into the river. Jax followed right behind her, unable to stop himself from laughing as they splashed through the cool water. She dove in and started swimming away from him, and he followed, his head going beneath the surface as he picked up a fast stroke and grabbed her feet. He twisted her around and opened her legs as he brought her body into his. Her arms and legs wrapped around him like a vice in an instant.

There was no more laughing from either of them as he kissed her hard and his tongue claimed possession of her mouth. His hands were on the small of her back holding her to him as she started to rock against him. One of his hands moved down to her bottom, his fingers tracing the lace edge of those panties that he loved so much. He kept on that path until he was able to pull back the material and his fingers were traveling down a path that made her moan into his mouth. He kept at it for a good while, and as he moved inside her, she moved harder against him.

"Jax." She said his name breathlessly. "I can't...I'm going to..."

"I know. I've got you," he said as her hands fisted in his hair. He was pretty sure there were a few casualties as she buried her face in his neck to muffle her cry. She tightened around his fingers, her body trembling in his arms.

Grace's grip in his hair slackened, and she rested her head on his shoulder as she attempted to catch her breath. Her fingers moved through the hair at the back of his neck, slowly and lazily making a circular motion.

Jax pressed his lips to her shoulder and placed a warm opened-mouthed kiss against her skin.

"That was nice," she said after a moment.

Jax pulled back so he could look at her. "Excuse me? Nice?"

"What's wrong with nice?" Grace asked, unable to keep her lips from quirking up.

"Oh, so this is funny to you?" he asked, trying to stay

serious. It was really difficult to do that when her eyes were lighting up and she was chewing on her lip to keep from laughing.

"*You're* funny to me."

"Well, prepare yourself, Princess, 'cause I'm about to show you just how not funny I can be." He began to make his way out of the water, Grace's arms and legs still wrapped around him. He palmed her bottom as he made it to dry ground and walked them back up to the house.

Flat surface. He needed a flat surface like ten seconds ago.

He spun around the yard while Grace started nibbling on his neck. He spotted his truck and made a beeline for it.

Desperate times and all.

Jax's house couldn't be seen from the street, there were too many trees sheltering the view, and his truck was parked at such an angle that no one randomly coming down the river would be able to see them, either. He just prayed no one was going to show up in the next ten, okay, twenty minutes.

"Stay here for a second," he said, popping the hitch and sitting her down on it. He disentangled himself from her arms and legs before he ran around to the cab of his truck and opened the door.

Nothing, there was *nothing* to lay her out on.

"Hey, Jax," Grace called out.

"Yes?" he said, looking under the seats.

"There are blankets in the back of my car."

"Why didn't you say anything before?" he said, slamming his door shut and running over to her car.

He grabbed both and came back over to her. He hopped up on the hitch and stood up in the back of the truck. He held on to two of the corners of the first blanket, popping it up in the air and letting it float down to the floor. He repeated the same process with the second, stacking them on top of each other so that there was a little extra padding.

When he turned back to Grace she was grinning at him.

"A little anxious, are we?"

"You have no idea," he said, dropping down to his knees beside her. "Come here." He leaned toward her, grabbing her head in his hands and kissing her.

She pulled back still grinning and scrambled back toward the blankets, giving him an awesome view in the process. The second she was flat on her back he was straddling her legs and working the lace down her thighs. And then he stopped when he realized exactly what he didn't have on him.

"Shit," he said, resting his face in the bend of her neck. "I don't have a condom."

He was going to cry. He was actually going to start weeping at any moment.

"I do," Grace said in his ear.

He pulled back and looked down at her. She was grinning up at him with the sexiest smile as she reached in and pulled not one but *two* condoms out of the cup of her bra.

"I'm beginning to think you came over here with these nefarious intentions in mind," he said as he grabbed the condoms from her hand.

"I have absolutely no idea what you're talking about."

"Liar."

"Scoundrel."

He kissed her as he went back to working the lace down her thighs. Then he was unhooking her bra and she was pushing the wet fabric of his boxer briefs down his thighs. He had the condom on in record speed and then he was inside of her, both of them moving together. She knew his body. Knew what he wanted, and when he wanted it. She knew just what to do at exactly the right moment. And he knew her body just as well. Knew where to touch her, what speed, what movement would send her flying over the edge.

Grace bent her knees, placing her feet on either side of Jax's hips, her nails digging into his lower back. She was saying his name and other things fairly incoherently and then she arched up into him, her body contracting around him. And that was it. All of it, *everything* set him off as he continued to move in her. He came, hard, and collapsed onto her.

"That was perfect," Grace said a moment later, her hands moving up and down his spine.

"It wasn't just *nice*?" he asked, propping himself on his elbows and looking down at her.

"No." She laughed, shaking her head. "But you know what would be nice?"

"What?" he asked.

"Doing that again."

"And again, and again, and again," he said, right before he covered her mouth with his.

Chapter Fourteen

Small Minds vs. Big Hearts

Grace had been so busy with the café and Jax that she hadn't really seen anyone, especially Preston. She hadn't had any quality time with him for weeks. So on Friday, she packed them both a lunch and headed over to his office.

Preston and his father worked out of an old red Victorian house that had been converted into offices. The top floor was entirely the Matthews Law Firm. Benjamin Matthews opened the firm twenty years ago, and it had been only him practicing the law out of the office until Preston graduated last year. With Preston on board, Mr. Matthews wasn't working himself into the pavement anymore.

"Knock, knock," Grace said, tapping on the door frame.

Preston looked up and dropped his pen on the stack of papers he was going over.

"Why if it isn't the elusive Grace King," he said, leaning back in his chair. "I didn't think you made public appearances without a week's notice these days."

"I know I'm horrible, but I brought a peace offering." Grace held up a bag of food.

"Do you have the roasted chicken sandwich that's covered

in gouda, bacon, and avocado in there?" he asked, narrowing his eyes at the bag.

"Yes."

"Peach cobbler?"

"Yes."

"Dr Pepper?"

"Yes." She grinned. "What do you think this is? My first rodeo?"

"All right, you're forgiven," Preston said, stacking up his papers and moving them to the side of his desk.

"Well, that didn't take much." Grace sat down in a chair across from him.

"You know I'm pretty forgiving when it comes to your peach cobbler. Besides, I haven't ventured out into the land of the living that much these days, either."

"Oh." Grace grinned. "So, I'm not the only one who's happily coupled up."

"Nope," he said, giving her a very uncharacteristic shy smile. Which caught her off guard because Preston didn't do shy. He was Mr. Confidence.

"What's with that look?" Grace asked, pulling out his sandwich and handing it to him.

"Nothing." He shrugged. He put the sandwich down before he unwrapped the bright orange wax paper.

"Preston, fess up." Grace grabbed her own sandwich and then pulled out the two cans of soda at the bottom.

He was still staring down at his sandwich when she put the can in front of him.

"It's different with Baxter," Preston finally said, looking up at her. "I know it hasn't been that long, but I could see myself spending the rest of my life with him."

"Why do you look so somber about it?"

"This is a small town, Grace."

"With small minds," she finished.

"Not everyone is like my family. Not everyone is as accepting as my parents and my brother and sister."

It was true. When Preston had come out to his family, none of them turned their back on him. They'd all been completely accepting of him. It hadn't changed their opinions of him in the slightest.

"Baxter hasn't told anyone in his family," Preston continued. "There would be a huge fallout if everything became public knowledge."

"With his family?"

"With everyone. Not just on his part, but mine, too. Most of the people here would look at me like I was a different person."

"You told Jax," Grace said. "He didn't care. He doesn't see you as any less of a person."

"Yes, but Jax is different. He actually likes me now *because* he knows the truth and that I've never been interested in you as anything other than a friend. And besides, Jax is a good guy." Preston took a bite of his sandwich.

"Jax picked up on the whole you and Baxter thing," Grace said.

"He did?" Preston asked as he swallowed his bite hard. "When?"

"A couple of weeks ago."

"Do the other guys know?"

"He said he's not sure. But he was sure of the fact that none of them would care. That none of them would look at either of you any differently."

"Yeah, that's easy to say," Preston said, shaking his head.

"Preston." Grace reached across the table and grabbed his hand. "The people that matter, the people that care about you and love you, they aren't going to care."

"And what about the people who do care?"

"They aren't worth any of your time and energy. Look,

all I've known my whole life is people looking down their noses at me because of the mystery of my father. I'm not going to sit here and tell you that it doesn't still hurt when I hear someone call me a bastard. It does. But we have to find our worth in ourselves, not in what other people think."

"When did you get all wise?" Preston asked, giving her a small smile.

"When I got the man of my dreams. I finally have Jax in my life, and I wouldn't let somebody else's thoughts or opinions keep me from him. Not ever. So don't let anybody keep you from who you want to be with."

"Thanks, Gracie. And I'm really glad that Jax finally figured things out," Preston said as he started in on his sandwich again. "That whole unrequited love thing didn't really look good on you. But that sex glow you've been rocking lately really brings out your complexion."

"So we've moved on from the serious portion of this lunch?"

"Yes." He nodded, grabbing his soda and popping the top.

And for the next half hour Grace filled Preston in on life with Jax, baby Trevor, and the developments at the funeral home with the internal Missy Lee investigation. Apparently Tara's sleuthing skills were pretty good, because she'd found out that Missy was in fact dating someone new.

The mystery man hadn't been revealed yet, but he was someone Missy had gotten Botox for. The proof of Missy's recent foray with a needle didn't take all that much effort in detective work. No, her inability to move her eyebrows and her puffed-up mouth were proof enough for that. And the woman was now accessorizing with an ever-changing line of jewelry that was well into the thousands.

"Are my old eyes deceiving me, or is that Grace King?"

Grace turned around to see a man who would be the spitting image of Preston in about thirty years. Benjamin Matthews was just as tall and lean as Preston. He wasn't as muscular as Preston but he wasn't doing too bad for someone in his midfifties. He was still very trim, with a tanned face from all the hours spent sailing in the Gulf, and hair just as blond as Preston's. He was also the very definition of a Southern gentleman.

"Mr. Matthews," Grace said, hopping up from her chair and walking into his open arms.

"How are you, darling?" He wrapped his arms around her and gave her a kiss on the head.

"Good."

"You're looking good," he said, holding Grace out at arm's length and looking at her. "Preston tells me that you and a certain deputy have started dating."

"We have." Grace grinned.

"And I hear that Brendan and Paige had their baby."

"Yes, sir, Trevor was born on Wednesday morning. Paige, Brendan, and Trevor got to go home this morning."

"Good. I'm really glad to hear everyone is doing well. You and Jax should come over for dinner sometime. Diane would love to see you. Maybe if the two of you come, Preston will be more likely to bring Baxter by."

"Ooo-kay." Preston came around the desk. "On that note it's time for Grace to go. Let me walk you out," he said, his eyes going big and his mouth going firm.

"Bye, Mr. Matthews," Grace said as she was ushered out the door.

"They haven't met him yet?" Grace whispered as they descended the spiral staircase that ran through the middle of the house.

"They've met him, just not as, you know. We aren't exactly ready for things to be that out in the open yet."

"There isn't *any* out in the open," Grace said. "You guys are under a big rock. What aren't you telling me?"

"Grace, you know I've never introduced *anyone* to my

parents, let alone a guy. That's a pretty big step, a huge step. One that could quite possibly make it real."

"No more fantasy land."

"No more fantasy land," Preston repeated, shaking his head.

"Well, take it from a girl who knows," Grace said, patting his arm, "the reality is so much better than the dream."

And just like that everything turned into a nightmare. As Grace and Preston rounded the last flight of stairs, they froze at the top of the landing. Waiting by the front door was one of the very last people whom they would want overhearing their conversation. And judging by the smirk on his smug face, Hoyt Reynolds had heard everything.

"Oh, shit," Grace whispered.

"Whispering isn't going to help you," Hoyt said, shaking his head. "Sound travels down this staircase. I never would've figured you for a homo, Matthews. I always pegged you as a panty chaser. I thought for sure you at least scored with the slut over there. Just goes to show how wrong a person can be."

Grace couldn't breathe. This wasn't happening.

Was. Not. Happening.

"Luckily for me I don't give a shit as to what you think," Preston said.

Grace looked up at Preston, and his strong angular jaw was set. Unmoving. Unbudging.

"I'd be careful if I were you, Matthews, you never know when things might be repeated."

"What things?" Preston asked, shrugging his shoulders. "I have no idea what you're talking about."

"All right, pretty boy, if that's the way you want to play, then *fine*." Hoyt drew out the last word.

Preston didn't say anything as he slid his hand to the small of Grace's back and steered her down the last flight of stairs.

"Your *fantasy land* is about to end," Hoyt said as they passed him. "And it's going to end painfully."

When they walked outside, the hot, humid summer day hit Grace in the face. The sticky air didn't help with the nausea that was creeping into her stomach.

"Oh, God, Preston," she said, burying her head in her hands as they rounded the building where she'd parked. "Oh, God, oh, God, oh, God, oh, God."

"Grace," he said, softly grabbing her shoulders and turning her to him.

"This is all my fault." She looked up at him.

"Both of us were talking; this isn't your fault. Calm down."

"He knows Preston. He *knows*. He heard us. This isn't going to stay a secret. He's going to tell."

"I know," Preston said, nodding his head somberly. "I know."

"I'm an idiot."

"Stop it," he said forcefully. "And you're not an idiot. I'm pretty sure all of the damning evidence came out of my mouth, not yours." He pulled her into his arms.

"You stop it," she said, pushing at him.

"Stop what?" he asked, not letting her push him away.

"Comforting me. I'm the one who should be comforting you."

Preston just sighed, shaking his head. "We can't change it, Grace. We can only go on from here."

But as Grace pressed her face into Preston's chest she was scared because she had no idea where this whole thing was going to go on to.

* * *

It took Bethelda less than twenty-four hours to find out about Preston and report on it. Grace was pretty sure Hoyt had gone straight down to her office to inform her about it. Bethelda had probably spent a little bit of time trying to snoop out if Preston had been seen with any guy in particular. But he and Baxter were discrete about their relationship, so no one really knew about them.

Well, no one who would tell Bethelda anything about it anyway. But even with her lack of information, the article was pretty damning.

THE GRIM TRUTH

GOING DOWN IN FLAMES

It's horrible what this world is coming to. These days, people's idea of what's morally acceptable is really morally reprehensible. Mirabelle is a small, Southern community with conservative people. But our simple ways and good-natured ideals have been corrupted for years.

Immoral women are running around tempting every man that they see into their beds. Illegitimate offspring are accepted into the fold with our innocent children, like it's the norm, like their sinful nature is perfectly okay. Well, it isn't, and neither is the newest shameful indiscretion that has hit our town.

Flamboyant Peacock, formerly Mr. Big Shot, is coming out of his well-dressed closet. He rolled back into town a couple of months ago with Esquire attached to his name and now he thinks he's the end all be all and that he can get away with whatever he wants, and damn the consequences.

Well, *damn* might be the key word because our baby face lawyer appears to be naïve to the consequences of his lifestyle *choices*, and by that I mean that Mr. Peacock is a homosexual. And apparently there is more than one in our fair town, because Mr. Peacock has a boyfriend.

Who this boyfriend is, we aren't sure. And none of our sources can confirm anything at the moment. What they can confirm is that Mr. Peacock has been seen hanging around Little CoQuette, Deputy Ginger, and their immoral band of friends. So keep an eye out, because you never know what evil is hiding just around the corner, or in the closet as the case may be.

On Saturday night, Grace had just pulled into her apartment parking lot when her phone rang.

"You free tonight?" Preston asked.

"Yup. You want me to come over?"

Jax was working late. He was behind on paperwork and was going to spend a couple hours at the sheriff's office, so her evening was wide open.

"No. I want to go out. Unlike some people, I refuse to hide."

"Oh, no. What happened?"

"Baxter said he wants to lay low for a little while. I told him that's perfectly fine, but he's going to be by himself while he does it."

"Preston." Grace said his name softly as she closed her eyes and shook her head.

"No, none of that. There will be none of the 'oh, let's pity poor outted Preston.' Not tonight, not ever."

"Okay, what do you want to do?"

"Dinner and then drinks at Shep's. I'm calling Harper next. You call Mel."

An hour later they were all sitting around a table at the

Floppy Flounder. There were a few not so covert stares in their direction. But Preston didn't even bat an eye. Maybe because they were all too busy laughing their asses off at Harper who was telling a rather entertaining story about her latest blind date.

She'd been set up with a friend of her cousin Janelle's boyfriend. He lived in Thomasville, Georgia, so they'd met up at a restaurant in Tallahassee because it was about half-way for both of them.

"So I get to the restaurant and he's sitting at the bar, two drinks in, and flirting with this waitress who looked to be about twenty."

"Oh," Grace said, shaking her head. "That's never good."

"No, it's not. Especially when he's thirty-five." Harper frowned.

"I thought Janelle said he was twenty-five," Mel said.

"I thought so, too," Harper said darkly. "She also failed to mention that he's recently divorced."

"Oh, jeez," Grace said.

"How recent?" Preston asked.

"The papers were signed last week." Harper reached for her drink.

"Seriously?" Mel asked.

"He apparently wants to get back in the game before he loses all of his."

"Oh, dear," Preston said before he took a bite of his hamburger.

"He also told me I had a *banging* body. He just loves a girl with curves. Apparently his ex-wife was a stick figure, and one of the reasons they got divorced was because she didn't want to have kids for fear of getting fat. He was a pretty big fan of my birthing hips, though."

"He did *not* say you have birthing hips?" Mel said, out-raged as she took another bite of her fried oyster salad.

"He sure did."

"I can't believe he talked about kids on the first date," Grace said.

"I can't, either, and if talking to him wasn't headache inducing enough, he reeked of cologne. His clothes were saturated in enough of it to choke a horse." She held up her hand in a wait-for-it gesture. "And he was wearing a button-down shirt that was unbuttoned to the middle of his sternum. He had enough chest hair sticking out to recarpet my apartment."

"Gross." Mel and Grace flinched in unison.

Grace wasn't completely opposed to chest hair. Jax had a smattering of it and she found it totally sexy. Well, she found *him* totally sexy.

"He also wore a thick gold chain. And every time he moved it ran through his chest hair." Harper shuddered. "At one point he leaned over and multiple hairs were caught in the links, which then fell in his food."

"Oh, my God," Mel said horrified while Preston and Grace promptly burst out laughing.

"So when's the next date?" Preston grinned as he swirled a fry in his ketchup and popped it into his mouth.

"When hell freezes over," Harper said, glaring at Preston.

"Why does your cousin hate you?" Grace asked.

"That is a very good question. I think it might have to do with me putting frogs in her bed when we were little."

"So she thought she'd send you a couple frogs now?" Mel asked.

"Wow, payback really is a bitch," Preston said.

"No kidding," Harper said, taking a long and healthy sip of her beer.

"You know what else is a bitch?" someone said from behind Grace.

Grace froze, her entire body winding up with tension.

She didn't need to turn to see that Chad was standing next to the table.

"Prissy little queers?" someone else asked.

Oh, fantastic. Judson was here, too.

"No one wants to look at you or be forced to listen to you flap your mouths, so why don't you two leave," Harper said with the 'you are below me' eyebrow raise she did so well.

"No one asked you, heifer," Chad said.

"And no one gives a shit as to what you think, either." Grace turned to look at him.

"Oh, Grace, I'd be careful if I were you. Your deputy isn't here to protect you," Chad said, reaching out and stroking her cheek.

Preston was on his feet in a second, standing in between Grace and Chad. Everyone in the restaurant was looking at them in silent fascination.

"Get away from her," Preston said.

"Oh, look, he's getting his fancy feathers all in a flap." Chad sneered.

"You're a disgusting disgrace to this town, Matthews," Judson said right before he spit in Preston's face.

There was a collective gasp from everyone in the room, but Preston didn't even flinch.

"Excuse me." Stacey Frampton came to the group. "You guys are going to need to leave. As it turns out, disgusting disgraces aren't welcome here."

"You see that," Judson said, looking at Preston. "You're not welcome."

"I wasn't talking to Preston," Stacey said, shaking her head. "I was referring to you and Chad. Leave. Now."

"Are you serious?" Chad asked, looking down at Stacey.

She was at least a foot shorter than him, but she didn't move.

"Yes, I'm serious. We have a very different view of

what's disgusting, Chad, and you and Judson here are at the top of the list of things that turn my stomach."

"You're not the owner. You can't kick us out," Judson said. "And I'd like a burger and fries. Now." He snapped his fingers her face.

Preston reached back behind him and grabbed the other half of his burger, and then he dropped it at Judson's feet. Ketchup and mustard splattered out across the floor and landed on Judson's boots.

"There you go," Stacey said. "Would you like a doggy bag to take it with you?"

Judson made a move like he was going to punch Preston, but all of a sudden Burley Adams was standing behind Judson, grabbing his fist and hauling him backward.

Judson was a fairly built guy, six foot and a couple of inches. But he looked more than insubstantial next to Burley Adams, who was about six foot eight and one of the biggest, beefiest men that Grace had ever laid eyes on.

"It's time for you to go," Burley said.

"What the hell are you doing? Get your hands off me." Judson struggled in Mr. Adams's firm grip.

"I don't think so. Because you see that woman over there?" Burley asked, pointing to Mrs. McFarlane behind the bar. "See, she *is* the proprietor of this establishment. And she wants you out of here. And if you know what's good for you, you'll leave as well, Chad. Otherwise we will call the authorities down here." Mr. Adams let go of Judson. "Because here's the thing, Preston is ten times the man that the two of you are put together."

"Yeah," Wallace Boone said, standing up from his table. "You boys should be ashamed of yourselves."

"Disturbing people while they're minding their own business." Eighty-year-old Mrs. Banners shook her gray-haired head.

"I respect him a hell of a lot more than either of you," Mr. Banners said as he gave both Judson and Chad the evil eye. "Stupid little jerks, the both of you."

Everyone else in the room just nodded their heads as they glared at Chad and Judson.

"And neither of you are welcome here ever again," Mrs. McFarlane said, pointing toward the door. "And as far as I'm concerned, any of the rest of you that share the same small-minded views as these two can get out of my restaurant as well."

Chad and Judson gave Preston one last long look before they turned and walked out the door.

"Here you go, son," Mr. Adams said, handing Preston his handkerchief. Preston took it and wiped at his face where Judson had spit at him. "Not everyone thinks the way those two idiots do. And I meant what I said. You're a better man than a lot of the people in this town. And if anyone ever pulls a stunt like that again, you're going to have more than just me at your back."

"I'll be there," Wallace said.

"Me, too." Stacey nodded. "You want another burger?"

"It's on the house," Mrs. McFarlane said. "Damn, was it ever worth it to see all that food fly across the floor."

"Let me clean this up and I'll be right back with your food," Stacey said as she grabbed a dirty plate from the table behind them.

"I'll get that." Preston made a move to bend down.

"Oh, no you don't," Stacey said, shaking her head. "When Judson demanded food and snapped at me, he was lucky I didn't break a plate over his head. If anything I owe you for not getting charged with assault and battery."

"At least let me help you."

"Preston, sit down. I mean it," Stacey said, pointing to the table.

"What the hell just happened?" Preston asked, sitting down and looking more than a little shell-shocked.

"I think some of the people of this town just accepted you for who you are," Grace said, reaching across the table and patting Preston's hand.

"I guess so." He nodded, looking touched.

* * *

Grace had called Jax and told him about the article that Bethelda had written. She also told him that she was going out with Preston, Mel, and Harper for dinner and drinks. Preston picked Grace up at her apartment, so Jax said he would come and get her at the Sleepy Sheep when he finished at the office. He'd had a pretty good day, busy, but good. He was looking forward to a beer before he took Grace home. He was also looking forward to spending all day Sunday with her.

He'd stopped by his house to change and was at the Sleepy Sheep just before ten. As he made his way to the bar he noticed the Red Sox playing on the TV. Normally he would've shaken his head at it, but something was going on that was causing Grace to lean across the counter. Her perfect bottom in the air as she tried to get a better look at the screen.

"Yes. Go. Go. Go," she screamed.

He also didn't mind her saying those things. Though he did prefer it when she screamed *yes* in bed, and under him.

"Whoop." She pumped her fist in the air as a Red Sox player ran across home plate. She turned to Bennett and smacked both of his hands that were in the air.

As her hands came down her head turned and her eyes landed on Jax.

"Hey, baby," she said as her mouth broke out into a grin and she slid off the stool. "My boys are killing it up there." She nodded to the screen as she walked toward him.

"As long as they aren't *killing it* against the Yankees, I'm okay with that. And I thought that I was your boy," he said, stepping into her.

"You're my man," she whispered as she grabbed the front of his shirt and pulled him down to her. She kissed him slowly, her tongue running across his, the faint taste of beer lingering when she pulled back.

"I can handle that." He ran his palms up her arms to her elbows. "You having a good night?"

"Yeah," she said, biting the corner of her lip nervously. "There was a small incident at dinner."

"What kind of incident?"

"The Chad and Judson kind."

Grace didn't even wait for a response before she launched into the story. When she got to the part where Chad had touched her, Jax stopped breathing. When she told him that Judson had spit in Preston's face, the very last of Jax's good mood was gone.

"Why didn't you call me?" he asked when she finished.

"Because there was nothing you could do about it. Besides, there were enough people there that were on his side," she said, smiling at him. And then she proceeded to tell him about how all of the people at the restaurant came to Preston's defense.

"Really?" he asked, looking over at Preston who was currently talking to Shep.

"It was amazing, Jax."

"It sounds like it."

"Come on." She beamed, pulling him toward the bar. "Let's get one more drink and then go home."

"Will do," he said, following her as his good mood magically started to come back.

* * *

"Baby, you have to wake up."

"No," Grace moaned into her pillow. "Sleep. No work today. Remember?"

They'd wound up staying at Shep's until midnight, Jax only having one beer, Grace having one too many.

Okay, maybe four too many.

Her head was pounding and her eyes refused to open.

"Grace," Jax said, trying to roll her over, "wake up."

"What time is it?" she asked, feeling like she'd only had her eyes closed for a few minutes.

"Almost three."

Okay, so she'd had them closed for less than two hours. Really, at this point it was the same difference.

Why did Jax suddenly hate her? He'd seemed like he'd been a pretty big fan of hers when they'd gotten home from the bar and rolled around for a good hour before they'd passed out.

"Why? Why are you waking me up? Why are you so mean to me?"

"Grace, something happened," he said softly.

Grace opened her eyes and rolled over so she could see Jax. The dim light from the hallway lit up the grim expression on his face.

"What happened?" she asked, trying to speak around her heart, which was suddenly lodged up around her throat.

"Preston is in the hospital. Someone attacked him."

Chapter Fifteen

Revenge

What?" Grace asked, sitting up in a panic.

"He stayed at the Sleepy Sheep until closing, and someone jumped him when he left. Shep found him. I'm going down there to talk to Preston."

"I'm coming with you," she said, throwing off the blankets.

Jax stood up and held out his hands for her to grab. When he pulled her up, he pulled her into him. He didn't say anything. He just held her as he pressed his lips to her temple and rubbed his hands up and down her back.

"I don't understand people," Grace said against his chest.

"I don't, either. I'm going to do everything that I can to figure this out, Grace."

"I know," she said as she kissed his jaw.

They pulled apart and got dressed. They were out the door ten minutes later. When they got to the hospital they found Shep sitting in a chair in the waiting room, his long legs stretched out in front of him. Mr. Matthews was pacing back and forth, running his hands through his thoroughly tousled blond hair.

"Grace," Mr. Matthews said when he saw her. He crossed the room and pulled her into his arms.

"How bad is it?" she asked.

"The doctors are still looking at him. I haven't seen him yet. But...but Shep said it was pretty bad."

Grace pulled back from Mr. Matthews and looked at Shep.

"He was barely conscious when I found him," Shep said sadly.

"Oh, God," Grace whispered. "Where's Mrs. Matthews?"

"In Tuscaloosa visiting her sister. I don't want to call her until I have something to tell her. I just...I just don't know what to do," he said helplessly. "Why would anyone do this? It just doesn't make sense. Preston didn't deserve this; no one does."

"I know," Grace said sadly.

"Who responded to the call?" Jax asked.

"Deputy Hough," Shep said.

"Where is he?" Jax asked, looking around.

"He had to make a call. He said he'd take Preston's statement when he was done getting checked out. So we're just waiting," Mr. Matthews told Jax.

It was another thirty minutes before Dr. Flint came out to tell them about Preston. He had a concussion, four cracked ribs, a black eye, and his left wrist was fractured. Not to mention that his body was covered in cuts and bruises.

While Mr. Matthews went to see Preston, Jax and Deputy Hough talked to Dr. Flint to get an official statement. Then they went to talk to Preston. About ten minutes later Jax, Deputy Hough, and Mr. Matthews came back down the hallway.

"Can I go see him?" Grace asked Mr. Matthews.

"Yes, he's in room one twenty-four. I need to go call Diane," Mr. Matthews, said pulling out his phone and walking toward the doors that led out of the emergency room.

"I'm going to go in to work today," Jax told Grace.

"I figured as much." Grace reached up, touching his cheek affectionately. She knew her man. He was determined to figure out who did this.

"I'll take Grace back," Shep said.

"Thanks," Jax said to Shep. "Roy and I are going to go down and see if we can find anything at the Sheep." He turned back to Grace and kissed her. When he pulled back he tucked a piece of her hair behind her ear. "He looks pretty bad, Grace. Prepare yourself."

"I will. I'll see you later," she said before she turned and walked down the hallway.

She pushed open the door to a dark room. There was a dim light coming from a lamp in the corner; it wasn't a lot but it was enough to show just how bad Preston's injuries were. His right eye was swollen shut, he had a split lip, a gash above his left eyebrow, and bruises across his cheeks and jaw.

"Grace," he rasped out.

"Hey, no talking." She came up to his bed.

"My voice box is fine," he said as his one good eye looked up at her.

"Yeah, but your ribs aren't," she said, fighting desperately to not start sobbing. It didn't work, her voice caught anyway.

"Hey, no crying." He winced as he reached out for her.

"Preston, stop moving," Grace said as she slid her hand into his.

"I'm fine, Gracie." His voice cracked around the lie. He closed his eyes as tears streamed out of both his eyes and his hand tightened around hers.

Fine? *Fine?* He was broken. And someone had done this to him. Some ignorant, evil, twisted person had hurt him, just because he was different.

God, it was such bullshit.

Grace reached up and pushed his hair back off his forehead. There was blood matted in the blond locks.

"I'm so sorry, Preston," she whispered. "You didn't deserve for this to happen to you."

Preston opened his eye again as the tears continued to stream down his face.

"Jax said he's going to do everything he can to figure this out. And I know he will. He's going to get whoever hurt you."

Preston didn't say anything. He just swallowed hard and nodded. She leaned down and pressed her lips to his forehead.

"I love you, Preston, for all that you are." She sat with him for a couple more minutes, gently stroking his hair back. He closed his eyes and before he fell asleep Grace said good-bye. "I have to go," she told him. "Besides you need to rest. I'll come see you later today."

"All right," he said, not opening his eyes.

Grace gave him one last kiss on the forehead before she headed out of the room. She shut the door softly, and when she turned she ran smack into Baxter. He reached out for her shoulders and steadied her.

"Is he okay?" he asked, looking like he was barely holding himself together.

Grace shook her head, the tears falling freely again. "They broke him, Baxter."

Baxter looked at the door for a second before he closed his eyes, defeated. "I messed up," he said, opening his eyes again. He was crying now, too. "I messed up royally. I let my fear get in the way of everything."

"It isn't too late. Fix it."

"What if I can't? What if he won't forgive me?"

"He loves you and love can forgive a lot of things," Grace said.

"Yeah?" he asked, reaching up to wipe at his eyes.

"Yeah." She nodded before she reached up and hugged him hard. He hugged her back and they stood silently for a second. When they let go, Baxter took a fortifying breath and walked into the hospital room.

* * *

Preston had been lucid when Jax talked to him. He remembered walking out of the bar, heading toward his car, and then being hit over the head. He hadn't been able to make out any faces, but he was pretty sure it was two guys and that he'd been beaten with something that wasn't a fist. He thought they used something smaller than a bat but still pretty damn hard. And he remembered that it had glowed slightly in the dark, like maybe it had been white.

Jax and Roy came up with nothing at the Sleepy Sheep. There wasn't anything left behind in the parking lot that looked like it could've been used as a weapon.

Whoever had hurt Preston had stolen his wallet. But Jax suspected that whoever had done it had just wanted to make it look like a mugging. There was no need to beat someone senseless when you already had what you wanted. No, Jax was pretty sure this was a hate crime.

And he knew exactly who was on top of his list.

After the incident at the restaurant, Jax was going to look into Chad and Judson. Same with Hoyt, as he'd started this whole mess by outing Preston to Bethelda, and subsequently the whole town. Grace had told Jax about Hoyt's parting words in the stairwell. Yeah, that left him pretty damn suspicious, too.

Jax went home to change into his uniform. He found Grace just getting out of the shower. She had a towel wrapped around her waist and another in her hair.

"Hey, baby," he said, pulling her into his arms. He reached up and grabbed the towel from her hair and threw it on the bed. He held her head in his hands, his fingers sliding into her wet hair, and kissed her. "You have no idea how much I wish I could spend the day with you." He rested his forehead against hers.

"I have a pretty good idea," she said, running her hands up his chest.

"What are your plans today?"

"I'm going to go over and see Brendan and Paige and the baby, then go back to the hospital to sit with Preston. Call me when you're done."

"Will do," he said, holding her to him for just a minute longer. But he really didn't want to let her go. Not now, not ever.

* * *

Chad lived over on the north side of town, in a small house about the size of the one that Jax rented. It was in about the same condition, too, maintained but not anything impressive. Chad's truck was parked outside when Jax pulled into the driveway. He went up the porch steps and knocked, waiting for a minute before the door opened.

Chad's mouth turned up in that arrogant, smarmy way of his as he looked out the screen door.

"Can I help you?"

"Just need to ask you a few questions," Jax said.

Chad merely raised his eyebrows.

"Where were you last night?"

"Why? Did something unfortunate happen?"

"Preston Matthews was attacked, and after your public display of hatred at the Floppy Flounder, you're a suspect."

"So something happened to the queer? I wouldn't say that's unfortunate. I'd say that's an act of righteous justice. But I wasn't involved."

"Where were you?" Jax repeated.

"With my girlfriend. Here, at my house."

"I'm going to need to get her name."

"Missy Lee," she said, coming to the door.

Not a lot of things shocked Jax, but this sure as hell did. Missy Lee was old enough to be Chad's mother. She was wearing one of Chad's shirts and nothing else.

Okay, this was highly disturbing on *soo* many levels. Jax tried not to let his surprise and discomfort at the situation show on his face.

"How long have you been here?"

"Since eleven o'clock last night," she said.

"And neither of you left?"

"Nope." Chad grinned. "We were busy all night. Is there anything else I can help you with?" Chad asked.

"I'll let you know," Jax said.

"I can't wait." Chad took a step back and slammed the door.

God Jax hated that guy. But if Chad had been with Missy all night, then he hadn't attacked Preston, and Jax needed to move on. Jax turned around and walked to his truck, but he slowed as he passed Chad's truck.

Chad worked for Marlin Yance Construction, the same company Bennett worked for. The bed of the truck had a couple supplies in it, a few wooden beams, and some PVC pipe, nothing that anybody would really worry about getting stolen. Chad's tools were most likely locked up in the metal box at the back of the bed, that or in his truck.

Jax didn't see anything suspicious, but that PVC pipe sure did give him an idea. Judson Cocker worked with the stuff, too, and it would've fit the description of a possible weapon Preston described.

When Jax showed up to Judson's apartment, he didn't see Judson's truck anywhere in the parking lot. There was no point in waiting around when Jax had no idea when Judson would be back. Jax headed out for Hoyt's place, but as he was driving he spotted Judson's truck in front of the Mira-belle Methodist church.

What a hypocrite.

Jax parked and got out. He looked into the back of the truck and found exactly what he was looking for.

There was a stack of PVC pipes. Jax leaned over to get a better look and found a red smear on the end of one.

* * *

Judson's truck was seized, and he was brought into the sher-iff's office. He didn't have an alibi. He said he'd been asleep and claimed that someone had to have planted the bloody PVC pipe in his truck. He hadn't been the one to do that to Preston, he had no idea who had, and he didn't really care. He refused to say anything else.

But it didn't matter. The searching of Judson's truck proved to be very helpful. And they found plenty of other incriminat-ing evidence, and for more than just Preston's attack.

A red flyer with the Bethelda article that had been attached to Grace's car was shoved between a backseat cush-ion, and the same black car chalk that had been used to write on her windshield was in the glove compartment. And then there was that blessed pipe.

Normally it took time to get DNA results back from the lab, but Sheriff Dawson pulled some strings to get this test moved to the top of the pile. A hate crime where somebody was beaten was a pretty big deal in comparison to other crimes.

The results came back within twenty-four hours. It was Preston's blood, along with some of his hair. And the only fingerprints found on the PVC pipe were Judson's. To top it all off, Preston's blood was found on the floor of Judson's truck. So his story of someone stealing the pipe, beating

Preston, and then putting it back wasn't enough to explain how it got into his locked truck.

The problem was, Preston was pretty sure two guys had attacked him, and the only other suspect was Hoyt Reynolds. When Neal Sanders brought Hoyt in to talk, Hoyt had pointed every single finger he had at Judson.

Hoyt said that Judson had always had a problem with Grace. He said that she'd turned Judson down in high school and many times after that. Judson had always been real bitter about it, too. When Grace had started her relationship with Jax, Judson had gone into a rage. But Hoyt hadn't known about the flyers, though it didn't surprise him.

Hoyt had known how upset Judson was after the altercation with Preston at the Floppy Flounder. Judson had been humiliated. Hoyt had never thought that Judson would go so far to get revenge against Preston, but apparently, he said, you sometimes just didn't know a person.

Jax wasn't in the room when they questioned Hoyt, but he and Baxter were on the other side of the glass and they heard everything Hoyt said.

"He's full of shit," Jax told Baxter. "He's just like his father."

"I know," Baxter said, furious. "I bet you anything that son-of-a-bitch attacked Preston."

Jax was pretty impressed that Baxter hadn't hit someone at this point. If it had been Grace that had been hurt, Jax would've gone crazy. There would've been no rational thought at all.

It had been two days since Preston's attack and he was doing better. He was home from the hospital and Baxter was currently staying with him. Indefinitely.

Baxter had no more reservations about making his relationship with Preston public. He didn't care what anyone thought anymore. But as it turned out, when he came out to his family, they said they'd always known. They told him it hadn't changed anything before, and it most definitely changed nothing now.

"The only evidence we have points to Judson," Jax told Baxter as they stared through the glass and into Hoyt's smug face.

"I can't wait to see how Judson's going to take it when he finds out his friend completely ratted him out," Baxter said.

"Oh, it's going to be interesting," Jax agreed.

* * *

And interesting it was.

"That piece of shit framed me," Judson roared. "I had nothing to do with this. Hoyt is the one that's always had a problem with Grace."

"Why?" Jax asked.

"You'd have to ask him." Judson snarled.

"So he didn't help you out with any of this?" Jax asked.

"I didn't do any of it," Judson said.

"It sounds to me like Hoyt is who you should be investigating, not my client who's innocent," Burt Norwood said. Burt was Judson's lawyer, and he was just as slimy as Judson.

"Right, I understand." Jax nodded. "But the thing is, all the evidence we have points to you, Judson, and nothing points to Hoyt. So if you were to confess and tell us about Hoyt's part in all of this..." Jax trailed off.

"I. Didn't. Do. It," Judson repeated.

And that was all Judson said through the rest of questioning. So he was the only one brought up on charges for attacking Preston and harassing Grace. He was released on bail, and Judge Mendelson ordered that Judson had to stay in Atticus County while awaiting trial.

* * *

Grace and Lula Mae were catering a dinner for Keith Reynolds. Hoyt's father was the Atticus County school superintendent, but up until about three and a half years ago he'd been the principal of Mirabelle High School. He had worked in the school district for twenty-five years, and a commemoration dinner to honor him was scheduled for Thursday.

Mel had been one of the teachers put in charge of the event, and she hired the café to cater. Grace wasn't enthusiastic about doing anything for Keith Reynolds, but she'd do anything for Mel.

"I'm not okay with this," Jax had told her the night before. "I don't want you anywhere near that worthless piece of garbage. I know Hoyt was involved in the attack on Preston, and Judson said that Hoyt is the one who always had a problem with you. Which means Hoyt probably helped with what happened to your car. He's a loose cannon, Grace, and he's capable of hurting you."

"In a room full of people? Come on, Jax, be reasonable. This dinner is tomorrow. I can't bail out on Mel. She's counting on me and Lula Mae."

"Fine. Cook the food but get somebody else to serve it."

"Jax, I'm not going to do that, so stop it. I'm going to be fine," she'd said, kissing him on the cheek.

"I still don't like this." He'd huffed.

And because he didn't like it so much, he was going to be at the banquet when he got off work to play bodyguard. Not that Grace minded, because she always liked to have Jax around. And if she was honest with herself, she really didn't feel comfortable being in a room with Hoyt or anyone in his family.

Mr. Reynolds was very much like his son with his thick blond hair, tall and lean stature, and arrogant as all get out.

He'd always been the biggest prick to Brendan, and Grace had no forgiveness for anyone who messed with her family.

Mr. Reynolds had always been fairly indifferent to Grace, but then again she'd never really done anything to garner the attention of the principal. She stayed out of trouble. Well, except for the rumors that had been spread about her. Grace wasn't sure if Mr. Reynolds had ever heard the rumors, but if he had, he'd never involved himself in such matters.

Dolores Reynolds, Mr. Reynolds's wife, was a grade-A bitch. She'd pretty much looked down her nose at most of the people in Mirabelle ever since she moved there. She'd never been particularly friendly to anyone. Whenever Grace saw her, the woman always had an unpleasant sneer on her face, kind of like she smelled something particularly foul. So that was either the expression the woman always had, or was just the expression she had when Grace was around.

Grace and Lula Mae spent most of the week in the kitchen preparing the food for the dinner, while Callie Armstrong and Rebecca Parks worked the front of the café. By four o'clock on Thursday, they had Lula Mae's SUV and the little space in Grace's Bug loaded up, and were heading over to the community center.

The dinner was for over one hundred guests. White linens covered the tables and unlit tea lights floated in clear round globes at the center. Panky was arranging blue and yellow flowers at the podium at the back of the room.

"I'm almost done and then I'm all yours," Panky called out to them as she snipped the end off a sprig of greenery.

"No rush," Lula Mae said. "We have to set up first anyways. We're going to need your help to dish stuff out tonight."

"Now you know if you want someone to dish stuff out you would need Pinky here, as the woman has no filter on that mouth of hers."

"Then how about you do it with a spoon?" Lula Mae asked.

"Now that I can do."

Mel showed up just after five with all the beer and wine. She didn't get to enjoy the night. Nope, she was the bartender. That's what happened when you were one of the lowest men, or women in this case, on the totem pole. And she hadn't been the only one forced into free service. Other teachers were in charge of various tasks for the night, all of them recent hires. They weren't the ones being honored, so what did it matter if they didn't get to sit down and eat their dinner? It didn't.

Mel wasn't the biggest fan of Superintendent Reynolds, either. For the last year she'd been trying to do a hands-on project to get the kids more excited about math. She wanted to show them how math could be used to build things.

Mr. Reynolds wouldn't even take the time to meet with her, sending her an e-mail stating there wasn't enough room in the budget. He refused to meet with her so she could show him her plan of paying for it. He didn't have the time. He was kicking off his reelection campaign, so what he apparently did have the time and budget for was a dinner celebrating him.

Asshole.

The guests started rolling in just before six. Grace was relighting one of the flames under the chafing dishes when she felt a prickling at the back of her neck. She looked up to find Hoyt Reynolds staring at her, his eyes full of hatred as he sipped his beer.

"I don't like the way he's looking at you," Lula Mae whispered in Grace's ear as she set a pan of lemon, basil, and goat cheese chicken in one of the already warmed chafing dishes.

"Don't worry about it," Grace said, moving on to the next dish.

Grace didn't want to give Hoyt any credit for his attempt at intimidating her.

"I wouldn't even be doing this if it wasn't for Mel," Lula Mae said under her breath. "Keith Reynolds deserves about as much honor as a horse's ass."

There was no love loss for Lula Mae toward the Reynolds family, either.

It was just after six o'clock when Mitch Bolinder, the principal of the high school, made his way up to the podium.

"I just want to welcome everyone here tonight," Mitch said, adjusting the end of his tie. "We are here to recognize a great man, a man who is an asset to our fine community. But first, let's eat."

The guests got up from their tables and filed down the food line. Grace, Lula Mae, Panky, and the English teacher, Mia Grant, served the food. The chatter echoed in the room, people laughing and carrying on as they dug into their food.

"This is just absolutely delicious," the music teacher, Karen Wilson, told Lula Mae as she came up for seconds.

"Why thanks, sugar," Lula Mae drawled as she scooped up some rosemary potatoes.

"How's that great-grandbaby of yours doing?" Karen asked.

"He's doing just fine."

"And Brendan and Paige?"

"All good, exhausted but good. Trevor has a set of lungs on him that could wake the dead." Lula Mae smiled. "So he's giving them a run for their money."

"Oh, I'll bet," Karen said before she moved on.

The line died down, and as Lula Mae and Panky took the empty dishes to the kitchen, Grace started to put out the desserts. She was just setting out a tray of her chocolate hazelnut mousse when an odd vibe went through the room. Grace looked up to see Judson Coker stumble up to the empty podium.

Oh, fantastic. He was drunk.

"This can't be good," Lula Mae said, coming up behind Grace.

Grace hadn't seen Judson since the incident at the restaurant. He'd just been released on bail the day before.

Judson leaned over and hit the top of the microphone with his palm, a dull thrum echoing through the speakers.

"So ya'll are here to honor Superintendent Keith Reynolds," he slurred. "An *upstanding* man, an *upstanding* husband, an *upstanding* father. Well why don't we give a nice, big round of applause to his backstabbing, conniving son who managed to get out of being punished for that little queer Preston Matthews's attack. Well done," Judson said, clapping his own hands together. "And while we're at it, why don't we recognize Keith Reynolds's other child, as she's currently here servicing all of you. But the King women's ability to service men is no secret to anyone. So why don't you come up here, Grace, and congratulate your *father*."

Everyone was silent and staring transfixed at Judson, everyone except for Mr. Bolinder, who was making his way toward the podium. He unplugged the microphone and turned to grab Judson's arm.

Grace's heart was pounding so hard in her throat she thought she was going to choke.

"No need to show me out," Judson shouted as he pulled his arm away. "I'm not making this up, either," he said as he made his way toward the door. "Keith Reynolds showed up in town and Grace King was born nine months later. Coincidence? I think not." Judson pointed to Grace. "So take a look at the bastard daughter of this man who y'all think is so great."

All eyes in the room turned to Grace, and she was lucky she didn't pass out.

Chapter Sixteen

The Truth

Jax had ten minutes left on his shift. He was parked and filling in the last of his paperwork. That day he had dealt with a guy exposing himself at the beach to a bunch of college girls, a group of drunk guys who were tailgating at the Piggly Wiggly and harassing people as they were coming and going from the store, and more speeding tourists than he could count, all of whom had given him a hard time. Apparently, forty-five miles per hour really meant sixty-five where they were from.

Jax wasn't sure how accurate any of his paperwork was as he was more than a little preoccupied. He was waiting for the clock to wind down so he could head over to the community center. Grace was there with that asshole, and he wanted to be there to make sure she was okay.

"Seventeen, what's your location?"

"Seventeen, at Mayfare and Seventh."

"Domestic disturbance at 4290 Partridge Road. Deputy needed on location."

This was going to turn out real well. That was his

parents' house. This was all he needed to deal with tonight. Why couldn't the call have come in ten minutes later?

Sherry Lynn was new to Mirabelle, so she had no idea that she was calling Jax to his parents' house, and as he didn't want to broadcast that to everyone on duty, he kept it to himself. He would've called for backup, but the other deputies on patrol were nowhere near him, and both of them were responding to other calls.

"Ten-four," he said, putting the truck in gear.

It took him less than two minutes to get to the house where he'd grown up. His grandmother had owned it so there was no mortgage to be paid every month, probably one of the few reasons Haldon Anderson was still there. If something was free, he was all about it. But the house didn't look the way it had when Jax's grandmother was alive.

The sun hadn't set yet, so all the disrepair was easy to see as Jax pulled into the driveway. Weeds had invaded the yard years ago, and it was going to take much more than a lawnmower to wage war against them. A rusted pickup truck sat abandoned on the side of the house, the driver's door hanging off the hinges and springs popping through the vinyl seats. Beer cans littered the front porch along with multiple ash trays that were filled with cigarette butts. The wooden planks on the porch sagged down to a dip that ran up to the front door. The mesh on the screen door was completely gone, yet the metal frame was still attached to the doorjamb, doing absolutely nothing to keep out the mosquitoes.

Jax cut the engine and got out of his truck. A loud smash and yelling greeted his ears.

"Fantastic," he mumbled as he made his way up the rotting front steps.

Before he even had the chance to knock, the front door swung open and Haldon Anderson stood in front of Jax. His brown hair was long and greasy and his jaw was covered in many days' worth of stubble. A gray T-shirt and dirty jeans hung off his wasted frame and he held a beer can in his hand.

"What do you want?" he sneered out the door.

"Someone called in a domestic disturbance."

"Probably that good for nothing busybody Connie Applewood. Why don't you mind your own damn business, you stupid bitch!" Haldon screamed. The smell of his beer and cigarette-soaked breath hit Jax like a punch in the face.

"How about you calm down," Jax said. "What's going on here?"

"Nothing that concerns you. Because nothing that concerns me concerns you. You get that? So why don't you just hop back into your little justice mobile and get the hell out of here?"

"Where's Mom?"

"What part of 'this doesn't concern you' don't you understand? I said get off my property. No one, and I repeat *no one,* gives a shit as to who you are, what you are, or what you do."

"I'm going to have to see her before I leave."

"Patty!" Haldon bellowed, not turning around. "Your worthless, piece of shit son wants to see you."

Patty came out into the hallway, her wispy red hair hanging around her pale, mousy face. Her green eyes, the exact same green as Jax's, were bloodshot and watery, and her mouth was in a grim line. She looked right through him, absolutely no emotion on her face when she saw him.

"You don't need to be here. Everything is just fine," she said in a hollow voice.

"Did he hurt you?"

"Your father has never laid a hand on me."

Well, that was a bold-faced lie. Jax had seen Haldon smack her around more times than he could count.

"Don't you go calling me his father. He's not my son.

He's not *anything* to me. He's not *anything* to anyone. Never has been, never will be. Do you understand that? You're *nothing*."

This wasn't the first time Jax had heard those words, and he certainly doubted it would be the last. Without fail, Haldon always ripped into his son.

Every. Single. Time.

"So like I said before, get the fuck off my property," Haldon said.

"Gladly. But you need to quiet down and stop bothering the neighbors."

"I don't care about the damn neighbors." He took a sip of his beer.

"I get it. You don't care about anyone or anything. But if you don't stop it, you're going to be not caring from the inside of a jail cell. So calm down," Jax said, looking at Haldon.

Haldon didn't say anything, just continued to glare. Jax knew that was probably all he was going to get out of his father, so he turned around to leave.

He didn't even make it off the front porch before the beer can pegged him in the back of the head. It was less than halfway full, but there was still enough cold beer in the can to spill down the back of his neck and soak into his shirt.

"Worthless piece of shit," Haldon said. "That girl you're screwing is going to figure that out soon and leave, and then you're going to be all alone, not caring about anything, either."

Jax didn't turn around, he wasn't going to do it, wasn't going to show that anything Haldon said affected him.

It was just too bad it did affect Jax, affected him more than even he knew.

* * *

Keith Reynolds was Grace's father?

He couldn't be. It just couldn't be right. She didn't believe it.

Grace turned to her grandmother and under the shell-shocked expression Grace saw the confirmation. It was in Lula Mae's eyes, right there, plain as day. Lula Mae had known that Keith Reynolds was her father.

Lula Mae grabbed for Grace's arm, but Grace pulled away shaking her head.

"You knew," she whispered.

"Gracie," Lula Mae pleaded.

"I have to get out of here," she said, going into the kitchen and grabbing her purse. She went out the side door and ran out of the community center as fast as she could.

Her grandmother had known who Grace's father was. All this time she'd known and never said a word. When Grace was fifteen she asked Lula Mae who her father was. She'd said she didn't know. She'd lied.

Did her grandfather know? Did Brendan? Were they all keeping this secret from her? Had they all known her father was Keith Reynolds?

And God, Hoyt was her brother. Just the very thought made her skin crawl. She was related to that jerk, too. Oh, how the gifts just kept on giving.

Grace couldn't say she'd wondered who her father was for twenty-four years. It probably hadn't been a conscious thought until she was three or four, but he'd been missing from her life for twenty-four years. Now she knew who he was, and she felt emptier than she had before.

People had always speculated that Grace's father was a married man, but now Grace knew it for a fact. And was it ever painful.

Grace held the memories of her mother near and dear to her heart. But this tarnished those memories. It made

Grace doubt her mother. Made her doubt *everything* from her childhood.

Grace wanted Jax. She needed him so desperately it was hard to breathe. She needed his arms around her. Needed to bury her face in his chest and hold on to something that was real. Hold on to the one person she was sure of. Because it sure as hell wasn't her mother, and it wasn't her grandmother for that matter, either.

Grace pulled off to the side of the road and dug around in her purse until she found her cell phone. She called Jax and waited through the rings, but he didn't pick up. She didn't trust herself not to lose it in a voice mail, so she hung up and texted him.

Finished early. See you at your place.

When Grace pulled up in front of Jax's house, the porch light was on but the house was dark and empty. Which was fitting because that was exactly how Grace felt at the moment. When she got inside she went through the house, turning on all the lights as she went. Apparently she thought that the more lightbulbs that were burning the faster she'd get a clue.

She was wrong.

She was so thoroughly confused that she was surprised her head was still on straight. She wasn't sure how long she paced through the house, searching for some sort of answer.

Maybe that was the problem. She was searching for the answers when really she needed to figure out the question.

She'd found out who her father was.

She'd found out that her mother had been part of an affair.

She'd found out that she'd been born out of something dirty.

She'd found out that her grandmother had lied to her.

But when it came right down to it, what did her knowing change?

Her father had never wanted to be a part of her life. She was under no illusions he was going to suddenly want to know her now. She had absolutely no desire to know him.

The world hadn't fallen out from under her feet. The ground was just unsteady, shaking. But she was still standing, and she was going to continue to stand.

Grace wasn't sure how long she'd been pacing, but she was in the hallway when the front door opened.

"Grace," Jax called out.

She rounded the corner, and when she saw him she found her solid ground. She launched herself at him, grabbing his face in her hands and kissing him. His arms wrapped around her and she was suddenly pushed up against the wall. Jax's hands slid up under her dress and he pulled her legs around his waist.

Jax was kissing her with a desperation that matched her own. Like she was his safe haven and he wanted to crawl inside of her, to be inside of her.

Did he sense her need for him? Or did he need her just as much as she needed him? She wasn't sure, but she didn't have any desire to come up for air long enough to ask. She didn't want to talk. She wanted Jax. Wanted him to make her forget the night. Wanted him to make her not think about anything that hurt. Wanted him to make love to her. Wanted him to *love* her.

He was still in his uniform and as she ran her hands up his shoulders, she realized his shirt was damp and he smelled like beer. But the whys to those questions flew to the back of her mind as one of his hands made its way to the apex of her thighs. She moaned into his mouth as he pulled back from the wall, carrying her down the hall as he stroked her between her legs.

When they got to the bedroom he pushed her up against the wall again, using its leverage to keep her pinned there with his body. His hands disappeared from her body, and then they were at the front of his pants where he undid his utility belt and put it down on the nightstand.

All the while Grace was pulling at this shirt, untucking it from his pants and fumbling with the buttons. When she reached the top she pushed it off his shoulders and then started working his white T-shirt up his abdomen. Their mouths separated as she pulled it off and a second later her dress was up over her head and joining his shirts on the floor.

Jax reached down and fumbled with the drawer on the nightstand before he pulled it open and grabbed a condom. He shoved his pants and boxer briefs down and put the condom on. His mouth came down hard on hers, his tongue thrusting into her mouth as he pulled her panties to the side and entered her. Grace cried out into his mouth, her back arching as he began to move.

Nothing about what he was doing to her was soft, gentle, or sweet. What he was doing was hot, intense, mind blowing, and exactly what she needed. Jax was exactly what she needed. He always had been and always would be.

He moved in and out of her with perfect thrusts that made her breath catch. His hands were gripping her thighs, his long fingers digging into her skin as he held on to her.

"Jax," she gasped, pulling her mouth from his.

His mouth latched on to her neck, sucking and kissing, and making her say his name louder, and louder. Grace came first, her grip on Jax's shoulders tightening as she held on to him. He followed her over the edge a second later, his face still buried in her throat.

When he caught his breath he pulled back and looked at her. He brushed her hair back from her face and looked at her, his beautiful green eyes holding hers.

"I love you." Grace wasn't sure why at that moment

she decided to open her mouth and say it, but she had. She couldn't stop herself.

Jax's hand stilled at her ear where he was tucking her hair back. The openness that had been in his eyes a second ago was gone, like a door had slammed shut.

"I...can't," Jax whispered.

Everything in Grace fell away in that instant. She'd thought she'd already survived the bombshell of the night. But was she ever wrong. Jax had just blown her life wide open with those two words.

"Can't what? Can't love me?" She couldn't breathe. Her lungs hurt and her head was spinning.

"Grace," he said, shaking his head.

God, he was still inside of her and he was telling her he wasn't in love with her. She was hollow, empty, abandoned.

He didn't love her.

"Put me down." She pushed at his shoulders. "Just put me down."

His hand dropped from her thigh and she unwound her legs from his waist, bringing her feet down to the floor. The hollowness intensified a thousand-fold as Jax took a step back and pulled out of her body.

How had she gotten it so wrong? How had she mistaken everything?

He didn't love her.

She reached down and grabbed her dress from the floor, feeling entirely too exposed in just her bra and panties. Jax tucked himself back into his pants and pulled up the zipper as she pulled her dress over her head.

"What was this to you? Just a way to pass the time?" she asked, wrapping her arms around herself, trying desperately to hold herself together.

"Grace." He ran his hand through his hair.

"What was this?" she asked, getting louder. She wanted

to start throwing things. To make things shatter into a million pieces so that everything around her resembled how she felt inside. "Where did you see this going, Jax? Did you always see this as temporary? There was no thought of a future with us?"

"I don't know what I thought about the future," he said.

"Meaning you didn't think about it at all."

"I'm not good enough for you, Grace. I'm not good enough for you to love."

"Not this *crap* again," she shouted.

"I'm not, Grace." He shook his head. "I'm not what you need. I'm not that guy. I'm not the guy that gets married and has a family. I never have been. I don't know how to be that guy. I don't know how to love."

"That's bullshit," she said. "You're scared of loving someone. Scared of letting someone in enough to hurt you. You're a coward. I know what it's like—"

"You don't know anything," Jax yelled, cutting her off. Something had changed in his eyes. Something that Grace had never seen before. Something that scared her. "You have a father, Grace. Oliver is your father. And yes, your mother died when you were young, and I'm not saying that wasn't painful, but you had Lula Mae, too. You had Brendan. I had no one.

"I had a father who hated me, and a mother who could've cared less. The only person I had, died when I was five and then I had to learn to fend for myself because I had no one. So don't you dare compare your daddy issues to mine. And don't you dare call me a coward. You have no idea what I went through."

He didn't know what she'd gone through, either. He didn't know that she'd found out who her father was. He didn't know what she'd been through that night. And she wasn't going to tell him. It didn't matter. What was it going to change? When it came right down to it, he didn't love her. Couldn't love her. And what if he never did?

"You're right, Jax, I have no idea what it was like for you. But you're wrong when you say you had no one. And if you're too blind to see that, too blind to see all the people that care about you, that love you, then I can't do anything more to convince you."

"I didn't ask you to."

"You're right." She nodded. "You didn't. You didn't ask me to do a lot of things, like love you. But I went and did it anyway. Stupid me." Her voice caught as she reached up and swiped at her eyes. "You didn't answer my question, what was this to you? Were you just with me until you got me out of your system? Until you were tired of sleeping with me? Because for me, this was it. *You* were it."

"I was never going to marry you."

Grace froze. There it was, the answer to all the questions, the answer that broke her.

"Grace," he said, taking a step toward her, his hand outstretched.

"Don't." She took a step back and held her hand out to stop him. "I love you, but I wish I didn't. I wish I'd never let you in."

"I never meant to hurt you."

"You didn't hurt me, Jax, you destroyed me. We're done."

"I know." He nodded slowly, not meeting her eyes.

She stepped around him and walked out of his room, out of his house, out of his life. And he didn't ask her to stay. He didn't do anything. He just let her leave.

Chapter Seventeen

The Fallout

How had that happened? How had everything just gotten so royally fucked up?

Jax had walked in the door and Grace had pretty much tackled him. She'd started kissing him and holding on to him, and he realized he needed to be inside of her like he needed his next breath. The sex had been incredible, all consuming, and just explosive. And then everything went to hell. Really everything had gone to hell much earlier in the evening; taking Grace up against the wall had just been a small reprieve from the pain of his childhood memories. And as it turned out the calm before the actual shit storm hit.

After he'd left his parents house he'd been so completely messed up. That was how it always was after he saw them. He felt like he was that helpless little five-year-old again, and Jax didn't do helpless well. He didn't do a lot of things well. And how things ended with Grace had been a disaster.

He hadn't been lying when he said he didn't know how to love. And being with her hadn't made him forget the truth, hadn't made him forget the fact that he wasn't the one for her. He'd just been waiting for the day Grace was going to figure it out and end things. And that's exactly what had happened. He'd been fooling himself starting a relationship that was doomed to end from the beginning.

But what else was he supposed to do? Being with her had been out of this world amazing. Nothing compared to waking up next to her in the morning. To pressing his face into her neck and breathing her in. To finally have someone to come home to. But he was just some guy in her life for a little while. It had always been just a matter of time, and the clock had finally caught up to him.

Jax had watched Grace walk away from him more times than he could count. But nothing had hurt as bad as this time. Nothing had hurt as much because this time Grace was walking out of his *life*, and that killed him.

* * *

Grace wasn't sure how she got back to her apartment before she lost it. Maybe it was just her desperate need to get as far away from the cause of her pain as possible. Whatever she was holding on to didn't last long. The second she walked in the door of her empty apartment she was done for.

She didn't have the strength to go into her bedroom, not only because the twenty feet looked like miles, but also because he'd slept in her bed so many times, the night before being just one of them. Those sheets and pillows would still smell like him. She just couldn't deal with that. She couldn't deal with anything.

He'd thought he wasn't enough for her. It was that belief that had kept him from being with her in the first place. But as it turned out, it was that *she* wasn't enough for *him*. If she had been enough, he wouldn't have been able to stop himself from loving her. And that obviously wasn't the case.

Grace wasn't sure how long she lay on the couch before

she fell asleep, but she woke up sometime later when someone knocked on the door. There was light peeking in through the edges of the blinds and it hurt her eyes. She slowly sat up, wrapping the thin blanket that she'd slept under around her shoulders. Her back was sore from sleeping curled up on the couch, and her head was throbbing from the hours of crying.

She felt like a zombie. She wasn't even human anymore, which wasn't that surprising as she'd just had her heart ripped out of her chest. She was shocked she was still breathing. Surely without a heart she'd stop breathing. Maybe then the pain would end, and she desperately wanted the pain to end. But that just wasn't going to happen.

She'd thought she'd been in for some pain when she found out who her father was. But that was nothing. No, having the one man she loved more than anything tell her that he didn't love her had been a category five hurricane that decimated everything in its path. Grace was never going to recover. There was no rebuilding after that kind of devastation.

Grace looked out the peephole to see Brendan on the other side of the door, wearing a look that was the perfect mix of concerned and pissed off.

Of course.

She opened the door and groaned when the full force of the sun hit her eyes.

"Hey," she croaked, stepping back so he could come in.

He stepped into her tiny apartment, shutting the door behind him. He pulled her into his arms and Grace lost it again, sobbing into her big brother's chest.

"Oh, Gracie," he said as he rubbed her back. "It's going to be okay."

"He doesn't love me," she hiccuped. "He never has."

"He's worthless, Grace. He always has been."

"What?" Grace asked, pulling back from Brendan and

looking up at him. She was pretty sure Brendan was mad at Jax, but not enough to say he'd always been worthless.

"Keith Reynolds isn't good enough to love you. He's a horrible man and your life has been better without him."

"I wasn't talking about him," Grace said, shaking her head. "I thought...I thought you were here because of Jax." Saying his name was like a punch in the stomach.

Brendan froze. "What happened with Jax?" he asked slowly, trying to mask the anger in his voice. He was unsuccessful.

Grace pulled back from him, shaking her head sadly as she tried to get her mouth to start working. She didn't want to say it out loud. Didn't want it to be true. But it was.

"We...we aren't together anymore," she whispered, choking on the words.

"What?" Brendan asked.

"He doesn't love me." Grace looked away from Brendan's face. She couldn't do it. She couldn't deal with this right now. Who was she kidding? She was *never* going to be able to deal with this.

"He's an idiot, Grace," Brendan said, putting his fingers under her chin and forcing her gaze up. "If he's too stupid to realize how amazing you are, he doesn't deserve you."

"Would you have been able to move on? If Paige had left or you'd lost her in the accident. Would you have been able to move on?"

"No," Brendan said without hesitation. "She's the love of my life."

"He's mine, Brendan. Jax is the only man I've ever been in love with, and he'll always be. You say he doesn't deserve me. But why don't I deserve him? Why can't I have him?" she asked, rubbing at the pain in her chest.

"I don't know, Gracie."

"Did you know about Keith Reynolds? Did you know he was my father?"

"No," Brendan said, shaking his head. "I had no idea. Grams called and told me what happened."

"She knew, you know. She knew the whole time."

"She told me that, too," he said sadly.

"Did Pops know?"

"No."

"I feel like I'm drowning," she said, swiping at her streaming eyes. "It's everything, Brendan. Learning who my father is, finding out what Grams kept from me, what Mom kept from me, Jax…Jax not loving me. It's too much. I can't…I just can't deal with this."

Brendan didn't say anything, he just pulled her into his chest again and let her cry her eyes out.

* * *

Jax was struggling. He'd probably gotten about two hours of sleep the night before. The cold, empty sheets next to him had made his chest ache, but that was nothing to the pain he felt when he'd woken up alone, without Grace. Since that first night they'd been together, he'd only missed out on sleeping next to her for a handful of nights. He was so used to the peace of falling asleep next to her and the pleasure of waking up pressed against her body.

But not today. Today he'd gotten nothing. That void was never going to be filled again, because Grace was the only one that could fill it, and she was gone.

He'd driven over to the house under construction before the sun had even come up. He was off from work for the day and he needed to do something to distract from the emptiness that was consuming him. The emptiness that was so deep it hurt.

He'd always planned on working on the house that day. Shep, Bennett, and Tripp showed up around nine to help out.

"What's wrong with you?" Shep asked after he'd been there for about thirty minutes.

"Nothing." Jax carried a piece of the wood flooring over to the saw.

"Bullshit," Shep said, folding his arms across his chest. He leaned back against one of the wooden pillars that supported Jax's house. "Did something happen with you and Grace?"

"I don't want to talk about it."

"What did you do?"

Jax didn't answer; instead he turned around and turned on the saw, drowning out anything Shep was going to say to him. When Jax turned it off a couple of minutes later, Shep was still leaning against the post, one of his eyebrows raised over his sunglasses, staring at him.

Jax continued to ignore him and walked over to the cooler to grab a bottle of water. But this time when he turned around he was greeted with much more than Shep's inquisitive gaze. Brendan was standing in front of him, looking more pissed off than Jax had ever seen him. Jax didn't have enough time to react before Brendan punched him in the jaw.

"What the hell?" Shep said as Brendan tackled Jax to the ground.

Brendan got in a few more hits as they wrestled around, but so did Jax. And it felt good. It felt good to let out some of his anger. It didn't matter that the target didn't deserve it. Nothing really mattered.

"You stupid son-of-a-bitch," Brendan said as he got in another good hit.

Jax didn't get a chance to retaliate, because a second later Brendan was pulled off him. Shep was holding Brendan back while Bennett and Tripp stood to the side, ready to jump in and hold Jax back if they needed to.

"What's going on?" Shep asked.

"Do you have any idea what you've done to Grace?" Brendan bellowed at Jax. "You broke her."

Jax didn't say anything, he just wiped at the blood that was flowing from his cut lip.

"What did you do to Grace?" Shep asked, his face mirroring a lot of the anger that was on Brendan's.

"You're a real piece of work to do that to her last night of all nights," Brendan said, disgusted. "To tell her you don't love her on the night she found out who her father was."

"What?" Jax asked as his stomach dropped somewhere below his knees.

Shep's hands stopped restraining Brendan, either because he was in shock or because he was all for Brendan beating the shit out of Jax.

"You didn't know?" Brendan asked.

"She didn't tell me."

"You didn't give her a chance before you dumped her?"

Technically, she'd been the one to end things, not that he'd given her any choice. But she'd been the one to say *we're done*, two words that would haunt him for the rest of his life.

"Who is he?" Jax asked.

Brendan stared at him for a second, probably deciding whether he was going to answer or not. "Keith Reynolds."

"Shit," Jax said, shaking his head. Really it couldn't have been a worse person.

"My sentiments exactly."

"How did she find out?" Jax asked.

"Judson showed up at the dinner last night, drunk off his ass, and he announced it to everyone there."

Well, Grace's need when Jax walked in the door was starting to make sense.

"How did he know?" Shep asked.

"I don't know," Brendan said, shaking his head.

"So it might not be true?" Jax asked hopefully. Grace

being related to the Reynolds family would be a massive blow. He sincerely hoped it was all a lie.

"No, it's true," Brendan said grimly. "Grams told me about it this morning. She knew the truth."

Grace's life had been ripped apart last night, and Jax had made it five thousand times worse. That sounded about right.

"I'm through with you, Jax," Brendan said as he took a step back. "I don't want anything to do with you." He turned around and walked to his truck.

Well, Jax was just fucking things up left and right wasn't he?

* * *

After Brendan left, Grace dragged herself to the shower and stayed there for an hour. The hot water made her feel somewhat human again, but that lasted only until she stepped back into her room and looked at her empty bed. She stripped it and promptly threw the sheets and blankets into the washer. Then she stuffed the pillow that Jax had always used to the back of her closet.

The clean sheets and blanket on her bed didn't make her feel any better. If anything, they made her feel even emptier.

Grace was in the kitchen making a cup of tea and some toast when there was another knock on the door. She looked out the peephole to find her grandmother. She closed her eyes and took a deep breath before she opened the door.

"Will you let me talk to you?" Lula Mae asked, looking so thoroughly heartbroken that Grace couldn't say no. Relief flooded Lula Mae's face as Grace stepped to the side and opened the door wider.

"I'm making peppermint tea, do you want some?" Grace asked as she closed the door and went back to the kitchen.

"Yes, please." Lula Mae took a seat at Grace's small dining room table.

Neither of them said anything as Grace fixed both mugs and set them on the table with the toast. She sat down and blew lightly on her tea as she waited for her grandmother to speak.

"Your mother wasn't perfect," Lula Mae finally said. "But she had a big heart, and she loved with all of it. You know, I liked Brendan's father when she first brought him home to meet your grandfather and me. Crayton had seemed like a good guy. She was so far in love with him she wasn't able to see straight. But then she found out she was pregnant, and he left her without a second thought. She was devastated."

Grace had known all of this, well not the part where her grandparents had liked Crayton. That was a surprise.

"She never got over it, having the one man she loved walk out on her, especially when she was carrying his child."

Grace could relate to that. She knew how her mother had felt, except for the whole pregnancy thing. Grace wasn't sure how she would function if she were pregnant with Jax's child. Probably not at all.

"She didn't date after that. She didn't have a lot of time while raising Brendan, but I think she just couldn't do it. She couldn't let herself be that vulnerable to get her heart broken again.

"A few years later Keith Reynolds came into town for a job interview. She'd gone out one night and met him. He was sweet and charming and exactly what she thought she wanted. Your mother wasn't a one-night-stand kind of girl, but she'd had one too many drinks and she went back to his hotel room.

"She didn't know he was married. He wasn't wearing a wedding ring and he never alluded to it. He claimed he was in town on vacation. I don't think he realized just how small Mirabelle was when he came down for the interview for principal. Apparently, he only came down to try to up the ante for another school he was trying to get hired at. He'd never planned on moving here."

"How did Mom find that out?" Grace asked.

"Well, Keith left without a word. Your mother found out she was pregnant a month later. Two months after that, Keith Reynolds moved to town with a wife and a son who wasn't even two years old. She told him, not because she wanted him to leave his wife, but because she wanted him to know she was going to have his child. He told her he wanted nothing to do with either of you," Lula Mae said sadly.

Grace's eyes burned and she looked down at the table as her tears fell and ran down her cheeks.

"She didn't want you to ever doubt that you'd been wanted," Lula Mae said, putting her hand over Grace's. "She wanted you enough for two parents, and so did your grandfather and I. There was never a moment that you were looked at like a mistake. She felt that if you knew who your father was, you'd think that."

"She was right," Grace said thickly.

"Grace." Lula Mae said her name softly. Grace looked up into her grandmother's warm loving eyes.

"Your mother loved you from the second she found out about you. She never regretted having you. Not once. Not ever. You were a gift to her. She always looked at you that way. In the end, you and Brendan healed her broken heart. It was the two of you, and she never doubted her life with the two of you in it.

"She went through a lot of heartache, but for her, it was always worth it to have her children. And she never looked back on her decisions with regret. She loved you, and leaving the two of you when you were both so young was the hardest thing she ever had to do."

Grace flipped her hand so she could hold her grandmother's. She squeezed lightly and her grandmother repeated the gesture.

"I'm sorry I didn't tell you, Gracie. But your mother asked me not to, so I followed her wishes. There were a lot of times I went back and forth on it. Especially when you asked me straight out, and I hated lying to you. But it was what your mother wanted."

"I understand." Grace nodded. "It still hurts, but I understand. Especially now."

"Especially now what?"

"It hurts when you find out someone doesn't want you, that someone doesn't love you. A father is supposed to love his child, and when he doesn't, it's painful. Sometimes not knowing is better."

"Grace?" Lula Mae asked.

"I thought that finding out about my dad was bad. It didn't even break the ice."

"Sweetie, what happened?"

"Jax doesn't love me," she said, and bit her bottom lip in an attempt to keep it from trembling.

"What are you talking about?"

"Last night...we...we broke up. It's over. We're over. I always thought when I finally got him I'd get to keep him. That he'd be mine. But he went into the relationship knowing there would be an end. I wish I never knew what it was like to be with Jax. I wish I didn't know what it felt like to *breathe* with him beside me. But I know now, and there's no going back."

No going back ever, and it was going to torment Grace for the rest of her life.

* * *

The news that Keith Reynolds was Grace's father spread around Mirabelle like wildfire. And as was typical of Bethelda Grimshaw, she poured fuel on the fire.

THE GRIM TRUTH

TROUBLE IN PARADISE

For years the good people of Mirabelle have wondered who Little CoQuette's father is. Well, the mystery has finally been revealed and it's more than a little troubling.

CoQuette's mother, Jeze Belle, was a loose, immoral woman. Jeze started bed hopping at a very young age, so it's no wonder she had her first out-of-wedlock child when she was eighteen, and the second bastard child came along only six years later. It's been speculated that CoQuette's father was a married man, and as it turns out he is.

Superintendent Charming MyAss moved down twenty-five years ago when he was hired as the principal of the high school. He worked there about twenty years before he decided to run for superintendent. He's up for reelection this year, but how many people are going to vote for him now that they know he has an illegitimate child running around? For all we know, CoQuette is just one of many.

At a dinner honoring Superintendent MyAss, Wrongfully Accused showed up to spill the beans. Wrongfully Accused has been friends with Charming MyAss's son, Loyal MyAss, for over twenty years. Apparently Loyal MyAss has been known to get drunk on more than a few occasions, and his loose lips are going to sink his daddy's ship.

According to Wrongfully Accused, it's been no secret in the MyAss household, that Charming MyAss is CoQuette's father. MyAss's wife, Friendly MyAss, has a habit of getting drunk off of a few too many gin martinis and throwing Charming MyAss's infidelity in his face, that along with one of her drinks. It would appear that the MyAss family has a problem holding their secrets, their liquor, and their pants up for that matter.

Grace couldn't escape the knowing looks wherever she went. Some people looked disgusted, like the confirmation that her mother had slept with a married man made Grace less of a person. Others looked at her with pity. Grace didn't care for either sentiment. Really she didn't care what anybody thought of her. People were entitled to their opinions, and she was entitled to think they could shove those opinions right up their asses.

The constant ache in Grace's chest was just as bad a week after she and Jax broke up. She'd had to learn to just deal with the pain, because it wasn't going anywhere. She ventured out only when it was absolutely necessary. She hadn't seen him since she walked out of his house. There was no doubt in her mind that the first time she saw him she was going to fall apart, and she had absolutely no desire to deal with that.

She'd hung out with Mel, Harper, and Preston on alternating nights, but she knew she wasn't much company. They didn't want her to be in her apartment all by herself every night. So to stop their loving but annoying babysitting routine, she'd started working late at the café. This worked out well for Grace for another reason. It meant she was at the café for less hours during the day dealing with people and their stupid looks.

On the Saturday night that was one week and two days after the breakup, or the day Grace's heart had been ripped out, Grace was making two dozen cupcakes for Annie Madison's son's second birthday. Apparently Carson loved trains, so Grace was taking up time laying tracks on every cupcake.

The kids at the party weren't going to pay much attention to the details, they were all under the age of five, but Grace needed a distraction.

She finished decorating at nine and cleaned up her mess. She was drying the last cupcake tin when there was a knock at the side door. Grace turned around to see Shep on the other side.

For one fleeting second her stomach had flipped; she thought Jax might be on the other side of the door. It was a stupid thought. He wasn't going to be stopping by ever again.

"Hey, stranger," Grace said as she unlocked the door and pulled it open wide enough for him to step inside.

"Hey, Gracie." He gave her a sad half smile as he pulled her into a hug and kissed the top of her head. "What are you still doing here?"

"Staying busy so I don't go crazy." She pulled back and walked over to the tray of cupcakes. "You working tonight?" she asked as she put the cupcakes into a box.

"Yeah, but we weren't that busy so I left."

"Not busy? It's a Saturday," Grace said, looking at him skeptically.

"All right, so it was busy. Austin is working tonight and my dad said they could handle the crowd."

"And you just happened to drive by and see the light on?"

"I figured you were either going to be here or at your apartment. I haven't seen you in a while."

"I haven't seen anyone." She pulled the refrigerator door open and slid in the cupcakes.

"Yeah, I figured."

It was taking everything in her not to ask how Jax was doing. Not to ask if he was struggling as bad as she was. Paige had told Grace about the fight between Brendan and Jax, though Brendan wouldn't have been able to hide it considering he had a bruised cheek and a cut above his left eyebrow. Grace hadn't heard how Jax fared. Brendan was furious with Jax, and as of the moment the two of them weren't on speaking terms. So the only person she could really get news from was Shep, but in the end knowing wasn't going to help her, so she kept her mouth shut.

"You done here?" Shep asked.

"Yeah." Grace nodded, turning to look at him.

"You have plans for tonight?"

"No, but I don't really feel like going anywhere. Not in a seeing people type of mood."

"I know. I was thinking we could hang out at your place," he said.

"Will there be alcohol involved? Because I could really use some tequila."

"Already in my car," he said, giving her one of his customary Shep grins. "You got any spare cupcakes?"

"Sure do."

"All right, I'll meet you at your place."

"You know, you really don't have to spend the night baby-sitting your best friend's pathetic sister," she told him.

"First of all," he said, taking a step forward, "you are not my best friend's pathetic sister. You're *my* pathetic friend. And I hate seeing you like this. Second of all, I'm not going to be babysitting you. I'm going to get drunk with you. And third of all, I might have my own sorrows to drown, so you won't win the award for most pathetic of the night."

Grace rolled her eyes and was surprised when the first genuine smile she'd had in days curved her mouth up.

* * *

"Ready? One. Two. Three. Shoot," Shep said right before they licked the salt off their hands, threw back a shot of tequila, and picked up a wedge of lime to suck.

It was after midnight and they'd had more shots than Grace could remember. She'd stopped counting after five. They were currently sitting on her sofa, her coffee table being used as a bar and for cupcake wrapper disposal.

"So why are you sad and pathetic?" Grace asked, looking over at Shep.

"I didn't say sad and pathetic."

"You said pathetic. Pathetic is way worse than sad. So tacking that on doesn't make it that much different."

"I suppose you're right." He studied her for a second before he turned back to the movie playing on TV. It was one of those ridiculous guy comedies, but as there wasn't a love story in it, she was fine with it playing. Grace was pretty sure Shep wasn't going to answer her, but after a moment he cleared his throat and turned back to her.

"Before my grandfather died he told me I needed to stop messing around."

"With women?"

"With my life," he said, shaking his head sadly. "He told me that my grandmother changed him. That loving her, and being loved by her, was the best thing that ever happened to him. He said that settling down in life isn't about settling, but about being with the one person that makes waking up every day a gift."

Grace's eyes were watering. Damn Shep and his philosophical insights into life.

"Have you ever had that?" she asked, blinking hard.

"I thought I did once."

"Hannah?"

"Hannah." He nodded. "But she wasn't mine to keep, at least not at the time. She's the girl that I've compared every other girl to. Because she's the only girl I've ever loved."

"Why didn't you ever go after her?"

"I didn't want to hold her back."

"That's stupid."

Shep laughed. "It was almost twelve years ago. I was a different person when I was eighteen. She's probably a different person now, too. Most likely she doesn't even think about me anymore."

"But you think about her," Grace said.

"Yeah, I do. And I love the girl that I knew all those years ago. It's quite possible I'm holding on to something that doesn't exist anymore."

"If that's the case, then I'm screwed," she said, closing her eyes.

"No, you're not, Grace," Shep said softly.

"You still love Hannah after twelve years." Grace opened her eyes. "And you only had her in your life for a couple of months. Jax has always been in my life and I've loved him since I was six. You think you could be holding on to something that doesn't exist anymore. But Jax doesn't love me, so I'm holding on to something that never existed. So you tell me, how am I not screwed?"

"Well, when you put it like that."

Grace laughed, unable to stop herself, and after a second the laughs turned into sobs.

"Shit, Grace," Shep said, pulling her into his arms and letting her cry on his chest. "He's an idiot."

"Everyone keeps saying that. Yet I'm the one who feels so stupid."

"I wish I could tell you something that would make you feel better."

"You don't have to," she said, shaking her head. "Thanks for being here."

"Always, kiddo," he said, kissing her hair.

* * *

Jax still couldn't sleep the whole night through. Every night, he'd wake up searching for Grace, desperate to pull her into his chest, but she wasn't there. More often than not, he found himself curled around the pillow that still smelled like her. But it wasn't enough. It wasn't anything in comparison to her.

God, he missed her.

He missed the little things. Walking into the bathroom after she showered, with the smell of her soap lingering in the air. Driving in his truck, her hand in his while she hummed along to the radio. Coming up behind her while she was cooking and pressing his nose into her hair. Kissing the hollow of her throat. He missed her smile, her laugh, the sound of her voice.

Everything felt empty. He felt empty. It had been ten days without her, but it felt like years.

Jax occupied his time working on the house. Brendan obviously hadn't been around, but Shep showed up a few times to help. He didn't ask any questions, or say anything really. Bennett was there on occasion, too, or sometimes Tripp, but for the most part it was just Jax, working alone.

Everything was finished except for the kitchen. For some reason he saved it for last. He was working on installing the cabinets that morning with Shep and Bennett, and when they finished they moved on to the countertops. The new appliances were scheduled for delivery that week, and then everything would be done.

Jax had been working on the house for eight months. Eight fucking months of grueling work, but as he looked around at it, he felt nothing.

"I'm going to go get lunch," Jax said, needing to get out of there. "Burgers okay?"

"Works for me," Bennett said.

Shep only nodded. Not making eye contact with Jax before he turned back to the counter.

Jax called in the order to Bubba's Burgers as he got in his

truck, but the place was packed when he got there, so he took a seat at the bar and waited for the food.

"Tough break, Deputy."

Jax looked over as Chad slid into the seat next to him.

Yeah, this wasn't going to end well.

"I don't care about whatever it is you're about to say. So why don't you go bother somebody else."

"I thought we could commiserate together. You know, two guys that have been screwed over by Grace King."

Jax stilled.

"I had no idea you two split. Was it because she was sleeping with Shep? Or did that happen afterward?"

"What?" Jax asked, turning to Chad before he could stop himself.

"Oh, you don't know. Well, that's just perfect." Chad grinned. "Apparently, Shep's Mustang was outside of Grace's apartment all night and well into this morning. Someone even saw him leaving looking thoroughly used up. You can read all about it in Bethelda's blog."

Jax's ears were ringing so loud he could barely hear the little waitress who handed him his order a second later.

Jax grabbed the bag of food and walked out of the restaurant. He sat in his truck for a full minute before he grabbed his phone and pulled up the Web site.

THE GRIM TRUTH

THE WHORE DOESN'T FALL FAR FROM THE TREE

A little over a week after finding out who her father is, Little CoQuette is out stirring up trouble and proving that bad choices are hereditary. It's no secret that CoQuette has been playing around in Deputy Ginger's bed recently. But she's apparently gotten tired of the redhead, because she's moved on to different pastures.

Wild Ram is the newest conquest on CoQuette's post. Wild has run the local watering hole, the Den of Iniquity, with his family for years. Wild has his own reputation for tempting a plethora of women into his bed, probably some at the same time. He's a known heartbreaker and he shows absolutely no remorse for that. And that's not the only thing that he lacks morals on. He's also one of Deputy Ginger's best friends, or at least he used to be, that probably isn't the case anymore.

An eyewitness says that they saw Wild Ram's Mustang outside of CoQuette's apartment late last night and when he left this morning he apparently looked ravaged. It would appear that CoQuette has taken after both of her parents cheating ways.

Jax sat there stunned. He thought something was up, as Shep had barely been able to look at him all day. But he couldn't fucking believe that Shep would do *this*. That he'd sleep with Grace.

The ringing in Jax's ears was getting louder and louder and when he pulled up in front of his house five minutes later it was all white noise. Jax ran up the stairs two at a time and when he opened the front door all he saw was Shep leaning against the counter, a stupid, smarmy grin on his stupid, smarmy face as he talked.

Jax crossed the room and Shep saw him a moment before he clocked him in the jaw.

"I can believe you slept with her," Jax said as they both went down to the floor hard, but Jax only got in a few hits before Shep had him in a headlock.

"Listen, listen," Shep said as he struggled to restrain Jax.

"I can't believe you. I always knew you'd screw anything in a skirt, but not her, not Grace."

"I didn't sleep with her, you moron," Shep said, tightening his hold as Jax continued to try to fight. "So do you want to talk about it or continue to flail around like an idiot? Because I'm bigger and stronger than your punk ass."

Maybe it was the loss of oxygen to his head, but Jax stopped struggling. Shep pushed him away and got up.

"I don't think you have any idea how badly I want to deck you in the face right now," Shep said as Jax got to his feet.

"The feeling's mutual."

"You don't get to talk," Shep shouted. "Do you really believe that we slept together? Do you really think that of me? Of Grace, for that matter? She's in love with *you*. You want to know what happened last night? She was working at the café after nine, for the fourth night in a row, and I was worried about her. I don't like her working late. Not because I'm *in* love with her, but because I love her like a sister. We went over to her place, got drunk on tequila, and she cried on my shoulder because she thinks she's never going to get over your stupid ass." Shep pointed his finger at Jax.

"I don't get you," Shep said shaking his head and still yelling. "I don't get how you can have the woman you love in front of you and not do anything about it. And don't you dare claim to not love her, because you told me you did the night you got drunk after she slapped you at the bar. When I drove you back to my house all you did was talk about her. Talk about how much you love her, and that she was the only woman you would ever love.

"And you know what, Jax, it didn't even take you saying it to make it painfully clear to *everyone* that you love her. Everybody who's worked on this house knows it," Shep said, indicating the walls around him with his arms. "Especially because of this kitchen. This is *her* dream kitchen. Do you think that fact has escaped anyone's notice? Because it hasn't. You built this for her." He paused to let that sink in.

"Do you want to ruin every relationship you have? You let Grace walk out of your life like she was nothing. Brendan's done with you. Was it your goal to piss me off, too? I screw anything in a skirt? Fuck you, Jax. You're *screwing* up your life. Is this what you wanted? A house to live in all by yourself for the rest of your life? Because if that's what you want, you're well on your way to it. How did you find out anyways?"

It took Jax a second to realize Shep had asked him a question. He was still trying to process the fact that he'd just gotten his ass handed to him.

"Find what out?" he asked unsure of what Shep was talking about.

"That I stayed at Grace's?"

Jax took a deep breath and let it out slowly. "Chad was at Bubba's. He told me about Bethelda's latest blog post."

Shep just looked at Jax dumbfounded before he reached up and pinched the bridge of his nose. He dropped his hand after a moment and shook his head. "Did you listen to the words that just came out of your mouth? You took the words of Chad Sharp and Bethelda Grimshaw over twenty-five years of friendship? Are you joking?"

"I...I wasn't thinking," Jax said, still dazed. "I haven't been..." not since he'd messed things up with Grace. That was the last time he'd thought clearly. The last time he'd felt even remotely good about anything. What the *hell* was wrong with him?

"No kidding. You need to get your shit together."

"Yeah." Jax nodded, rubbing his hands across his face. He just wasn't sure how to go about doing it.

Chapter Eighteen

Epiphanies in the Relish Aisle

Sixty-two-year-old Gene Fritch was a wealthy man. His family had lived on Mirabelle Beach since the 1930s and they'd accumulated quite a bit of the land. Over the last twenty years they'd built dozens of beach houses that they rented out. Five years ago they built the LaBella Resort complete with golf course, private pool, and spa. Harper worked there three days a week giving massages, and she was booked solid every day. The Fritches made a pretty penny during the summer, and the snowbirds kept them well in the black during the winter.

Well, Gene had died of a heart attack, and his funeral was going to be a finale of grand proportions.

Carla Fritch, Gene's third wife who just happened to be twenty-five years younger than him, was known for her theatrics. Gene's funeral was going to be the performance of her life, so she spared absolutely no expense. She ordered the funeral home to be filled with orchids, roses, and lilies. The café was catering almost five thousand dollars' worth of food, there was going to be an open bar, and a professional violinist and harpist were being flown down from New York to play music.

Paige was still on maternity leave, but she was going to come in and work for a little bit. Carla ordered the picture tribute, service folders, prayer cards, and every other thing she could possibly put her husband's picture on. It was well over eight thousand dollars' worth of stuff. There were going to be huge pictures of him stationed around the funeral home surrounded by the plethora of flowers that she wanted everywhere. Not to mention she'd ordered some of that creepy jewelry the funeral home sold. Carla was going to be walking around with her dead husband's thumbprint around her neck.

When everything was said and done, Gene Fritch's funeral was going to be over one hundred thousand dollars. To top it all off, he was going to be buried with another one hundred thousand dollars' worth of stuff: a gold crucifix from the 1500s, a Tampa Bay Buccaneers Super Bowl ring, a tie pin and cufflink set that was made of platinum and diamonds, a twenty-thousand-dollar suit, and a baseball signed by the Mets when they won the 1969 World Series.

Apparently good old Gene thought that he could take some of his riches with him to the afterlife.

The funeral was going to be on Thursday night. Gene was going to be lowered into his final resting place at dusk.

That gave Grace and Lula Mae a good couple of days to plan everything out and start prepping. The day of the funeral, Grace and Lula Mae showed up at the café at six in the morning and cooked for a solid nine hours. They had Lula Mae's SUV and Grace's Bug loaded up with everything before four and had two hours to set everything up before the service started.

"Grace," Lula Mae said as she stacked the shrimp cocktail on a platter, "I need you to run over to the store. I forgot the ketchup for the cocktail sauce and we need more fresh strawberries for the mousse cups."

"Anything else?" Grace asked as she grabbed her purse.

"If the fresh pineapple looks good get two of those and we could use some more cilantro."

"I'll be back," she said as she headed for the front door.

Grace pulled into the parking lot of the Piggly Wiggly five minutes later. She grabbed a handheld basket and headed for the produce. She got the strawberries, pineapples, and cilantro. The service started in twenty minutes, so she rushed over to the condiments aisle, rounding the corner and running smack-dab into a solid chest, the very same solid chest that she loved.

"Grace," Jax said as his hands grabbed on to her arms to steady her.

Why did the first time she saw him have to be then? Have to be when she couldn't take a second to really deal with it?

"Jax," she said, inhaling sharply. "Sorry, I, uh, wasn't watching where I was going." She took a step back.

"It's okay," he said as his hands fell from her shoulders.

She wanted to wrap her arms around his neck and press her mouth to his. To kiss him until neither of them could breathe anymore. But that wouldn't accomplish anything except ripping her heart open even wider.

God, she missed him, everything about him. She missed wearing one of his T-shirts and smelling like him all day. She missed drinking coffee with him in the mornings, the feel of his fingers in her hair, and his hand at the small of her back. She missed waking him up in the middle of the night to make love. But it hadn't ever been love to him. Just sex because he didn't love her.

"I have to go," she said, needing to get away from him before she started crying in front of the relish display. She stepped around him, and as always he let her walk away.

* * *

Jax still felt the warmth from Grace's skin on his hands, still had the scent of her in his lungs. He'd had her in front of him. Literally had her in his hands, something he'd wanted since he'd let her walk away from him weeks ago, and he hadn't done anything to make her stay.

There were so many things he wanted to say to her. That he was a moron for starters. That he should've never let her go. That he missed her so much it was physically painful to be without her. That he was miserable. That she was everything to him.

That he loved her.

Jax couldn't remember telling anyone that he loved them. He might've told his grandmother at one point, but he wasn't sure. For him, the very idea of saying those three words was terrifying. He'd always thought that saying it would make it real, make it possible to let someone in, make it possible for someone to hurt him.

Parents were supposed to love their children unconditionally, to take care of them, protect them. Jax had never had that. He'd never known love from his own blood, so he'd always thought he wasn't capable of it, that it wasn't part of his DNA.

He was a fucking idiot.

He'd been loved for most of his life, and it might not have been by a family that shared his blood, but it was most definitely by a family that would bleed for him.

He'd had Claire, Lula Mae, and Oliver who'd always treated him like a son. Brendan and Shep who were more like brothers than anything else. Brothers who had helped him through the darkest times in his life, who had helped him build a house because they wanted him to have a home, brothers that called him on his bullshit when he was too blind to see what was standing right in front of him. Well, what *had* been standing right in front of him.

Jax had been there the day Grace came home from the

hospital. It was a couple of months after his grandmother died, and seeing her had been the first real moment he'd felt hope. She was so small, and perfect, and he wanted to protect her like he'd never been protected. And somewhere along the way, he'd fallen in love with her.

Who was he kidding? He'd always been in love with her. The love he had for her at age twenty-nine was definitely different from the love he'd had at five, but it had always been there.

Jax had been running from his love for Grace for a long time. *Too long.* He wanted to tell her as she stood in front of him, but she'd looked up at him with so much pain in her eyes that it had literally taken his breath away.

"I thought you were going to get the beer."

Jax turned and looked at Bennett who was holding a bag of chips and a jar of ranch dip. They'd gone up to the house that afternoon and Bennett helped Jax install the appliances that had been delivered. Afterward, they'd grabbed a pizza to take back to Jax's. The Yankees were playing the Angels so they were going to watch the game and drink beer. Jax had just been missing the beer part of the equation so they'd stopped by the supermarket.

"I ran into Grace." Literally.

"Oh." Bennett nodded. "How'd that go?"

"I'm an idiot."

"Well, Shep and Brendan are pretty likely to agree with that statement."

"Yeah." Jax nodded, running his hand through his hair and turning back in the direction Grace had gone.

"Go after her. Talk to her."

"She's working tonight."

"Oh, yeah, that funeral for Gene Fritch."

"Let me go get the beer," Jax said as he turned around and headed toward the refrigerated section. Well, at least he had the night to figure out how to get her back.

* * *

"All right, what's going on with you?"

Grace looked up from stacking another tray of cookies. Harper was standing in the kitchen doorway, her hands folded under her ample breasts and a frown on her lips.

"Seriously?" Grace asked, raising her eyebrows.

"Besides the obvious." Harper waved one of her hands in the air. "Something happened. Your mood has gotten funkier since I saw you yesterday."

"I saw Jax," Grace said softly. And she felt like she'd been ripped in half for the last three hours.

"Here?" Harper looked over her shoulder at the crowded hallway.

"No, earlier tonight at the store," Grace said as she started stacking cookies again. "Where's Mel?"

Even though Gene Fritch hadn't been the one to hire Harper, nor had he really had anything to do with the spa, technically he had been her boss. Harper had to come to the service, so she dragged Mel along with her.

"I don't know. I got cornered by Tarvis Fritch, one of Gene's disgusting grandsons, and I only just got away. Who hits on someone at a funeral?"

"Creepers."

"Exactly. And don't think I'm going to let you get away with that little subject change."

Grace sighed and looked up.

"Okay, I'm not going to push you on this right now, but be prepared for Mel and me kidnapping you when this is all said and done."

"I have to help my grandmother clean up first."

"Oh, no, you don't," Lula Mae said, coming into the kitchen. "Pinky, Panky, and your grandfather are here. We can take care of it." Lula Mae turned to Harper. "You take her with you when this is all finished."

"Yes, ma'am," Harper said, giving Grace a big "I won" smile. "I'm going to go find Mel." She turned around and left the kitchen.

Graced followed, carrying her newly stacked tray of cookies. She went out into the crowded hallway and into the viewing room.

Carla was standing by the casket, sobbing loudly as people hugged her. She was wearing a bright red dress and enough diamonds that Grace felt like she needed to put on her sunglasses to help with the glare.

Grace put the cookies down and then headed upstairs to use the bathroom. The one downstairs had a line ten people deep. When she walked out, she ran smack into Missy who was coming out of the casket display room.

"What are you doing up here?" Missy asked, narrowing her eyes at Grace suspiciously.

"Going to the bathroom. Do I need to ask permission these days?"

"You don't need to be up here," Missy snapped.

"Missy, can't you find something better to do than be a giant pain in everybody's ass?" Grace didn't wait for an answer before she sidestepped Missy and headed back down into the crowd.

* * *

It was almost eleven by the time Grace, Mel, and Harper got out of the funeral home.

"Where are we going?" Grace asked as she climbed into the backseat of Harper's car.

"Don't you worry about it," Harper said as she started the ignition. "So what happened when you saw Jax?"

Grace rested her head back on the seat and stared up at the ceiling. "Well, I *ran* into him and he put his hands on me to steady me. I miss his hands. I miss him," she said unable to stop her voice from cracking.

"Oh, sweetie," Mel said sympathetically.

"Did he say anything?" Harper asked.

"Well"—Grace pulled her head up—"I told him I was sorry for running into him. And he said, 'It's okay.' That's it. Well except when he said my name. I wanted to throw myself into his arms just as much as I wanted to run away."

"Ugh," Harper said, shaking her head. "I really just want to smack him."

"Me, too," Mel said.

"Look, I'm fine with us doing whatever tonight. But can we not talk about him? Please?"

"Talk about who?" Harper asked.

"I have no idea," Mel said.

"Thanks." Grace closed her eyes as she leaned her head against the seat again.

"But can we please talk about Tarvis Fritch hitting on Harper?" Mel asked. "Because that *has* to be discussed."

Grace couldn't help the smile that spread across her lips. Really, she couldn't ask for better friends. They were always just what she needed.

"Oh, jeez," Harper groaned.

"So when are you two going on a date?" Mel went on. "Is he going to take you out on his big fancy yacht. Seduce you under the light of a full moon."

"Shut up," Harper said. "He's disgusting. He kept leaning into me to talk, breathing on my neck." Harper shivered. "And he touched me. I'm going to have to burn this dress now."

"Oh, that's a shame. I like that dress," Grace said.

"I did, too," Harper said sadly.

The car slowed and came to a stop. Grace pulled her head up and saw that they were in front of Rejuvenate Spa and Salon, the other place that Harper worked.

"What are we doing here?" Grace asked as she unbuckled her seat belt.

"We're about to have a little fun of our own," Harper said, turning to Grace and grinning over her shoulder. "I asked Celeste and she said we could have free rein."

"Seriously?" Grace asked.

Rejuvenate was not a cheap place to go. On average they made about one hundred dollars per client.

"Yup." Harper grinned. "Let's go."

All three girls got out of the car.

"And I got some loot." Harper handed a bottle of wine to Mel.

"How did you get that?" Grace asked, unable to keep herself from grinning.

"She flirted with the bartender," Mel said.

"Never say I didn't do anything for you," Harper said as she unlocked the door and pushed it open.

All three girls stepped in and as Harper moved toward the alarm panel, Grace shut the door behind them.

Grace saw it a second before it happened. She turned to her left as a figure moved in the dark. There was a loud bang and someone was screaming as Mel fell to the ground, the wine bottle shattering on the floor.

Chapter Nineteen

One and Only

Jax was rubbing at the label on his beer bottle. Rolling and unrolling the paper as the game played in the background. The Yankees were up in the bottom of the eighth, but Jax just couldn't seem to care.

When he'd been with Grace, there were rewards for their team winning. She'd bought him a pair of Red Sox boxers and he had to wear them whenever they won. When the Yankees won, she had to wear a navy blue thong with NY embroidered on the front; there'd also been a matching lace bra.

"Why don't you just call her," Bennett said from his side of the couch. "I'm sure she's still up. You can go over and talk to her. Fix things."

"I don't know how to fix things," Jax said, shaking his head.

"Tell her that you messed up, that you love her."

Jax stopped rubbing the label and looked over at Bennett. Jax had never actually said those words out loud, or admitted it to anyone.

"I'm not an idiot. You loving Grace isn't a shock to

anyone besides you," Bennett said as he took a drink of his beer.

"Apparently not."

"Just tell her the truth."

"That easy?"

"I have no clue." Bennett shook his head.

Jax's phone started ringing in his pocket and he pulled it out. It was Baxter. Jax slid his thumb across the screen to accept the call.

"Anderson," Jax said.

"There was a B and E at Rejuvenate," Baxter said, getting right to the point. "The suspects have fled but three women walked in and one was shot. I was at the funeral with Preston tonight before I went on duty. I heard Harper tell Mel they were going to go over there with Grace."

Jax couldn't breathe. Panic so severe he thought he was going to black out filled his chest, constricting his lungs. Grace was in danger, possibly shot, and he wasn't there to protect her. He couldn't do it. He couldn't lose her. He'd just figured out she was it for him. He hadn't even told her he loved her.

"Is anyone on scene?" He was on his feet and heading toward his bedroom.

"No. I'm the closest and I'm ten minutes away."

"I'm leaving now," Jax said as he hung up and stuck the phone in his back pocket.

"What's going on?" Bennett asked from the other room.

"Someone was shot when they interrupted a burglary. Baxter thinks it was Grace, Mel, and Harper that walked in on it," Jax called out as he grabbed his gun.

When he walked back out Bennett was already at the door.

"What are you doing?" Jax asked.

"I'm going with you."

"Bennett you can't—"

"The hell I'm not," he snapped out.

Jax wasn't going to argue. He could barely focus on anything. The only coherent thought going through his brain was that he had to get to Grace. He kept picturing the accident last year. Grace hurt, and crying. This couldn't be happening again. She just couldn't be shot. And if it wasn't her, it was someone she loved deeply. Someone he cared about, too.

He needed to get to her. He had to get to her. He had to save her.

They were out the door and Jax turned on the police radio as he started up his deputy's truck. He backed out of the driveway and hit the lights and siren the second he got on the road. He tore through the streets of Mirabelle, but he couldn't drive fast enough.

"Be on the lookout for Chad Sharp and Hoyt Reynolds..." Mary Landers's voice said from the radio.

"Shit," Bennett said under his breath.

The panic coursing through Jax was beyond overwhelming, but after hearing those two names it intensified tenfold. Chad and Hoyt were involved with all of this. One of those two assholes had shot somebody. If it was the last thing he did he was going to make them pay. And if it was Grace they shot, they'd be lucky if he didn't kill them.

He needed to be next to Grace. He had to see that she was okay. He had to know that he hadn't lost her. Lost the only woman he ever loved.

He pulled into the parking lot and barely put the truck in park before he was out the door. Rejuvenate's alarm was blaring as Jax sprinted to the building. As he mounted the steps, Grace opened the front door.

The relief at seeing her was knee weakening. He was surprised he didn't fall to her feet and start crying. He wanted to wrap his arms around her and never let go. But that wasn't a reality in the current situation. She might not have been hurt, but somebody else was.

"Jax." She said his name through a sob. "It's Mel; she's been shot."

He grabbed her hand and brought her to his side. He pulled her into the building, Bennett following closely behind them. A small table lamp let off a dim glow. Harper was kneeling above Mel, pressing a blood-soaked scarf into Mel's shoulder.

Bennett was wearing a flannel shirt over his T-shirt. He pulled it off as he crossed the room, glass crunching under his boots. He came around to Mel's other side and kicked back some glass before he knelt to the ground. "Mel, it's going to be okay," he said calmly as he put his hands and shirt over Harper's trembling ones. "Understand? You're going to be fine."

"Okay," she whispered as tears streamed from her wide, terrified eyes.

"I got it," Bennett said, looking up into Harper's face.

Harper nodded and pulled her hands out from under his.

It was when Harper turned away that Jax saw it, the flare of barely contained panic in Bennett's eyes. It was a look that said, *not her, anybody but her.* But Bennett got it under control as he looked back down to Mel.

Harper slowly got to her feet, and when she stood, Jax saw that her knees were cut and bleeding. She'd been kneeling in the glass. She'd taken about two steps before her knees buckled. Jax let go of Grace and lunged forward, catching Harper before she hit the ground. He braced her back with one of his arms and put the other behind her knees.

"What's the glass from?" Jax asked as he carried Harper to the couch in the corner.

"A bottle of wine," Grace said as she followed him.

"Harper," Jax said as he sat her down. "Are you okay?"

"I just . . . I got a little light-headed." She blinked her eyes rapidly.

"You're in shock. It's okay. Just sit here." He kneeled down in front of her.

"It was Chad and Hoyt," Grace said softly.

"I know." Jax looked up at her.

"How'd you know to come?"

"Baxter called. He knew you guys were here, and he was ten minutes away. Grace, who was it? Who pulled the trigger?"

"Chad."

Jax took a deep breath trying to calm himself. It really wouldn't have mattered who'd pulled the trigger, Jax would've hated the stupid fucker no matter what.

Jax looked up as a new set of flashing lights pulled into the parking lot. Baxter was getting out of his truck as the ambulance pulled in. The paramedics came into the room and loaded Mel onto a stretcher. Harper was going to need stitches so she went in the ambulance to the hospital. Neal Sanders, the other deputy working on the burglary cases, showed up just as the ambulance pulled out.

"Grace," Jax said, turning to her. She'd been glued to his side, but he needed to wrap his arms around her, to bury his nose in her hair and inhale deeply. So he did just that.

"Hmm?" she mumbled as she pressed her face into his chest and wrapped her arms around him.

"Bennett is going to drive you to the hospital in Harper's car," he said as he rubbed his hands up and down her back.

"Where are you going?" she asked panicked as she looked up at him.

"I have to stay here for a little while. As soon as I take care of things I'll be there, okay?"

"Okay." She nodded. "Jax, I—"

He didn't let her finish. No, he'd needed to press his mouth to hers. Grace's hands gripped his hips as he held on to her for dear life. His mouth slanted over hers and he kissed her with every ounce of himself, with all the need that had been building in him since she'd left, with the desperation that had almost killed him in the last twenty minutes.

"God, I've missed you," he said, resting his forehead against hers.

"I've missed you, too," she whispered.

He pulled back and looked at her, palming the side of her face in his hand.

"There are a thousand things I need to tell you. I—"

"Jax," Baxter called from the front door. "We're going to need you to get in here."

"Okay." He spared Baxter a glance before he turned back to Grace.

"It's okay," she said, putting her hand over his. "We'll talk later."

"Later," he nodded as he brought his mouth down to hers for one last kiss.

* * *

The same scratch marks that had been on all the locks for the other burglaries were on the locks at Rejuvenate. Chad and Hoyt had broken in through the back door. The alarm had the same sixty-second delay as the others, so Chad and Hoyt had gotten into the building less than a minute before the girls had.

Rejuvenate sold a fancy line of jewelry that cost about one hundred dollars for a bracelet, and almost one fifty for a necklace. The makers of the jewelry claimed that different stones would help the wearer with different traits, such as patience or memory. It was all a load of crap in Jax's opinion, but apparently the stuff sold like crazy. Rejuvenate had over ten thousand dollars' worth of the stuff, but Chad and Hoyt hadn't had a chance to get it before they were interrupted.

It had taken four hours to get a search warrant for Chad's and Hoyt's houses. When Jax and the deputies searched their places they found enough evidence to put the guys away for a long time. They had pills from the pharmacy, merchandise from the specialty shop, paintings and antiques from the beach houses. They'd accumulated quite a collection. And to top it all off, Preston's wallet was found in Hoyt's house.

* * *

It was after six in the morning by the time Jax got to the hospital. Grace was curled up on a couch wearing green scrubs. Her head rested on the back of the couch and her eyes were closed. Mel's fourteen-year-old brother Hamilton was next to her, his head resting in Grace's lap as he slept. Grace's hand was in his hair, like she'd been soothing him to sleep and had fallen asleep herself.

Bennett was sitting across from Grace, also wearing a set of green scrubs. They'd apparently gotten more blood on themselves than Jax had. He'd only had some on his T-shirt but he'd had a spare in his truck. Bennett was awake, nursing a cup of coffee. He stood when he saw Jax and crossed to him.

"How's Mel?" Jax asked.

"Out of surgery. The bullet didn't hit anything vital. She woke up a little while ago to talk to Deputy Hough. He already took everyone's statement. Mel's parents are with her in the room."

"Good," Jax said as some of the tension left his shoulders. "Where's Harper?"

"Preston took her home. There wasn't really anything else to wait around for."

"Really," Jax asked, raising his eyebrows. "Then why are you still here?"

Bennett hesitated for just a second before he spoke. "I was waiting to talk to you. You find anything?"

"Just the stuff they stole. Not them," Jax said, shaking his head in disappointment.

Bennett's mouth flattened into a thin line and anger flared in his eyes. "If I ever come across that son-of-a-bitch I'll kill him."

"Get in line, man," Jax said, clapping Bennett on the shoulder before he walked over to Grace. He leaned over and pressed his mouth to her neck. "Baby, wake up," he whispered.

She stirred and slowly opened her eyes. She had to blink a couple of times to adjust to the hospital's fluorescent lights.

"Hey," she said, straightening and reaching for him. She placed her hands on either side of his face and brought his mouth to hers. When she pulled back a second later she rested her forehead against his.

"How you doing?" he asked.

"Better now that you're here."

"You ready to go home?" he asked, pulling back.

"I don't want to leave him." She indicated Hamilton.

"I'll stay with him," Bennett said.

"You sure?" Grace asked, looking over at Bennett.

"Absolutely." He nodded.

And there was a look in Bennett's eyes that said he wasn't going anywhere anytime soon.

* * *

The second they were in the truck, Jax reached across to Grace and she climbed into his lap gladly. He held her to him, and his mouth found hers. He kissed her passionately, his fingers winding into her hair and his tongue moving against hers. God she'd missed his hands on her. His mouth on her. He pulled back a couple minutes later and buried his face in her hair. It felt so good to be back in his arms. Like she was home again.

"I don't want to let you go, but we need to talk and I really don't want to do it in a hospital parking lot."

"Then let's go," she said, looking up at him.

He kissed her softly on the mouth before his arms loosened and she climbed out of his lap. She settled on the other side of the truck missing his arms already. When she was all buckled in, he put the truck in reverse and backed out of the parking lot. When they were on the road, he grabbed her hand in his and rubbed his thumb back and forth across her knuckles.

A thousand thoughts had gone through Grace's head all night, and she'd barely had a chance to process anything. She didn't know what Jax was thinking. Where his thoughts were on where they stood. What he wanted. How he felt. But with the way he'd been holding her, touching her, and kissing her, she thought that maybe he wanted to be with her, that maybe he loved her.

But until those words came out of his mouth, she wasn't going to risk her heart again. She couldn't be with him if he didn't love her. She couldn't put her heart into something knowing it was just going to get broken.

Grace was surprised when he turned off and started driving toward Mirabelle Beach, but she didn't say anything.

When they pulled into the parking lot, the sun had just started to make an appearance over the water. Jax helped her out of the truck and they both slipped off their shoes, leaving them in the cab of the truck before they walked out to the beach. The waves crashed against the shore and the warm breeze blowing from the Gulf blew Grace's hair around her face. The sand was still cool under her feet, and it felt good running between her toes.

Jax was quiet next to her. Her hand was in his again and he'd picked up the rubbing motion across her knuckles. When they reached the wet sand they turned and started to make their way down the beach, the water lapping up around their feet as it rolled in and out. She knew him well enough to know he was trying to figure out where to start. So she patiently waited and gave him his time.

"I screwed up," Jax said after they'd walked for a couple of minutes. He stopped short and she turned to him. She settled her hands on his chest as he put his hands on her waist and pulled her into his body. "For so long I thought I only *wanted* you. I've never really gotten anything that I've wanted, so I never thought I'd get you. And then when I finally did, it didn't seem real," he said, shaking his head.

"You were the dream, not the reality, and it was just a matter of time before I woke up and you were gone. But when that happened, when you left, when I let you walk away... forced you to walk away," he said, closing his eyes and shaking his head. When he opened them again a moment later they were filled with so much pain that Grace's heart hurt. "I was in a nightmare without you. I was wrong when I thought I only wanted you. I *need* you. You're the most important person in my life. I love you, Grace King."

Finally.

Grace threw her arms up around Jax's neck and pulled herself up so she could bury her face in his throat.

"I love you, too," she whispered. "So much."

He took a deep breath and held her to him.

"I'm so sorry," he said, kissing her temple. "I wish I could go back to the first time you'd told me, that I could've appreciated it fully, that I'd told you I love you, too. Because I did, I loved you then."

"It's okay, Jax," she said, pulling back so she could look up into his face.

"I'll never take you for granted again. I swear."

"Jax?"

"Yes."

"Kiss me," she pleaded.

And he did just that.

* * *

Jax brought Grace back to his house, where they made love. It was different that time. So much more than all the other times they'd been together. And it was all because of those three little words. Except those words really weren't so little; they were monumental and they changed everything.

He loved her.

And he proceeded to tell her that over and over again as he touched her, and kissed her, and moved inside of her. He hadn't been the only one saying it, either. Every time she said she loved him he thought his heart was going to burst. It was the most wonderful feeling to hear those words coming across her perfect lips.

For Jax, finally admitting that he loved Grace, letting her love him, was undeniably the most life-changing experience he'd ever had, and he never ever wanted to go back.

* * *

Something was ringing over and over again. When it finally stopped it was replaced by a heavy pounding that got louder and louder.

Then the ringing was back.

Ringing. Hammering. Ringing. Hammering.

"Jax," Grace moaned into his chest. "What's going on?"

"Hmm?" he said, turning into her.

"What's that noise?"

"Someone's at the door," he groaned as he pulled away from her and got out of bed.

"Tell them to go away." She grabbed a pillow to hold on to since she couldn't hold on to Jax anymore.

A drawer opened and shut and the sound of Jax walking down the hallway was drowned out by the incessant noise coming from the front of the house. It stopped a moment later and voices echoed down the hallway.

"Grace," Brendan bellowed. "I'd like to talk to you."

Grace bolted up suddenly wide awake.

Fantastic. Brendan sounded pissed.

Grace got out of bed and grabbed one of Jax's T-shirts and a pair of shorts from the drawer that still held some of her clothes. She walked down the hallway, passing the trail of clothes that she and Jax had left behind as they made their way to the shower when they walked in the door that morning. They'd stayed under the warm spray for a good while before Jax turned off the water and carried her, dripping wet, to his bed. She never even had a chance to get cold before he covered her body with his and made love to her. Twice.

"What's different this time?" Brendan asked a tad bit aggressively.

"I'm in love with her. I realized I always have been."

Grace paused just before she rounded the corner. Jax had told her he loved her more times than she could count within the last few hours. But every time he said it, her heart fluttered. And the fact that he was telling Brendan was a big deal.

"So you finally figured it out?" Brendan asked, sounding slightly mollified.

"Yeah. I screwed up pretty big. And not just with her. I'm sorry, man."

"I've had my head up my ass before," Brendan said. "We're good."

Grace rounded the corner just as they slapped hands and came in for a quick man hug.

"Does that mean I'm off the hook, too?" Grace asked.

Brendan pulled back from Jax and looked down at his little sister. The pissed-off look was back in full force for only a moment before it crumpled and was replaced with a look of worry, followed by relief. He crossed over to her and pulled her into a breath-stealing hug.

"Why didn't you call me?" he asked, holding on to her.

"It was the middle of the night," she said, and wrapped her arms around him.

"I don't care." He pulled back and held her shoulders in his hands. "You've had everybody freaking out. Grams called me on the verge of a nervous breakdown because Mindy Trist came into the café this morning talking about the shooting."

"Shit." Grace winced.

"Yeah, Grams thought that maybe you'd just stayed out late with Harper and Mel, and that's why you weren't in, but when you didn't answer your phone, she started to panic. I think Pops is on the verge of a coronary. So unless you want to kill our grandparents, please call them."

"All right, all right, I get it. Next time someone shoots at me, I'll call you."

"That isn't funny," Jax and Brendan said at the same time.

"Brendan, I'm fine."

"It could've just as easily been you that had gotten shot," Jax said from behind them.

Grace turned and looked at him, his face dark and foreboding.

"What happened?" Brendan asked.

"Why don't I fill you in while Grace calls your grandparents?" Jax took a step back toward the kitchen. "You want some coffee?"

"Sure," Brendan said, giving Grace a quick peck on the forehead before he let her go and followed Jax.

It took Grace a good twenty minutes to reassure her grandparents. She called in and checked on Harper, then Mel, who was awake and doing pretty good for someone who'd just been shot. Grace promised to stop by the hospital later that day. When Grace hung up she went to the kitchen to join Jax and Brendan.

"Mel's doing good," she said as Jax fixed her a cup of coffee. She looked up at the display above the stove. It was almost one, so she and Jax had gotten about four hours of sleep before Brendan showed up.

"You going to see her?" Jax asked as he handed her the mug.

"Yeah, and Grams said they had to leave some stuff at the funeral home last night." She settled into his side. "So I'm going over there to pick it up."

"I need to go down to the station. See what's going on." Jax slid an arm around her.

"I hope they lock those two assholes up and throw away the key," Brendan said.

"Got to catch them first. And those two are as slimy as they come," Jax said, his grip on Grace tightening as he kissed the top of her head.

* * *

Jax dropped Grace off at the funeral home at three to get her car, but she didn't go inside to grab the stuff from the café. She was too anxious to see Mel. Besides, the funeral home was on the way back from the hospital so she was just going to swing by and grab everything before she went back to Jax's.

Mel was sitting up in bed watching TV when Grace walked into the room. Her arm was in a sling and her curly hair was piled on top of her head. Grace dropped her purse on the chair and hugged Mel as tight as she could without hurting her.

"I'm so glad you're okay." Grace sniffled as more than a few tears slid down her nose. "I was so scared."

"Me, too," Mel said, holding on with her one good arm.

They stayed that way for a little while before Grace pulled back, running her fingers underneath her eyes.

"No more crying," Mel said as she wiped at her own.

"I'll try." Grace sat down in the chair next to Mel's bed.

"So you and Jax are back together." Mel grinned.

"How did you know?"

"Harper."

"Of course."

"And," Mel pressed, waving her good hand in the air. "What happened?"

"He told me he loves me," Grace said, chewing on her bottom lip.

"Oh, Grace, that's wonderful. But what's with the nervous lip biting?" Mel frowned.

"While you were off getting shot I was getting back together with my boyfriend."

"Okay," Mel said, shaking her head. "Enough with that. I'm going to be fine, and life goes on. I couldn't be happier for you."

"I'm really glad you're okay." Grace was unable to stop her eyes from welling up again.

"What did I tell you about crying?" Mel asked sternly as her eyes started to water.

The two women finally composed themselves after another couple of tear-filled minutes.

"Apparently word travels fast," Grace said, eyeing Mel's goodie pile as she threw a tissue in the trash. On the table next to Mel's bed sat a teddy bear, four different flower arrangements, multiple boxes of chocolates, and a bouquet of balloons reaching for the ceiling, drifting back and forth in the current from the AC.

"Most of that's from my students."

"Nice," Grace said, pulling a pint of cookie dough ice cream from her purse.

"Ice cream? You're officially my second favorite."

"Who's number one?" Grace feigned offense.

"Well, I really like the teddy bear."

"Who got you that?" Grace asked as she dug around for the two spoons.

"Bennett," Mel said softly.

Grace stopped digging in her purse and looked up at Mel. "He came back?"

"He didn't leave the hospital until about eleven this morning."

"What?" Grace asked. "What's going on between the two of you? Have you been holding out on me?"

"No," Mel said, shaking her head. "I haven't been holding out because nothing is going on. I mean the man is gorgeous, there's no doubt, but really what chance do I have?"

"You're gorgeous, too. Have you looked in the mirror lately? Well, I mean not today," Grace said, letting her mouth twitch.

"Oh, thank you. You're making me feel so much better."

"Seriously, Mel, you're beautiful. What makes you think you couldn't get him?"

"It's nothing, Grace. We're just friends. I find him attractive. End of story."

Oh, Grace was fairly sure this wasn't the end of the story. It was just the beginning.

"Really? So your voice gets all warm and dreamy when you talk about all your friends?"

"It did not," Mel protested.

"It so did, *'Bennett,'* " Grace simpered.

"Shut up and find the stupid spoons," Mel snapped.

"Well, no need to get crabby or anything." Grace grinned as she went back to her digging.

Huh, Mel and Bennett. That wouldn't be a bad thing at all.

Not. At. All.

* * *

Jax stopped by King's Auto after he dropped Grace off. He was more than slightly nervous as he got out of his truck and walked into the shop, but really it was now or never.

"Didn't I just see you?" Brendan asked as he came out from behind a car.

"Yeah, you got a minute?" Jax asked, nodding toward the office.

"Yup." Brendan pulled his gloves off.

"Well, if it isn't the man of the hour." Oliver stood up and rounded his desk. He pulled Jax into a hug and slapped him affectionately on the back.

"I didn't do anything," Jax said, shaking his head as Oliver pulled back.

"Nonsense." Oliver waved off Jax's words. "Brendan told me that as soon as you found out what was going on you drove like a mad man to get to my granddaughter."

"Did Bennett tell you that?" Jax asked, looking over at Brendan.

"Yup, he said he was scared for his life."

Oh, Jax was sure that Bennett was scared, but he was pretty sure it had nothing to do with Jax's driving.

"I was scared for mine, too. I had to get to Grace. As it turns out, I've always been trying to get to her. I know that now," Jax said, looking at both men.

Brendan's eyes narrowed, but a slight smile curved the side of his mouth. Oliver just looked at Jax, his expression neutral except for the twinkle in his eye. Jax took a deep breath before he continued.

"I messed up with her before. Messed up when I let her doubt for a second how I felt about her."

"And how's that?" Oliver asked.

"She's it for me. I love her and I want to spend the rest of my life with her. And I'm hoping the two of you will be okay with that."

"Uh, I'm sorry, son," Oliver said. "I'm not *okay* with that."

Jax's stomach promptly fell down somewhere to the region of his feet.

"Me, either." Brendan shook his head.

"Thrilled would be a better word," Oliver said, looking at Brendan.

"Or elated," Brendan offered as his mouth split into a huge grin.

"Ecstatic." Oliver nodded and smiled. "Jax, you've always been part of our family. You falling in love with Grace is a gift."

Jax breathed a sigh of relief and shook his head. Falling in love with Grace sure as hell was a gift, and Jax was going to treasure it.

* * *

Grace stopped by the funeral home just after six that evening. She'd wound up staying with Mel longer than she'd expected to, so when she pulled up in front of the funeral home it was empty, everyone having gone home for the night. But Grace had a key so she could let herself in. She really wouldn't have bothered stopping by, but she was going to have to go into the café early the next morning to make up for the day she'd missed, and some of the stuff she needed had been left behind.

The funeral home was an old, two-story Victorian house. It might've been creepy if it wasn't painted a cheerful butter cream yellow. Grace didn't see the place as creepy, but she didn't want to be locked in after hours. There were still dead bodies in there after all. But the sun was still clearly in the sky and she was only going to be inside for five minutes.

Grace unlocked the front door and made her way to the beeping panel to disarm the alarm. She flipped a light switch and the hallway that led to the kitchen filled with light. She put her keys down on the counter and as she reached for the first pile of café items, cold metal jabbed into the side of her head and a hand came up and covered her mouth.

Chapter Twenty

Out of the Frying Pan and Into Hell

There are so many things I want to do to you." Chad's hot breath slapped against Grace's ear, making her stomach heave. "So many things," he said as he pressed his body into hers and forced her to move out of the kitchen and up the stairs. "But there isn't enough time for all that fun at the moment."

"Just put the bitch somewhere where she won't be in the way," Hoyt called out from a room down the hall on the second floor.

"That's what I'm doing," Chad snapped back as he threw Grace into the supply room. She fell forward into the shelves, her hands fumbling for purchase, but it was useless. She hit the shelves and a sharp pain radiated through her head. "You scream and I'll shoot. Understand?"

She nodded. She'd never been more terrified in her life, and if she opened her mouth she'd probably throw up.

"Hold out your hands," he said, pulling a roll of duct tape from the shelf.

She stuck them out and they shook as Chad wound the tape around and around. He tore off a thick piece and slapped it across her mouth before he pulled her down the hallway and threw her into the bathroom.

* * *

A few new developments had been made in the burglary cases. Hoyt and Chad had definitely had a source on the inside of Lock and Load to figure out the logistics to the systems. Too bad Judson had no idea what information he'd been supplying. Judson had been brought in again, and this time it appeared that Judson was telling the truth when he said he wasn't involved.

Chad and Hoyt still hadn't been seen by anyone, nor did anyone have any information on the pair. The sheriff's office was putting in all available resources to look for the assholes, but they'd probably hit the road the night before. All Jax could hope for was that there might be one last thing that they'd need to take care of. One last thing that would get them spotted. One last thing that would get them caught.

Jax stopped by Shep's house on his way back from the station. Things were still a little rocky between them, and Jax knew he was the one who needed to fix it.

Shep didn't say anything when he opened the door and saw Jax on the other side. He just opened his door wider so Jax could step in.

"I'm sorry," Jax said when Shep turned around. "I'm sorry for hitting you. And for thinking you would ever sleep with Grace. And for what I said about you sleeping with anything in a skirt."

"Water under the bridge," Shep said, shaking his head. "I heard about the shooting. I stopped by and saw Mel. Glad she's okay."

"She's lucky it wasn't worse. We're all lucky it wasn't worse."

"Did you fix things with Grace?" Shep asked, folding his arms across his chest.

"Yeah, I—" His voice caught and he stopped. Jax cleared his throat and tried again. "I'm going to ask her to marry me."

"It's about damn time." Shep grinned. "Congratulations, man," he said, and held out his hand. When Jax grabbed it, Shep pulled him into a hug. "You deserve her," Shep said when he pulled back. "You deserve to be happy, too."

"I'm beginning to realize that."

Jax and Shep talked for a couple more minutes before they both headed out the door, Shep to the bar, and Jax home to Grace. Just that very thought made him so freaking happy.

He was halfway there when his phone started ringing. He pulled it out and answered.

"Anderson."

"We have a problem," Baxter said. "Hoyt and Chad were seen going into the funeral home."

"It's after six, no one should be there." Jax turned and started heading toward the funeral home. If Chad and Hoyt were armed and someone was there, they'd have a hostage situation on their hands.

Baxter hesitated for just a second, the last second Jax had before his entire world came crashing down.

"Jax, Grace's car is parked outside."

The world was spinning and Jax couldn't take air into his lungs, which was a problem considering the fact that he was driving.

"I'm three minutes away."

"Meet me in the back," Baxter said before he disconnected.

After the longest three minutes of Jax's life, he pulled into a parking lot across the street from the funeral home.

Jax snuck around to the back of the building and tried to

focus on what he was doing, tried not to let the fear choke him. But that was hard to do when Grace was in that building with two men who wouldn't hesitate to hurt her. He had to get to her. Had to make sure she was okay.

God, this couldn't be happening twice in less than twenty-four hours.

When Jax got to the back, Baxter was waiting for him.

"I called Mr. Adams," Baxter said. "He met me down the street and gave me the keys. I figured a quiet entrance was our best bet. Neal is on his way."

Jax just nodded, unable to move his jaw.

Baxter unlocked the door and opened it quietly. Jax walked into the room, gun drawn, as Baxter followed with his own gun out.

They walked through the room and opened the door into an empty hallway. They made their way through it and passed the kitchen. Jax looked inside to make sure it was empty. The light was on and Grace's keys were sitting on the counter. A sharp pang hit Jax in the chest, but he pushed past it.

A floorboard creaked overhead and voices traveled down from the second floor. Baxter nodded his head toward the other end of the hallway.

Back stairwell, he mouthed as he went off on his own.

Jax nodded as he continued toward the front of the house. He edged along the wall until he got to the funeral home's main viewing room. He checked to make sure it was empty before he moved past it. He eyed the stairs, praying he could get up them without alerting Chad and Hoyt.

He put one foot up and breathed a sigh of relief when it didn't make a sound. He continued up, one painful step at a time. When he reached the top he saw Baxter coming down the hallway from the left, checking the rooms as he went. Jax went right and headed toward the noise coming from the next room.

Hoyt had his back to the door as he ripped at the lining of one of the coffins. Hoyt's gun was laying on top of the closed coffin next to him and within reaching distance.

"Put your hands up and turn around slowly," Jax said as he came up behind Hoyt, angling himself so that he had the doors to the room within his line of sight.

Hoyt froze and did as he was told.

"So you found us," Hoyt said through a look of sheer loathing. "Well, one of us at least. Too bad you didn't find Chad first as he's the one who's taking care of your whore."

"Get down on your knees."

"Funny, that's what Chad was planning on making her do, too," he said as he slowly got down.

"Lie down with your hands behind your back." Jax still had his gun leveled on Hoyt when Neal came into the room.

"I got him," Neal said as he pulled his cuffs out of his belt.

Jax went back out into the hallway and stopped dead. Chad was coming out of a room, using Grace as a shield as he held a gun to her throat. There was duct tape around her wrists and across her mouth, and tears were streaming down her face.

Black dots clouded Jax's vision as he felt like he'd been ripped in half. So this was what dying felt like.

"Let her go," Jax said.

"I don't think so." Chad shook his head. "You see, you have what I want and I have what you want."

"And what do you want?" Jax asked.

"To get out of here with the stuff I came for. But you're currently blocking my path."

Hoyt and Neal were in a room in the front of the house, but the back of the house had a balcony that ran across the second floor. Out of the corner of Jax's eye, he saw through the window in the room to his left. Baxter was currently crossing the balcony, most likely headed for the room that was next to Chad.

"So if I let you go, you'll let her go?"

"Like that's going to happen," Chad said, shaking his head.

"If you don't hurt her, I'll let you walk out of here with whatever the hell you want."

"What if I want her, too?" he asked, sliding his hand down to her breasts.

Grace winced as he touched her, closing her eyes and taking a deep breath through her nose. Jax wanted to launch himself across the room and rip the fucker's arms out of their sockets.

Come on, Baxter, he mentally pleaded.

"Let her go, Chad," Jax repeated.

"No."

Something creaked in the room next to Chad and he moved automatically. As his body turned, he lowered the gun from Grace's throat. Chad was about twenty feet away, and Jax had shot at much smaller targets from a much farther distance. Jax pulled the trigger once, and Chad's gun fell to the ground only a second before he did, cradling his shoulder and screaming.

Grace pulled forward and fell against the wall. She tried to scramble away from Chad into an empty room, but her bound hands didn't let her get very far.

Baxter came out of the room and grabbed the gun that Chad had dropped. Since Baxter was taking care of Chad, Jax went to Grace.

"Are you okay?" Jax asked as he pulled Grace farther into the office.

She nodded, tears still streaming down her face, and her entire body shaking. She was breathing hard through her nose, and Jax was pretty sure she was about to pass out.

"Look at me and breathe," he said, cradling her face in his hands. "I'm going to get the tape off."

He pulled at it slowly, Grace's warm, rushed breath washing out over his knuckles. When her mouth was free she started gasping for air.

"Breathe baby, you have to breathe," he said as he started to work at the tape on her wrists.

The second her hands were free she threw her arms around Jax and clung to him. She sobbed into his throat as he wrapped his arms around her and pulled her into his lap.

"You're okay," he said over and over again.

* * *

The flashing lights were giving Grace a headache. Well, it was probably that and all the crying she'd done, but really what else was to be expected when a lunatic held her at gunpoint. Grace wasn't sure how long Jax held her on the floor of that office, but when they finally went downstairs, Chad and Hoyt were gone. Hoyt was taken directly down to the sheriff's office; Chad had to make a trip to the emergency room first.

The parking lot was filled with multiple sheriffs' cruisers, an ambulance, and a crowd of people. Jax had refused to leave her side and was currently standing guard next to her as the paramedic looked at the cut over her eye.

"I think you'll just need a few butterfly stitches," he said, gently probing her forehead.

She winced when he disinfected the wound. Jax had his hand at the small of her back, and Grace was grateful for it. The only thing keeping her grounded was the sure, steady weight of his hand.

"He didn't do anything else to you?" Jax asked as the paramedic applied the last bandage.

"No," she whispered.

He nodded, none of the tension leaving his face or shoulders.

"Grace!"

She looked up as Brendan, Oliver, and Lula Mae crossed the parking lot.

"Oh, thank God," Lula Mae sobbed, pulling Grace in for a hug.

Grace looked over her grandmother's shoulder at Brendan and Oliver who were both wearing matching expressions of worry.

"You shot him?" Brendan asked, looking at Jax.

Jax nodded. "He'll be going away for a very long time."

"It better be for the rest of his lousy, miserable life," Oliver said, shaking his head. He looked over at Grace and promptly started to cry.

"Pops, I'm okay," Grace said as Lula Mae pulled away and Oliver took her place.

"I know." Oliver held her. "But I've already lost one of my girls. I can't do it again, Gracie."

"I need to go talk to some people," Jax said as he started to step back from the group.

"Oh, no you don't." Lula Mae grabbed him and pulled him in for a hug. "Thank you, Jax. You saved her life," Lula Mae cried as Jax wrapped his arms around her.

Jax looked up and locked eyes with Grace. "Grace is my life."

* * *

Jax and Grace headed to the station so Grace could give her statement. When they arrived Jax had to give his own statement, and he looked more than a little bit panicky when he had to leave her side.

"I'm fine," she said, giving him a small smile.

"All right." He gave her a kiss on the forehead before he walked down the hall.

Grace told Lieutenant Lancaster exactly what had happened from the moment she walked into the funeral home. She was surprised she'd been able to remember everything past the blind panic that had consumed her for the majority of the time, but she somehow managed to get through the story.

Grace and Jax didn't get home until after midnight. She was exhausted and all she wanted to do was crawl into bed and not move for days.

The second she walked in the door she headed for the bathroom. They'd given her a lot of hot tea at the station and it had made its way to her bladder on the ride home. When she finished washing her hands she dug a hair tie out of the drawer next to the sink. Jax hadn't moved any of her stuff when they'd been apart.

She pulled her hair up and grabbed a washcloth, soaking it in cold water before she wiped the dried tears from her face. Mascara and eyeliner had smudged under her eyes and she washed that away before she ran the cool cloth to the back of her neck. Her skin was still crawling from where Chad had touched her and she wanted to wash that off, but she needed to talk to Jax first.

When she opened the door she saw Jax in the bedroom. He was sitting at the edge of the bed, his arms resting on his knees as he stared into his open hands. He didn't say anything as she sat down next to him, just continued to stare at his hands.

"Jax?" she asked, reaching out and putting her hand in one of his.

His long fingers closed over hers as he shook his head. "He had a gun to your head," he whispered thickly.

"I'm okay," she said.

He turned to her, tears streaming down his face. "But what if you hadn't been?"

"Oh, Jax," she said, inhaling sharply. Grace had never seen Jax cry, not once, and he was crying for her.

"I keep seeing it . . . seeing you . . . bound . . . with his arms around you . . . touching you . . . and that gun . . . God, that gun . . ." He closed his eyes and turned into her, wrapping his arms around her and placing his head over her heart.

Grace pulled her legs up onto the bed so she could wrap herself around him. She rested her head on the back of his neck, one of her hands stroking his shoulders, the other in his hair.

"I can't lose you . . . I can't . . . do it," he choked out.

"I know. I can't lose you, either. I love you, Jax." She kissed the nape of his neck.

"I love you. I love you. I love you," he said over and over again.

They both cried and held on to each other, neither of them wanting to be the first to let go.

Epilogue

All You Ever Wanted

Jax was busy at work all week dealing with the aftereffects of the burglaries, the shooting at Rejuvenate, and the disaster at the funeral home. Every morning, he left the house with Grace at seven and didn't get back until after nine.

Apparently Missy Lee had been stealing from the dead for years. She would take a necklace, or a gold watch, or a ring here and there. She'd pawn the items whenever she'd go on one of her big trips, but not too much to draw attention to herself. While she waited to pawn them, she'd stashed them at the funeral home, hiding them in the lining of the display caskets and inside the urns. She'd stolen all of the stuff that Gene Fritch had wanted to be buried with.

Missy had let Chad in on her secret. When Chad and Hoyt were identified at Rejuvenate, they knew they needed to get out of town, but they decided to liberate Missy's contraband before they did so. They'd been hiding out in an abandoned gas station across the street from the funeral home waiting for their perfect opportunity, which Grace had provided.

Missy Lee didn't take very well to being backstabbed.

The second she'd found out what Chad and Hoyt had been up to, but after she'd already been presented with insurmountable proof of her own theft, she squealed like it had been nobody's business. In the end, all three of them were going to pay for their crimes.

Jax might've been working long hours, but he stayed in constant contact with Grace, calling her and texting her. He knew she was okay for the most part, but he had a desperate need to see her, to touch her, to hold her. He'd come apart when he saw Chad holding that gun to her head. He'd broken right in half, and having her in his arms was the only way he felt whole.

Whenever Jax was in the same room as her, he had to be touching her. Whether it was his hand at the small of her back, his fingers in her hair, or his legs tangled with hers as he held her in bed. He knew he'd never get tired of touching her; never get tired of her warm, soft skin beneath his hands. He loved how she responded to his touch, how she reached for him and curled into his body. He loved the contented sigh that escaped her mouth even when she was asleep.

He just loved her and he was ready to prove it in every single way.

* * *

It was a little over a week after the funeral home incident, when Grace and Jax had a Sunday off together. They slept in that morning, Grace sprawled across Jax, using his chest as her pillow. When they got up, Jax asked if she'd like to go see the finished product of his house. Grace hadn't been inside for over a month and she was excited to see it.

Jax was anxious as they drove up and it only intensified the closer they got. Grace knew he was nervous about the house. He'd never gotten approval from his parents, and showing her something that he'd put so much of himself into was probably more than a little nerve-racking for the guy.

But Grace had full faith in what he'd created. She had full faith in him. He'd worked on the house with his own hands, kind and gentle hands that she loved. There was no way those hands hadn't created something amazing.

The outside was finished, too. Jax had painted the exterior a dark gray, with white trim and a bright red door.

"Wow." Grace smiled at him. "It's beautiful."

"Well, you like the outside. Let's hope you like the inside, too." He led her up the steps.

"I'm going to love it," she said, squeezing his hand reassuringly.

"All right." He smiled at her nervously before he put the key in. The lock clicked and he pushed open the door.

The air-conditioning was running. Cool air wrapped around Grace as she stepped through the door. She couldn't help the small gasp that escaped her lips as she walked into the hallway. It was painted in the dove gray she had picked out. Hardwood floors stretched out toward the living room and into the brightly painted red room next to where Jax was standing.

"That'll be the office," Jax said, pointing to the room.

"I like the Boston Red Sox's red." She grinned.

"It's just red," he said, shaking his head. "Nothing Boston about it."

"Mmm hmm." She grinned as she made her way down the hallway to explore more. "Oh, Jax," she said as she came into the living room, "it's beautiful."

The ceilings were vaulted. Amber wooden planks came together from the front and back of the house. The dove gray walls made all of the white edging pop. Grace spun around slowly, taking it all in, and when her eyes landed on the kitchen, she stopped, stunned.

"Oh, my God," she breathed, covering her mouth with her hands.

It was her dream kitchen, down to the very last detail. The same hardwood as the rest of the house covered the floors. The countertops were black granite. The cabinets a creamy off-white and a couple of the ones above the counter had paneled glass doors. The refrigerator was housed in the same wood as the cabinets and it blended in perfectly. There were two ovens stacked on top of each other built into the wall, and an eight-burner stove sat in the middle of the back counter.

The sink was on the right wall with a window above it. There were two islands in the middle of the room. One had a wooden rack hanging above it and it had already been filled with all her pots and pans from her apartment. The other island was set up as a bar, with a light gray granite counter-top and bar stools lined up on one side.

It was perfect. Had he built it for her?

"Jax?" she whispered through her hands as she turned around to look at him.

He was standing right behind her, and his hands came up to grip her elbows and pull her hands away from her mouth.

"I've never really had a place to call home. Where I grew up with my parents, that wasn't a home," he said, shaking his head. "It wasn't a place that I felt safe or loved. The first time I ever really felt safe was at your grandparents' house. You came along a very short time after. I remember seeing you for the first time, and you were so small and innocent, and all I could think was how beautiful you were.

"You brought something into my life, Grace, something I'd never known before. I didn't know what it was at five, but you changed me. I was always drawn to your grandparents' house growing up, but it wasn't because I found my home there, it was because I found my home in you."

Tears were falling freely down Grace's cheeks, and Jax reached up to run his fingers beneath her eyes.

"This kitchen was always part of the plan. *Your* kitchen was always part of the plan. And it's because *you* were always part of the plan, it just took me a little while to figure it out. I built this house for you, every part of it. I wanted to give you what you gave me. Because, Grace, you're my home. The place I feel safe and loved and wanted. The place where all the brokenness from the past goes away and it's just you and me.

"I denied my feelings for you for so long, but when it comes right down to it, you're undeniable. I want to spend the rest of my life with you," he said, reaching into his pocket and pulling out a small velvet box as he got down on one knee.

"Jax," she whispered, trying to remember to breathe.

"Grace Elizabeth King, will you marry me?" he asked as he flipped open the box.

She didn't even look at the ring, because she couldn't take her eyes off his.

"Yes." She didn't hesitate. She'd never been surer of anything in her life.

The smile on his face was like nothing she'd ever seen before. He grabbed her hand and slid the ring on. Then he was on his feet, pulling her into him and bringing his mouth to hers. She wrapped her arms around his neck as his hands went down to her thighs and he pulled her legs up around his waist. He walked her backward and sat her down on one of the islands in the middle of the kitchen.

He pulled back and buried his face in her neck. "I love you, Grace. I love you so much," he said as he kissed her throat.

"I love you, too," she said, resting her chin on his shoulder.

Her arms were still wrapped around his neck, giving her a perfect view of the ring. It was beautiful. The diamond was over a karat and it was set in a platinum band.

"You bought me a princess cut diamond?" she asked, unable to stop herself from laughing.

"Yup," he pulled back, grinning at her. "I always told you that you were a princess. I thought it was pretty fitting."

"It's perfect. I can't believe you." She shook her head. "I can't believe you did all this," she said, indicating the kitchen with her hand.

"I wanted to give you something, something like you gave me."

"You already did, Jax." Grace smiled, reaching up and touching his face. "The only thing I've ever wanted was you."

When Bennett Heart returns from Iraq, it seems like everybody in Mirabelle wants to see him with the town sweetheart, Melanie O'Bryan. He's not sure he can be the man Mel needs—but he's willing to give it a fighting chance...

Please see the next page for a preview of

UNSTOPPABLE

Prologue

The Calm in the Storm

The pain was incredible. It was like someone had drilled a hole into her shoulder. And she was cold, oh so unbelievably cold.

She'd been shot. At least she was pretty sure she'd been shot. She'd heard the gun go off and then someone had been screaming. Was it her scream? Was she screaming now? She thought she was. She felt like she was. Or was the screaming all in her head?

No. No, there was definitely something blaring. A loud piercing noise, and it wasn't in her head. It was everywhere.

And she was flat on her back. When had she fallen? She didn't remember going down. Just opening her eyes to a world of pain.

"We're at Rejuvenate," a panicked voice said. "We walked in on Chad Sharp and Hoyt Reynolds breaking in; they shot Mel. They shot her."

Okay, so she *had* been shot.

"Oh, God, oh, God, oh, God," another panicked voice said. This voice was much closer. It was above her.

The room was dark; blurred images were moving around in a dim light but she couldn't make them out.

Warmth was leaking out of her. She could feel it spreading out over her shoulder. There was pressure, pressure on her shoulder, pressure over the pain. Someone was trying to hold her together.

She closed her eyes. Maybe then the pain would go away. Maybe then she'd be okay.

"Mel, look at me," the panicked voice above her said.

She opened her eyes and tried to get past the pain. Tried to come back. Harper, it was Harper above her. She focused on Harper's face. There was blood smeared on Harper's cheek and she was crying.

The rest of the room slowly came into focus. The loud blaring was the alarm and Grace was on the phone, talking to someone.

"Mel, say something. Please," Harper begged.

"I'm scared," she whispered.

"I know, I know," Harper said, her voice shaking along with her hands.

"Jax is here," Grace cried out, shooting across the room.

More voices, and the floor underneath Mel shook as many someones walked across it. And then someone was kneeling on the other side of her. Mel looked up into the last face she'd expected to see.

Bennett.

He had piercing bluish gray eyes and they were intently focused on her.

"Mel, it's going to be okay," he said calmly as he put his hands over Harper's trembling ones. "Understand? You're going to be fine."

"Okay," she whispered as tears streamed from her eyes.

"I got it," Bennett said, looking up at Harper.

Harper nodded and pulled her hands out from under his. And then Bennett was in Mel's face, his calm, beautiful eyes staring straight into hers and his voice the only thing she could hear.

"Stay right here, Mel. I've got you. I promise."

Chapter One

The Scruffy Man and the
Curly Haired Girl

It had been eight weeks since Melanie O'Bryan had been shot, eight weeks since she'd gone to a spa after hours and walked in on a burglary in progress. She'd been with her two best friends, Harper Laurence and Grace King. It wasn't like the three girls had done anything wrong; Harper was a massage therapist who worked at Rejuvenate and was able to go in and out of the spa as she pleased. They'd just been in the wrong place at the wrong time.

Mirabelle, Florida, was a small beach town. Its six hundred square miles boasted a population of about five thousand. Even though there were very few saints in that five thousand, the burglary spree that had hit the town was not the norm. Chad Sharp and Hoyt Reynolds had stolen hundreds of thousands of dollars from over a dozen businesses and houses.

No one had known who was behind the burglaries until Mel, Harper, and Grace had walked in on the one at Rejuvenate. Chad and Hoyt had gotten away that night, but their greed caught up with them, and so had the law. Now the two thieves were sitting behind bars, awaiting trial. They were pretty much guaranteed life in prison.

It had been Chad that shot Mel in the shoulder. The bullet hadn't hit anything vital, but it landed her in physical therapy for the past six weeks. She'd actually just finished her last session the day before. Her shoulder was still sore for the most part, but little by little she was getting back to a full range of motion.

Things were slowly returning to normal for Mel. It was the middle of August and school was starting on Monday. Mel and the other teachers had just a spent a week planning, and she couldn't wait for her students to be back in the classroom.

It was just after four on Friday when Mel pulled up in front of her little two-bedroom house. It had belonged to her grandparents and when both of them died, the house had passed down to her. Otherwise Mel wouldn't be a homeowner because her salary as a math teacher at Mirabelle High School didn't bring in the big bucks. She'd always loved the little buttercream yellow cottage with its robin-egg blue shutters and doors, and the front porch swing where she spent hours.

Mel grabbed her purse and groceries from the trunk of her black Jetta. She had just enough time to put everything away, jump in the shower, and get ready for tonight before Grace and Harper came over. There was a crawfish boil over at Slim Willies and they were going to head over together. But only after they spent a little while catching up on each other's lives. They'd all been so busy lately that they hadn't really gotten to see each other.

Mel had been best friends with Grace since birth. Well, since two months after Mel's birth, as that was how long it took Grace to join the world. Their mothers had been best friends as well, so Mel and Grace had no choice and really they wouldn't have wanted it any other way. They'd been pretty inseparable over the years, and when Harper moved to Mirabelle in the sixth grade, they eagerly accepted her into the fold. Mel was lucky to have Grace and Harper in her life, and she thanked God for them on a regular basis.

Harper was a massage therapist, and she'd been booked solid all summer with clients. Mirabelle had a fancy little resort out on the beach called LaBelle. They tended to draw in clientele with a pretty thick pocketbook. Harper also worked at Rejuvenate, the spa in downtown Mirabelle where Mel had been shot. Between the two places, Harper barely had enough time to think, let alone go get dinner.

Grace had been busy planning her wedding to her fiancé, Deputy Jaxson Anderson, and really it was about damn time. The girl had been in love with her stubborn redhead since she was six years old and they'd only just gotten together last April. It had taken Jax a while to figure out he was in love with Grace. The boy had always been ridiculously protective of her, but in his stupid boy mind he'd thought that he wasn't good enough for her. He'd finally gotten a clue.

These days if Jax had a spare moment it was spent with Grace. His protective instincts had intensified a hundredfold. Grace had had her own run-in with Chad Sharp and Hoyt Reynolds. When the two thieves tried to rob the funeral home, they'd taken Grace hostage and Jax had a real wake-up call when he had to watch Chad hold a gun to her head.

A chill ran down Mel's spine. She'd never been terrified of guns before, but now the thought of them made her just a little light-headed and she tended to break out in a sweat. Not to mention the very thought of Chad had her stomach in knots.

Mel fumbled with her keys at the door. She took a deep breath and got past the sudden fear that had gone through her. Chad was in jail, and he couldn't hurt her.

She opened the door and when she walked into her house,

the air conditioner was a welcome relief to the humidity that was Florida in the summer. She locked the door behind her and made her way down the hall, dropping her purse on the dining room table and going into the kitchen. She put her bags on the counter and headed for the cupboard to grab a glass. She filled it with ice water and downed half of it before she pressed the cold glass to her forehead.

Really there was no point in taking a shower to wash off all of the stickiness from the day. As soon as she walked outside again, the heat was just going to coat her skin and frizz up her hair. Mel had long, honey-blond corkscrew curls that were a royal pain in the ass to maintain.

But Bennett Hart was going to be at Slim Willies, and even if it was just for five minutes, Mel wanted to look halfway decent.

She might've had a small crush on the guy. Small being that whenever he was around she went all warm and gooey and felt like a freaking sixteen-year-old again.

But really how could she not? He was gorgeous, all six feet and however many inches of him. And he had muscles everywhere. Toned arms and legs and abs of wonder. And don't even get her started on his eyes. They were some sort of icy gray blue that sucked her in. He had dark blond hair that he kept cut close to his skull. He hadn't let it grow out after he got out of the military.

But he had gotten a little more lax with the shaving of his face. Mel had always been a sucker for a scruffy man, and Bennett had perpetual five o'clock shadow on his square jaw.

Not to mention he was there the night Mel had been shot. But she'd liked him long before that fateful night at the spa. Him saving her life hadn't started those feelings.

When the 911 call had gone through to dispatch, the closest deputy to the scene was ten minutes away, so the deputy called Jax. Jax had been hanging out with Bennett that night and both of them rushed over to Rejuvenate. At the time, Jax and Grace had been broken up and Jax had no idea what had happened, just that someone had been shot and that Grace was at the spa. When the two men got there Mel was lying on the ground, Harper kneeling over her, holding a bloody scarf to the bullet wound.

Mel had never been more terrified in her entire life. The pain had been unbelievable and she'd been on the brink of passing out when Bennett showed up. He'd been so calm and talked Mel past the panic. His voice had been the only thing that had grounded her.

But it was just a crush. *Only* a crush. He didn't like her back. Well, not as anything more than a friend, so it really wasn't anything.

Then why was she going to spend an hour fixing her hair before she saw him?

Mel put all of her groceries away before she went into the bathroom and promptly stripped down. She hesitated in front of the mirror as she walked to the shower, her amber eyes dipping down to the scars on her right shoulder. There was one the size of a dime where the bullet had gone in, and then three around it about the size of pencil erasers. The three other scars were from the surgery needed to fix her injury.

She reached up and touched the bullet wound, her fingers tracing around the small pucker on her skin. Even if her arm healed completely, the scar would always be there. Would always be there to remind her of that awful night.

Mel dropped her hand and got in the shower. The hot water poured over her and as she stretched her arms up to wash her hair, the tight pain in her right arm made her wince. It might still hurt but it was loads better than it had been.

When she got out of the shower she grabbed her blow dryer. She stood in the bathroom wrapped in her towel, methodically drying her hair and doing her best to shape the curls to a manageable style.

She put a light coat of makeup on and when she finished she went into her bedroom. Mel stood in front of her opened closet, staring at her clothes and trying to figure out what she was going to wear. The winning combination was a flowing, knee-length, green, cotton skirt and a white V-neck shirt.

Mel went into her kitchen to uncork a bottle of wine. If the girls were going to talk, they were going to be drinking as well. That was just how it was.

She grabbed three glasses from the cabinet, the corkscrew from the drawer, and the wine from the fridge. The kitchen had a view of the front yard, and as Mel finished pouring the wine she saw Harper's car pull up. Grace got out of the passenger side, and the two girls made their way up the front porch.

There'd never really been a chance for the three friends to share clothes growing up or now for that matter. Grace came in at a whopping five-feet-four. She had light blond hair and a heart-shaped face that framed her blue eyes and pouty lips. She was fairly tiny with her A-cup bust and slim waist, though she did have a fairly round butt that she was proud of and that Jax was pretty fond of. She was wearing tight jeans that accentuated said rear and a cute little hot pink tank top that only she could pull off. Said tank top would've looked more than somewhat scandalous on Mel and just downright indecent on Harper.

Harper had been a little overweight when she first came to Mirabelle, and most of the boys in school weren't very nice about it. But it had only taken her a few years to grow into her body. Now, she was all curves. Men had absolutely nothing negative to say about how her D-cup breasts filled out a shirt, or anything for that matter. She was currently wearing a formfitting light blue dress that made her violet eyes pop and looked incredible with her long black hair.

Yeah, Harper didn't have any issues catching a man's eyes these days. Problem was, no one was catching her eye.

Mel was at least the same height as Harper, both of them being five-feet-seven, but that was where all the similarities stopped. Where Grace had most of her curves below the waist, Mel's were above. She had a decent C-cup, no real butt to speak of, and thin legs. But at least she had good thighs and calves, so she didn't have a lot of complaints.

Mel put the bottle of wine on the counter and went to open the front door.

"Oh, no," Harper said as soon as she saw Mel. "Oh, no, no, no, no, no. You get your skinny ass in that room of yours and change," she said as she and Grace came into the house.

"What's wrong with this?" Mel asked, looking down at herself.

"It's flirty. You don't want flirty. You want *sexy*," Harper said, grabbing Mel's hand and pulling her down the hallway.

"Yeah, you need to show off those legs of yours," Grace said as she shut the door and followed them.

"That's what's going to help you in your man-catching endeavors."

"What man-catching endeavors?" Mel asked, coming to a sudden stop.

"Bennett," Grace coughed.

"Excuse me?" Mel asked, rounding on Grace.

"Oh, don't even deny it," Harper said as she now began dragging Mel into her bedroom. "You *soo* want to have that man's babies."

"Oh. My. Gosh. It isn't anything," Mel said a little bit too loud.

"Whatever you say. Now take off that skirt," Harper said, letting go of Mel's hand and looking at her.

"You're being ridiculous." Mel shook her head. "My skirt is fine."

"You don't want fine, you want *fine*." Except Harper pronounced it *fwine*. "And you wouldn't be this resistant if Bennett were asking you to take off your skirt."

Yeah, if Bennett were asking her to take off her skirt, she'd be completely naked in three seconds flat.

"Strip. Now," Harper said to Mel.

"I'm going to go get something for us to drink," Grace said, leaving the room.

"The wine's already poured and on the counter," Mel called out after Grace as she pushed her skirt down her thighs.

"Pretty pink panties?" Harper asked, raising an eyebrow.

"Just find me something to wear so you'll shut up."

Harper turned to Mel's closet and started looking through her wardrobe.

"No, no, no," Harper said as she pushed hanger after hanger aside.

"Wow, those are nice. Were you planning on someone seeing those tonight?" Grace asked, coming into the room with all three glasses of wine. She handed one to Mel and smirked as she looked at Mel's undies.

"Are the two of you quite finished?" Mel asked before taking a sip of her wine.

"We're never finished," Grace said as she handed Harper a glass of wine and then sat down on the bed.

"I see that teddy bear he got you is still on your bed," Harper said, turning to them and taking a drink of wine.

Okay, so Bennett might've brought Mel said bear when she was in the hospital. And it was possible that she'd slept with it every night since. It was just because it was soft and cuddly and...

Yeah, she was pathetic.

"Look, it's just a silly crush so let's not make anything of it, okay. We're just friends. Nothing's going to happen and I'll get over it."

"Uh-huh," Harper said, raising an eyebrow. "Just friends," she said slowly.

"He doesn't have feelings for me beyond that," Mel said.

"How do you know? Have you asked him?" Grace asked.

"No, and I'm not going to. And neither are the two of you," Mel said, staring at her two friends pointedly.

"Who?" Harper asked, trying to look like she was mildly offended.

"Us?" Grace asked innocently.

"We would never." Harper turned back to the closet and resumed her hunt.

Yeah, Mel didn't believe that for a second.

"What about her jean miniskirt?" Grace asked.

"Ohhh, that would look really good with this orange tank top or this green V-neck with the stripes," Harper said as she continued to push through the hangers. "Take your shirt off, too," she demanded, not even turning around.

"I'm going to need more wine," Mel said, and took a fairly large gulp before she put her glass down and did as Harper ordered.

* * *

Bennett Hart had been back in Mirabelle for just over two years now. He'd moved back after his honorable discharge from the air force. He'd enlisted when he was eighteen and spent eight years in the service before he was shot down in a helicopter in Afghanistan. There were eleven people on the mission that day; only Bennett and the co-pilot survived, and both of them had barely escaped with their lives.

Bennett's injuries had been extensive: six broken ribs, a fractured right foot, gunshot wound in the left shoulder, and shrapnel to the right thigh. Just a fraction of an inch over and it would've hit his femoral artery. Yeah, he knew just how lucky he was to be alive, but that didn't stop the survivor's guilt. How could it? He'd watched as his best friends, his brothers, died and there'd been absolutely nothing he could do to save them.

He still had the nightmares. Still woke up in a cold sweat screaming as he fought with his pillows and sheets like they were the demons that had taken his friends. At least the nightmares didn't happen on a nightly basis anymore, so that was progress. But that day would haunt him for the rest of his life.

These days Bennett took things easy. Well, easier. There were a certain number of hazards that came with working in construction, but he wasn't being targeted on a daily basis. He'd picked up a thing or two in the military, and building schools and hospitals had stuck with him. Now he mainly worked on remodels with businesses and houses. It was more than just a job for Bennett. He liked working with his hands, liked creating things.

It was good being home in Mirabelle, too. Good living close to his dad and stepmom.

Bennett's parents had divorced when he was four. Bennett's mother Kristi ran off to Arkansas with a man she'd had a fairly extensive affair with for years. She was now married to him and they had three children together. She sent a card every year on Bennett's birthday, which he never opened. Besides that, he had absolutely no contact with her.

Bennett's father, Walker, had remarried when Bennett was six. Jocelyn had been the one to pack Bennett's lunches in school, teach him how to cook, and sit next to his father at all of his baseball games and his graduation. She'd always been much more than a stepmother to him, and for all intents and purposes she was his mother. He'd started calling her mom not that long after she'd married his dad.

Bennett had also fallen back in with a good group of guys

he'd gone to high school with. Brendan King, Jax Anderson, and Nathanial Shepherd were all a year older than him, but they'd all played on the Mirabelle High baseball team together. The three guys had been best friends since preschool, or something like that, but they'd welcomed Bennett into their fold and through them he'd gotten a whole other family.

It had been hard for Bennett at first, hard for him to let anybody into his life. When he'd first moved back to Mirabelle he kept himself pretty isolated from everyone except his dad and mom. Losing his friends in Afghanistan had nearly destroyed him. It took him a while to realize that the country roads of Mirabelle weren't the same thing as the deserts of the Middle East. Yes, tragedies happened every day, but his friends weren't getting shot at.

Well, except for that one time a couple months ago.

Bennett had made a couple of close friends in Mirabelle over the last two years and Melanie O'Bryan had become part of that inner circle. She was a sweet girl. Maybe just a little soft-spoken but she had a quiet confidence. And she had this sassy sarcastic side to her that came out every once in a while. She'd drop these one-liners that tended to shock the hell out of him.

And damn did she ever have a killer smile, with dimples that made Bennett never want to turn away from her. She was a high school math teacher, and from what Bennett had heard she had the patience of a saint and was loved by her students. It wasn't that surprising. Mel was just a good person. A *great* person.

When he'd walked into that spa all those weeks ago and seen her bleeding out on the ground, it had taken everything in him to stay calm. All he'd been able to think was *not her*. But Mel was strong and she'd survived it, and Bennett thanked God for that every time she was around, and even when she wasn't.

Mel had a knack for popping up in his thoughts a lot, and holding his attention whenever she was in the same room as him. So it came as absolutely no surprise to him that he zeroed in on her the second she walked up onto the deck of Slim Willies. She was wearing a skirt that showed off her killer legs and a gauzy purple and blue flowery tank top that gave just a hint of cleavage. Her hair was down, her curls framing her pretty face and running over her shoulders and down her back.

Bennett was so distracted by Mel that he completely missed what Brendan had just said. The two men were standing at the outside bar waiting for a drink.

Brendan King was Grace's older brother. He was a mechanic at King's Auto, and he and his grandfather owned the place. Brendan and his wife Paige had just had their little baby boy Trevor two and a half months ago, and they were taking advantage of a night out. Paige's mother Denise was on babysitting duty.

"Sorry," Bennett said, clearing his throat and focusing on Brendan. "What was that?"

Brendan turned and looked over his shoulder. Bennett let his gaze travel back to Mel. She along with Grace and Harper were joining the table where Jax and Paige were sitting. Mel looked up as she pulled a chair out, and her eyes locked on Bennett's. Her cheeks flushed a soft pink and she smiled at him shyly. She waved and Bennett couldn't stop himself from smiling and waving back.

"Huh," Brendan said, facing Bennett again. "When did that happen?"

"When did what happen?" Bennett asked.

"You and Mel?"

"There is no me and Mel."

"Oh, really? So you just get smiley for all the pretty girls?"

"I didn't get smiley," Bennett frowned as he looked at Brendan.

"Right."

"And we're just friends," Bennett said as he tried to get the attention of one of the guys behind the bar.

There was a group of about ten college girls that the two bartenders were giving a little bit too much attention to. They were loud, bordered on obnoxious, and were all processed to about an inch within their lives. Their dark tans were fake, too much time spent in a tanning bed. Their makeup was on thick and their clothes were on light. They gave off more than a glimpse of their flat stomachs, and their breasts spilled out of the top of their too tight shirts.

They did absolutely nothing for Bennett.

His eyes automatically found Mel again. She was laughing. Her head thrown back as her shoulders shook and a huge smile lifted up her mouth. Mel had a natural sun-kissed tan and her skin glowed. He wasn't even sure if she wore makeup or not. And he liked the way she dressed. Her clothes gave off just a hint of the sexiness that he was sure lay beneath. She was modest, and real. She was beautiful.

"Just friends?" Brendan said skeptically. "Okay, whatever you say."

* * *

"You know he keeps looking at you," Grace whispered in Mel's ear.

"Shut up," Mel said, kicking her under the table. "He is not."

"Yes, he is," Grace said, pinching Mel's leg.

"Ow, don't pinch me." Mel rubbed the now sore spot on her thigh.

"Then don't kick me."

"What are you two talking about?" Paige asked, leaning across the table.

Jax had gotten drink orders from Grace, Mel, and Harper before he'd joined Bennett and Brendan at the bar. So only Mel, Grace, Harper, and Paige were at the table.

"Bennett," Grace said.

"Mel has a little crush," Harper said.

"What part of *shut up* do you not understand?"

The deck was filled with people and the band had started playing, so it was loud. There wasn't really a chance that they would be overheard, but talking about Mel's *crush* in public made her really nervous.

"Don't worry." Paige grinned. "I won't say anything."

Mel loved Paige and did trust her not to say anything. Paige had fit right in with their little group after she moved to Mirabelle over two years ago, and she'd quickly become a very close friend.

Paige had long, dark brown hair that fell in messy waves, gray eyes, and freckles across her nose and cheeks. She was tall and her running habit had kept her legs in amazing form; it had also melted off almost all of her pregnancy weight.

"He's really cute," Paige said as she looked over at the bar. "You should totally go for it."

Cute? No. Bennett Hart was sexy as hell in a way that made Mel want to put her mouth all over his body.

Oh, dear, she should *not* be thinking about that.

"Can we *please* not have this conversation right now?"

"Oh, look how red she's getting," Harper said. "She *really* likes him."

Yeah, that's why she was blushing and not because she was thinking about how lickable his abs probably were.

"I hate you all," Mel said, and buried her face in her hands.

"No, you don't," Grace said. "You love us dearly."

"That's debatable."

"Fine, no more harassing Mel...right now. But we will have this conversation later," Paige said.

"Count on it." Grace grinned.

"So school starts next week?" Paige asked.

"Yeah, on Monday. I'm looking forward to the kids being back. Sitting in that empty room all week was making me crazy."

Mel was glad that they'd changed subjects because when she glanced up again, Bennett, Brendan, and Jax were at the table, beers in hand.

"Here you go," Bennett said, sliding a bottle in front of Mel.

"Thanks." She smiled up at him.

"So what's making you crazy?" he asked as he took the seat directly across from her.

Out of the corner of her eye, she saw the matching smirks on Grace's and Harper's faces. At least they kept their mouths shut.

"The kids not being there. It's too quiet."

"I'll bet." Bennett nodded as Brendan and Jax sat down, too. "Too much quiet makes me crazy, too."

"Jeez, this place is crowded."

Mel looked up to see Nathanial Shepherd and Tripp Black standing at the other end of the table. Nathanial Shepherd, who everyone called Shep, worked at his family's bar the Sleepy Sheep. He was tall with thick, shaggy black hair and piercing blue eyes. His jaw was covered in what could only be described as ten o'clock shadow and his arms were covered in tattoos. He had the whole bad boy image down to a tee.

Tripp Black had moved to Mirabelle over a year ago when he landed the job as fire chief. He had dark brown eyes and thick brown hair. He was also a man of the perpetual scruff.

"Yeah, good luck getting a drink unless you're going to flash something. But I feel like your legs could get you fast service," Brendan said, looking at Shep.

"Aww, come on, Brendan," Shep said. "You know you're the pretty boy around here."

"Who are you calling a pretty boy?" Brendan asked before he took a pull on his beer.

"You. You going to do something about it?"

"Nah," Brendan said, shaking his head. "Because we both know the truth."

"That Jax is the prettiest of us all?" Shep said.

"Exactly." Brendan nodded.

Mel wouldn't exactly say that any of the men around her could be termed pretty. Hot was a better word. Hot and incredibly built. Yeah, all of them were ridiculously good looking, but none of them had ever inspired the feelings in Mel like Bennett.

"I'm not even going to comment," Jax said, shaking his head as he put his arm around Grace and pulled her close to him.

"That's because you have a maturity level higher than these two put together," Paige said, pointing to Shep and Brendan.

"I have no idea what you're talking about." Brendan smirked and pulled Paige in to give her a loud smacking kiss on the temple.

"Let's start heading up for dinner," Grace said, pointing to the line behind them. "You guys should start." Grace pointed to Paige, Brendan, and Bennett. "You, too, Mel." She winked.

Mel really wanted to glare at her, but chose not to draw attention to Grace's not so subtle grouping. She got up from the table and followed behind Brendan and Paige, and Bennett fell in by her side. She tried not to think about how that made her heart flutter a little bit.

It cost twenty-five dollars to get into the crawfish boil, but the food was all you could eat and the live band was sure to provide hours of entertainment. The line for food was already pretty deep when the four of them made their way to the end.

"So how's the new superintendent?" Brendan asked.

The former superintendent, Keith Reynolds, had tendered his resignation during the summer. It had been a pretty big scandal in Mirabelle when it was revealed that Keith Reynolds was Grace's father.

Brendan's father, Crayton Dallas, had walked out on his mother Claire before Brendan was even born. Six years later Claire had Grace, and no one had known who Grace's father was. Turns out it was Keith Reynolds. Keith had come down to Mirabelle twenty-five years ago to interview for a job as the high school principal. He never intended on taking the job; he'd only come down to get another school interested in him. He never told Claire that he was already married. He'd said that he was down on vacation. Claire had made her own mistakes that night, but she never looked at Grace with regret.

It had also been a pretty big blow to the Reynolds family when it was discovered that their son Hoyt was involved in the string of burglaries around town. Hoyt was one of the men who held Grace hostage at the funeral home; it made matters more complicated that he was her half brother.

Mel had never been a fan of anyone in the Reynolds family, especially Keith. She hadn't liked him when he was the school principal or when he'd become the superintendent. He was a cheating, pompous ass who had never wanted anything to do with his daughter.

Grace had been better off without him in the long run, but really the girl hadn't had the easiest life before she found out who her father was. Claire died of breast cancer almost fifteen years ago. Grace had known her mom for only ten years.

"I haven't really had that much contact with Superintendent Stafford. We've had a couple of faculty meetings and he seems to know what he's doing. We have another on Friday to see how the first week of school goes. So far I think he's better than his predecessor."

"Well, anyone is better than that piece of scum," Brendan said with disgust.

It would come as no shock to anyone that Brendan was incredibly protective of his little sister. And he hadn't been the only one. Grace grew up with Brendan, Jax, and Shep constantly playing overbearing protectors. They'd even played that role with Mel and then Harper when she'd showed up.

"Were you able to get permission to do that project?" Brendan asked.

Another reason Mel despised the former Superintendent Reynolds was that he never had time to talk to his teachers, or it would be more accurate to say that he never made time. Mel had wanted to do a hands-on project with her students. He told her there wasn't enough money in the budget, and he wouldn't even look at her plans to pay for it.

"I haven't asked yet," she said, shaking her head.

"What project?" Bennett asked.

"I wanted to show my students how math can build things. And the bookshelves in the library are in desperate need of being fixed. Some of them should be trashed all together."

"You want to rebuild them? Have you ever done anything like that before?" he asked as they all moved up in the line.

"No, I was going to ask the woodshop teacher Mr. Coryell for help, but he retired over the summer."

"You know that power tools can be tricky, right?"

"Don't worry, I'm not going to let any of the students lose a limb." She smiled.

"Well, I was concerned about *your* limbs, too," he said as his mouth quirked up.

Oh, if he only knew what she wanted to do with all of her limbs. Like wrap them around his body and not let go for hours. And now she was blushing again. Where was a cool breeze when a girl needed one? They were right on the beach, but the air was too humid to do anything for her reddening face.

"Well, if you need any help let me know," he said.

"Really?" Mel asked surprised, and maybe a little bit too excited.

"Yeah, for the sake of the safety of your limbs," he said, grinning.

Holy cow was that man's smile lethal. She was pretty sure if she were using heavy machinery when he was around she'd probably smash her finger or something. If he smiled at her like that, she'd probably be losing those limbs he was so worried about.

But no pain no gain, right?

"I'll keep you posted," Mel said as she turned away from Bennett to look forward.

Paige was grinning at Mel, whereas Brendan was looking at Bennett with what could only be described as a bemused *I told you so* look.

Mel *really* wanted to know what that was all about.

THE DISH

Where Authors Give You the Inside Scoop

From the desk of Debbie Mason

Dear Reader,

While reading CHRISTMAS IN JULY one last time before sending it off to my editor, I had an "oops, I did it again" moment. In the first book in the series, *The Trouble with Christmas*, there's a scene where Madison, the heroine, senses her late mother's presence. In this book, our heroine, Grace, receives a message from her sister through her son. Grace has spent years blaming herself for her sister's death, and while there's an incident in the book that alleviates her guilt, I felt she needed the opportunity to tell her sister she loved her. Maybe if I didn't believe our departed loved ones could communicate with us in some way, I would have done this another way. But I do, and here's why.

My dad was movie-star handsome and had this amazing dimple in his chin. He was everything a little girl could wish for in a father. But he wasn't my biological father; he was the father of my heart. He came into my life when I was nine years old. That first year, I dreamed about him a lot. The dreams were very real, and all the same. I'd be outside and see a man from behind and call out to him. He'd turn around, and it would be my dad.

I always said the same thing: "You're here. I knew you weren't gone." Almost a year to the day of his passing, my dad appeared in my dream surrounded by shadowy figures who he introduced to me by name. He told me that he was okay, that he was happy. It was his way, I think, of helping me let him go.

I didn't dream of him again until sixteen months ago when we were awaiting the birth of our first grandchild. I "woke up" to see him sitting at the end of my bed. I told him how happy I was that he'd be there for the arrival of his great grandchild. He said of course he would be. He wouldn't be anywhere else.

A week later, my daughter gave birth to a beautiful baby girl. When I saw my granddaughter for the first time, I started to cry. She had my dad's dimple. No one on my son-in-law's side, or ours, has a dimple in their chin. He used to tell us the angels gave it to him, and we like to think he gave our granddaughter hers as proof that he's still with us.

So now you know why including that scene was important not only to Grace, but to me. Life really is full of small miracles and magic. And I hope you experience some of that magic as you follow Grace and Jack on their journey to happy-ever-after.

♥ ♥ ♥ ♥ ♥ ♥ ♥ ♥ ♥ ♥ ♥ ♥ ♥ ♥ ♥

From the desk of Kristen Ashley

Dear Reader,

Usually, inspiration for books comes to me in a variety of ways. It could be a man I see (anywhere), a movie, a song, the unusual workers in a bookstore.

With SWEET DREAMS, it was an idea.

And that idea was, I wanted to take a hero who is, on the whole, totally unlikable, and make him lovable.

Enter Tatum Jackson, and when I say that, I mean *enter Tatum Jackson.* He came to me completely with a *kapow!* I could conjure him in my head, hear him talk, see the way he moved and how his clothes hung on him, feel his frustration with his life. I also knew his messed-up history.

And I could *not* wait to get stuck into this man.

I mean, here's a guy who is gorgeous, but he's got a foul temper, says nasty things when he's angry, and he's not exactly father of the year.

He had something terrible happen to him to derail his life and he didn't handle that very well, making mistake after mistake in a vicious cycle he pretty much had no intention of ending. He had a woman in his life he knew was a liar, a cheat, and no good for anyone and he was so stuck in the muck of his life that he didn't get shot of her.

Enter Lauren Grahame, who also came to me like a shot. As with Tate, everything about Lauren slammed into my head, perhaps most especially her feelings, the disillusionment she has with life, how she feels lost and really has no intention of getting found.

In fact, I don't think with any of my books I've ever had two characters who I knew so thoroughly before I started to tell their story.

And thus, I got lost in it.

I tend to be obsessive about my storytelling but this was an extreme. Once Lauren and Tate came to me, everything about Carnal, Colorado, filled my head just like the hero and heroine did. I can see Main Street, Bubba's Bar, Tate's house. I know the secondary characters as absolutely as I know the main characters. The entirety of the town, the people, and the story became a strange kind of real in my head, even if I didn't know how the story was going to play out. Indeed, I had no idea if I could pull it off, making an unlikable man lovable.

But I fell in love with Tate very quickly. The attraction he has for Lauren growing into devotion. The actions that speak much louder than words. I so enjoyed watching Lauren pull Tate out of the muck of his life, even if nothing changes except the fact that he has a woman in it that he loves, who is good to him, who feeds the muscle, the bone, the soul. Just as I enjoyed watching Tate guide Lauren out of her disillusionment and offer her something special.

I hope it happens to me again someday that characters like this inhabit my head so completely, and I hope it happens time and again.

But Tate and Lauren being the first, they'll always hold a special place in my heart, and live on in my head.

Happily,

Kristen Ashley

♥ ♥ ♥ ♥ ♥ ♥ ♥ ♥ ♥ ♥ ♥ ♥ ♥ ♥

From the desk of Rebecca Zanetti

Dear Reader,

I'm the oldest of three girls, and my husband is the oldest of three boys, so we grew up watching out for our siblings. Now that we're all adults, they look out for us, too. While my sisters and I may have argued with one another as kids, we instantly banded together if anybody tried to mess with one of us. My youngest sister topped out at an even five feet tall, yet she's the fiercest of us all, and she loses her impressive temper quite quickly if someone isn't nice to me.

I think one of the reasons I enjoyed writing Matt's story in SWEET REVENGE is because he's the eldest of the Dean brothers, and as such, he feels responsible for them. Add in a dangerous military organization trying to harm them, and his duties go far beyond that of a normal sibling. It was fun to watch Matt try to order his brothers around and keep them safe, while all they want to do is provide backup for him and ensure his safety.

There's something about being the oldest kid that forces us to push ourselves when we shouldn't. When our siblings would step back and relax, we often push forward just out of sheer stubbornness. I don't know why, and it's sometimes a mistake. Trust me.

SWEET REVENGE was written in several locations, most notably in the hospital and on airplanes. Sometimes

I take on a bit too much, so when I discovered I needed a couple of surgeries (nothing major), I figured I'd just do them on the same day. Why not? So I had two surgeries in one day and had to spend a few days in the hospital recuperating.

With my laptop, of course.

There's not a lot to do in the hospital but drink milkshakes and write, so it was quite effective. Then, instead of going home and taking it easy, I flew across the country to a conference and big book signing. Of course, I was still in pain, but I ignored it.

Bad idea.

Two weeks after that, I once again flew across the country for a book signing and conference. Yes, I was still tired, but I kept on going.

Yet another bad idea.

Then I returned home and immediately headed back to work as a college professor at the beginning of the semester.

Not a great idea.

Are you seeing a trend here? I pushed myself too hard, and all of a sudden, my body said...*you're done*. Completely done. I became sick, and after a bunch of tests, it appeared I'd just taken on too much. So at the end of the semester, I resigned as a professor and took up writing full time. And yoga. And eating healthy and relaxing.

Life is great, and it's meant to be savored and not rushed through—even for us oldest siblings. I learned a very valuable life lesson while writing SWEET REVENGE, and I'll always have fond memories of this book.

I truly hope you enjoy Matt and Laney's story, and

don't forget to take a deep breath and enjoy the moment. It's definitely worth it!

Happy reading!

Rebecca Zanetti

RebeccaZanetti.com
Twitter @RebeccaZanetti
Facebook.com

From the desk of Shannon Richard

Dear Reader,

When it comes to the little town of Mirabelle, Florida, Grace King was actually the first character who revealed herself to me, which I find odd as she's the heroine in the second book. I knew from the beginning she was going to be a tiny little thing with blond hair and blue eyes; I knew she'd lost her mother at a young age and that she was never going to have known her father; and I knew she was going to be feisty and strong.

Jaxson Anderson was a different story. He didn't reveal himself to me until he literally walked onto the page in *Undone*. I also didn't know about Jax and Grace's future relationship until they got into an argument at the beach. As soon as I figured out they were going to end up together, my mind took off and I started plotting everything out, which was a little inconvenient as I wasn't even a third of the way through writing the first book.

Jax is a complicated fella. He's had to deal with a lot in his life, and because of his past he doesn't think he's good enough for Grace. Jax has most definitely put her on a pedestal, which is made pretty evident by his nickname for her. He calls her Princess, but not in a derogatory way. He doesn't find her to be spoiled or bratty. Far from it. He thinks that she should be cherished and that she's worth *everything*, especially to him. I try to capture this in the prologue, which takes place a good eighteen years before UNDENIABLE starts. Grace is this little six-year-old who is being bullied on the playground, and Jax is her white knight in scuffed-up sneakers.

Jax has been in Grace's life from the day she was brought home from the hospital over twenty-four years ago. He's watched her grow up into the beautiful and brave woman that she is, and though he's always loved her (even if he's chosen not to accept it), it's hard for him think that he can be with her. Jax's struggles were heartbreaking for me to write, and it was especially heartbreaking to put Grace through it, but this was their story and I had to stay true to them. Readers shouldn't fear with UNDENIABLE, though, because I like my happily-ever-after endings and Grace and Jax definitely get theirs. I hope readers enjoy the journey.

Cheers,

♥ ♥ ♥ ♥ ♥ ♥ ♥ ♥ ♥ ♥ ♥ ♥ ♥ ♥ ♥ ♥

From the desk of Stacy Henrie

Dear Reader,

I remember the moment HOPE AT DAWN, Book 1 in my Of Love and War series (on sale now), was born into existence. I was sitting in a quiet, empty hallway at a writers' conference contemplating how to turn my single World War I story idea, about Livy Campbell's brother, into more than one book. Then, in typical fashion, Livy marched forward in my mind, eager to have her story told first.

As I pondered Livy and the backdrop of the story— America's involvement in WWI—I knew having her fall in love with a German-American would provide inherent conflict. What I didn't know then was the intense prejudice and persecution she and Friedrick Wagner would face to be together, in a country ripe with suspicion toward anyone with German ties. The more I researched the German-American experience during WWI, the more I discovered their private war here on American soil—not against soldiers, but neighbors against neighbors, citizens against citizens.

A young woman with aspirations of being a teacher, Livy Campbell knows little of the persecution being heaped upon the German-Americans across the country, let alone in the county north of hers. More than anything, she feels the effects of the war overseas through the absence of her older brothers in France, the alcohol troubles of her wounded soldier boyfriend, and the disruption of her studies at college. When she applies for a teaching job in hopes of escaping the war, Livy doesn't realize she's simply traded one set of troubles for another, especially when she finds herself attracted to the school's handsome handyman, German-American Friedrick Wagner.

Born in America to German immigrant parents, Friedrick Wagner believes himself to be as American as anyone else in his small town of Hilden, Iowa. But the war with Germany changes all that. Suddenly viewed as a potential enemy, Friedrick seeks to protect his family from the rising tide of injustice aimed at his fellow German-Americans. Protecting the beautiful new teacher, Livy Campbell, comes as second nature to Friedrick. But when he finds himself falling in love with her, he fears the war, both at home and abroad, will never allow them to be together.

I thoroughly enjoyed writing Livy and Friedrick's love story and the odds they must overcome for each other. This is truly a tale of "love conquers all" and the power of hope and courage during a dark time in history. My hope is you will fall in love with the Campbell family through this series, as I have, as you experience their triumphs and struggles during the Great War.

Happy reading!

Stacy Henrie

♥ ♥ ♥ ♥ ♥ ♥ ♥ ♥ ♥ ♥ ♥ ♥ ♥ ♥ ♥ ♥ ♥

From the desk of Adrianne Lee

Dear Reader,

Conflict, conflict, conflict. Every good story needs it. It heightens sexual tension and keeps you guessing whether a couple will actually be able to work through those serious—and even not so serious—issues and obstacles to find that happily-ever-after ending.

I admit to a little vanity when one of my daughters once said, "Mom, in other romances I always know the couple will get together early in the book, but I'm never sure in yours until the very end." High praise and higher expectations for any writer to live up to. It is, at least, what I strive for with every love story I write.

Story plotting starts with conflict. I already knew that Jane Wilson, Big Sky Pie's new pastry chef, was going to fall in love with Nick Taziano, the sexy guy doing the promotion for the pie shop, but when I first conceived the idea that these two would be lovers in DELICIOUS, I didn't realize they were a reunion couple.

A reunion couple is a pair who was involved in the past and broke up due to unresolved conflicts. This is what I call a "built-in" conflict. It's one of my favorites to write. When the story opens, something has happened that involves this couple on a personal level, causing them to come face-to-face to deal with it. This is when they finally admit to themselves that they still have feelings for each other, feelings neither wants to feel or act on, no matter how compelling. The more they try to suppress the attraction, the stronger it becomes.

In DELICIOUS, Jane and Nick haven't seen each other since they were kids, since his father and her mother married. Jane blames Nick's dad for breaking up her parents' marriage. Nick resents Jane's mom for coming between his father and him. Jane called Nick the Tazmanian Devil. Nick called her Jane the Pain. They were thrilled when the marriage fell apart after a year.

Now many years later, their parents are reuniting, something Jane and Nick view as a bigger mistake than the first marriage. Their decision to try and stop the wedding, however, leads to one accidental, delicious kiss, and a sizzling attraction that is as irresistible as Jane's blueberry pies.

I hope you'll enjoy DELICIOUS, the second book in my Big Sky Pie series. All of the stories are set in northwest Montana near Glacier Park, an area where I vacationed every summer for over thirty years. Each of the books is about someone connected with the pie shop in one way or another and contains a different delicious pie recipe. So come join the folks of Kalispell at the little pie shop on Center Street, right across from the mall, for some of the best pie you'll ever taste, and a healthy helping of romance.

Adrianne Lee

♥ ♥ ♥ ♥ ♥ ♥ ♥ ♥ ♥ ♥ ♥ ♥ ♥ ♥ ♥

From the desk of Jessica Lemmon

Dear Reader,

A *quiz:* What do you get when you put a millionaire who avoids romantic relationships in the same house with a determined-to-stay-single woman who crushed on him sixteen years ago?

If you answered *unstoppable attraction*, you'd be right.

In THE MILLIONAIRE AFFAIR, I paired a hero who cages and controls his emotions with a heroine who feels way too much, way too soon. Kimber Reynolds is determined to have a fling—to love and leave Landon Downey, if for only two reasons: (1) She's wanted to kiss the eldest Downey brother since she was a teen, and (2) to prove to herself that she can have a shallow relationship that ends amicably instead of one that's long, drawn-out, and destined to end badly.

When Landon's six-year-old nephew, Lyon, and a huge account for his advertising agency come crashing into his life, Landon needs help. Lucky for him (and us!) his sister offers the perfect solution: her friend, Kimber, can be his live-in nanny for the week.

The most difficult part about writing Landon was letting him deal with his past on *his terms* and watching him falter. Here is a guy who makes rules, follows them, and remains stoic . . . to his own detriment. Despite those qualities, Landon, from a loving, close family, can't help caring for Kimber. Even when they're working down a list of "extracurricular activities" in the bedroom, Landon puts Kimber's needs before his own.

These two may have stumbled into an arrangement, but when Fate tosses them a wild card, they both step up—and step closer—to the one thing they were sure they didn't want...*forever*.

I *love* this book. Maybe because of how much I wrestled with Landon and Kimber's story before getting it right. The three of us had growing pains, but I finally found their truth, and I'm *so* excited to share their story with you. If Landon and Kimber win your heart like they won mine, be sure to let me know. You can email me at jessica@jessicalemmon.com, tweet me @lemmony, and "like" my Facebook page at www.facebook.com/authorjessicalemmon.

Happy reading!

Jessica Lemmon

www.jessicalemmon.com

About the Author

Shannon Richard grew up in the Panhandle of Florida as the baby sister of two overly protective, but loving, brothers. She was raised by a more than somewhat eccentric mother, a self-proclaimed vocabularist who showed her how to get lost in a book, and a father who passed on his love for coffee and really loud music. She graduated from Florida State University with a bachelor's in English literature, and still lives in Tallahassee where she battles everyday life with writing, reading, and a rant every once in a while. Okay, so the rants might happen on a regular basis. She's still waiting for her Southern, scruffy, Mr. Darcy and in the meantime writes love stories to indulge her overactive imagination. Oh, and she's a pretty big fan of the whimsy.

Learn more at:
ShannonRichard.net
Twitter, @shan_richard
Facebook.com/ShannonNRichard